MW00396215

Beta Sigma Phi
To Make Donations
435-673-1516

Books by the Author

The Blue Chair

35¢ Thrills

Hothouse

Merry-Go-Round

Merry-Go-Round

a novel by

Joyce Thompson

CROWN PUBLISHERS, INC.   NEW YORK

Copyright © 1982 by Joyce Thompson

All rights reserved. No part of this book may be reproduced
or utilized in any form or by any means,
electronic or mechanical, including photocopying, recording,
or by any information storage and retrieval system,
without permission in writing from the publisher.
Inquiries should be addressed to Crown Publishers, Inc.,
One Park Avenue, New York, New York 10016
Printed in the United States of America
Published simultaneously in Canada
by General Publishing Company Limited
Library of Congress Cataloging in Publication Data
Thompson, Joyce.
Merry-go-round.
I. Title.
PS3570.H6414M4 1982   813'.54   81-9903
ISBN: 0-517-543419   AACR2
Book design by Camilla Filancia
10 9 8 7 6 5 4 3 2 1
First Edition

Many ingenious lovely things are gone

That seemed sheer miracle to the multitude,

Protected from the circle of the moon

That pitches common things about.

WILLIAM BUTLER YEATS

"Nineteen Hundred and Nineteen"

With thanks to:

DAPHNE ABEEL

JACK JAMISON

PAUL KOMAR,
*Department of Oceanography,
Oregon State University*

ELAINE MARKSON

KEITH OIEN

THE DUANE PERRON FAMILY

PAUL STEELE

ALEXANDRA THOMPSON STEELE

JILL THURSTON

Chapter 1

$\mathcal{I}$ never knew my mother had a lover.

That she'd had a husband, and dallied with him in the usual way that people do, I was always forced to acknowledge, since it was an a priori condition of my own existence. They weren't making test-tube babies in 1948, when I was born, or 1947, when the grappling that conceived me must have taken place. Somebody had to provide the Y chromosome that gave me a penis and a draft card, and I always took it on faith it was the same guy in the picture next to Verna's on my dresser, the one with the pith helmet.

The pith helmet is dazzlingly white, shaped like a splay-lipped bowl, and I always imagined the face under it looked something like mine. The guy in the picture has round steel-rimmed glasses and a not-too-kempt beard. He must have moved just when the photographer shot, because the features are blurred to indistinction, so it's like trying to make out a face through half a dozen layers of mosquito netting. In the sixties, I wore wire rims and had a lot of facial hair myself. Like father, like son. I also drank a lot, something else I figured was part of my patrimony.

Drink was my daddy's undoing. When he was in Panama helping make engineering repairs on the Miraflores Locks and I was still too little to know my own name, much less his, he and his buddies used to amuse themselves nights by striking macho/American poses in Panama City's native bars. One night the natives were particularly restless, or the Americanos were particularly ugly, and hostilities broke out. Before it was all over, my father shot a Panamanian in the gut, but not before he, the Panamanian, inserted his shiv between my daddy's ribs. All hell broke loose. In the confusion that followed, with the wheezing sirens of the *policía* approaching fast through the hot tropical darkness, with a high-spirited bar fight teetering on the brink of becoming an international incident, two of my father's cronies carted him away from the scene of the crime, hauled him down the street to another bistro, propped him up on a barstool and ordered him a double bourbon. Before the bartender could pour his shot, my old man fell over, dead, on the bar.

It was swift, specific justice, crime and punishment both inside an hour's time, and whatever pain it caused my mother, neither the loss nor the circumstances much bothered me. I couldn't miss a man I didn't know, and instead of the drab reality of an alcoholic sire around the house, belching and beating on me when he was in his cans, I was free to fantasize my father into a romantic hero, a kind of D'Artagnan of the Canal Zone. In my distant replays, my father was always in the right. In one version, fully imagined, with lots of bad dialogue and good swordplay, he's defending the honor of womanhood. In another, his victim is really a Russian spy. When Bunny O'Toole, who weighed a hundred and sixty-five pounds and had a moustache in the seventh grade, used to give me crap for getting A's in school, I was able to congratulate myself for the self-restraint that let me keep the killer instinct that was genetically mine from running wild. Both the moustache and the aggression were covers for the harelip that was congenitally Bunny's.

At any rate, I grew up believing I had no rival for my mother's affection. She worked for me, lived for me, smiled for me, reserved her soothing woman's touch solely for the healing of my skins and sprains and ego lacerations. Or so I thought. I would have shared her, if grudgingly, with a father whose right preceded mine, but to learn, even after I was twenty-nine and she was dead, that another man, a stranger, had evoked those same smiles, or better, had taken comfort, or worse yet, pleasure, from her cool hands and actually known secrets of her anatomy I only guessed at made me feel utterly betrayed. It was an even worse feeling than finding out your woman's been making it with another guy. I know, because I've been there, too.

No matter what promises you make or vows you take, no matter what the love songs say, you always know, deep down, that your lover isn't really *yours*. She belongs to herself, and you belong to yourself, and any rights you grant or joint tenancy agreements you draw up are really only provisional and artificial. A mother is different. A mother belongs to you. You lived inside her body, deeper than any lover ever reached. Utterly dependent, you survived by her grace. She was the center of your universe. She changed your diapers and tickled your toes, she watched your teeth and your values come in. She knows every wart and mole and scar on your body, and most on your soul besides. Now that's intimacy. There is a tendency, perfectly normal, I think, to want to beat the shit out of any stranger who dares to breach that intimacy.

Except that by the time I found out about him, my mother's lover was safe from retribution, being already dead,

3

and trying to make it up to me from beyond the grave. He left me everything he had.

I was living in Boston at the time and driving cab. The woman I'd been living with for four years had dumped me recently enough and painfully enough that I was still resolutely and defensively celibate. I lived in a one-room basement apartment on Marlborough Street and kept an old army blanket tacked up over the one window. I had a hot plate and no refrigerator. The mold I was growing on the shower curtain was prospering and had started to colonize the walls of the stall. At night, after I took my cab back to the garage and had a hamburger, the greasier the better, at some sad café, I went home and sprawled on my cot and smoked cigarettes and drank Gallo Hearty Burgundy in defiance of the boycott because it was cheap and good and produced a hangover a man could be proud of, and read trash detective fiction, Dostoevsky excepted, until I fell torpidly asleep. I took the sheets and my clothes to the laundromat once every two months or so. My dissolution was deliberate and perversely satisfying. The generally disgusting condition of my person and my habitation was protection against becoming involved with anyone or anything. If I was tempted to ask anyone home, the thought of her reaction to the two-inch-long waterbugs I kept as pets was enough to bring me to my senses.

Why, even given a genetic predisposition to booze and homicide, would a relatively healthy, relatively attractive young man with a reasonably good set of sixties liberal credentials and a doctorate in mathematics deliberately adopt such an unhealthy, unattractive way of life? The answer is absurdly simple. I'd just sustained the cruelest blow of my life. It wasn't Barbara's defection after four years, though that was a bummer, or my mother's death from bladder cancer, which was pretty hard, too, but the sudden and incontestable revelation that there were people in the world smarter than I was. Than I am. The news almost killed me.

The standardized tests they give you all through school had always assured me I was in the top one tenth of one

4

percentile in the whole United States in smarts. The numbers didn't lie. By the time I was fifteen, I'd skipped two grades. I sailed through algebra. Trig was fun. The calculus opened like a flower for me. Whatever deficiencies I had or disappointments I suffered were amply compensated by the knowledge that I had a good, an excellent, brain. So what if you're handsome (or athletic, or amiable)? I'm smart. Who cares if your cock is twelve inches long when erect? I've got a respectable member *and* an exceptional head. Einstein, move over. Make room for me.

Only it turned out I wasn't Einstein. I wasn't even Barney Crews. Things got a little harder by graduate school. I didn't always intuit the proofs anymore; sometimes I had to work at it. My mathematical muse began to require some courting. That's okay, I told myself, a little pushing doesn't hurt. It makes you grow. I believed my capacity for growth was infinite. The test scores said so.

What the test scores didn't do was to divide that one tenth of one percentile into smaller, finer gradations. If I was in the top one tenth of one percentile, Barney Crews was in the top one hundredth. When the variables started to trudge for me, they were still dancing for Barney. While I was pushing Sisyphus' rock uphill, Barney hadn't even broken sweat. Barney Crews was an execrable little creep with a sunken chest, a big ass and no sense of humor. But Barney Crews was smarter than I was. And Barney Crews wasn't even the smartest person possible, he wasn't the smartest person in the world.

We shared an office at MIT, a stall really, just big enough for two desks, one file cabinet, two bookcases and two bodies. If one of us ever had a student coming in to confer, the other one had to leave. Which was okay. I didn't like being in the office when Barney was, anyway, first because, especially in the winter, Barney stank. A kind of too-sweet smell that had nothing to do with perfume steamed off Barney or his clothes and tainted every cubic centimeter of air in our cell. It wasn't sweat, not even old sweat. I'd known Barney Crews for two and a half years and never once seen him sweating. It was a less healthy smell than sweat, more as if he were decomposing as he sat there. Maybe it was the smell of genius, his damn facile little brain cells combusting. Whatever it was, it smelled like the bottom layer of a compost pile, it smelled like human silage.

The other reason I couldn't stand to be in the office with him was that when he worked, he crossed one leg over the other and swung the top leg back and forth in long, constant arcs, rhythmic as a metronome. You could have hooked him up to a motor and used him to generate electricity. No matter where I sat or how I turned my chair in those close quarters, it was impossible not to see that swinging leg. I'd rotate so it wasn't in my central vision, I'd glare at the book or paper on my desk, but the shadow of that swinging foot was always there, polluting the periphery. It drove me crazy. Once I asked him if he was masturbating. Barney just looked up and said no.

Those are probably just excuses. Probably I could have stood the smell and the weird hyperkinesis of his left leg if I'd been confident that Barney was dumber than I, or even no smarter, but for a long time before I faced the truth, I was haunted by a persistent unease, a nasty, gnawing, ever-present, unarticulated suspicion that this person I despised was actually my superior at the one thing that mattered most to me. I didn't want him to know it. I didn't want to know it myself. So, much as I could, I stayed away. When we were both there working in the office, hunched over our separate desks, it was painfully clear to me that while Barney's mechanical pencil was constantly in motion, responding to uninterrupted output from his brain, mine was subject to long spells of inactivity while I wrestled with the problem at hand. I didn't have to see Barney to know his fluency was greater than mine. He used a hard lead in his pencil and I could hear it scratching away across the paper. Never once did I hear him erase. When I had to be there with him, killing an hour or two between inconveniently scheduled classes, I took to reading the newspaper or simply doodling prolifically, so my pencil would sound as inspired as his.

That meant I had to work at home, and working at home, constantly and obsessively, was one of several big things that helped drive Barbara away.

The end of my academic career came one bitter cold, lead-skyed January day. Barney was wearing his earmuffs as he sat at his desk. I was trying valiantly to crack a proof, having promised Barbara I'd work during the day, like I used to and was supposed to, and save my nights for her. The leg, the pencil and the decomposition process were all well under way. I smoldered with frustration. The problem was inscrutable to me, and Barney impinging on my consciousness made it impossible to think. I threw down my pencil and swore out loud.

Barney swiveled in his chair to face me, palely surprised, and pulled his earmuffs off. "Something wrong, Sky?"

His voice was as mild as his smell was strong. I growled back something about being stuck. Barney unslung his swinging leg and stood up. "Let me see, Sky. Maybe I can put you back on the right track."

I said, "Don't bother," but that didn't stop him from leaning over the paper on my desk and reading the equations. His pencil scanned the lines, then stopped. "Nothing to it, Sky. Here's where you went wrong. Look . . ."

I wasn't about to look. What my subconscious had known for months suddenly surfaced and presented itself to my conscious mind, formulated something like, "This fucker is smarter than you are, Schuyler." That was it. I swiveled my desk chair as hard as I could and nailed Barney just above the left knee. It took him by surprise and he went down. I think he hit his head on the wastebasket. The temptation to kick him while he was down almost overwhelmed me, but I resisted, grabbed my jacket and bolted out the door. My last memory of MIT is of Barney Crews sitting on his big ass on the floor, stunned, staring after me like a wounded Eagle Scout.

Barbara left. My mother died. I got a job driving cab. If I couldn't be the smartest one in the game, then goddamn it, I wasn't going to play at all. The only good thing to come out of

7

it all was that I finally felt I understood my father a little better. The guy my old man killed had probably offered to help him.

Chapter 2

I could fill a page or maybe two with zeros, interposed between a decimal point and the lonely digit one, if I was to try to give you an accurate numerical representation of the incredibly minute chance that what did happen, would. It's as useless to speculate what might have become of Schuyler of the Marlborough Street self-abnegation as it is to wonder what George Patton would have done if he'd passed his span in time of peace, or what outlet the fervor of Khomeini might have found if he'd been born an Episcopalian in, say, Nebraska. I cite these two as examples not to suggest that there's any comparison to be made between me and the great men of this world, but only to point out that destiny, an unexpected coalition of time and event, can play its part in the lives of lesser men with lesser tales to tell. What happened, did. Here's how.

I rarely opened my Marlborough Street mailbox, having lost the key, and when I did jimmy it open with my pocketknife once every couple weeks or so, usually found the letters and cards inside addressed to that direct-mail Everyman named Occupant. The only bill I ever got was from the electric company, since when I left MIT, I'd torn up all my credit cards and tossed them in the Charles, in a kind of solemn and self-dramatizing rite signifying my withdrawal from the race to prosper, and the light bill arrived in my mailbox with comforting regularity the fourth day of the first week of every month. It was March 17 I opened my mailbox to find a letter addressed specifically to me from the law offices of Terence Ruggle, Esq.; I remember because I'd taken a fare to South Boston and got hopelessly entangled in traffic along the Saint Patrick's Day parade route. The letter said simply that I should visit Ruggle in his office as soon as possible.

I figured there were only two reasons a lawyer would want to see me: one, that MIT was after me for breaching my contract; or two, that Barney Crews had decided to charge me with assault. Maybe, in my recklessness, I'd hit him harder than I thought, permanently crippled his swinging leg, the seat of his genius, and thereby ruined a brilliant career. I was understandably reluctant to go see Ruggle, but a few days later, curiosity got the better of me, and I did.

Ruggle's office was in Central Square at an address belonging to a flight of stairs papered with handbills that ascended narrowly from the street between storefronts up to a level of small, sad offices one would never, from below, suspect were there. The lawyer's lair was neighbored on one side by an abortion-counseling service and by a professional palmist on the other. His office was very tiny, furnished with desk, chairs and file cabinets he might have bought wholesale off the set of *The Maltese Falcon,* and his windows so caked with grime that little light came in. Ruggle was chewing on the soggy end of a cigar he must sometimes have smoked, from the stale smell of the office, the abundant yellow in his white hair and on his teeth. He was short and square, a stolid gnome, and guessed immediately, when I entered, that I was Schuyler Rykken.

I joined his handshake warily and, when invited to sit, sat tentatively on the edge of his wooden chair. He regarded me with the satisfaction of an entomologist having captured a long-sought species of beetle. "Well, Rykken."

"Well?"

He put his cigar down on the lip of a plastic ashtray filched from some bar and folded his hands on the faded green blotter in front of him. "I suppose you know about the bequest," he said.

I didn't, but I learned. According to Ruggle, a man named Jack Willets had left me, in his last will and testament, a little money, a merry-go-round and six adjacent lots in Kilchis County, Oregon. I suggested he must have dug up the wrong Schuyler Rykken.

"You the only son of a Mrs. Verna Rykken, 2171 P Street, Boston?"

"She's dead now, but I was."

"Then you're my man."

I protested again; I'd never heard of Jack Willets, much less met him.

"Look, Rykken, if I'm satisfied you're the beneficiary here, and I am, why should you fight it? Maybe the guy picked you out of the phone book, for all I know. Do you want to settle this business or not?"

"Make it quick," I told him. "I left my cab in a truck loading zone."

At his own slow pace, Ruggle sprung his bulk from the desk chair and extracted a file from the mostly empty top drawer of a scarred metal cabinet, then spread its contents on his desk, and lip-read through, stopping to share the salient points with me.

"Says here I'm supposed to see the estate through probate . . . take my fee from liquid assets . . . deal with the tax folks . . . transfer deed to you." He looked up. "Not that I expect there'll be much cash, but the property might be worth something."

"Did *you* know Jack Willets?" I asked him.

"Never met the man myself. He did his business with me by mail."

I was still clinging to probability and insisted there'd been some mistake.

"Rykken, it was my job to find the heir. I found him, and it's you. If you don't take your inheritance, the state will. You don't want that to happen, do you?"

"I suppose not."

"Then I'll just go ahead and settle this thing up. You should be hearing from me in a couple weeks time."

"That's all?" I asked him.

"That's all," Ruggle said, "except for this." He took a

sealed envelope with my name on it out of the file and handed it to me. "I don't know what's in it," he said. "It was attached to the will."

I put the letter in my pocket and climbed down from Ruggle's office, got back to Green Street just in time to talk the meter maid who was writing the citation out of ticketing my cab. I'd just inherited a merry-go-round, I told her, and wasn't quite myself.

"First time I ever heard *that* one," she said, and rewarded my originality by relenting, ripped off the half-written ticket and crumpled it into a ball. "Okay," she said. "Go on. Get out of here."

I got in the cab and went.

Chapter 3

*J*ack Willets was my mother's lover.

That's what the letter said. As soon as I hit the street, a tiny blue-haired lady tried to hail me, even though my light was off. She was old and carrying an enormous potted philodendron and looked as if she were about to expire, so I picked her up. She wanted to go to Pleasant Street. After I dropped her off, since I was on the right side of the river, I headed on out to Mount Auburn Cemetery, up the hill to a spot Barbara and I had discovered one Sunday in our picnicking days. It was close to the Poets' Corner, where all the nineteenth-century literary lights repose. Just downhill from Hawthorne and the Alcotts, there's a big terraced plot with a kind of frilly Victorian phallic marker for the family and smaller but no less ornate headstones for the individual dead. The kinky thing about it, what first caught our eye, was the stone dog, lying on a granite pedestal inside a big glass box, just waiting for someone to throw him a granite stick to fetch. Barbara and I spent hours trying to figure out if he was really a stone dog, or a real dog dipped in plaster, with real doggie bones and doggie organs sealed inside. We called him Rocky Rover.

I went and sat beside him to read my mail. Mount Auburn Cemetery had never seemed a ghoulish place to me, more like a museum than a graveyard, but my skin prickled a little when I opened Willets's letter.

Dear Schuyler, [it said]
Maybe your mother finally told you about me, and maybe not. Verna was the greatest joy and the one love of my life. Many times, I offered to make an honest woman of her, and to be a father to you, but she didn't want to marry again, and preferred to leave things as they were. I hope you will understand that our intimacy was really a beautiful thing.

In Verna's memory, I'm making you my heir. I have no one else.

Sincerely,
Jack Willets

This early in spring, on this gray day, there was no other living person in Mount Auburn Cemetery. The few intrepid tourists who come each year with their Nikons to shoot the sleeping place of poets were still back home in Omaha Magic-Markering their AAA maps. The grass was newly mowed and the dead around me were just that, quietly and irreversibly dead, so long dead, in fact, that everyone who ever loved, or hated, or mourned for them was equally dead. Their gravestones were superfluous and silly, a field of granite flowers planted on a forgotten hillside. I sat there on the grass next to Rocky Rover's glass kennel, quite literally not knowing what I was supposed to feel, or what I felt, until at dusk the grounds keeper came chugging up the hill in his sepulchral golf cart and chased me out before he locked the gate.

I'd lived with Verna eighteen, twenty years, and never once suspected I wasn't the only man in her life. I combed my memory for a nook that Willets might have occupied, but the past was inscrutable, or I was too young and insensitive when I was living it to have recorded the proper clues. There was symphony one night a month in season, after she got a little bit ahead financially, and Thursday bridge with the girls, complete with a Friday breakfast recap of every bid, a couple of weekends on the Cape with women friends, but no one time or place I could pick out and say yeah, that had to be it.

And now the mysterious stranger I couldn't place or even imagine had bequeathed me, not a million bucks or a fat stock portfolio, no gold watch or sensible memento, but a merry-go-round. A merry-go-round, for god's sake. It made me question my mother's taste in men. What I knew about carousels would have filled an advertising matchbook, with room left over for a big response coupon. They have horses, don't they?

I'd never even ridden one.

Chapter 4

*B*arbara liked crepes. I offered her crepes. Barbara liked to have reservations. I made a reservation. I even shaved off the new beard that had started to come in, more through inertia than by design. It looked like hell anyway, needed another two weeks at least to deserve the name beard. No more slapdash Schuyler. I was smooth-faced and on my best behavior.

We agreed to meet at a creperie on Boylston Street; Barbara was coming straight from work. It wasn't a place I'd hang around by choice, white walls and dark wood and copper things, with a fashionably dense jungle of flora suspended from the rafters, all designed to serve as a stage set for the sort of people who regard eating as some kind of gala social event and not a basic biological need. In the four-plus years since we'd first met, Barbara had become more and more that kind of person. It happened gradually. First she started to wear makeup. Then it was skirts. Then she got her hair, which was perfectly good, perfectly beautiful hair, cut off and what was left of it tortured into a shape that hair would never think of assuming left to its own devices. She bought electric curlers and brassieres with lace on them. Finally it was high heels. I protested every step of the way. Come on, Barbara, you don't need all that crap. You're fine the way you are.

Only Barbara didn't think so. "Come on, Sky," she said back. "I'm pushing thirty. You can't blame a woman for wanting to look her best."

I made the mistake of pointing out that those two statements did not a syllogism make.

"I don't care about your damn logic, Schuyler. If it makes me feel better to curl my hair, by god, I'm going to do it. Besides, they don't want some aging hippie hanging around the office. I'm an account executive now."

"So why don't you just get a crew cut and buy yourself a nice pinstripe suit? Then you'd fit right in with the rest of the boys." I said that. I'm not especially proud of having said it, but I did. It sounds like sexism, but (he protests) it really wasn't. I would have voted for Barbara for president, if she'd decided to run. I just didn't think much of the advertising business in general, and cordially detested most of the particular "boys" who were her colleagues. In her enthusiasm for making it in a man's world, Barbara tended to overlook the sad fact that a lot of men are jerks.

Thinking about it as I waited, I could see that our roads had been diverging for a long time before they forked for good. Still, I was hoping for some kind of miracle. I wanted to get back together again. I wanted her to come to Oregon with me.

Then suddenly she was there, coming through the glass door, her eyes searching before she spotted me, her natural Barbara-gait not entirely crippled by the two blocks of wood strapped to her feet, her Barbara-look not quite obscured by the expensive effort to resemble everyone else. I had to admit she did it well; she was an excellent specimen of the type, and mine weren't the only eyes that followed her. Soon enough, she found me, and I saw her, after a moment's hesitation, decide to smile.

"Schuyler." She gave me her hand to shake. "Have you been waiting long? I got hung up at the office."

"It doesn't matter," I said. "My time is cheap."

"Still down on yourself, I see."

"Realistic."

"Jesus, Sky, when are you going to grow up?"

And there we were, picking right up where we left off. Only our forcible physical separation had stopped the fight. My hackles were rising fast, ready for round 437, but I smoothed them back down. I hadn't seen Barbara in months. In theory, at least, I still loved her. "Always the adversary," I said.

Barbara swallowed whatever smart rejoinder was itching to come out and touched my arm, gently. "I'm sorry, Sky. We aren't even seated yet, and I've already picked a fight."

My arm tingled where she touched me. I wanted her to touch me some more. "It's my fault, too."

She smiled then. "You're right." And laughed. "You have a gift for making me mad. But let's declare a truce. Old friends ought to be able to have dinner together without starting World War Three."

Old friends. It made me feel like the faded photograph at the back of the album, flaking at the edges. All right. I stuck out my hand, to start again. "Sure. Long time, no see, Barb. You're looking great. What's new?"

For the first time, she looked me in the eye. "What I *wanted* to say, Sky, is that I'm sorry about your mom. She was a good woman. I loved her, too."

Her words struck up against a core of unrelieved grief inside me and bounced away. All the time my mother was dying, I wanted to call Barbara, wanted her to hold me and help me feel what was happening. But I was too proud, and it was too soon. Now that I had her sympathy, it was simple and meaningless. I watched the guy in the chef's hat tossing crepes over the big central fireplace so I wouldn't have to look at her. "Thanks for sending flowers," I said.

The maître d' got to my name on his list and led us to a balcony table where there was lots to look at besides each other. Below us, people at a couple dozen tables were forking crepes and sipping wine and, presumably, relating to one another somewhat better or worse than we were.

"I wanted to come to the memorial service, Sky, but I was afraid it would be awkward."

I nodded.

"I felt like I was letting you down. But I figured if you really needed me, you'd call." She played with her empty water glass. They hadn't got around to filling it yet. Her nails were the color of tomato juice, and much shinier.

"Verna picked an inconvenient time to die," I said.

Barbara tossed her head, so that the elaborate configuration of curves and curls bounced of a piece. "You sound so hard, Sky. It isn't like you."

"I don't feel hard," I told her. "In fact, I don't feel much of anything."

We'd backed ourselves into a hard place, and both knew it. There was no way we could do death and pretend it was the weather. We either had to treat it right or let it go. I changed the subject. Through the ordering and the salad and the creamed chicken crêpes, we talked about Barb's adventures in the ad biz, about the rising price of grass (Barbara, moving up in the world, was developing a nose for cocaine) and the disappointments of the Carter presidency. We kept it light, and neither one of us drew blood. By the time we were waiting for dessert, I was mellow enough to start my pitch. "By the way, it seems there was another death in the family. You're looking at an heir."

"I thought you didn't have any relatives."

"I thought so, too. Actually, this guy was Verna's paramour." It was the first time I'd said it out loud, and it sounded a little sudsy, but Barbara had a secret penchant for soap opera. She was enchanted. "Before or after your father?" she wanted to know.

"After, I think. After me. And I never guessed."

"A woman has her secrets, Sky." Barbara sounded so knowledgeable I winced. I'd been faithful to her for four years, in my fashion. Was it a mistake? I tried to tell her how betrayed I felt, which was definitely a mistake. The dessert crêpe we were splitting, a gooey affair, arrived in the middle of Barbara's dissertation on a woman's right to a little happiness. After we'd stated and restated our positions on the subject, without achieving synthesis, she finally asked what I'd inherited.

"Two thousand dollars, six lots in Kilchis County, Oregon, and a merry-go-round," I told her.

Barbara laughed. "He must have been something."

"I don't know anything about him. *Nada.*"

"But a merry-go-round, Sky, that's wonderful. I love them. They were always my favorite ride at the fair." Barbara seemed genuinely interested, and her cheeks flushed prettily. It seemed like a good time to ask.

"Listen, I'm going to head out to Oregon in a couple of weeks and have a look at my merry-go-round and my land. The two thousand should buy some kind of car and pay for gas. You want to come?" I couldn't tell if I sounded casual or desperate. Barbara was quiet for approximately forty-five seconds, so I assume she gave it some thought.

"I'd like to, but I can't. It's getting crazy at work right now."

"You've got vacation coming, don't you?"

She shook her head. "I went to Bermuda in February. I really needed a change of scene." She held her wrist out and studied it. "I guess my tan's all gone by now."

"You could take a leave of absence."

"I just landed an airline account, Sky. First one the agency's ever had. I'm not about to turn it over to someone else."

"Not even for a couple of weeks?"

Her eyebrows were apologetic.

"What you're saying is, your job is more important than anything else."

At least I forced an old-Barbara gesture out of her. She combed the hair back off her forehead with her fingers, never mind the curls. "I guess so," she said.

We finished dessert in silence. On the street, Barbara said, "You want to come over to my place for a drink or something? We could talk."

I didn't know what she had in mind, but I knew by then what she didn't. "I don't think so, thanks. Not tonight."

It was hard to tell if she was disappointed or relieved. She darted forward to give me a quick peck on the cheek, changed her mind and kissed me for real on the mouth. Then she pulled back just a little to look at me, close enough to make me dizzy. Even tinged green by mercury vapor, even with all that junk on her face, she was beautiful. She stroked my cheek with one finger. "Give me a call when you get back from Oregon, okay?"

Beautiful, but not mine. "I may not be coming back from Oregon," I said.

Barbara stepped back a little more to put three feet, a stranger's space, between us. For a moment, she looked surprised, and then the cover-girl mask came back in place. A dazzling smile. "Well, good luck, Sky. Send me a postcard when you get there."

"Sure, Barb," I said. "I will."

Chapter 5

*A*merica's been done. You know the trip: every hippie who's ever made it from New York to California with a flag on his backpack and a guitar in his pillowcase, whether he plays or not, ends up thinking he's a cross between Woody Guthrie and Alexis de Tocqueville, full of insights on the state of the nation that must be shared; every clod who puts a couple thousand miles on the odometer thinks he's the new Tom Wolfe. I have a lot of faults, but that's not one of them. I didn't discover the country, I simply drove across it. My travelogue will be brief.

Early May, early morning, I load the van. The van is an old Ford Econoline, boxy as a freight car, is ten years old and weighs three quarters of a ton, with eighty thousand miles showing and probably a few more that don't. Loaded with all my stuff worth moving, it's still half empty. There's a pound of good grass, supposed to be Colombian and paraquat-free, in the giant-economy-size box of Tide, right next to the case of Pepsi-Cola in the back. The box with my mother's ashes in it, a nagging disposal problem, I fit under the second seat and try to forget. To my landlord I leave my mold garden and the dinosaur dust motes under the bed. I get on the Mass. Pike in Allston, heading west.

We stop in eastern Pennsylvania, at a county fair in progress, just long enough for me to ring enough Coke bottles on the dusty midway to win a lavender stuffed panda the size of a five-year-old child, which I strap in the front passenger seat and carry all the way to eastern Washington, where I make a present of it to a cute redheaded hitchhiker I pick up, asking and receiving nothing in return. The panda is important because it abets my illusion that my mother joined me on my trip.

Who's to say she didn't? I'm as rational as the next man, have no traffic with astrologers or tea-leaf seers, entertain no fond hopes of a life beyond the present, have never sent or received a telepathic message. I walk under ladders with impunity and subject my perceptions to rigorous tests of reason. Yet I believed, and still believe, that Verna rode along with me for a while. Could I have touched her ? I don't know. Could a third party have photographed the two of us together in the front of the van? Probably not, but all the same, sometimes early in the morning or just near dusk, I was sure I felt her there in the passenger seat beside me, a contented fellow traveler who felt no need to speak. I'm willing to attribute the magic to my own brain, to concede she was there because my own mind conjured her, that I needed to be with her, and so somehow created her from air, from memory and desire, to meet my need. At last it was possible for me to mourn her.

It was the sense of her presence that led me to visit her hometown of Butte, Montana, though she quietly evaporated on my way into town and didn't come back until I was well out of it. I wanted to see why she left, and I did. Even the nineteenth-century boomtowns of New England, their factories extinct now, gates barred and windows broken, seem more alive and full of hope than Butte. I drove up the steeply graded streets, past tired company houses clinging to the hill, past tired-looking children playing without much enthusiasm on tired-looking porches, and tried to picture my mother as a little girl, dusty and exhausted, jumping rope or playing halfhearted uphill hopscotch, or simply sitting on the steps, trying to daydream her way out of Montana.

"I can't remember not knowing I was going to leave," she told me once. "The sooner the better. I picked Boston because my school books came from there."

She was a reverse pioneer, retracing the westward course of her forebears, defining frontier for herself. "If I'd stayed in Butte," she used to say, "I would've ended up a miner's wife or an old maid schoolteacher. By the time I was fifteen, I could tell my daddy was getting itchy for a son-in-law. He didn't believe in birth control, just making the little bastards legal."

So she came to Boston and met my father and fell prey to one of the oldest scams in the book, deferring her education in order to finance his. What she ended up as in Boston, after forty years, was sole proprietor of the tobacconist's franchise in the Suffolk County Courthouse, pushing Life Savers and smokes and morning carry-out coffee. The last few years, she had a little microwave oven in her cubbyhole and heated up plastic sandwiches for the bailiffs and judges who liked to work through lunch and didn't care too much for their digestion. The bladder cancer preceded her eligibility for Medicare by a couple of years, so it cost her everything she'd lived for just to die. Driving out of Butte, I found myself hoping that Jack Willets had made her happy.

Someplace high in the Idaho mountains, Verna jumped ship. We'd been climbing steadily for miles, till the needle on the van's heating gauge was almost off the charts. To keep it from boiling over, I let it coast in neutral every time we hit a downhill grade, and every once in a while, I had to pull over and stop to let it cool down and catch its breath. The rest of the time we chugged slowly, steadily upward, doing twenty-five, thirty miles an hour. Log trucks were passing me on uphill grades. The van groaned in her fever.

Finally it seemed like we were on top of the world. The mountains were close enough to touch, and the road wrapped around them like a piece of string. Here and there short, sharply vertical trails shot off from the road between the trees, so that if one of the big trucks gained too much momentum and lost control, the driver could bail out there and use the grade for a kind of ultimate emergency brake. If you lost control going the other way, you were out of luck. There was no shoulder, only a fragile-looking metal retainer, most places, and beyond that, a sheer, straight drop whose bottom you couldn't see from the road. Bound west, I was glad to hug the mountainside, with a whole lane's width of space to make up for miscalculations. The air was noticeably thinner way up there.

It was about ten in the morning and the sun was shining, not the yellow-hot passionate sunshine of the prairies or the malevolent oven-sun of Arizona, but a kind of silvery whimsical mountain sunshine, thin as the air. The road curled around the mountainside, and I followed it into the middle of an encompassing, low-slung cloud that was dumping hail like crazy, turning the road slick and silver. Inside the cloud, the light refracted every which way, so the roadway and the mountain seemed as effulgent as the sky. The hailstones played percussion on the roof, but that only accentuated the silence of the place itself. The cloud filled the deep valley to my left and overflowed it and I felt that if I drove through the railing and clear off the road into the mist, I wouldn't fall.

It was nature outdoing Cecil B. DeMille. It was gorgeous. It was there my mother's spirit, or ghost, or presence or whatever you want to call it decided to get off. I felt her go. I'd kind of hoped by that time she'd make it out to Oregon with me, but the decision about where to spend what remained of eternity was clearly hers. As strongly as I'd felt her presence before, I sensed her absence now. "Verna?" I said. "Mom?" I don't know what I expected to happen. Nothing did. A deep, resonant nothing that persuaded me a decision had been reached.

I stopped the van inside the storm and dug around under the seat until I found the cardboard box that had her ashes in it. She'd left me a note formalizing her desire to be cremated, but it contained no instructions for what to do with the residues that survived the fire. It hadn't really occurred to me there'd be any until the mortician called me up to find out what I wanted done with them.

He made his best pitch to sell me an urn and a nice eye-level niche in a well-kept mausoleum that probably gave him a kickback and only when pressed conceded that he was required by law to release the ashes to the family of the deceased upon request. I mentioned scattering, and he managed to convey the impression that he was gagging on his end of the phone. "Have you ever *seen* human ashes, Mr. Rykken?"

I hadn't, and didn't want to, but I had some reservations about the mausoleum business, too. I told the guy I'd be by to pick the ashes up. He gave them to me in a box meant to contain dill pickles. I took it home and stashed it out of sight on the top shelf of my closet. It was harder than one might think to fix on an appropriate place for ancestor disposal. Downtown Boston was definitely out. On the Common, they'd arrest me for littering. I considered Cape Cod, Truro or Coast Guard Beach, if only because there it might be possible to find a lonely stretch where I could scatter in peace, but Verna never particularly liked the ocean, and my own memories of the beach included a high wind off the water that could spit the damn things back in my face.

Ultimately, I deferred deciding, and stopped opening my closet door. By the time I left Boston, I'd almost succeeded in forgetting they were there. Almost, but not quite. Still unresolved, I packed the pickle box into the van when I left town.

Now I was able to feel that my irresolution was really inspired patience. Here, in the mountains of Idaho, my mother chose to rest, and I would comply with her wishes. Of course, at one level, I was pretty sure it was me who was doing the choosing, but in either case it was a clear, compelling choice, much preferable to any of the alternatives. Melting slightly as they touched, the hailstones left watermarks on the box, darker brown than the surrounding cardboard. I took the box up to the metal roadside railing and tried to see through the mist. From the coolness of the vapor that breathed up the canyon wall onto my face, I could tell it was a long way down.

I was reluctant to open the box and see the ashes, maybe have to touch them. Finally I decided I'd just loosen the overlapping flaps and heave the whole thing over the side. It was a big enough drop that the contents were bound to spill out on the way down, and cardboard *is* biodegradable.

In the split second after I tossed the box over the edge, I had a strong, almost desperate sense of the loneliness and isolation of the place, and nearly repented my action. But death is lonely anywhere. And it was done.

The hail stopped. The cloud brightened to pure gold around me, and I took it for a sign of cosmic approval, a kind of meteorological amen. A truck came roaring around the last blind corner into view, and the driver honked peevishly at my impromptu parking job on the narrow roadside. I would have been a good deal less embarrassed if he'd surprised me taking a leak. I rushed back to the van, climbed in and started her up. A few more convolutions of the upward spiral and the road began to descend. I left the cloud above and behind me and emerged into summer again, fully divested, no longer student, or lover, or son.

My head was light, and the blood felt thin in my veins.

The colors of the trees and the sky and the roadside undergrowth and the rocky places on the mountainside seemed almost surreally vibrant. I flipped on the radio and found a signal, filled the van and my head with syrupy country western plaints and came off the mountain singing.

Chapter 6

*B*uilding permits required. That's the first thing Kilchis County had to say to me, or anybody else, entering its precincts. It kind of irked me. After traveling 3,178 miles to get there, I figured I deserved a better greeting. O weary traveler, home at last. Give me your tired, your poor. At least a Welcome, Stranger. Anything but this authoritarian business about building permits. It made me want to climb out of the van and build something impermissible right there on the county line, which was invisible, of course, a surveyor's abstraction. The trees of Kilchis County didn't look a damn bit different than the trees of whatever county I'd just left behind.

That's all there were—trees. Big tall conical trees, firs, I know now, but didn't then. One evergreen looked the same as the next to me. When I was a kid in grade school, after I got past the triangle-on-a-popsicle-stick stage, I used to draw Christmas trees with their branches pointing down. So did everybody else in the fifth grade. It was an artistic convention to make your Christmas trees with the branches pointing down, and no one in South Boston ever questioned it. All the branches on the Kilchis County evergreens pointed up. They got their cone shape by a trigonometric progression of upward-pointing branches, each angle, top to bottom, a little less acute, each branch longer than the last. How much else had I been misbelieving all these years?

24

Besides the trees, there was the road, and my second impression of Kilchis County was that it didn't give a damn about its roads. This one was chewed up pretty badly, all pocked and crevassed, with nothing anybody sane would call a shoulder on it. Way up in the space between the tops of the trees on the left side of the road and the tops of the trees on the right was a narrow strip of dead-white sky that ran parallel to the road and mirrored it. Folks in Oregon, I learned later, have a way of attributing the weather to strangers. They'll say to a visitor, "Well, I see you brought the sunshine with you," or "Gee, fella, how come you brought us rain?" I brought rain. I wasn't a hundred yards into Kilchis County before it started to drizzle. I turned the wipers on. It was June, the rest of the country was suffering from drought, but in Kilchis County, water was falling out of the sky.

The road progressed in a series of connected perpendiculars that passed for curves because they were slightly rounded at the corners, and because the highway boys had posted yellow curve caution signs here and there along the way to make it official. Usually the signs are curvier than the road, but in this case, the road builder put the arrow painter to shame. Usually, too, if you add fifteen to the posted speed limit, you're driving safely, but that kind of arithmetic nearly got me killed in Kilchis County. It took me one good spin-out to learn that when the signs said 20 mph, 25 meant suicide. There was no sun to set, but the strip of white above the road turned slowly gray, then darker gray and the trees dimmed down from dark green to simply dark, and I knew it was time for my headlights. I could see the raindrops falling through the beams.

Then, another corner, another surprise. No more trees. No anything. The land heaved up from the road on one side and plunged down into a gully on the other. Beyond the gully, it rose again, hills semicircular, like the inside of a bowl. It was nothing more or less than a clear-cut, but I was ignorant of logger-talk and free to choose my own name for it, and what came to mind was devastation. Not a tree stood anywhere, though I could make out the shapes of the rejects, lying on their sides like bodies of the dead left unburied on the battlefield. Here and there, huge knots of decapitated roots rose up, hundreds of arthritic fingers clawing dusk. What I thought at first were gravestones, dense as at Arlington and lighter gray than the surrounding nightfall, turned out to be thousands of tree stumps, already weathered white.

Into the trees again. Better visibility through the clear-cut had made me overconfident, and the van picked up speed on a slight downhill grade. A curve sign warned me, but I charged ahead until my headlights picked out the stand of trees rising in front of me. The road veered sharply left, and it took all my strength and speed to stay with it. My tail end swung out and the tires shrieked and suddenly two luminous red eyes were staring back at me through the rain. A deer stood dead ahead, mesmerized by the lights, not moving a muscle as I sped toward her. I hit the brake so hard I could hear everything in the van shift, myself included. After a couple of preliminary shudders, the Ford stopped just six feet from the deer. We stared at each other. The fear I saw in her eyes matched the fear I felt in my body.

I shut off the headlights and released the deer from her spell. In the darkness, I could just make out the form of her motion, fleeing, hindquarters bobbing up, a flash of tail, and then she was safe in the woods again. I recognized that frisk of rump from the animation in *Bambi*. They really got it down. For me, life imitated art; I'd never seen a living deer before.

Eventually, the road got straighter and first one farm-house, then clusters of two or three appeared beside it, lighted. The green glow of televisions inside shone out and gave each house a kind of aura in the dark. Finally and without ceremony, my road dumped me on the Pacific Coast Highway, 101, with a signpost pointing south to the city of Kilchis. Since it was dark, I couldn't see the ocean, but I could hear it, a continuous low roar that wasn't the engine and wasn't the rain and wasn't any part of me. It came from my right, an unfamiliar direction for oceans. Heading south from Boston, the ocean was always on my left. The west was backward.

Kilchis City clings to 101 for dear life. Being the widest place in the road for fifty miles, north or south, brings in the occasional hungry tourist or weary traveler, without whom it would have shrunk right along with the logging industry and the fishing industry and the dairy business in the last twenty years. With only thirty-four hundred people to boast of, Kilchis wasn't what I'd normally call a city, but it thought it was, and compared to anything else I'd seen lately, I guess it had the right.

Kilchis had one major main street, called Main Street, running south, and two other quasi-main streets with different names on either side of it that were one way north. Downtown proper was three blocks long, enough for a Montgomery Ward's, a drugstore, a hardware store, two or three cafés, a dimestore, a beauty parlor and a Mode O'Day Fashions. A minor case of urban sprawl accommodated two car dealers, two banks, a dentist and a feed store. There were three gas stations, all showing the same inflated price per gallon, and three cinder-block buildings, one pink, one blue, and one yellow, each purveying a different house-brand Christianity. A text war evidently raged among them. Each one had a sign on the lawn with a biblical quotation painted on it, and they seemed to be in competition over who could make people feel worst. Asked to judge, I would have given the honors to The Wages of Sin Is Death, not so much on the strength of the threat, since the wages of life is death, anyway, but for its niggling vision of God as bookkeeper, too dumb to make His subject and His verb agree. People seeking comfort from religion presumably had to find it in another town.

Leaving the little knot of main streets tied around the highway, I probed the living sections of the place—wide, sanitized streets lined with old frame houses and tidy ranches, a squat hospital and a sprawling high school built with late fifties cinder-block economy. Occasionally my

27

headlights illuminated a plaster of paris flamingo standing one-legged on a lawn, or a ceramic sea gull perched on a roof. The people of Kilchis drew their blinds at night. The lawyer had told me my merry-go-round was someplace in or around Kilchis City, but I couldn't imagine where. I was hungry and tired and depressed by the rain.

The Treetopper Inn was right on Main Street, and called attention to itself with one of the more amazing signs I'd ever seen outside of Revere, Massachusetts. When a blue neon woodsman wields his blue neon ax, a pink neon tree falls over dead, to be resurrected with the next blink. Up and down, up and down the tree goes, once every twenty seconds, three times a minute. What really won the Treetopper my custom, though, was the name of the bar. They called it the Hemlock Room. Discreetly, I smoked a fat roach in the van, then sprinted through the rain for the door. Two minutes inside convinced me they'd never heard of Socrates or how he died. On the paneled wall behind the bar was a sign that read HAPPY HOUR EVERY FRIDAY NITE— HEMLOCK COCKTAIL SPECIAL 90¢.

I wanted to eat and I wanted to drink. All the barstools were full, and I wasn't looking for conversation anyway, so I took myself to a small table behind the bar. The dope was taking hold. Merry-go-round where? Willets, Jack. Some kind of idiot, to choose a place like this. My mother? Oh Mommy, Mama, Mother, alone in the Idaho mountains. Silenced by their silence. Don't leave me alone. I'm afraid of the dark. And while you're at it, make it stop raining, too. The neon woodsman's blue ax falls and falls again, once on the window, once against the wall. Postpone wondering what I'm doing here. Is it all because Barney Crews can do a prettier proof? Is smarter than me? Well, this proves it. I've come to Kilchis City, Ma.

Ready to order?

Who me? Yes, thanks, I'd like it all, a plateful of prospects and a pocketful of rye. Special of the decade. No, make that the century. I'd like a brain better than Barney Crews and a woman warmer than Barbara was on a cold night and oh, yeah, bring me a side of life eternal, please. Replay the past and make my daddy live. Failing that, a hemlock cocktail please. I won't recant. The porches of Kilchis City are too damn small.

Uh, you want something, fella?

You're not kidding.

Want to start with a drink?

I do. I do. She's sort of pretty, actually, in a plain way. A strange way. Wearing a naked face on a slim body, no glop and goo. She has lines like I have lines, apprentice lines, just coming in, only they make her look like a little kid who's very tired and needs a big nap. Plain hair, dark brown, pulled back in a braid.

Bourbon on the rocks, no water. In honor of my father, I order that. Bourbon on the rocks, no water, was his drink.

Eating, too?

Uh huh.

She hands me a greasy menu and goes off to get my bourbon. The jukebox is on and the sound's off on the baseball game on the TV set above the bar. Pitcher twitches on the mound, runner steals second in apparent synchrony with Tom T. Hall. I know all the sentimental ballads this year. Remember me? I just drove cross-country.

I was looking at ten, twelve backs along the bar, heavy-shirted, strong-looking, hunched-at-the-shoulders backs whose front sides were wholly absorbed in getting drunk. My bourbon came.

Want to order now, or shall I come back?

I hadn't looked at the menu, except to see that all the prices had been crossed out twice on their way up. What's good?

Clubhouse sandwich.

Okay.

Chowder?

Sure.

Pencil scratches pad. She's gone. Dangling from the barstools, the men's legs were long, their pants short, socks white, feet dressed in soft moccasins. Their ankles seemed fragile and defenseless outside their boots. I watched their legs twitch and swing around the metal stools. I drank my bourbon in memory of my father who died in a bar in Panama for reasons that remained obscure to me. In memory of my mother, out of her pickle box and wafting down the chasm with the hail.

My chowder came. I thanked the waitress. Every time she approached my table, some of the men swiveled slightly on their stools to look at me. I had no intention of abusing the waitress. I was deep in my own thoughts. The chowder was a ripoff, canned. The pieces of clam were small as spiders. Potatoes soggy lumps afloat in grayish liquid. Beware of gray chowder: it may contain hemlock.

She comes back with the club sandwich. How's my chowder?

Not too well, thanks. I'm still looking for the clams. Maybe she's got a microscope?

She starts to say something. Maybe she's sorry. Maybe the cook's sick, or drunk. I don't get to hear because the occupant of the last barstool dismounts and comes to snarl at me. No way to talk to a lady.

I don't know if she's a lady or not, but I don't say so. I do say I'm not holding her responsible for the lousy chowder.

Am I trying to start something?

Not at all. I ask him if he's ever had the chowder here. I lift up the bowl and suggest he try to find a clam, if he's so interested in my soup.

When he tosses the chowder in my face, it confirms my suspicion there are no clams. The waitress laughs. I have potato in my hair. I ask her to bring me a towel. My antagonist is younger than I am and a whole lot bigger. He's wearing red suspenders and his face would almost be pretty, it's so young, except he's spoiling it by scowling. Am I going to let him get away with that, he wants to know.

Eleven faces, old, young, but mostly middle-aged are staring at us from the bar. He suggests we fight.

I tell him I'm not in the mood.

He calls me a coward.

I tell him the chowder was no loss.

He asks me if I'd like a knuckle sandwich.

I tell him I've already got a clubhouse.

He throws my sandwich on the floor. Not anymore, I don't.

I tell him he's going to pay for my dinner. Plus a 15 percent tip.

Make me. Nyah nyah nyah.

Maybe the cops will.

His daddy's the sheriff.

Good. Maybe he'll spank you when you get home.

Until he grabs the front of my shirt, I have no intention of fighting him. He's got eleven seconds at the bar, and the last time I looked, I was alone. While he's pulling me up by the shirt front, I insert a knee in his stomach. It surprises him. It surprises me. He staggers back, puts his hand on a chair for balance, then decides it'd be a good idea to break the chair over my head. He looks like a berserk lion-tamer, holding the chair by the leg and waving it at me. We dance around the table for a while, stepping on pieces of sandwich. I consider turning the table over on him, but it seems a little drastic. The only other choice is to wait for him to move and then react. By now I'm wondering how he'd look without his front teeth.

It becomes an academic question, because about this time the bartender, who's a big guy with an even bigger gut, comes waddling over and stands beside me, facing my crazy friend. Okay, Tommy. Game's over. Time you were goin home like a good boy.

Make me, Tommy says.

Hell yes, I'll make you, the bartender says. But I'd rather not.

Just let me smash his head in first. You heard what he said.

He said the chowder stinks. He's right.

Move it, Frank, or I'm gonna hit you too.

Frank nods sideways. While Tommy's busy insulting me, two guys from the bar get up and sneak up behind him.

Frank nods again, and they grab his arms.

Now you put that chair down, boy, and go on outside and cool off. It ain't this fella's fault Judy Lynn got herself engaged to some other guy.

Tommy pouted. He put the chair down. There was no way to save face and he didn't try, just wilted like a whipped puppy. Frank the bartender put a fatherly arm around his shoulder. You owe me six-fifty, Tommy. Three and a quarter for the meal this fella ordered, and three and a quarter for the one he's gonna eat.

Make it five-fifty. I don't want seconds on soup.

The men on the barstools turned back to their drinks. Tommy took out his wallet and handed Frank a ten. Keep the change. It's all I got.

Thanks for dinner, Tommy.

He glares at me.

I'm sorry about Judy Lynn, but don't say so. Tommy doesn't appear to be in the mood for condolences, especially mine. He goes back to the bar, swigs down the rest of his beer, grabs his jacket and stalks on out of the Treetopper Inn.

Chapter 7

*T*hanks. Me to Frank.

Sorry about that, fella. Frank to me.

My table looked like somebody threw up on it. Actually, it was the remains of the chowder, but in any case, it wasn't a place I wanted to sit back down. I noticed a few potato shards afloat in my bourbon. Frank noticed, too.

"You come on up and sit at the bar and I'll fix you another drink," Frank said.

"I think I'd like to wash up first."

He pointed me off to the men's room and I went. In the

mirror I looked greasy and gray. Flecks of potato were stuck in my eyebrows and hair. I put my whole head under the faucet and let the water run. My shirt was beyond halfway measures. It needed a laundromat. I dried my face and polished my glasses as best I could on the strip of roller towel that pulled out of a rusty dispenser on the wall. Next to it, a vending machine offered condoms in all colors of the rainbow and a couple interesting textures that promised your partner new transports of delight. Fifty cents bought you a two-pack. At a quarter a throw, that had to be the cheapest sex around. I was still pondering what a mauve condom would look like on a human member when one of the bar sitters came in to relieve himself. He was an older guy with a couple days growth of beard and a spot of blood red on the white of his right eye. His hands were big and looked like they'd been chopped out of a hunk of raw meat by someone who didn't carve too well. Next to him, Tommy looked like a cream puff. I pulled out my comb and applied it to my wet hair while he stood at the urinal.

As he zipped and flushed, he looked over his shoulder at me. "You got a cool head, son. Tommy don't. Ever since his girl went off to college and sent him one of them Dear Johns, he's been tryin to pick a fight with everything that moves."

"No harm done," I said. "I needed to wash my shirt anyway." We walked on back to the bar. At Tommy's vacant seat, Frank had set me up another bourbon, more generous than the first. Frank moved down the line, keeping everybody full. When everybody was, he came back up to my end of the bar. "Drink okay?"

"Yeah. Thanks." When Frank smiled, I noticed that apart from the four front, top and bottom, his tooth supply was pretty scarce, alternating craggy brown molars and bare pink stretches of gum. His hair stood straight up in a crew cut gone to seed. His eyes were small in a big face, and close together. "Tommy's a hothead. He don't handle his liquor too well. Apart from that, he's a nice kid."

I raised my glass and rattled the ice cubes. "To Tommy. A real nice kid." I slugged down some of the bourbon, enough to convulse my tongue and make my eyes consider watering, and assumed that was the end of the conversation, but Frank hovered, wiping big hands' on the stained lap of his apron. "Ain't seen you around here before," he observed.

"Nope," I said.

"You stayin or just passin through?" When Frank narrowed his eyes, they all but disappeared into the pink bags underneath. He may have looked like an ex-marine, but he had an auntie's nose for gossip. I volunteered nothing. "Staying. Awhile."

"Where you from?" he asked, and I wondered before I said it how Boston would sound. As impossibly exotic, in the Treetopper, as Alexandria or Dubrovnik, I thought, a small bomb dropped among the barstools, but I underestimated Frank, his worldliness and his complacency. When I said Boston, he nodded knowingly. "Red Sox," he said. "Them Bruins. Paul Revere come from around there, didn't he?"

"Yup," I said.

"Always wanted to see Boston," Frank said. "And Philadelphia. And Washington, D.C. You been to Washington, D.C.?"

"Yup," I said.

"I went, I'd give them congressmen a piece of my mind. You see the president?"

"The president was watching a football game."

Frank nodded thoughtfully. "I expect they gotta relax sometime, just like the rest of us." He paused to savor his own profundity, then shook his head slightly, just one jerk toward his right shoulder, three parts wonder, six resignation. Then he rammed a chrome neck into a bottle of Old Crow and topped off my drink. "Business or pleasure?" he said.

I looked into my glass, ice cubes gone now, full of straight warm fire. "Drinking?" I said.

"Bein in Kilchis. You here on business, or for fun?"

"Where does a person have fun in Kilchis?"

Frank slapped his palm flat on the bar. "You're lookin at it. Unless you bowl or sing barbershop. Some folks do that.

Me, I got a voice like a tomcat in an electric storm. I drink."

"I thought bartenders had to stay sober."

"If they wanta stop fights, they do." Frank laughed. "Sometimes you let 'em get a little too far just to see what's gonna happen. Hell, I'm as curious as your next guy. You wanta see, can a guy fight? What's Harry gonna say next? You let 'em go a ways."

"Anybody ever get hurt?"

"Nothin big. About twice a year we send guys over to the emergency room. That ain't bad, considerin we're open every night except Christmas and July Fourth."

The waitress came out of the kitchen and put a plate down in front of me. A hamburger was on it, bleeding grease, and a mountain of thick, ridged french fries rose beside it. "Cook ran out of chicken," she said. "He made you a hamburger instead."

"Fine," I said.

"Ketchup?"

"You didn't answer my question," Frank said. "Business or pleasure?"

"I guess you could call it business."

"What kind of business you in?" Frank was closing in. He kept testing for the right button to push to make me spill my story.

"Between jobs," I said.

"Ever tend bar?"

"Never did."

"Don't have to be a big bruiser. A good waitress can stop most fights better than a man," Frank said.

"That's good to know."

"Marty there's had some college," Frank said. "Not too many jobs around here use yer education, down here. Unless yer alma mater is the school of hard knocks."

I had a sudden feeling I was seeing us in black and white, me and Frank at the bar, on a television screen. A recurring horizontal tic passed through us. We were on *Playhouse 90*. It was about 1955. My part was written for James Dean. A taller Ernest Borgnine could have played Frank, or a younger

Walter Brennan. Twenty years before, we might have passed for profound. I decided to screw up the script a little. "Anybody disco in Kilchis?" I asked.

"Some of the kids, maybe. Only other dancin's at the VFW. They get some big-name polka bands over there." Frank sized me up. "You go to college?"

"A couple of years," I said.

"I wanted my boy to go down to OSU," Frank said. "But he wouldn't buckle down to the books. Always messin around with engines. He's got him one of them funny cars," Frank said. "Only it ain't so funny anymore. He's close to twenty-six and never had a steady job."

Someone down the bar hailed Frank and asked for beer. When he came back from the tap, he lowered his voice almost to a whisper and said, "I think he smokes that pot."

I found myself wondering if Frank was a narc. Or maybe he was selling something. I wasn't about to find out. I made a sound that combined a good number of consonants and vowels and couldn't be construed as meaning much of anything one way or another.

"Sometime I'm gonna try it," Frank confided. "Sometime the sheriff's out of town. Can you imagine? I'm a grown man. I fought a war and raised two kids and I never smoked a funny cigarette." He grinned. "My brother-in-law's the sheriff."

That made Tommy his nephew. I kept my mouth full of hamburger. When Frank tried to fill my glass for the third time, I put my hand over it. "No more. Thanks."

Frank returned the bottle to the enclave of bottles behind the bar. "Smart man knows his limits. Where you stayin?"

"I don't know yet."

"Hotel's around the corner. It's clean. There's a couple motels south of town, but they like to rent their rooms twice a night, if you know what I mean. Rains like this, kids got no place to go."

When I got up from the stool, the floor was less solid than I expected. My system was used to the slow, steady infusion

of red wine, mellowed by the smoke of funny cigarettes, but
bourbon, straight, was a stranger, a higher order of proof,
Barney Crews. The floor felt marshy and stuck to my shoes.
"Let me pay you for the hamburger," I mumbled.

"Tommy already paid. Drinks, too. In fact, I made a
profit."

I was trying to remember where I left the van. I got a few
feet from the bar before Frank called after me. "Hey, fella,
what's yer name?"

He had me for a minute, then I picked four syllables out of
the air and said them out loud. "Schuyler Rykken." Around
the corner, I wrote the same four syllables in the hotel
register, and for eight bucks got a room with a shower down
the hall. A framed place mat on the wall above the bed
showed me that Kilchis County (pop. 18,000), famous for
Fish, Milk, and Fir Trees, was larger than several of the
eastern states. The Gideons, famous for Bibles, had left one
by my bed. When I climbed in, I concluded the Hotel Kilchis
was famous for damp sheets. On the other side of the
venetian blind, the wind sprayed rain against my window.
The bourbon swayed me to sleep unlovingly, and I don't
remember dreaming.

Chapter 8

*S*undays are the undoing of the existential man. I've
always believed religion was invented specifically to euphe-
mize the day of anomie into a day of rest. Consider. Every
other day of the week, the world carries on a commerce that
would include you if you wished to be included. Sundays
negate that potential, make the illusion of possible inclusion
impossible. The library is closed. The liquor stores are
closed. The shopping malls are locked up tight. Alone, of

which you can be proud, becomes lonely, which scares the shit out of you. And time. Minutes attenuate, and the hour approaches infinity.

In the late afternoon, sometime around five or six, if you've survived that long, the Void takes off its cosmetic philosophical mask and gives you a peek at the *real* horrors— the face without features, space without time, darkness unmitigated by the faintest hope of light, the definitive message that there is no definitive message, which isn't so bad in the middle of a busy day when you formulate it in words, and then can feel courageous answering your formulation with a neatly executed cosmic shrug, but can stop your liver and make your stomach ache on a Sunday when the awareness doesn't come in words at all, but as a kind of neurological blight, a suppression of the senses for lack of input, a conviction that all your constituent molecules might just as well fly apart and start rearranging themselves into something else right now. The weak take refuge in taverns, churches, museums and the movies. The strong test themselves by going to parks filled with lovers and children or simply stay at home and clutch the bedpost till Monday rolls around.

Sunday is the worst day because it can also be the best. In the Barbara years, it was a day of newspapers and steak and eggs, triple-header lovemaking, long naps or long walks along the river, long drives in the country, long talks about the states of the world and our souls. When I was a kid, Sunday was the one day I had my mother to myself, and as an adult, a day I often visited or called her. If my father had lived to spend a Sunday with me, I liked to pretend we would have played catch or changed the oil or taken things apart for the sheer joy of putting them back together again. In better days, I pitied Barney Crews, who had no family and no friends, his Sundays, with only orders of infinity interposed between himself and nothingness.

It was Sunday when I woke up alone in Kilchis City. I hadn't known it was Saturday night when I went to bed, but when I woke up, I guessed immediately it was my least favorite day. The quiet, for one thing, an absence of hustle, no horns honking in the streets, no sense of urgency. Spirits leaden, not just from burned-out bourbon, but in response to an internal calendar that recognized instinctively the seventh day. I lifted one slat of the blinds and saw it had stopped raining, but the sky was still all cloud, a pale, dull white. The neon woodsman on the Treetopper Inn sign was unlit and not chopping. There wasn't a body moving on the slice of Main Street I could see.

What time it was I had no idea, but I figured the more of the day I spent sleeping, the less I'd have to spend living, so I climbed back between the clammy sheets, closed my eyes and counted whatever apparitions happened by. I remained unremittingly conscious. Then, as a practical matter, I masturbated, without any very clear fantasy to make it fun, no plot, only a few poorly conjured images of breasts and thighs that belonged to no one in particular, hoping I might sleep after, but I didn't. I read the Kilchis City phone book cover to cover, but even that didn't do it. Jack Willets was still listed, a number with no address; I kept turning back to the W's, reading that number. It was a current phone book. Finally, I picked up the receiver, got an outside line and dialed. It rang once, twice, three times while my heart raced, before a woman's voice, recorded, informed me the line had been disconnected. If I wanted assistance, I should stay tuned. I did. After a space of seconds, a living operator, a man with a young, smooth voice, came on the line and wanted to know if he could help. I asked him if there was a new number in place of the old. Pages rustled, then he said, "I'm sorry. Our records show service has been terminated. There is no new listing for that party." After I thanked him and hung up, I found a pen in my jacket and drew a line through Willets, Jack. It was the kind of thing you do on Sundays.

Hunger finally drove me out of the hotel. There was some food in the van, tag ends of cheeses, an aging egg or two, some sausage festering in the cooler, but I didn't feel like eating them, even though it was the last possible day any of it could be considered ingestible. Since there was no one to reprove me, I decided to be wasteful, and took myself to Kilchis's other café, the Skyway, for breakfast. It was grander than the Treetopper, or had been in the thirties, when plastic was the new miracle. Flat, stylized chrome clouds were suspended from the ceiling, while here and there, electric suns in brushed chrome visors shone among them, and the green plastic booths, incised with black floral tracery, were mostly full of churchy looking families who, having fed their souls, were ready to do the same for their stomachs. A towheaded little girl of three or four in the next booth kept peering over the seat back at me; she was bucktoothed, like a rabbit, and I wiggled my nose at her. She laughed, then ducked away.

It was always my rule in Boston never to go to a restaurant alone without a book. It was a way to watch without seeming to, a way to seem to prefer to be alone. I felt the lack in Kilchis, with nothing and no one to look at besides my fellow patrons. In Kansas, where I'd never be again, I stared boldly, but in Kilchis, where I might be staying, it seemed unwise. People could stare back. Did, in fact. My rabbity observer was simply more obvious, less devious than her elders. After I had my coffee, before my omelet came, I went to the postcard rack by the cash register and left a quarter for two views of Kilchis picked at random. It was a small price for appearing to be connected in this world.

Now to write; I'd paid to have that task to do. The first was easy—I'd send it to Barbara. Never mind that we were washed up as lovers; by four years of faithful service, I'd earned the right to write her anytime, from anywhere. I half wanted to tell her about my mother, her brief resurrection and final resting place, since Barbara and my mother had become friends independent of me, but the message space, two and one-quarter by two inches, wasn't enough to make even a start on that one, small as my writing is. With the child in the next booth watching closely, I settled for: *Kilchis is the next Atlantic City. Wildly exciting. Wish you were here.* Because it pleased me to think of her current boyfriend, if there was one, reading it and worrying, I signed myself, *Love, Sky.* Then added, *P. S. Write me General Delivery, Kilchis, Oregon.* I doubted that she ever would, but I went through the ritual as if it were important, which it was, if not for communication, as a method of killing time.

The second card was harder; I seemed to have overestimated the number of my friends by one. Past Barbara, it was lower echelons of acquaintances—the taxi dispatcher, maybe, or my landlord. I had a good relationship with an assistant librarian in the Popular Fiction section of the Boston Public Library, but I didn't know her name, and she didn't know mine, and since I'd most likely never see her again anyway, it seemed like the waste of a stamp. An old Greek ran a sub shop near my place on Marlborough Street and used to talk to me a lot while I waited for my cold-cut submarines. He looked so much like Anthony Quinn and spoke with such a heavy accent I thought for a while I'd found myself another Zorba, until I realized that, put in plain English, the sum total of the guy's wisdom seemed to be, Put lots of oil on everything. It makes it taste better. I didn't know his address.

Finally and in desperation, I addressed the second card to Barney Crews at MIT. *Dear Barney,* I wrote, *It's nice here at the asylum. Remember, I'll be looking for you when they let me out. Schuyler.* With that my omelet came, and I put the postcards aside. It wasn't until my plate was cleared and I was working on my third cup of coffee that I actually looked at the pictures on the front. One, the one I'd sent to Barney, showed a very green field with lots of black-and-white cows grazing. The other was an aerial view of a thin neck of land surrounded by water on either side—on one, by what appeared to be ocean, gray-green and energetic, ruffled with whitecaps. The water on the other side was glass-calm and deeply blue. Only one building stood on the land, on a kind of mini-promontory that veed out on the ocean side. The shoreline around it looked ragged, as if it'd been eaten away by big teeth. I turned the card over to read the legend: *Near present Kilchis, what remains of Seasound City—a few trees and a pavilion housing a carousel, miraculously spared from destruction by the sea.*

When the waitress, who had thick arms and a thick waist and big blue plastic glasses with a metal butterfly stuck to one lens, made her fourth round with the coffeepot, I handed her the postcard and asked her if she knew the place. She squinted at the picture, then slowly smiled. "Why, sure, that's Seasound and the merry-go-round. I used to ride on it when I was a girl."

"Is it hard to get there?"

"'Bout five miles. You just turn right by the Arco station and twist with the road until you see the sign. Not much out there anymore, though, and the merry-go-round's not running since Mr. Willets died."

"Did you know Jack Willets?" I asked.

"Sure. He come in here when he got tired of his own cookin. Real nice man, but a little strange."

"How strange?" It hadn't occurred to her yet to wonder why I wanted to know, so I kept the questions coming.

"Never married for one thing. Lived alone. I invited him over to my place a couple times, for a home-cooked meal. I'm a widow," she explained. "My hubby was killed in a logging accident—nine, ten years ago now. It can get kinda lonely, you know? Only old Jack, he wasn't too much for the ladies. He used to kid about havin his heart permanently broke, before he come out here. He was from back east somewheres. Boston? Somewhere back there, anyway." The waitress had a fond look on her slightly puffy face. She was a nice woman, but Willets was right—no match for Verna.

"Anyway, he never did give me a tumble," she said. "But he loved the kids. Every kid in town knew Jack, and he knew them. Not that there's so many kids around anymore." She shifted her weight and leaned against the green plastic back of my booth. "The young folks don't stay around here. They graduate high school and boom, they're gone off to Portland or Corvallis or somewheres, just like that, lookin for work. They don't come back, neither, except to visit the folks at Christmastime. Seems like the only people havin babies in Kilchis these days is the hippies." She remembered her audience then, and looked at me quickly to see if I was of that persuasion. I nodded her on, but now she studied me, and wasn't going to budge until I'd accounted for myself. "*You* know Jack Willets?" she asked.

"Not really," I told her. "I never met the man. But he was a friend of my mother's. She told me if I was ever out this way, to look him up."

"Well, you're a little too late for that, son. But tell me, where's your mother from?"

"Boston," I said.

"They go to school together, or what?" She was trying to sound nonchalant, I think, but it came out belligerent. It dawned on me she was still jealous of a dead man.

"I don't know how they knew each other," I said. "It was before my time."

"Oh, well. . . . You want some more coffee?"

"Half a cup, thanks." She poured it full. "He must have been quite a guy, huh? I mean, my mother always said good things about him."

"Jack Willets was a gentle man," the waitress said. I don't know how she meant it, exactly, but she said it in two separate words, so I figured she wasn't talking about his table manners. "Too bad he's gone. He'd've liked to've seed you, son." It was the first of her smiles that was meant for me, and I recognized she was doing me a kindness of her own, just like my half-truths were meant to spare her pain. Suddenly I was over the line between using her and liking her, only I didn't know how to say so. "Coffee's good," I told her.

"Hot, anyway," she said. "Say, you bring us this bad weather?"

"I don't think so. It was here when I got here."

She gazed out at the pale white sky pressed against the restaurant window. "Wouldn't know it was June, would you?"

"No," I agreed. "Does the sun ever shine here?"

"From time to time," she said. "From time to time. When the sun shines here, it's the most beautiful place in the whole world." She laughed a little laugh that was younger than her body. "Course, it don't happen all the time. That's what makes it special. And what keeps the California folks away. Otherwise we'd all get trampled in the rush. Rain's the only protection we got."

"Sounds like you don't think too much of Californians."

"That's a fact," she said. "They come nosin around up here, lookin for ways to spend their money. They had their way, Oregon'd be one big RV park, with them condomimiums all along the ocean for the rich folks to enjoy, and hands off for the rest of us. Thank God for the rain." Since I was learning something, I didn't interrupt. Her voice softened a little. "Livin here's somethin like bein poor," she told me. "When you haven't got much money and you get a new pair of shoes, them shoes are somethin special. They make you feel like a queen. You take 'em off and put 'em up somewheres you can admire 'em. If you got new shoes every week, it wouldn't be the same. Weather's like that too. Too much sun, a person don't even notice sunshine anymore. It don't gladden his heart." She looked at me hard, almost pleading, naïve and wise in equal measure. "You see what I'm sayin?"

I nodded vigorously. I would have tried to keep her talking all afternoon, if she was willing, but a voice bellowed out of the kitchen, "Yvonne, dammit, where are you, woman? There's three orders backed up here, gettin cold."

Her body tensed and she hollered back, "Hold your horses. I'm comin." More quietly, she said to me, "Fella owns this place's a regular slave driver. Law says I'm entitled to a fifteen-minute break. Reckon I just took it." She moved off slow and steadily, obedient but uncowed, and making the difference clear. "Nice talkin to you," she turned to say, before she was wholly waitress again, serving food and wiping tables.

9   *Chapter 9*

C. D. Horner was in groceries in Saint Louis.* At first, there was only one store, a small neighborhood market called Horner's Corners, with three apartments, one large and two small, occupying the upper floors of the tall frame building. The largest of the three domiciled Horner, his wife and baby daughter until business prospered and Horner acquired a second, then a third and finally a fourth market, a small chain, and built a new house for the family on a hillside, with a ballroom on the top floor and more bedrooms than could be filled even if all the relatives visited at once. Horner was rich, not Carnegie or Rockefeller or robber-baron rich, but rich enough to buy his way into the local social register and watch his daughter graduate from the city's best academy for young ladies, shoulder to shoulder with other girls whose fathers' money smelled less new.

In 1906, after twelve years of taking only Sundays off, Horner allowed himself to be persuaded by his brother-in-law to come west on an elk-hunting expedition, and when their itinerary brought them to coastal Oregon, he first laid eyes on the peninsula, shaped something like the shell of a razor clam and clinging to the mainland by a thin clam neck,

* Most of the historical information in this chapter comes from a pamphlet I found in the library, *The Story of Seasound*, Kilchis County Historical Society, 1967, 58 pp.   S.R.

that separated Kilchis's deep, sequestered bay from the restless turmoil of the Pacific Ocean to the west. His eyes saw four miles of unspoiled ocean beach curve grayly toward distant hills, a thousand feet wide, with sand as soft and fine as granulated sugar, saw the great ocean spitting around two jagged rock islands that stood like molars in a giant mouth, whose lips were the land. He saw the elevation of the seaward dunes, huge sand hills rising a hundred and fifty feet above the beach, topped with tall, tough, wind-resistant pines. An inner eye showed him the future, if only he would make it happen—a sumptuous resort of grand hotels and palatial second homes atop the dunes, residents and guests all millionaires, at the very least, sipping champagne and dancing in the moonlight beside the sea.

In Horner's vision, it rivaled Atlantic City and put Palm Springs to shame. Seasound City, for so he christened it when the only inhabitants were clans of Scotch broom, beach grass and wild scrub pines, gulls and crows seaward and, on the bay side, kingfishers, would be the jewel of the Pacific Northwest, playland of wealthy moguls, a little bit of cosmopolis amid the indigenous torpor, and he, J. D. Horner, would be its patriarch and patron. He would develop it.

Having seen the land and dreamed the dream, Horner was hooked. He made the brother-in-law, till then manager of the second of the Horner's Corners markets, his business agent and left him behind in Oregon with a commission to acquire the land, while he hopped the first train back to Saint Louis to liquidate his assets and tell Mrs. Horner the good news: they were out of groceries and into real estate. What Mrs. H. thought of her husband's midlife volte-face, whether she made the move willingly, with resignation or under protest is unrecorded, but move they did, leaving the mansion on the hill and their daughter, lately matriculated in Stephen's College, behind in Missouri to finish her finishing. The elder Horners headquartered in Portland while the sale was finalized, the peninsula platted, an engineer hired to deflect fresh water from hilltop springs five miles away, the copy written and handbills printed, offering prospective buyers the chance to invest in the newest, the biggest and best summer resort on the whole Pacific Ocean, Alaska to Argentina.

It was also, in 1906, the least accessible. The automobile was not yet the vehicle of choice. Most folks regarded it with considerable suspicion. No cars, no roads. The Pacific Coast Highway didn't exist, the rail line from Portland to the coast was not yet completed and no road connected Kilchis to Seasound City overland. The only way to reach Horner's seaside paradise was by water—a four-day voyage, dock to dock. The entrepreneur bought himself a steamboat to ferry prospects a hundred miles down the Columbia, from Portland to the river's mouth, and a second hundred across open ocean from Astoria south to Kilchis Bay.

Shipping the lumber and the work force in, Horner had built an elegant hotel to house his guests. Brilliantly white, artfully porticoed, its pantries stocked with caviar, its tables set with heavy silver, cut glass and Lenox china under massive crystal chandeliers, the Seasound Hotel was set upon the peninsula's highest rise to overlook the ocean. Of the prospects who didn't succumb to seasickness, some bought lots and began to build homes of their own on the sand cliffs above the beach—homes fanciful and strange, resembling gracious southern mansions or Japanese pagodas, English country homes or small medieval castles, columned Greek temples, Spanish haciendas, homes of Victorian ornateness or Georgian austerity. An unparalleled architectural miscellany flowered on the dunes.

For recreation, Horner built tennis courts and a larger-than-Olympic-size swimming pool, housed from the elements by a large wooden structure christened, with a Victorian flourish, the Natatorium. A wave machine roused artificial surf in Horner's pool to give swimmers the illusion they bathed in the ocean while sparing them exposure to the icy water and rapacious undertow of the real thing. A dance pavilion hosted seaworthy popular bands. The completion of the railroad to Kilchis and the building of a road from there to the peninsula brought more settlers and the start of a business district to Seasound.

In 1911, a Frenchman named Thibault announced his intention of bringing to Seasound City a carousel. Horner was pleased with the proposal and wanted Thibault's merry-go-round placed by the hotel, near the resort's other amusements, but the Frenchman declined to build on sand and explored the peninsula until he found what he believed to be a solid lot with a vein of bedrock under it and a stand of sturdy pines to help stabilize the sandy soil, for which J. D. Horner charged him all of fifty dollars and considered him a fool for paying it. Frenchy Thibault, as he was known to locals, built a huge wooden barn around his carousel to protect it from the sea mist and the rains, and opened his amusement on June 21, 1912, to a crowd of appreciative riders.

When I arrived at Seasound sixty-six years later, there was no city, no business district, no hotel, no sidewalks or tennis courts, no sewer, no houses and no place to swim but the sea. Which was where everything else, everything but Frenchy Thibault's merry-go-round, had ended up. Winter storm tides had eaten up the beach, consumed the dunes and swallowed up the man-made monuments that crowned them, even twice breached the peninsula itself, just south of where the merry-go-round stood, though the county had paid to close the gap, since the ocean tides were damaging the oyster beds inside the bay. Seasound City was not, when I arrived, even a ghost town; nothing remained for ghosts to haunt.

Later, exploring, I found what artifacts were left—huge slabs of sidewalk upended on the beach, cement chewed away from the egg-size cobbles, so that they stood in round relief; cast-iron radiators and lengths of pipe corroded into fantastic shapes by salt and weather; enameled parts of iceboxes or stoves, spotted with rust; and, here and there, buried for winters in the sand, a bent spoon or a broken goblet, but that first day I saw only my merry-go-round, orphaned among acres of stiff, man-high broom and salmonberry, with nothing to suggest it had not always been alone. Though Frenchy had built inland, leaving the sandy promontories to his more optimistic, view-hungry neighbors, the merry-go-round stood now on a little delta of its own carved out of the dunes and had a magnificent view, if what you like to look at is water, billions of gallons of green, nervous water, flexing into whitecaps, bombarding land.

What I saw first was a big wooden building, something like a barn and something like a giant, pitch-roofed shed. Up close, I could see what paint was left blistered on the boards, waiting to pop under pressure of the wind and flake away, and the boards themselves silvered by weather to an all-encompassing organic gray. The roof had been shingled once and still was, after a fashion, with every other shingle, more or less, in place and sprouting a gray-green seaside lichen, smooth as spray paint. Horizontal shutters, hinges bleeding rust, covered the window holes, and the whole structure, while basically sound, looked kind of sad. It had the feeling of a ruin to it, of a temple that's outlived the religion it was built to serve. I saw a signpost, but no sign. Skeleton trees, spined by leafless branches, rose up fifty, seventy-five feet out of the sand, gray as driftwood, and as dead.

I wanted to see the inner sanctum, of course, the central mystery, but I didn't have a key and didn't know where to get one. A massive chain looped the double doors together by the handles and a padlock that looked like it meant business held the ends together. It crossed my mind to smash the lock—maybe one of the big beach rocks hurled hard enough would do the job—but much as I kept reminding myself all this was mine, I still felt vaguely criminal poking around there, as though I trespassed and would be punished if caught. Finally I decided to see if I could pick the lock. I pulled out all the attachments on my pocketknife and took the lock in hand. No picking necessary. Someone had filed through one side of the crosspiece just above where it fitted in the lock. It swung back easily. I unlaced the chain and tugged at the doors. They were swollen with damp and cried out when I opened them.

It's hard to describe what I saw, because seeing takes place all at once, and description requires things to be put in order according to values the eye by itself doesn't recognize. First there was dimness, and a fraction of a second for the lens to open before I could see anything at all. Then, I suppose, the carousel shape, its round peaked roof and flat round platform and the uprights connecting the two. The muffled forms of the horses, pale and shapeless. They'd all been draped, with sheets, with painter's drop cloths or faded blankets, the way furniture is draped in empty houses so that in the shadows, it looked like a ghost-go-round. I walked deeper inside, all around the carousel, and in the far corner found a little screened-off cubicle with something like living space behind it, a narrow cot with a sturdy metal frame, probably World War I surplus, with a damp and lumpy mattress showing its buttons and naked stained ticking, a bedside table with one club foot, evened by a stack of old magazines, vintage *Playboys* mostly, the pinups soggy and pocked with the imprint of the table leg. A Baby Ben, its hands and numbers faintly luminous, was run down on the table, keeping no time. I picked it up and wound it, to make the minutes move again. It'd stopped at ten to ten, and that seemed as good a time as any; I had no watch to set it by and no particular reason to want to impose the world's notion of time on Baby Ben. Its tick was companionable, and I felt as if I'd performed a small miracle.

I spotted a single light bulb over the bed and did a second miracle. The light showed me a sawed-off chest of drawers and a provisional closet, jury-rigged of twine, a couple of cardboard cartons full of moldering paperbacks, a plastic dishpan with assorted plates and cups and odd-lot silverware inside, a battered black footlocker under the bed, the accouterments of a life at least as spartan as the one I'd lived on Marlborough Street, and considerably neater besides. The clutter of beer cans and stomped-out cigarette butts on the dirt floor, the couple of used condoms I found under the bed I judged, rightly, were not Jack Willets's mess, but belonged to whoever sawed the lock. Kids, probably, and not overly sensitive, if they'd been making it in a dead man's bed.

I tried to imagine them, passionate on the mildewed mattress, tender by the harsh light of one bare bulb, witty and whimsical, maybe, as they smoked a lazy cigarette after, but it didn't work. My imagination failed me. Love, in my limited experience, is never so oblivious of death.

I turned away from imponderables, toward the machine. The screen didn't reach to the ceiling, so a little light spilled over into the main part of the building, where the merry-go-round stood. I mounted the platform this time, closed my hand around a supporting pole. It was brass, warmer and denser to the touch than I'd expected. At the center of the circle, in the doughnut's hole, was an octagonal box, painted a faded green and festooned with chipped gilt. One panel, a door, stood open and I went inside to have a look at the works. My pupils opened wide to use all the light there was, and I saw a small electric motor, red paint dimmed by a thick film of grease, that seemed to be the god of the machine. It drove a giant flywheel that turned a rod that drove a gear that interlocked with another smaller gear that made a vertical rod go up and down, and so on, a simple, elegant mechanism that I studied with gratitude and pleasure because it was linear and logical and inexorable and implied things I wanted to believe about cause and effect and human perspicuity.

I traced the linkages several times, admiring the design. Here was something capable of being understood, something efficient and utterly predictable, a triumph of reason. That it existed to drive wooden horses round and round, up and down, only proved to me that as a species we're considerably more ingenious at solving problems than at stating them in the first place. No matter how frivolous the application, the technology was beautiful, and just seeing it helped to stabilize a reeling brain.

My brain *did* reel. I read over what I've written down and find I haven't really conveyed that. Writing makes sequential what should be simultaneous, permits no true profusion, no overloading of the senses as happens in life. Reporting one detail, a hundred others are excluded. A well-made sentence confers motives that may or may not exist in reality. I've written that I saw this and did that, as though there were some pattern to my actions. There wasn't. There *was* a brown tinge to the shadows, a silence inside the sea roar that unnerved me; there *was* a feeling of opening a tomb, to find it already desecrated; there was a certain clamminess to the air; there were questions and regrets. The beer cans were Olympia. The cigarette butts were Marlboros. There was fear.

As I crouched beside the starter motor, checking it out, I had the uneasy feeling I was being watched. I listened, but heard nothing move. At last I half turned and saw it, one glassy green eye, one flared nostril, peering out from underneath a sheet. They belonged to the middle horse in the row behind me. For a minute, maybe two, I stared back, not moving. Afraid to move. Then I made myself laugh out loud, an odd sound in that quiet place, and not entirely convincing. The green eye was cold and clear, a no-bullshit kind of eye, and I found its look accusing. Paranoia, I told myself. Stupid nerves. Get up and show that horse who's boss. I got off my haunches and pulled back the sheet just far enough to expose a wooden head and neck dressed in a carved silver bridle set with glass jewels. The neck arched forward, the teeth were bared inside florid red horse lips, wooden hooves stretched out in a gallop, flashing nostrils gulped air, the carved mane curled backward on the extended neck, all plunging forward against a wind of great velocity. In the damp, in the quiet, where nothing moved, the green-eyed horse raced against a perpetual gale. Motion and stillness, both things were true. I reached out to touch the shining yellow neck, half expecting to feel hot flesh. The wood was cool and solid. The green eye never blinked.

Chapter 10

*S*ummer came back on Monday. The sheets on the hotel bed felt a little drier when I woke up. Sun scorched the mist and finally burned it away. Kilchis City looked better in a better light. It had to do with shadows. Lacking a distinct light source, there are none, and without shadows, everything looks flat. The flaws show. A play of light and shade gentled the edges of Main Street's cracker-box buildings, lent them idiosyncrasy and mass, a hint of mystery. Shadows improved Kilchis. Sun improved Schuyler. I woke up optimistic, as if some nagging organic imbalance that was getting me down had been righted by a change of weather. One morning's despair is another's status quo.

After a shower in the communal bathroom down the hall, I went back to the Skyway for breakfast, hoping, for continuity's sake, to build on my acquaintance with Yvonne, but Monday must have been her day of rest. An unsmiling young woman wearing an engagement ring with a diamond so big it had to be fake served me monosyllabically instead. She had extremely large breasts and was young enough to suppose that was all she was going to need in life. She certainly hadn't developed a personality to match her chest. When I asked her where the courthouse was, she pointed.

I've seen public buildings that forbade smoking and spitting, bare feet and dogs, but I'd never before encountered one with a sign that said, CALK BOOTS PROHIBITED. WEAR STREET SHOES PLEASE. Acceptably shod, I entered. The Registry of Deeds was downstairs, past the Tax Collector and the typing pool, past the Health Department where screaming babies waited for their shots, way back in a windowless corner furnished in must and brown. The registrar herself looked like a jaundiced raisin, with dentures that loosened noticeably as she spoke until she sucked them back in place, in a never-ending cycle of spit and suck. I was the only person in the office, and judging from her loquacity, she was glad to see me.

Since Willets's Boston lawyer had been in touch, she already knew a good deal about me, and when I told her my name, she unleashed a prodigious monologue, punctuated occasionally by a nosy question.

"Rykken . . . Norwegian name, Rykken . . . used to know a Torkel Rykken when I was young . . . don't suppose he was any relation though [spit] . . . funny people, Norwegians . . . I know, I married one [suck] . . . you like lutefisk? I hate it [spit] . . . my husband had a foul temper [suck] . . . didn't see it often but when he got mad [spit] look out [suck] you got a temper, boy?"

"Well, sure. I suppose so. Doesn't everybody?"

"Not like the Norwegians [spit] I know, I married one [suck] believe me, you would have thought he was the calmest [spit] most peaceful man on earth [suck] except when he got riled [suck] he only got mad at me [spit] once in forty-two years but that was [suck] enough . . . cracked two ribs and knocked out half my teeth [suck] I never crossed him again . . . I heard you got in a little [suck] altercation over at the Treetopper Saturday [spit] night and that you [suck] handled yourself real [spit] well . . . course [suck] maybe it wasn't you. . . ."

"I think it was me."

She cackled happily. "See there now [spit] I told Frank it must have been [suck] the young fella that inherited [spit] the merry-go-round [spit] from Jack Willets and I was [suck] right." She clapped her hands and sucked again, for emphasis. "Course maybe you take after your ma. Your mother Norwegian?"

"No."

"What then?"

"Part Irish, and something else. English, I think."

"Aha. That saves you, see. The Irish is your safety valve. You drink [spit] a lot?"

She was a raisin with little berry eyes, a bird who wanted

to pluck secrets from my heart. She fluttered with excitement, astute old witch. "Sometimes I drink," I said.

"Good answer, boy. Sometimes he drinks. Ha ha. You have the look of a drinker, son, and I [spit] can always tell. A quiet drinker, I'd say . . . you should get out more [suck] socialize. Life's too short to brood, you [spit] know."

"Have you got the key? They said in Boston you'd give me the key."

She opened her palm and showed it to me, then closed her fingers around it. Holding it for ransom. "What's [suck] your hurry? Got to slow down . . . impatience kills a man . . . your merry-go-round'll [spit] still be there ten minutes from now or twenty or next year. You going to [suck] keep it running or are you [spit] going to sell?"

"Do you think anyone would want to buy it?"

She made her mildly sinister laughing noise again, and her berry-eyes smiled. "There's plenty of folks would buy it in a minute, *if*," she said.

"*If* what?"

"If they build the other jetty."

I didn't get it. "What other jetty?"

"The one they should have built when they built the first one." She cocked her head and gave me a wicked smile. "You don't know much, do you, boy?"

"Not about jetties."

"Not about lots of things." (For expedience's sake, I omit the sound effects henceforth. Imagine them.) "See, the Corps told them they should build *two* jetties, back in ought-nine. But Congress wasn't about to pay for two jetties in Kilchis County, Oregon, and the city fathers wouldn't do it, either. They sat around and bellyached about it till 1921. Then they scraped together enough to go ahead and build *one* jetty. Next hard winter, old King Neptune started snacking on Seasound City. Had the hotel for breakfast and the Natatorium for lunch. And all those fancy houses." She shook her head, obviously on Neptune's side. "They were fancy, too. And now they're gone. All gone." For a minute she could see them, all the fancy houses, in her mind. Then she opened her fist, just a little, to tantalize me with another glimpse of the key. "There's folks been paying taxes on lots out there that've been underwater for thirty years and more. Don't want to lose title, just in case the Corps can make the ocean spit it back up."

"Another jetty would do that?"

"That and one hell of a lot of fill, my boy. Pardon my French. There's those that say it could be done."

"It doesn't sound exactly cost effective to me," I said.

"Shows how much you know. Just how much undeveloped coastline you figure's left in this country, my boy? How much?"

I shrugged.

"Damn little," she said. "They build another jetty and that sandbox of yours is a gold mine."

"Let's hope they build it then. How about giving me the key now?"

She put the head of the key in her mouth and used it to push her teeth back in place. "Your folks alive?"

I shook my head.

"Both dead?"

A different shake, affirmative. My patience was giving out. I felt violated by all the questions.

"That makes you an orphan," she said with a kind of emphatic delight. "You need some mothering, you come see me. Call me Mom. Everybody does. My youngest boy, he's been a county commissioner for nearly eighteen years now. Works upstairs."

"And he got you your job, right?"

"Wrong. I been the registrar of deeds here for forty years. My boy did keep them from retiring me when they were going to, a few years back."

"How many years?" I asked.

"Let's see." She used her fingers and my key to tick off memories. "That'd be eleven years ago, I guess. I'm seventy-seven now." She preened, patted her hair. "But everybody says I don't look my age. Just last week, Harvey Knox—he's one of the other commissioners—said, 'Mom, you don't look a day over sixty-five. And sharp as a tack besides.' I am, you know," she said.

She still posed with her hand behind her head, like a Dorothy Lamour pinup. It was a weird effect.

"You're supposed to tell me I don't look my age."

"Yeah."

"Go on," she said. "Tell me."

She was entirely too used to being obeyed, probably had the goods on everyone in Kilchis, after forty years of public service. Since she didn't have anything on me, though, I decided not to play. "Vanity, thy name is woman," I told her.

Her face fell, and her hand dropped out of the cutesy cheesecake pose. Then she laughed. "Okay. All right. I like you, boy." She handed me the key. "You come see me again. Come anytime. I might even let you buy me a cup of coffee." She grinned so I could see her plastic gums, ingenuously pink. "I may not be pretty anymore, but I know everyone and everything that happens in this town." It sounded less like a boast than a simple statement of fact. I didn't doubt it for a minute. "You will come see me?"

I'd never been propositioned by a septuagenarian before, but she was hard to refuse. "I might," I said, "if I can call you something besides Mom."

Her crinkly yellow skin turned faintly pink, and her laugh was incongruously girlish, almost a giggle. "Well, my Christian name is Barbara. I suppose I could let you call me that."

"On second thought, let's make it Mom."

She shrugged a knobby thin shoulder. "Suit yourself, boy. Everybody does."

"Thanks for the key, Mom," I said. "I've got to go now." It wasn't really disloyal; I'd always called my mother Verna, because she liked it better that way.

"I'll see you, boy," Mom said, and sucked her dentures back in place.

Chapter 11

*A*n impulse to settle, what I recognized as my pallid male equivalent of a nesting urge. I'd felt it before, moving into new dorm rooms or new graduate student apartments, a strong desire to put my living space in order, to organize my possessions in such a way that their arrangement would both predict and serve a way of living. From past experience, I knew the impulse was apt to be short-lived; except when Barbara and I set up housekeeping, when the momentum lasted a record four months and experienced an annual renewal that resulted in painting the bathroom or buying a new rug, the longest my homemaking urges ever persisted was about three days. Since I had the energy, I figured I'd best put it to use.

I'd decided to live at Seasound with the merry-go-round, where I'd have no rent to pay. On Moving Day, I pulled the van up close to the door and turned the radio up high to give me a beat to work by, opened the shutters to let in light. In town, I'd bought plastic garbage bags and begged half a dozen cardboard cartons from the local liquor store. The first task was to dispose of Willets's stuff, and the big trick was to do it without violating his privacy. I was getting to be an old hand at doleful dumping, having had the responsibility for Verna's effects after she died, but that was a little different, since I'd known her well, and because her women friends obligingly assembled one Sunday afternoon to help me out, claiming as keepsakes pieces of clothes that fit them, or knickknacks they'd always admired. All in all, we'd made quick work of it.

I was even quicker with Willets's things, none of which had any personal meaning to me, no memories attached. In less than an hour, the deed was done; I'd decided what to keep (table, chair, dresser) and what to dump (books, clothes, linens, cooking things, old cans of paint and stiffened brushes, his bed) and the place stood ready to receive my things instead. His battered black trunk was the only hang-up. Finally, without opening it, I stowed the footlocker in a bit of dead space behind the merry-go-round engine, where some tools and a couple cans of oil were also stored, where it would be out of sight and mind.

Then, in a burst of efficiency, I unloaded the van, unpacked my suitcases and dispersed my possessions, treating each assignment of place as if it were a great decision, sagely made. I unbolted the van's third seat and brought it in to be my temporary bed. When I was done, the little encampment didn't look much different than it had before. Still, I was enormously pleased with myself. As a final touch, I took the photographs of my parents, long my household icons, from the bottom of the last suitcase and set them up on the dresser. For the first time, I noted how ill-matched they seemed—my father young, blurred and bearded, and my mother ripely middle-aged, as I best remembered her. He might have been her son.

On to the merry-go-round. There was a solid rim below the canopy that made a kind of circular frieze, with six gilded frames of equal size around the circumference, and in daylight, I could see that the pictures inside them, of bustled ladies and side-whiskered gentlemen, nymphs dancing to the tune of pipe-playing centaurs, were in tough shape, the surfaces scored with cracks and chipped, the images almost obliterated by time and damp. They made the carousel look her age.

The animals, by contrast, were beautifully kept. One by one, I pulled off sheets and blankets until I'd exposed the whole menagerie—eighteen horses in all, a tiger, a rabbit and a gilded chariot pulled by a pair of arching, leaping fishlike creatures, a dream of dolphins, maybe, copped from some medieval bestiary. The tiger wore a purple-and-gold saddle and stood ferociously, one big paw raised, each claw carved sharp and separate, but its expression was ingenuous, and it wore a gentle smile around the pointed teeth, as if it knew it was a pussycat. The rabbit was foolish and distinctly unrabbitlike, though it was a disturbingly good caricature of vapid humanity. Its wooden ears drooped in opposite directions, one forward, the other back.

The horses overwhelmed me, so many of them, each subtly different from his fellows. Their coats were every color, their harnesses embedded with artificial jewels of every kind, rubies and sapphires, topaz, emeralds, amethysts and diamonds. The overall impression was magnificent—splendor, profusion, gaiety—but I wanted something more than an overall impression; this was my merry-go-round, and I wanted to establish intimacy, to take possession of it with my senses. It was a hopeless task, of course—only time could acquaint us properly, but I was determined to try to speed the process up, breathed deeply to slow myself down and began to circle the platform, touching a purple haunch here or green ear there, with my brain set to catalog details.

I saw that some of the horses were handsome, some proud, some small-headed and swift- and mean-looking, some oddly childlike, with primitive expressions of goodwill. I saw that some had carved tails, while others wore thick swags of real horsehair, coarse to the touch. I saw that each horse had a different and characteristic gait, and that none was particularly horselike; the carved legs pranced or kicked, stretched or curled according to the whim of the carver, with little respect for nature. Their wooden hooves were shod.

As I slowed down, the horses speeded up, and I saw them each as one cell of a complex animation, arrested in motion between one instant and the next. My mind brushed an Einsteinian nub, and I perceived time and motion as interchangeable forces, not similar, but same. My horses were wave and particle at once. I felt their urgency, their need to move. I turned the motor on, took the brake off, engaged the clutch. The whole mechanism groaned, coming to life, the flywheel turned, rods pumped, gears meshed in two simultaneous cycles of revolution, and after a delay that seemed as long as the six days or sixty billion years of creation, the big wooden platform began to rotate slowly, the horses pumped up and down, up and down, chasing each others' tails.

It was a silent parade until I remembered music and opened the back of the band organ (Wurlitzer 1912) to see what I could do. It, too, had been electrified, and when I threw the switch, a huge cylinder spiked with tiny nails and pocked with tiny rectangular vents began to rotate; somewhere out of sight, bellows sucked air; the brief electrical hum was replaced by music—parade music, march music, full-bodied and ebullient, music with waving colored flags and marching feet and stamping hooves implicit in it. The horses raced in synchrony with it, and the whole merry-go-round seemed to speed up to keep time with the invisible band. I climbed on a purple horse and rode, rode till I was tired and dizzy, holding two thoughts at once: how truly beautiful it was, and how utterly absurd.

When I threw the brake, the revolutions of the platform, the rise and fall of the horses slowed gradually until they stopped. For a moment there was music without motion. The organ wheezed and sighed when I turned it off. Everything was still again, and quiet, the horses nodding in their dream of speed, waiting for the next time I set the wheels in motion, made the band play and let them run. I was their master now.

Chapter 12

*I*t wasn't the ideal way to meet new people. I was flat on my back, constrained as a mummy in the shroud of my down sleeping bag, which had, in the course of summer travels through hot country, started to smell pretty ripe, when their voices woke me up. When I opened them, my eyes blinked into the beam of a flashlight trained on my face. I didn't know where I was or who was there with me, only that I was utterly vulnerable to whatever was coming down, with my wits uncollected and my vision uncorrected, glasses somewhere out of reach.

A voice spoke. Male. "Who the hell are you?" Words challenging, but tone uncertain? I hoped so.

I worked a hand out of the bag to shield my eyes. "How about pointing that light someplace else?"

A short hesitation, then the beam dropped to the floor, drawing a circle of light with the shadow of feet and knees inside it.

"I said, 'Who are you?'"

"I'm thinking. Give me time." I struggled to sit up, hugging the sleeping bag tight around my waist. I wasn't wearing much, only a T-shirt and a loose-fitting pair of undershorts with big red hearts on them, a valentine joke from Barbara, the only clean ones left.

"Maybe we ought to get out of here," a female voice suggested.

"Before you go, how about getting the light?"

The flashlight sought out the pull-cord and a hand grasped it. The overhead light came on, and the voices acquired bodies. One was much bigger than the other. I felt on the bedside table until I found my glasses, put them on and became visually literate again. A boy and a girl. He was dark, she was blonde. He was angular, she was round. He was holding a six-pack of beer against one hip and she was holding tightly to his arm.

"I'm a better host with my pants on," I pointed out.

The boy had green eyes and full lips, generous features, carved but not chiseled. His straight dark eyebrows almost met above his nose as he glared at me. Something about the way he stood, body tensed but imbalanced, made me think he was as surprised as I was.

"I'm harmless," I assured him. "How about tossing me those jeans?"

"Who are you?"

"Schuyler Rykken." Schuyler Rykken smiled and held out his hand. "Who are you?"

62

"Name's Tony Silber."

"You going to shake my hand or not?"

He passed the flashlight to the girl and his shaking hand connected with mine, both wary of the old bone-crusher ploy.

"Are you the Welcome Wagon, or what?"

"We could put the sheriff on you for breakin in here."

"You come here often?" I asked.

"None of your business."

"Looks like you're going to have to find another place for your little parties." I got to my feet, pulling the bag with me and half-shuffled, half-hopped toward my jeans, hung over the chair. "I cleaned up after the last one, but you're out of luck. I didn't save your cans."

"Tony, we better go now." She was one of thousands of girls I'd seen in the last six months or so, all trying to look like Farrah Fawcett, hair blonded and full on the sides, with a big swatch hanging down over the forehead. Under the mane, her face was small and innocent.

"Don't go. By all means stay." I grabbed my jeans and hopped behind the shelter of the hanging sheet that made the closet, dropped the bag around my ankles and climbed into my pants, emerging clothed.

Tony was still looking irked to find his trysting place occupied. I told him to cheer up.

"What I want to know is, what right you got to be here pushin us around?"

"Property right, they call it. I own"—my gesture was a grand sweep—"all this."

"This place belonged to old man Willets, and he's dead."

"He left it to me."

Tony squinted. "You his kid, or what?"

"Nope. I never even met the man. He was a friend of my mother's." I pointed to Verna on the dresser. "A very good friend."

"Let's go," the girl said. "We're sorry we disturbed you." She tugged at Tony, but he didn't budge.

"You gonna keep her runnin?"

"Maybe."

"I worked for old man Willets," Tony said. "Three years I worked for him."

"You want a job?"

"Depends."

"On what?"

"Football practice," the girl said. "Tony's quarterback."

"Lots of things," Tony said.

"Tell me, did Willets make a living here?"

Tony laughed. "Hell no. Broke even, good years. He worked for the phone company."

"So much for that," I said. "You can sit down if you want. You'll have to drink your own beer, though. I wasn't expecting guests."

That embarrassed the girl. "Listen, Tony, we better . . ."

Tony sat down on the van seat and ripped the cardboard top off his six-pack. He opened one for himself and one for the girl. She sat beside him. "You want a beer?"

"Thanks." I popped my top.

Tony sprawled on the seat as he drank, in a pose that was meant, I think, to convey casual insolence and looked, instead, more like discomfort. It took him awhile to think of something to say, which was, "You're not from around here."

"How did you guess?"

"You talk funny."

"Kind of funny," the girl, a diplomat, amended.

We sat quiet for another spell, the beer our only excuse for keeping company.

"You married?" Tony asked me.

"No."

"You're not one of those fags, are you?"

"No."

He drained his can in one long swallow, then crushed it emphatically against his thigh. The aluminum crumpled like Kleenex. "I guess I wouldn't mind workin for you then, if you want me to. I know that machine pretty good."

"Pretty well," the girl said.

"Pretty good is good enough for me," I told him.

"He knows better," the girl said. "He talks wrong because he thinks it makes him sound tough."

"Jeannie. . . ." It was more a plea than a warning. His ruddy skin blushed darker. "She's always after me," he said. "Always tryin to improve me."

The girl touched his arm, possessive and unrepentant. "He's got a three point four average, but you'd never know it to listen to him."

Tony squirmed away from the proprietary hand. "Jeannie, sometimes it don't pay to show your brains."

"Doesn't, Tony," she said. "Sometimes it *doesn't* pay."

Chapter 13

*B*efore I got out of my sleeping bag, I smoked a joint for breakfast. Often my use of marijuana is purely recreational, but sometimes, if I smoke enough of the right stuff in the right spirit, it becomes therapeutic. I go down to some deep place inside myself where there are two Schuylers, and they have a little talk. They argue things out, and after one of their conversations, I feel as if I know my own mind better. The voices are always there, of course, always conversing among themselves, but straight, it's hard to hear them, or if a phrase or feeling does filter through, hard to identify the speaker, and unattributed insights are always suspect, almost worse than none at all. Most of the time, the rational, dutiful, predictable conscious self who operates on 10 percent brain power is simply excluded from the Parliament of Selves, like a child banished just when the conversation of adults gets interesting, eavesdrops, to no avail, the voices speak too softly or too fast, understands nothing. Is frustrated. Grass helps. It's a tool of better mental health.

I smoked in that spirit. The set of eyes both Schuylers shared stared up at the sheet of cobwebs clinging to the bare boards of the roof that sloped down over the bed. Pretty soon, the dialogue began.

"Kind of pretty," Schuyler One said. "Tenacity of spiders."

"Dump," Schuyler Two said. "The place is a dump."

"This place or Kilchis?"

"Both dumps," Schuyler Two said. "Conducive to intellectual paralysis."

"Oh, I don't know. I've met some interesting people."

Schuyler Two laughed rudely. "That's because the type is novel. *Dumbus rusticus*. They're like vampires. It's their purpose to make you like them. Pretty soon your syntax erodes. Your logic goes soft. Perspective, gone. You get dumb."

"You're a goddamn intellectual snob," Schuyler One accused.

"And proud of it. There is no MIT in Kilchis. There is no symphony."

"Damn phony. How often did Schuyler go to the symphony?"

"The point is, knowing it's there if you ever want to."

"I could always buy a stereo and play the classics at home if the passion ever stirs."

"That brings us to money."

"One of the primary arguments against civilization."

"Useful nonetheless. Do you really want to be a telephone lineman?"

"Is it worse than driving cab?"

"MIT would take us back."

"We've been through that."

"And should be past our adolescent tantrums. Lacking genius does not automatically preclude being useful."

"What's so bad about running a merry-go-round?"

"Barney Crews notwithstanding, we are still, statistically speaking, smarter than nine hundred ninety-nine out of every one thousand people. Is it moral to waste that power?"

"Well, hell, we could use it to make better bombs, or something useful like that. Maybe Edward Teller needs an assistant."

"There's teaching."

"Teaching somebody else to make a better bomb."

"It beats breaking your back to support another man's hobby. At least we should pick our own toys."

"All crap aside, tell me how you feel."

"All crap aside, lonely. You?"

"Lonely," Schuyler One agreed.

"Scared."

"Granted, scared, But scared of what?"

"Loneliness."

"Ah, loneliness. What if we found a decent job and a woman and maybe some friends?"

"Is that all you want out of life?"

"Is there more?"

"Creativity. Intellectual achievement. Also religion."

"Forget religion."

"I was just covering all the options."

"So what do you recommend we do?"

"I have no recommendations at this time."

"Since we're here, maybe we should stay awhile and see what happens."

But Schuyler Two didn't answer. Schuyler Whole got up and went outside to take a leak. It was high tide and the ocean leaped at the foot of the dunes. He was careful not to piss into the wind.

Chapter 14

My ad in the local paper for an artist to repaint the merry-go-round's dilapidated frieze brought out everyone in Kilchis capable of holding a color crayon. The president of the Kilchis Art Society showed me her velvet paintings of scenes from Indian life. A retired milkman with a gouty leg did portraits of moose, deer and elk respectively, against the same purple mountains' majesty. All of his subjects had such prodigious antlers, I concluded they must stand for something else in his subconscious iconography. He was self-taught and had neglected to teach himself perspective, so that mountain and moose had the same presence and weight, one simply superimposed on the other, with no imaginary space between them. Still, I preferred his paintings to the desolate children with limpid eyes the size of bottle caps effected by the keeper of the local hobby shop cum art supply store, or the slashing chartreuse and magenta "psycho-portraits" the high school art teacher served up, the sort of thing Edvard Munch might have done if he'd gone color-blind on a particularly bad acid trip. I put the moose on my list of possibles and kept looking.

There were the horse pictures painstakingly traced and colored by a thirteen-year-old 4-H Club member, female; the assistant librarian's flowers and fruit; the anguished spaghetti of a bearded young Jackson Pollack imitator who considered himself Kilchis's avant-garde. They weren't exactly what I had in mind. Nor were the smiling pastel sea gulls, the globby palette-knife surf, the pen-and-ink pines, or the melancholy bipedal beagle the local newspaper cartoonist drew, not without some wit and skill.

Exactly what was I looking for? Maybe naïvely, I'd just

assumed I'd know it when I saw it, I'd be strongly attracted and fall in love with someone's style, someone's images. Forced to formulate, I would have muttered, "Gibson Girls, maybe, or Edward Turner landscapes or well, gee, I don't know." I would have hired van Gogh or Seurat, Titian, probably, or Ingres, or Rousseau, and turned down Monet or Cézanne or Mondrian. If Andy Warhol had happened by and offered me multiple images of soup cans or Marilyn Monroe, I probably would have taken him up on it, not without some lingering reservations.

My gallery was the back of my van, parked in the public lot beside the library. I didn't want to make people drive out to Seasound, so advertised my intention to be in the parking lot 1:00 to 3:00 on three consecutive afternoons. To appear businesslike, I'd bought myself a stack of three-by-five cards at the dimestore, and religiously wrote down everyone's address and phone number, even if the stuff was dreck. I didn't have the heart to turn people down to their face, you see, and so resorted to "I'll call you." I could banish the image of the gouty mail carrier waiting by a silent phone better than I could deal with the reality of his hopeful old face crumpling with disappointment in my presence. Professional art jobs were scarce in Kilchis; the courthouse mural of a logging camp, dated 1936 and commissioned by the WPA, had been the last, so my talent search created quite a stir.

But yielded nothing by the third day when I closed up shop and locked the van. Supercilious Schuyler Two was busy berating Kilchis and his more optimistic namesake for having expected to find anything more than he did in such a godforsaken place. I was thirsty and took myself to the Treetopper for a beer. Marty, the woman who'd waited on me the night of the fight, brought me my pitcher. I paid her and started to pour myself a glass, but she hovered, watching me.

"You want a beer?" I asked her.

"What? No. What I want to know is, was that your ad in the paper, for an artist?"

"Don't remind me."

"You didn't find what you were looking for?"

"I've seen everything in the last three days but paint-by-numbers. Maybe even some of that. No, I didn't find what I was looking for."

"What were you looking for?"

"That's harder to say. I just inherited a merry-go-round. There are six framed panels for pictures, and the pictures that are in them have seen better days. I wanted new ones."

"Canvas or plaster or wood?" she asked.

"What's there now is wood. I figured I'd let the artist decide the details."

"But you didn't find your artist."

"No. Not unless I go with the moose man."

"You mean Bud Crimmins." She laughed. "He got a red ribbon at the county fair last year. Which says something about Kilchis."

"Who got the blue ribbon? Lydia Baxter and her chrysanthemums? Sarah Taylor's Day-Glo Indians?"

"I did," Marty said. She smiled just right, conveying pride and no pride at the same time.

"Well, well. So how come you didn't come round with your portfolio?"

She held up her order pad and pencil, one in each hand. "I work."

"I see. Tell me, are you any good?"

Marty shrugged. "My teachers used to say I had 'talent,'" the quotes were hers and she made them audible, "and I work hard. But I can't make a living at it." She paused to make a wry face, then added, "Yet."

"But it's a name I should look for. Marty . . ."

"Vanderhill. Sure. I figure there's about a point oh oh one percent chance I'll be famous someday," she said.

"Those are lousy odds."

"That's right," Marty said. "And I would have made a dynamite dental technician, too." She smiled a not wholly sunny smile, then poked her pencil through the hair over her ear. "But I enjoy my delusions. And waitressing is *so* much fun. You meet the most interesting people. Guys who fling bowls of clam chowder at each other, for example."

"That wasn't my fault."

"No." She sighed. "The fault of the species. The instinct for male dominance display is unbelievably strong around here."

"You sound like a feminist."

"I'm a painter," Marty said. "I don't like *ists*. Not even art-ists."

"Don't think I have anything against feminists," I told her. "I lived with one for four years. In fact, you might even say I'm one myself."

"Goody for you."

"Okay," I said. "Goody for me." The first halfway acceptable woman I'd met in Kilchis was turning out to be a bitch. Too bad.

Marty's voice softened. "When do you want to see my stuff?"

"You're deigning to apply for the job?"

"Checking it out," she said. "That's a little different."

"Okay. When can I see your stuff?"

Marty looked at the wall clock. "I get off at five. I could take you to my studio then."

"Fine. I'd love to see your studio."

She grinned at me. "I also live there. But I didn't want you to get the wrong idea."

Another guy came in and sat down at the bar. Marty went off to take his order. He was the first of many, a steady trickle of off-work loggers fresh from the woods that kept the taps running, the jukebox playing steadily. Marty hustled, keeping their glasses full, friendly but not flirtatious. I'd seen that knack in older women, of holding sexuality in abeyance without denying it, but never in someone so young. The men were comfortable with her, and she was comfortable with herself, warm smile, cool presence. Her motions were economical, and she had the gift of doing several things at once, running the tap with one hand, paying out change with the other, noting orders in her head, an efficiency that required intelligence. She came round once to see if I wanted a refill.

I found myself hoping she was a good painter. Schuyler Two was skeptical, asserting that the Kilchis County Fair and the Museum of Modern Art are even farther apart than the three thousand miles that separate them geographically. Schuyler One, getting slowly, pleasantly, afternoonly blitzed on Bud, hoped on. At ten to five, Marty circled back to my table and picked up the pitcher. "Why don't you pay up and leave? I'll meet you outside."

"Ashamed to be seen with me?"

"I hate explaining myself," she said. "Humor me."

I humored her, and spent the next quarter hour window shopping at the hardware store, eying the bedpans and trusses in the pharmacy window, legs warm to the knee from the beer, and having a terrific unrequited need to pee. Finally she appeared beside me, changed out of her yellow uniform into a faded pair of jeans, her hair hanging free and full of regular, loose, ridged waves from the braids. "This way," she said, and set off up the street in a long-legged stride I had to accelerate to match. We hiked four or five blocks into residential Kilchis, not talking much, before we turned into the driveway of a large blue house.

"Nice color, huh? My place is over the garage." The garage was freestanding and had an outside flight of stairs. We climbed.

The living room was her studio, furnished only with tools of the trade—two easels, a drawing table, a long workbench with palettes, knives and brushes neatly filed, a standing rack to organize her tubes of paint. A couple of hooded photographer's lamps aimed at the easels. Stretched, empty canvases leaned against one wall, finished paintings against another.

"Ready?" she asked.

I shook my head. "I have to use your bathroom first. Two pitchers."

She showed me the way. Her bathroom was so utterly, carelessly female it made my heart ache—the silly pastel underpants drying on the shower rod, shampoo and creme rinse and a plastic leg razor in a little colony on the edge of the tub, another unselfconscious encampment on the back of the toilet, bottles and jars, not as many as Barbara had, but enough to stir up memory and, with it, a sense of loss. It smelled like a woman's bathroom, too, tangy sweet and fresh.

Her paintings exceeded my wildest hopes. They existed in their own space between realism and abstraction, landscapes mostly, but terrains of shape and pattern more than of detail, not, à la Cézanne, an imposition of geometry on nature, but a celebration of nature's own brilliant and artless manipulation of geometrics. She wasn't afraid of color, but her palette was subtle. Her seas were all motion and energy, unlike any painted seas I'd ever seen, transcending the marine and taking on the universe.

"You've got the job if you want it," I told her.

For an instant she looked edified, then asked, "How much?"

"I was thinking of five hundred dollars." Actually, I'd been thinking of three, especially if I had to go with unforeshortened moose and elk, but I didn't want to offend her, and raised the ante absolutely as high as I could afford to go.

"That's not a lot for the amount of work involved."

"It's the best I can do. I don't want to offend you."

"Oh, I'm not offended," she said. "Just disappointed. What exactly did you have in mind for the panels?"

"I'd leave that entirely in your hands. Did the pope tell Michelangelo what to put on the Sistine ceiling?"

"As a matter of fact, he did." She smiled a real smile, not kind or obliging or amused, but one that expressed her own pleasure. "Actually, I'd kind of like to work on plaster, if I could fit the frames right and find a good fixative so the humidity wouldn't ruin it." Laughed. "I imagine everyone has a secret desire to do frescoes. I'd love for somebody to give me a whole wall."

Barbara was a creature who turned heads. Marty wasn't,

but in her own environment, a little flushed with thought, she grew more and more attractive. I envied her her evident passion for her work and remembered, painfully, the long ago time when mathematics had given me pure joy. "So will you take the job?" I asked.

"I'll have to think about it. I'd want to see the space first."

"What are you doing tonight?"

"Tonight I'm painting." She pointed at an unfinished canvas on one of the easels. "But tomorrow's my day off. I was planning to use it to get a grant application together, but I suppose I could spare an hour."

"What grant?"

"Just the state arts commission. It's only fifteen hundred, and there are only two for painters, but it's worth a try. They say you should apply for grants as regularly as you pay taxes. I usually don't get around to it, but this time I promised myself I would."

"I wish you luck," I said.

"It requires luck. I figure I could afford to quit work for three months on fifteen hundred bucks. And I could do a lot of painting in three months."

"Why no"—I chose words carefully—"why no patron to support you?"

She turned away from me and appeared to study the painting on the easel. "I was married once, if that's what you mean. Briefly. It didn't work out."

"I'm sorry," I said.

She turned back to me, her eyes opaque. "I'm not. It hurt a lot at the time, but I'm really much better off on my own. My husband claimed to believe in my talent, and to support my work, but somewhere deep down, he thought it was unnatural, if not obscene, for me to have something I cared about as much or more than him."

She stood back from the easel and eyed the painting in progress critically. I got the message that she was anxious to get down to work, and shuffled a few steps closer to the door. "I'd better be moving along. Got to feed the horses, you know."

She looked at me blankly.

"Bad joke," I said. "I'll see you tomorrow."

"Around two. I'll be ready for a break by then."

"You know how to find . . ."

"Everyone knows how to find the merry-go-round. I'll be there at two."

I said good-by. She'd already picked up a brush before I closed the door behind me. Going down the stairs, I imagined I heard her humming at her work.

Chapter 15

*D*espite her evident talent as an artist, despite her brusque, almost frosty way with me, it hadn't escaped my notice that Marty was a female person, a fit and healthy specimen not lacking in appeal. It was a good long time since I'd had any traffic to speak of with female persons, and even though logic told me there was scant chance an affair would start, much less prosper, my imagination turned amorous and I spent the night in a welter of improbable erotic dreams that would have done a thirteen-year-old virgin proud. Next morning I woke up sticky and ashamed and vaguely pleased with myself at the same time. I definitely needed a shower.

I was damned if I was going to check into a motel simply for the privilege of bathing. The proprietors of the two trailer parks, one north, one south of Kilchis on 101, both turned down what I considered my eminently generous offer of two dollars for twenty minutes of bathroom time. One did, however, suggest I try the Y. The YMCA was a sad-looking fake stone building in the heart of downtown Kilchis; passing by before, I'd taken it for the county jail. The Y had a pool, and for fifty cents, I could swim and shower.

"Trouble is," I told the matron at the desk, "I forgot to bring my shorts."

She produced a cardboard box full of strays abandoned in the locker room and I picked out a pair of green-and-white-striped trunks that looked as if they might fit.

The pool, Olympic size, glowed aquamarine, and the steamy air was redolent of chlorine. At the shallow end of the pool, marked off by yellow plastic floats, a pride of lardy-thighed young mothers were teaching their toddlers to float. Now and then, a less than buoyant child panicked when the water reached his nose and let out a shriek of terror. A handful of middle-aged ladies bobbed lazily in the deep end of the pool, their legs foreshortened into grotesquery by the way the water bent the light, and two boys in their early teens, muscles stringy on still-thin limbs, pursued each other up the ladder to the diving board and off its end in a constant cycle of splash and climb. My orphaned trunks were both briefer and tighter than what I would have worn in anything but extremity. I headed for the water as fast as I could and took a shallow running dive off the edge of the pool. The water felt good, benevolent and warm and thicker, somehow, than ordinary water, maybe only because I was used to swimming in the sea. A couple quick laps, from the deep end to the floats, left me breathing hard enough to consider quitting smoking for the three millionth time since I'd started at sixteen.

There were too few people in the big pool for it to seem like a public place, and when I surfaced after my laps, I found a couple of the toddler mommies staring. I plunged down again and swam underwater to the side of the pool, then made a quick exit to the showers.

Even after I was clean and dressed, it was still a long time until two. I wandered around Kilchis, on streets I was already coming to know all too well, and in my travels, discovered the County Employment Office. Inside, I read the posted list of job opportunities. I could be a shrimp picker or a choke setter, peel cascara bark, clean motel rooms, be a short-order cook or a hospital aide. The Chrysler dealership was looking for a salesman, and Safeway wanted a box boy. The county was rife with chances for an ambitious young man to make it big. The bureaucrat in his cage asked me if I wanted to register, and I told him I was just looking.

From the pavement, through the window, I watched the town's one barber give a crew cut. In my head, I could hear the hum of the clippers, the same kind that shaved me semibald in the second grade. I went into the Thrift Shop, and after much browsing, bought myself a set of salt and pepper shakers shaped like sea gulls, because I thought they were funny. Grover and Millard, I named them, after two great Americans. Grover had smaller holes in his head and was meant to hold the pepper. Outside the dimestore, a kid with a cardboard box accosted me.

"Want a kitten, mister? They're free."

"Are you kidding?"

"Just take a look." He thrust the box up under my nose. Three small bodies rolled with the motion of the carton. "Cute, ain't they?"

"Sure," I said.

"You can pick 'em up, if you want to."

"No thanks."

"I don't find homes for 'em by the time he gets off work, my dad is gonna drownd 'em."

Schuyler One was horrified. Schuyler Two said it was nothing to him. Two of the kittens, one gray, one striped, huddled together in one corner of the box. The third, all black, gave me a guilelessly impertinent stare with round green-gold eyes in a face made fat by its halo of fur. I reached out one finger to stroke its head, just once, and the kitten raised a tiny paw to cuff at it.

"Please, mister," the kid wheedled. "That's a real nice cat. I can tell he likes you."

"Uhm," I said.

"Pick of the litter. He really is."

I closed my hand cautiously around the kitten, its body smaller than it seemed under the fur. It gave a little squeal. "You're sure they're old enough to get along without their mother?"

"Six weeks, honest."

"What sex?"

"We think he's a boy. Feel yourself, under the tail there. We think those little bumps are balls."

"I don't need a lot of kittens," I said darkly.

"Hundred to one, it's a boy. If it's a she, you can always get him fixed anyway. Doc Benson only charges fifteen bucks."

I groaned. "What do I need a cat for?"

"Keep the rats away. Besides, a cat's good company."

"I haven't got a box to put him in." My last excuse.

"They'll give you one in the store there."

I held the kitten against my shoulder, and he worked his tiny claws in and out of my shirt. The kid was grinning up at me; he knew a sucker when he saw one. "I'd call him Lucky if I was you. On account of he's black."

"What do you feed a kitten this age?"

"Just a little milk, mister. Won't cost you much at all."

"All right. I'll take it," I told the kid. "But if it turns out to be a girl, I'll find you and wring your dirty little neck."

His neck was dirty, and so were his hands, but he didn't care. He grinned happily at me. "He's a real nice kitten. You take good care of him."

The dimestore gave me a box, and before I left town, I picked up milk and kitty litter. Now I was sorry I'd wasted two fine names on porcelain sea gulls, but by the time I got to Seasound, I'd found a third that pleased me for the cat. "Euclid," I told him, through the air holes in his box top. "That's your name. You hear?"

He answered with a weak but spunky mew.

Because it was sunny, Euclid and I sat outside to wait for Marty. The kitten was no bigger than some of the rocks in the dirt, but he could move fast in his spraddle-legged way, and wanted to nose or poke at everything in sight. When an ant hustled by, Euclid tailed him like an intrepid television detective. He wanted to strike, I could tell, and lifted his paw, but the task of coordinating his body and his senses was still so new he didn't have it quite down yet, and let himself be transfixed into passivity while the ant accomplished an unmolested retreat. After we'd played for a good long time, Euclid started to cry, not the communicative mews I'd gotten used to, but a high-pitched continuous wail of kitten anguish. At first the obvious eluded me; I diagnosed his malaise as being of the soul and tried to comfort him with petting and philosophy, but he was inconsolable, and his insistent unhappiness frightened me and gave me real pain. What was wrong with the damn cat? Why couldn't I help?

He was hungry—it was as simple and as basic as that, and I finally figured it out and poured him a saucer of milk. He stepped into it, then recoiled, surprised by the wet, and shook his paws dry, crying still. He nosed at the milk but wouldn't or couldn't drink it. I pushed his chin into the saucer, hoping he'd get the idea, but he only cried louder and longer. His little body seemed to be getting lighter by the minute in my hands, and I was genuinely afraid he'd starve, still urging the saucer on him when Marty drove up in an antiquated Volkswagen that could have used a new muffler.

She picked Euclid up and stuck her little finger in his mouth. He sucked on it. "You're cradle robbing," she told me. "This cat isn't weaned yet."

"The kid assured me . . ."

"The kid lied. Have you got a medicine dropper?"

I didn't. She rummaged through her pocketbook and came up with a plastic squeeze bottle half full of Visine. She sprayed the eyedrops out in the dirt and filled the bottle with milk, then cradled Euclid in one hand and offered him the bottle. "You've got to squeeze some out every once in a while," she said. "He can't really suck on this hard plastic."

A bottle and a half restored Euclid's good spirits. Because she'd come across with food where I'd failed, he seemed to develop a particular fondness for Marty, and played close to her feet as we sat in the sun.

"Adding to your menagerie," she observed.

"It was me or drowning."

"That's the oldest lie in the book."

"Because it's effective," I said. "You think I can claim him as a tax deduction?"

"Not if you call him Fluffy."

"Euclid."

"Hello, Euclid," Marty said. When she looked at me, I noticed that her eyes were an orange-brown, the color of tea. "So where are the panels?" she asked. "I'd like to see them."

The merry-go-round stopped her still. She'd never seen it before, and she simply stood and looked for a minute or two, then began a closer inspection. It was the horses that interested her, not the machinery. She climbed up on the platform and made the rounds of the beasts, occasionally saying something too softly for me to hear, completely absorbed by her study. When the tour was complete, she hopped off. "They're beautiful," she said. "This thing is priceless."

"Barely breaks even," I told her.

"Folk art," she said. "I wonder how long it takes to carve a horse."

She didn't expect me to know the answer. While I held Euclid squirming against my chest, she stepped back and circled the carousel, looking at the frieze this time around, then took off her sandals and climbed carefully onto the back of a cream-colored horse on the outer rim to inspect one panel, looking close and feeling the wood with her fingertips. When she got down she said, "The wood's thin. I could cut it out, I think, and lay in a plaster surface. You'd have to find a good tall ladder and build some kind of platform for the top."

"You'll do it then?"

"Five hundred plus expenses," Marty said. "You buy the materials." I must have winced, because she said, "It barely covers labor. I have to make some kind of profit."

"I see your point. I also see mine. I'm not exactly a rich man."

"You could always do it yourself."

"Sure. I also compose operas and tap dance on the side. Okay, you've got it. Expenses, too. I must be out of my mind."

She didn't disagree. "Don't worry. I'll earn it. And it

should be tax deductible, even if the cat isn't." She picked up her pocketbook. "Do you want a list of things to buy, or should I just give you the bill?"

"Get it yourself."

"I could use an advance, then."

I led her back to my living quarters and made her out a check for two hundred. While I wrote, she looked at my parents on the dresser, and the sea gulls beside them. She picked up Millard, the salt shaker. "Should I take this as an indication of your taste?"

"Everything in its place. I happen to get a kick out of kitsch." I handed her the check and she squirreled it away as deftly as a belly dancer caches tips.

"I'll work in the evenings. I can bring the lights out from my studio. Have you got an extension cord?"

"I'll get one."

"Good," she said. "I think I'll go for a walk on the beach now."

I held Euclid up in one hand. "Do you mind if we come?"

She brushed her hair back behind her shoulders. "Actually, yes. I need the thinking time."

"I understand," I told her, not sure that I did.

"Thanks, Schuyler," she said. "I'll start tomorrow night. With luck, I'll be done in a week or ten days."

"Whatever. Good."

She picked up the alarm clock and held it for a moment. "You might want to wrap this in a towel and let the kitten sleep with it tonight. He'll think it's a heart beating." She started to move away. I followed her back out into the sunshine and watched her slide down the dunes to the beach below. It was more than an hour before I heard her start the car and drive away.

Chapter 16

*T*he alarm clock deception didn't work; Euclid was too astute to mistake Baby Ben for Mom. In fact, the only place he was quiet and content enough to sleep was curled up in my armpit, not a bed I would have chosen, for obvious reasons, but one that suited him. I got little sleep myself, being mortally afraid of crushing him, and spent most of the night wakefully pondering the tyranny of the helpless. In the morning, I was stiff from trying not to move and wake the kitten and willing to take him back and get my solitude refunded. Finally, past dawn, I drifted off to an immobile sleep, and dreamed of giant moths flapping their wings against my face. I woke to find Euclid sitting on my chest and exploring my face with his paws. He kept his claws retracted, and his probings were gentle. When I opened my eyes, he made a little cat sound and started to lick my chin with his rough/soft kitten tongue. My frustration eased up some. Tyranny indeed! His bones were fine and light as a bird's under his fur, so fragile one tightly clenched fist would have broken them all. Somehow, in the past twenty-four hours, I'd become his guardian and protector, the person solely responsible for seeing that did not happen, for not doing it myself. To show me just how much he appreciated my loyalty, he peed on my chest.

Back to town, to get a ladder and an extension cord for Marty. I left a load of clothes sudsing at the laundromat while I did my shopping, and Euclid in his box, flaps open, in the van. The balance in my checking account was sinking fast; since leaving Boston, I'd done nothing but spend, and it made me nervous to have no source of income, present or predictable. My anxiety then came only in short stabs, when I wrote checks and performed the inexorable subtractions;

the reserves in my savings account, compounding paltry interest, stood between me and total insolvency.

I'd been a student, with scholarships and a loving mother through the sixties, and the seventies brought more scholarships, fellowships, assistantships and gifted student perquisites, finally a chauffeur's license and a Checker Cab to pay the bills. I'd never had my flirtation with indigence, never bummed around, hustled spare change, dealt dope or played the ukulele on street corners for my daily bread, and poverty still seemed vaguely romantic to me, something that might strengthen my character, increase my insight into the human condition or, at very least, furnish me a few good stories to tell the grandchildren I assumed I'd someday have. Inflation was raging, but being unemployed made me inflation-proof, right? Thirteen percent of nothing is nothing. Didn't Janis Joplin sing "Freedom's just another word for nothin left to lose"? Didn't Janis know? Here I was free, ten years too late, maybe, but truly free. If the wolves got too close to the door, I'd peel cascara bark, I'd clean motel rooms, I'd survive. I was proud of my courage, ignorant of taxes, and still believed, I think, that my test-verified superiority was a kind of safety net that would catch me before I fell too far.

Once again, writing makes a liar of me. What I write is true enough, but the tone is wrong, soured by hindsight. The cynicism comes from knowing the outcome; I wasn't cynical then, and I wasn't a fool, either. The risk was pure, the courage was real. There was a chance, then, that things would turn out differently, that at every juncture, events would knit themselves into a different reality, and I still do not believe that I was wrong to take those chances, or to make any of the decisions that I did.

Believe, please, in the integrity of Schuyler Past. He was no more a fool then than he is now, only foolish in different ways. His mind was clear, his heart pure, even his confusions sincere. His greatest fault was a lack of clairvoyance, and you can't condemn a man for that, the last I heard.

So. It was still a hiatus, a time between times, adrift from the old life, not yet anchored in the new. Like a skin graft, it took me awhile to "take" in Kilchis, and before I did my days were strange, longer and emptier and fuller of possibility than ordinary days. Errands became events, and meals. Every human contact, every four sentences exchanged with the man at the lumber yard, the loan of bleach from a grandmother at the laundromat, the bank teller's smile or the box boy's glare affected me profoundly. Marty, being the realest person in an unreal world, almost obsessed me. Mostly to kill time, I stopped at the post office on my way back to Seasound and asked for mail. The clerk handed me an envelope with the address of Barbara's advertising agency embossed in blue. As soon as I got to the van, I opened it and read.

It was typed, the only Barbara-scrawl her name at the bottom, but at least she hadn't dictated it to her secretary.

Dear Sky, [she wrote]
Got your postcard. Oregon does look beautiful. I'll have to come out and see it for myself, as soon as I can find some time. These airline people are running me ragged. The other night I had to make it clear that while my brain was for sale, my body wasn't.

It's funny, Sky, knowing you're gone. Even after we split up, while you were still here, I liked knowing I could find you if I ever needed you. Have I lost my best friend? Are you ever coming back?

Write back and tell me everything.

Love,
Barbara

It was meant to leave me guessing, I think, intended to titillate without committing. Barbara was always good at that, paying out a little line, ready to reel it back if she didn't like the way the current tugged. Predictable Schuyler was titillated, and didn't mind a bit. Now I had alternative fantasies, a choice of two, to contemplate while snuggling with Euclid in my narrow bed.

Chapter 17

*M*arty at work was Marty rampant. The spice-tea-colored eyes shone with a fierce light. Her hair was braided tight and the braids wrapped tightly around her head, so symmetrical they made her face seem slightly asymmetrical. She was thin inside a pair of men's overalls streaked and daubed with every color of dried paint, and said little except to talk about the problems of her work. The first night was not for painting, nor was the second. The old wooden paintings had to be cut away, and when they were, she laid down the first layer of plaster. She was always in motion, and her movements were steady and efficient. Occasionally, I'd ask her a question or offer her a beer, but she was so absorbed she scarcely heard me. I felt worse than useless; the work she was doing was hard, but she neither asked for nor needed my help.

It was past midnight when she came down from the ladder, all six panels plastered with a scratch coat. Again, I offered her a beer.

"Coffee please," she said. "I've got to drive home."

While I heated water on the Coleman stove, she circled the merry-go-round, studying her work critically. I brought her the coffee.

"Thanks, Schuyler. I think it looks pretty good. Tomorrow night I lay the second coat of plaster, if this one's dry. The night after, I'll start painting." She flexed her fingers and stretched her legs. Her face was pale and she looked tired. She swallowed the last of the coffee and handed me the cup. "Well, home to bed."

The second night's work, mixing and laying a second coat of plaster, took much less long. Marty was quiet, but accepted my offer of a beer. It was a warm night, and we went down on the beach to drink it. We sat in the loose sand at the foot of the dunes.

"I didn't realize this was going to be such a complicated process," I said.

She gave a thin laugh. "Neither did I. After I opened my big mouth, I had to read up on it and find out. I'm very nervous about the painting. I suspect wet plaster's pretty unforgiving."

"You've never done it before?"

"No." She was pressing a pattern of interlocking circles on the sand with the bottom of her beer can. "I've always wanted to, though."

I lit a cigarette and offered her one, which she declined. "You shouldn't smoke," she said.

"I suppose not." I took a long drag.

"Schuyler?"

"Yeah?"

"Do me a favor?" She sounded serious. I was hoping it was a favor of a personal nature. "Sure," I said.

"Don't watch while I'm painting."

"Okay. Whatever you say."

She turned to face me. There were short, wispy hairs all around her face that didn't get involved with the braids, and the sea air made them curly. "I'm not being temperamental," she said. "But it's a new medium for me, and I want to do it freehand, without a cartoon. It'll go faster, and I'll be able to make changes if something isn't working right. But it's going to take all my concentration."

"I understand," I told her. "You can even be temperamental, if you want."

"It's not my style." She smiled. "I know you live here, and it's your merry-go-round. I just don't think I could handle an audience."

86

"Stop apologizing. I know just what you mean. I used to share an office with another guy, only I could never work while he was there."

"What did you do?"

"You wouldn't believe it."

"Try me."

"Well, I used to be a mathematical genius."

"Not anymore?"

"I resigned. You want to walk?"

Marty lifted her can to weigh its contents, then finished it in one long swallow. "Not tonight, thanks. I want to get back to my studio and work some more on the sketches. I've also got to get my pigments organized."

"Sounds big," I said. "I'll walk you to your car."

The next night, I helped her get her plaster bucket, her tools and pigments up to the ladder-top platform before I left. She was full of sighs and apprehensive half-smiles. I could tell she was anxious to get started. "Well, wish me luck," she called down from her perch.

"Luck. When will it be safe to come back?"

"Give me four hours," she said.

"Shall I take Euclid?"

"He can stay."

I saw a G-rated nature picture, long on anthropomorphism and short on plot, at the Rialto, then nursed a pitcher of beer until the span of my banishment had elapsed. When I got back to Seasound, Marty's car was gone, she was gone. Inside, one of the spots was trained on the panel she'd completed. It was the view out from Seasound, a stretch of animated waves in the foreground, the two huge boulders rising black, and beyond them, the long blank horizon, sea subtly differentiated from a cold sky striated with a smudge of high, icy clouds. To the extreme left, a hint of the gray-blue hills that marked the curve of the coastline southward. Their misty, almost domesticated whimsy cast a chill of isolation over the central space of the painting where sea met sky without mediation.

I took it very personally. It was beautiful but made me feel deeply lonely. The empty center seemed to be an editorial comment on my own life, the vanishing point that vanished into nothing, the hills that tantalized but seemed unreachable. When Euclid popped out from under the platform and came to play with my shoelaces, I picked him up and held him close against me, grateful for his almost insubstantial warmth, for his aliveness, and aware too that even if he prospered and avoided accidents, even if he survived to enjoy the maximum cat's span of years, I would someday lose Euclid, outlive him and be alone with decades of loneliness to face. It made me want children suddenly, heirs of my own, eight or nine at least, to help fill the resounding silence that stretched before me.

I spent most of the next day trying to figure out what to say to Marty about the painting. From a business point of view, I was well served and had no complaints; aesthetically, I was knocked out; but personally, emotionally, I was numbly vulnerable, and felt I couldn't say anything without saying all. Finally, I hedged, wrote her a note that said, "Keep up the good work," taped it to the ladder and left before she came. I stayed away till midnight and came home more than a little drunk.

The spot shone on the second panel, the same scene but vastly different. The sky had cleared to a warm blue and the sun, though it wasn't in the painting, shone through it, danced gold on the waves and burned the mist off the southern hills. A progression of plump, fantastical cloud shapes blew across the sky. The horizon was still empty, but now seemed full of possibility. I laughed out loud, fed Euclid from the Visine bottle, and went to bed a happy man.

By the third night, I began to like the paintings being created in my absence, liked meeting them alone, liked the feeling of magic, the mystery of panels slowly filling themselves in through no perceived human agency. Third panel, same scene, the weather wintry, pale slate-gray, so that the rocks assumed a startling blackness. An unseen wind raked across the water, blowing foam, teasing the tops of the

88

breakers into vertical jets of spray. The hills were almost hidden by fog, and a V of migrating geese flew toward them through the white sky.

On the fourth night, I left her another note: "I begin to see the plan. It's wonderful." In the fourth panel, a quintessential sunset warmed her palette, giving the undulating water a pink sheen, dripping purples in the crags of the rocks, painting the banked clouds crimson above, delicately apricot beneath, where the touch of the sun was direct. Where there was blue, it was a fresh, translucent blue, and the hills were enveloped in a lavender mist.

It was night in the fifth panel, a moonlit night, the moon bright silver-white over the hills, backlighting the rocks, spreading silver over the water. Where the waves crested, they glowed faintly green with the clash of phosphorus, and in the moonlight, you could see the shapes of gulls at rest on the rocks. Somehow she'd managed layers of translucent blackness, a wholly visible night.

"God rested on the seventh day," my last note read. Only one panel remained blank, and try as I would, I couldn't guess how she would choose to fill it. It saddened me that the process was coming to an end. The movie changed midweek at the Rialto to a saccharine romance that I watched without seeing, and I sat through most of a preseason exhibition game, football, on the TV above the Treetopper bar before I headed back. How would it end?

The light source in the sixth panel is eastward, out of the frame, coming in from the space where the viewer stands. I guess that makes it dawn, early morning, anyway, and the scene has changed slightly, enough to add a strip of beach in the foreground, and on the beach, seen from the back, two figures walk. The figures are quite abstract, just two dark shapes against the sea, but unmistakably human shapes. They're close to one another but not touching. Nothing explicitly suggests it, but from the relative scale of the figures, it's possible to infer that they are male and female.

I put Euclid in his traveling box and got in the van and drove back to Kilchis, to Marty's studio. It was late, I hadn't been invited, but I wanted to see her. The job was done; she deserved feedback. I kept telling myself that as I drove and as I knocked at her door, the cat in my hands.

I heard the lock retract, and she opened the door, wearing a long dark cotton dress, a kind of hippie dress. Her hair was still braided, but the braids were unwrapped and hung down her back. At the sight of her, Euclid mewed recognition. She reached out her hands and took him from me. "Euclid," she said. "What a nice surprise. And Schuyler."

Now I paid for my impulsiveness, not knowing what to say. I stood in the hallway and tried to think on my feet. "I wanted to tell you I really like the paintings. I really do," I said. It was pretty weak, I'll admit, but she looked as pleased as if she'd just got a good review from Bernard Berenson. "Good," she said. "I'm glad."

"They're wonderful. What a great idea."

"Monet had it first, I'm afraid. I just adapted."

"Don't be so academic. Or so humble."

"Okay."

For a space of seconds, we smiled rather stupidly at each other. I was afraid she'd say good-night and close the door. "Can I take you somewhere for a drink? To celebrate?"

"No thanks," she said. "But you can help me celebrate. I bought myself a bottle of champagne. It's cheap, but so am I." She stood back to let me in, led me through the studio to a small yellow kitchen. The bottle was already open on the table, and she took a plastic glass from the drainboard and filled it for me.

"To fresco," she said.

"Amen. And to a job well done."

"Do you suppose Euclid would like some?"

"Don't corrupt him. I can't afford a cat who drinks bubbly."

Marty folded a leg under her and settled on a straight-backed kitchen chair, the kitten in her lap. "I'm glad you're satisfied, Schuyler. Of course, it's not perfect, but I'm pleased myself. The reality comes pretty close to what I saw in my head. I hope you don't mind if I photograph it for my portfolio."

"Whatever you like. It really deserves to be on display somewhere."

"After you're open for business, it will be."

"It's not exactly a gallery out there."

"No. But people will see it. And I'm ready now if anybody ever offers me a wall. More champagne?"

"Sure."

"So you think you got your money's worth."

"Absolutely. I'm just sorry I can't pay you what it's really worth."

She shrugged. "It's much easier to put a price on art before it exists than after." Euclid was getting restless confined to her lap, and she put him down to explore.

"About the last panel," I said.

Marty laughed, dismissive. "Oh that. I guess it's a little corny, but I wanted to get human figures in there somewhere. A merry-go-round is a human enterprise, after all. Do you like it?"

"I wondered if it had a message." There. It was out.

"Hmm. I hadn't thought about it. I never shrink my work. It just happens." She watched me over the rim of her glass. "Did you think it had a message?"

"I wondered. You put two people on the beach."

"It looked too lonely with just one. Too melodramatic. So I added a friend, and risked being overly romantic instead."

"Are you romantic?"

"Not especially. Not anymore. I think it tends to be a flaw in art."

"How about in life?"

"I suppose some people would think it's romantic to starve for art. People who haven't done it." She got up from her chair. "My foot's asleep. It always happens when I sit that way." She hopped on the numb foot. "How about you? What brings you to Kilchis?"

"Pure circumstance. And the fact that I've got no place better to be."

"What happened to your office?"

"I left. Before I came here. The two things aren't related. Not directly, anyway."

Marty sat back down, massaging her foot. Euclid clawed at the hem of her dress. "Are you lonely?" I asked her.

She looked from her foot to me. "I'd say that was impertinent, except I can see how you could get that idea, from some of my paintings." She picked up the cat again and brushed him against her cheek. "There are two answers to that one. Yes, I'm lonely, isn't everybody? And no, I'm not. I've got some good friends." She held Euclid up in front of her face and addressed him. "There are some interesting people around here. People who'd be doing something else if they lived in a city."

"You ever live in a city?"

"San Francisco. Eleven years. I liked it."

"Why Kilchis?"

"Because it's beautiful. And hard. You ask too many questions, Schuyler."

"Sorry. I didn't mean to offend you."

"There are two kinds of people around here," Marty said. "Runners from and runners to. You have to be careful not to get them mixed up."

"I won't ask which you are."

She smiled. "I'm both. Maybe everybody is. Would you like some scrambled eggs?"

I declined, afraid the offer was merely courteous. "It's past Euclid's bedtime. I'd better go." She didn't try to dissuade me. I was ashamed of my fantasies. In real life, she was cool, untouchable. I decided to let her be. "Let me give you a check for the rest of what I owe you."

"You can wait. I haven't added up my expenses yet. It's probably another fifty, sixty bucks."

"You sure you trust me? I might leave town."

"I'll repossess the paintings then."

We were at the door by then. When I took Euclid from her, our fingers brushed. It had been so long since I touched someone it almost hurt. She leaned against the doorframe. "I'm glad you like the paintings. It was nice of you to come tell me."

"Real nice," I said. "Good night." I turned away before she closed the door. With Euclid in my pocket, I walked slowly to the van.

Chapter 18

*T*hree days of rain, thunderous rain, huge drops that plummeted to the ground and bounced back, they hit so hard. The wind whipped them against the walls of the pavilion, so that it sounded like a steady shelling of sniper fire. The ruts on the road to Seasound filled with water and puddles approaching lake size appeared on the peninsula's one dirt road. My sleeping bag and clothes were clammy, my spirits doused. I'd seen it rain that hard in Boston for maybe half an hour at the most, and then clear or back off to a drizzle, but this went on and on.

Tony Silber tried to reassure me. It would probably stop for Saturday's Grand Opening, and if it didn't, people would come anyway. They were Oregonians, after all, and used to it. Thank God for Tony. He was the genius of the Opening, and his vision made it Grand. He had me mimeograph handbills, which he put in restaurants and bars and the windows of stores, so that tourists, passing through, would come. He bought a roll of purple tickets that said ADMIT ONE because, he contended, people like to keep their stubs for souvenirs. He persuaded me we needed door prizes, one for adults and one for kids, and helped me pick them out, a toy piano and automatic coffee maker he vowed that folks would love. He talked me into a food concession—hot dogs, popcorn, candy bars, soft drinks and coffee. He also talked me into hiring his girl friend, Jean, to make and sell the food. "You're lucky, Sky," he said. "She'll work for minimum wage."

Tony salaried himself at twenty-five cents an hour above minimum, because of his experience. He convinced me that I should stay out front and be visible, selling and taking tickets, getting to know my customers, while he, Tony, would run the ride. "Rides should be six and a half minutes long," he said. "That's what Mr. Willets used to do. He always said, 'Ten's too long, and five's too cut and dried.' I'll wear my watch, Sky. And don't worry, the rain'll stop."

Amazingly enough, it did. Saturday morning, the air shimmered blue, and the sun was out, pale but really there. Steam curled up from the pavilion roof. The ocean, reflecting the sky, was back to blue, and the whitecaps sparkled. Tony and Jean arrived earlier than they had to, around nine, to help set up the concession. Tony was excited and asked me so often if I was nervous that I finally was. Then he clapped me on the back and told me to relax. "Nothin to worry about, Sky. Not a thing. It'll be a great day. You'll see. I just wish old Jack Willets could be here to see it."

"He would have liked the new paintings," Jean said. "He really loved that view."

Even the horses looked excited, ready to run. Around ten-thirty Tony said, "How about it? Shall we let 'em get warmed up? Just for a minute or two?"

I nodded and he was off, starting the organ and the engine. The horses moved. Sun through the open window sparkled in their jewel eyes. Tony came out from the core and mounted a blue stallion. He called to Jean, and she leaped on the platform and rode beside him. Their laughter rose over the tumbled trumpeting of the organ, and they waved to me as they circled by. "Come on, Sky," Tony called. "Climb on and ride."

I watched until the green-eyed yellow horse I saw first of all came by and got on board and rode him. The music

94

entered and passed through me as we went up and down, and just for a few seconds, I could pretend to be a child, with all my senses filled, riding in and out of the sun. Tony whooped with delight and Jean let go of her reins and stood up in her stirrups as she rode. When our ride ended, it was a quarter to eleven, just fifteen minutes until opening time. We took Euclid and went to sit outside in the sun, waiting for the first riders to arrive. At a quarter past, we were still waiting. "What if nobody comes?" I asked.

"They'll come," Tony said. "Don't worry. They'll start coming any time now."

At eleven-thirty, the first two cars pulled up and started disgorging kids. Between them, we had three adults and seven kids and Tony marshaled them inside for their first ride free. Confidentially, to me, he said, "You've got to watch close so we only give 'em one free ride." I tried to memorize their T-shirts as they attacked the carousel and scattered, choosing their horses. More tires sounded outside, and a second stream of kids gushed in. A father carried his tiny daughter on his shoulder, seated her on the tiger and stood protectively beside her. When Tony judged the ride to be full enough, he started her up and I saw the machine as it was meant to be, dispersing joy. Jean sold her first cup of coffee. More kids spilled in and stood around the platform, watching intently. Tony slowed the ride and climbed on the platform, shouting, "You want to go again, it's thirty-five cents. Get your tickets from that man over there." He pointed at me, and I was deluged by shoving children and sticky coins, passing out purple tickets as fast as I could rip them off the roll.

Frank, the bartender at the Treetopper, ambled in and introduced his grandson, a chunky crew-cut boy of about seven. Frank pointed at the frescoed panels. "Them Marty's pictures?"

I nodded.

"She said she was doin some work for you. She's pretty good, huh?"

"She did a good job," I said.

"Hell, yes. And she's a good waitress, too. I don't care what people's hobbies is, so long as they do their job."

"You're very open-minded."

"I try to be. Hell, life's too short to go around with a lot of prejudices. Now, some folks around town probably wouldn't hire Marty, on account of she looks kind of like a hippie, but me, I got no complaints."

Another ride ended and another swoop of children interrupted Frank's remarks. I told him to get himself a cup of coffee and tell Jean it was on the house. He told me he was much obliged. They kept coming, plump mothers in pastel Bermuda shorts, T-shirted fathers with billed caps on their heads, grandmothers clutching pink sweaters around their shoulders, families of denimed hippies now and then, long-skirted moms and bearded dads, tourists with the look of tourists, more affluent than the locals, the fathers wearing cameras like amulets around their necks and always, without letup, children of all shapes and sizes, fat children and thin children, pretty children and ugly children, clean and dirty, short and tall, blond and dark, shy and brave, quiet and loud, fast and slow, every imaginable variety of child that Kilchis could produce.

Mothers stopped to tell me how they'd ridden the merry-go-round when they were kids and how glad they were that little Tommy or Beth or Sue or Justin got to ride it, too, and weren't those new pictures around the outside there and what time was the drawing and did you have to be present to win, and I'd try to make friendly noises in response while I sorted change and sold tickets. The pockets of my canvas apron grew heavy with coins. Jean was boiling up her second pot of wieners. Kids kept asking where was the bathroom and I kept telling them there wasn't one. All the time, the band kept playing, the horses kept running round and round.

Once there was a lull, which gave me time to worry about Euclid. I went back to my quarters behind the plywood screen and found him crying on the dresser with two small boys trying to coax him down. They'd just pulled out the bottom drawer to climb on when I caught them. I shooed them away and comforted the cat, then decided to put him in the van where he'd be unmolested for the rest of the afternoon. The sun was high outside, and warm, and people who came for the merry-go-round stayed for the beach, filling it with blankets and lawn chairs in little familial clusters. Parents sunned, read, dozed or drank beer while a ragged line of children accosted the surf, wading, shrieking, body-surfing on the bigger waves. Euclid settled on the dashboard of the van, in full window-warm sun and looked down contemptuously at the assorted family dogs that rooted around for bits of hot dog bun in the dirt, or lifted legs to urinate against the tires of the van.

As I turned to go in, a thin, shrill voice hailed me by name, and I swiveled to find Barbara/Mom, the troll from the courthouse basement, stepping spryly down from the passenger seat of a shiny red Chevy Bronco. She was wearing pink plaid slacks and her scant hair was tied up with a scarf. Rhinestones glinted at the upswept corners of her sunglasses. When I went to greet her, she took my arm possessively.

"I brought all three of my grandchildren," she told me. "Does that mean I get three free rides?" She laughed at my gravity as I tried to frame a reply. "That's all right, Schuyler Rykken. I'll pay my way. I'm not here to cheat you." Three kids, two boys and a girl, gathered around her, the oldest no more than twelve, already taller than she. "Children, this is Mr. Schuyler Rykken. He owns the merry-go-round now." They muttered wordless greetings and started to scatter until Mom summoned them to sullen order with a sharp whistle through her artificial teeth. "Slowly," she said. "Like gentlemen and ladies." To me, "They're not, of course, but someone has to make the effort." The driver of the Bronco, a shortish man, barrel-chested, round-faced, thinking about going bald, climbed out and joined us. "This is my boy Zeb, the county commissioner. He spawned these rascals here, and wishes he hadn't." We shook hands with mutual disinterest and professed to be pleased at the meeting. "Don't mind Zeb," Mom confided as she steered us

both inside. "He's a good boy. Very honest, but a little dull."
She eyed the concession stand. "Zeb, you go get yourself a
hot dog while I have myself a ride on the merry-go-round."

The commissioner obeyed. Mom watched the horses,
topped with chattering kids, and tapped her tennis shoes in
the dirt in time to the organ's tune. "Lord, it makes me feel
like a girl again. My grandpa used to bring us out to
Seasound in his Model A. We'd eat Sunday dinner at the
hotel and while the grown-ups had coffee after, my brother
and I got to ride the carousel. It had a brass ring in those
days. Where's your brass ring, son?"

"I guess I don't have one. What is it?"

She pointed to a spot below the outer frieze. "Hangs down
about there. If you catch it with a stick while you're riding,
you get another ride free. It's like another chance. Makes
life interesting."

"I'll look into it."

"You should also look into the next commissioners'
meeting. They're going to be talking about Seasound." The
platform creaked to a halt and children dismounted, while
others leaped on and raced for favorite steeds. "Excuse me
now," Mom said. "I want the rabbit." She hoisted herself up
and arrived at the rabbit from one side just as a small boy in a
blue T-shirt approached from the other. They conferred
between the wooden ears and evidently Mom prevailed
because she got on the rabbit, while the boy wandered on
among the horses until one caught his fancy, just as Tony
started her up again.

A flashbulb flared behind me. A very tall, very thin man,
one of the thinnest men I've ever seen, pocketed the exhausted bulb, then approached me, peering owlishly through
glasses so thick they distorted his eyes. "Harold Hopper,
Kilchis Signal," he said in a voice much bigger than his body.
"You're the new proprietor?"

"That's right."

"And you plan to keep it running?"

"I guess so. I haven't really thought too far ahead."

He pumped me for a story; I pointed out the paintings. He

wanted to interview the artist. I told him she wasn't there. I realized it hurt me that she wasn't there.

The band played on. The hours, like the horses, cycled by and at three, Tony stopped the merry-go-round and I, standing on the platform and feeling more than a little foolish, welcomed the crowd, thanked them for coming and raffled off the toy piano and the coffee maker. Frank the bartender's stolid grandson won the piano and asked if he could exchange it for a catcher's mitt. The winner of the Mr. Coffee flushed and giggled and nearly fainted for the public edification, while Harold Hopper took her picture. After the drawing, the crowd thinned out fast, and four o'clock closing time found the pavilion almost empty except for a clutter of candy wrappers, soda cups, mustard-stained napkins and assorted detritus. Tony and Jean and I settled wearily on the bench seats of the dolphins' chariot to count money and compare notes. Most of the take was in coins, and we sorted them carefully into dollar-size stacks before counting.

Combined receipts from food and rides totaled $270. Less $43.75 in wages for Tony and Jean. Less $40 for door prizes. Less $20 for various advertising expenses. Less $15 for tickets. Less $100 for food and hardware rental left me $51.25 profit before subtracting the day's expenditure of electricity.

"Not bad," Tony said. "We finished in the black."

"I'd call it gray," I told him. "And you can't eat gray." In fact, I was tired and discouraged at how little income so much work would yield.

Tony persisted in his optimism. "It'll only get better. That roll of tickets will last what's left of the summer. There's coffee and hot dogs left over. You don't have to give away free rides and door prizes every day."

I groaned.

"Come on, now. Wasn't it nice seeing all those people enjoying themselves?"

"At my expense."

"The horses enjoyed it," Tony said. "They needed the exercise."

"Are you nuts? The horses are inanimate objects, my friend."

He looked wounded. "I only meant they were made to be enjoyed."

"Yeah." I remembered Euclid then, confined to the van. "Get yourselves a beer out of the cooler, kids. I've got to rescue the cat." Euclid still crouched on the dashboard, a forlorn ornament. He was glad to be freed. As I climbed out of the van with him perched on my shoulder, I saw Marty's Volkswagen come chugging up the road. It had dried out enough in the course of the day that her tires raised some dust. Seeing her seemed to improve my circulation, speeded up the passage of my blood, but my feelings were mixed, and I had a small mean desire to hurt her if I could. I went back inside the pavilion before she pulled up, and was settled in the chariot with a beer before she came in.

She looked around at the garbage on the dirt floor. "Either you three are real slobs, or you had a good crowd."

"I counted almost two hundred people," Tony said. "It was a great day."

"I'm sorry I missed it. I had to go into Portland for art supplies. I tried to get back in time, but traffic was bad." She was wearing a skirt. Her bare legs were both shapely and pale.

"There's more beer," Jean said. "I'll get you one."

Euclid jumped down from my lap to sniff at Marty's toes. Still I said nothing and didn't move to make room for her in the chariot beside me.

"Schuyler's depressed," Tony explained. "He didn't make his fortune today."

Jean handed Marty a beer. Marty sat down on the platform at our feet and Euclid climbed onto her lap. "Your pictures are really fine," Jean said. "I wish I could paint like that."

"Practice," Marty told her. "Actually, I was hoping to get back in time to get a ride."

Chivalrous Tony jumped up. "I'll start her up again, shall I, Sky?"

"I don't want to put you to any trouble," Marty said.

"Oh, no trouble. Pick your horses, everybody." I stayed put. "Come on, Sky," Tony called. "Don't be a wet blanket."

"I'm not a wet blanket. I'm an old man and I prefer to let the dolphins pull me."

"Jesus, Schuyler." Tony laughed and turned to Marty, sidesaddle on a green horse. "You guys have a fight or something?"

"We hardly know each other," I told him. "Now shut up and start the damn thing, would you, if that's what you're determined to do."

"Hang on to your hats," Tony yelled, and the merry-go-round started to move. I maintained a dark silence as we rode. Tony executed a wild pantomime, running to catch a horse, climbing on over the backside, pretending to be scared. I didn't laugh. Once I looked at Marty. She was looking at me with what seemed to be amusement. After a while, she jumped off and stood back from the merry-go-round, studying the total effect, then deftly leaped back on and mounted the rabbit. I got up. "That's all." I went into the core and braked her myself, less gracefully than Tony did it.

Tony called to me from his mount. "You know, I thought you were a pretty good guy, Sky, considering your age and all, but now I'm not so sure."

"Maybe I can't stand the excitement."

Tony addressed Marty. "If you've got a date with him tonight, you're in for a real good time."

"We don't have a date." We said it almost simultaneously. Tony tried to smooth over the awkwardness. "Listen, we're going out for a pizza. Maybe you two'd like to come along."

Into the silence that followed, Jean said, "Tony's always trying to organize everybody. That's why they made him quarterback."

"I'm only trying to help Sky out. He's obviously dying to take this lady out, only he's too shy to ask her."

Marty looked at me. "Is that true, Schuyler?"

"You're an asshole, Tony," I said. "How do you know she wants to go out with me?"

"She's here, isn't she?" Tony said. He turned to face Marty. "You want to go out with him?"

"Well . . ."

"Jesus, grown-ups are so immature. Come on, Jeannie. Let's get out of here. They're beyond help." Tony grabbed Jean's hand and pulled her toward the door. He turned back to shout, "Don't you two kill each other now."

"Nice kids," Marty said. "I've seen them around Kilchis."

"Tony could stand a few lessons in tact."

"We could all use lessons in something. I could be less shy. You could be less temperamental."

"I'm not temperamental. I'm tired. I'm also depressed. You know how much I cleared today? Guess."

"A hundred bucks."

"Half that. You probably make more at the restaurant."

"On a good night. Friday or Saturday night when they're full up and drinking hard."

"Why aren't you working tonight?"

"I needed a break. Do you really want to be my Saturday night date, Schuyler?"

"I haven't had a date in years. Does that mean I pay for the drinks and bring you home at eleven?"

"If you like."

"I have a question," I said. "Why are we so damn difficult with each other?"

"I suspect it's partly sexual tension." She was looking at the dirt, at her sandal, not at me.

"Me Tarzan, you Jane. That kind of stuff?"

Now she lifted her eyes and half-smiled. "Something like that. Except, of course, we hardly know each other."

"True," I agreed.

"We might not like each other if we did."

"Also true."

"You know, Schuyler, that sixth painting just sort of

popped out of my subconscious. When you asked me if it was a message, I had to say no. I was too embarrassed to say anything else."

"It's hardly pornographic," I pointed out. "The people aren't even touching."

"No. But they want to," she said.

"So what's to stop them?"

Marty looked away again, at her toes, poking at a crumpled candy wrapper. "Lots of things. Nothing's simple, you know? Sometimes I don't even know how to act."

"Afraid of being hurt?"

"Oh, no. I'm not afraid of that. The good thing about being hurt is learning you can survive it. What I'm afraid of . . ." she searched for words, as if her fears were elusive. "I'm afraid of losing myself. I'm afraid of compromising, or being compromised." She looked at me quickly, to see if I understood.

"Go on," I said.

"I only mean that it takes a long time and a lot of effort to manage to know who you are and what you want and to live accordingly. I've got that pretty well down by now. But I don't know about testing it."

"Am I so threatening? If you've managed all that, you're way ahead of me."

"I wasn't bragging. The danger, you see, would be in caring."

"Ah," I said.

"I'm doing quite well on my own."

"Congratulations."

She gave the candy wrapper a swift kick that sent it flying. "I don't seem to be making myself clear." She turned then and walked the few yards to the merry-go-round, climbed on it and leaned against a blue horse.

"You seem to think I present some kind of threat to your well-being." I considered, then shrugged. "As far as I know, my heart is pure. I have no evil intentions toward you."

She led with her chin, like a defiant child. "Do you *have* any intentions toward me?"

"Well . . ."

She held the reins of the blue horse across her palm. "I'm not asking if you want to marry me."

"That's good."

"What I mean is, do you want me? Do you want to know me?" Her arms dropped to her sides and something lonely and difficult in her expression reminded me again of a child. I broke the vase, Mommy. I got a D in math. Will you still love me? She'd succeeded in making herself utterly vulnerable. It was stunning, and it scared me. I spoke gently. "You don't believe in romance, do you?"

"No, I don't. Where did that ever get anybody?" She didn't stamp her foot, but I half expected her to.

"Well, it makes a sunnier path to the bedroom, or wherever it is we're headed."

Her response wasn't verbal, it was aquatic. Her face screwed up, turned pink and tears poured down it. She seemed to wilt with the water loss, and sat limply on the edge of the platform, wrapped tight in her own arms, as if against cold.

I had no idea what to do, what would please or comfort, what insult. For a moment, I tried to imagine I was Marty, that I'd put myself in an indefensible position. That I was crying. It was risky, but I tried it, sat down beside her and carefully, steadily, as if it were my job to defuse a particularly sensitive bomb, slid an arm around her shoulder. That it was one of the first things I'd done right in a long time she told me physically, inching closer and laying her cheek against my shoulder. When she was ready to stop crying she did, sniffing loudly.

"Was it something I said," I said, "or something you ate?"

"God knows. I'm sorry, Sky. I must have needed to cry." She tossed her head toward the paintings. "I can get very wound up when I'm working. And when those people came out of my brush, it really upset me."

I patted her hair and kept my silence.

"It meant you'd crept through my defenses, damn it. That I was *interested*."

"I'm glad you're interested," I told her. "I probably don't have a lot to recommend me, when I look at it objectively. No answers, no friends, not much money. And I lied to you before. It turned out I wasn't a genius. Not quite. That's why I gave up math."

To my relief, she laughed. "Do you really worry about being a genius? Sometimes at three in the morning I torture myself wondering if I'll ever be a *great* painter, or merely adequate." A shadow of a frown drew her brows together and she wiped away a few extraneous tears. "You do agree I'm adequate?"

"More than," I assured her. "Much more."

"Well, I don't know about that. But adequate. The question is, is adequate enough?"

"No," I said. "The question is, are you getting better?"

Now that her mind was engaged, her body withdrew a little, making her autonomous. "Oh, yes," she said. "At least, I think so. It isn't always a nice clear progression. Sometimes even now I turn out a real dog."

"But in general."

"In general, yes. I'm getting better."

"As long as you're still getting better, you have a shot at greatness, or whatever you want to call it. That's Rykken's theorem."

"And you weren't?"

"I didn't think so."

"Maybe you weren't meant to be a mathematician," she mused. "Maybe you're really a genius at something else."

"Don't confuse me. I'm very good at being a failed mathematician by now."

She gave me a fey flower smile. "Are you any good at being a lover?"

"What kind of question is that?"

"Nosy. Are you?"

"I'm out of training at present. I'm also very good at being a monk."

"Religious?" She looked surprised.

"Just celibate. There's a certain satisfaction in swearing off things that've proved to be bad for you."

"Sex?"

"Women."

'So you have a past, too. We're really not so different."

"If we're not sufficiently different, then sex is out of the question."

Marty punched my arm, a punishment for being stupid. "You talk too much," she said.

I turned quickly to face her, using the element of surprise to good effect, kissed her a long kiss, half caricature, half sincere. Warm, moist, soft, clean—a kiss with many constituent sensations. Then I broke the clinch, rose and pulled her to her feet. "We both talk too much," I told her. "It's completely cooled my ardor. Spontaneity or nothing for me. Come on. Let's go get a pizza."

We did.

Chapter 19

*M*arty's bed was a firm double mattress on the floor of a tiny bedroom painted a noncommittal shade of rental beige. A tentative sort of dawn was sneaking in its one small window when I woke up. Marty, long hair spread artlessly behind her, was asleep beside me, one naked shoulder peering out from under the covers. I was naked myself. We had eaten pizza, pepperoni and mushroom, with a crust too thick and puffy for my taste. We had made love.

Our lovemaking was somewhat brief, more biological than aesthetic, I'm afraid, owing to my long abstinence and the usual confused excitement of first times, but it sent both of us soundly and swiftly off to a satisfied sleep, and I was lazily confident that my staying power would increase with practice.

My arm was captive under Marty's rib cage, and now that I was awake, it continued asleep. I tried to free it without waking her. Even asleep, she sensed the withdrawal, and when I'd worked the arm out, her whole body edged closer to mine, until the whole front of her was pasted tightly to the side of me. Asleep, she was not unlike Euclid in her quest for comfort, for contact; she even emitted little sleepy sighs that reminded me of him. Different from daylight Marty, or Euclid awake. Yielding and seeking, greedy for touch. My hand began to prickle back to life.

I liked my being awake and her being asleep. It had the feeling of being more wholly my own time than all the nights and mornings I'd lain in bed alone because then, whether I liked it or not, too much of my energy centered on wishing I weren't, so not enough was left over for productive meditation. Lying next to Marty, I thought about the Opening, what remained in my mind as a dazzle of brightly colored children sailing by on brightly colored horses, all orchestrated by the elation of brightly colored music playing on. And how I felt about it: gratified, silly, confused. The seductive properties of making people happy, not something the years in math had offered me. Impending poverty. Even, tenderly, as one recalls the past when it is past enough, Barbara, without regrets or any particular measure of longing. It was a great luxury to lie next to a semi-beautiful and wholly naked woman and think my own thoughts. How different from the pleasures and lusts of eighteen.

The time had come, I decided, to try again. I stroked Marty's slim body, the smallish breasts and stomach taut between the hipbones, turned her to her back and eased my weight on top of her, prodded gently for entrance until her hand woke up enough to guide me in. Slowly, more of her came awake, bit by bit, stirred into lazy motion and, finally, passionate response. My own body was less urgently selfish now, reawakened to patience and the subtleties of pleasure, and it was just right somehow, languid and intimate, not so hectic and embarrassed and loaded as it might have been, not, I remember feeling, like the start of an affair at all.

When it was over, Marty opened her eyes and smiled at me, and I kissed her on the nearest thing in kissing range— her eyebrow—enormously pleased both with myself and her. For a few drowsy seconds, I let myself feel guilty for having left the cat alone all night, but soon absolved myself and slept again in Marty's arms.

Chapter 20

*T*he Kilchis County Commissioners met on the third floor of the courthouse, in a room whose brown floor and dirty beige walls and generally dusty smell reminded me of the schoolrooms of my youth, except that here, in the adult world, we patrons sat on pewlike pine benches, while the commissioners and their staff people arrayed themselves up front, at a long table of a better wood. There were three of them, in a county too small for five, two being an impractical number in case of disputes, and the three sat in order of ascending height, which appeared to be, conversely, descending age. The tallest was the oldest, past retirement age in most lines of work, I'd say, with a forehead made high by hair loss and corrugated by life. He had small, watery blue eyes divorced by a massive nose the color of raspberry jam. Mom's boy Zeb sat beside him, in the middle, his average build gone to seed in middle age, so that his stomach overhung his belt and distorted the figures on his silkyish shirt. The youngest, handsome in a homogenized Scandinavian way, was dressed flawlessly if synthetically, and his haircut represented an inspired compromise between generational styles.

The oldest was the chairman, it appeared. Their meetings and their county were small enough that they didn't stand on ceremony, but proceeded with a meandering informality that often had the effect of leaving a newcomer like myself totally mystified. What they were talking about, I gathered eventually, was a lawsuit threatened against jointly the county of Kilchis and the Army Corps of Engineers by a coalition of folks whose Seasound properties had washed away with the tide. The idea was, it seemed, to demonstrate negligence on the part of the prospective defendants in having built only one jetty and thereby causing the offending currents to decimate the Seasound peninsula. What the prospective plaintiffs wanted was nothing less than the resurrection of their lots. By listening for a long time as the commissioners chewed on the problem I learned, what was tangential to them and central to me, that my hunk of high ground was considered to be the cornerstone of the projected resurrection.

The oldest commissioner had a cryptically prophetic manner, and opined, "It was the hand of God struck down that land." Mom's son was more pragmatic. "The whole thing's hogwash," he said. "They'd never prove a thing."

"They could get experts to testify against us," the youngest warned. "Geologists, oceanographers, engineers."

"We could rent us some experts, too," Zeb replied. "Hell, you can hire folks to say most anything you want to hear."

The youngest appeared to be the commission's Cassandra. "It's Orville Mason behind this, you realize," he told them. "He's paying the bills. And I hear he's so sure he's going to win and get that second jetty built he's already hired him an architect to draw up plans for his development out there. All he needs is old man Willets's place, and he's in business."

"Who owns that piece, anyway," the eldest thundered, "now that Willets is dead?"

Mom's son was pleased to know. "Left it to some kid from

Boston. He's got the merry-go-round runnin weekends now."

The kid from Boston squirmed in his pew, but no one fingered him. A staff person, male, laconic, late thirties, cast a new light on the matter. "We have to consider," he told his bosses, "how many jobs reclamation of that land could bring to the area. We'd be remiss if we didn't think of that."

Zeb slapped his palm down on the table. "Boy, you use the damnedest words. I bet you've got a fifty-cent word for piss."

"Several," the consultant claimed, "which I'll pass on, if you like, after we adjourn. But my point is, maybe we should join the plaintiffs in the suit against the Corps. Get ourselves off the hook and maybe help the local economy besides. Next year is," he pointed out, "an election year."

"So it is. So it is," Zeb chimed. "I hear it is. Jobs, eh? Well, it's a thought."

"I move," the youngest commissioner announced, "that we authorize Leroy here to look into just what he suggests, for the good of Kilchis County."

Zeb seconded.

"We have no business tampering with the Lord's work," the senior commissioner intoned. "Money is the root of all evil. Happy is he who has made peace with his God."

"How do you vote, Charlie?" Zeb asked.

"I abstain."

"Looks like the motion carries, then," Zeb said. "Leroy, you go ahead and look into this thing. We'll expect a report at the next meeting."

"Wait a minute," Charlie said. "Last I heard, I was chairman of this commission. Leroy, you look into this thing."

"Yes sir, Commissioner."

"It being lunchtime," Charlie said, "I declare us adjourned."

Before I left the building, I descended four flights of stairs to Mom's basement lair.

"You came to the meeting," she crowed. "Was I right? Did they talk about your land?"

"They did and I heard. I'm not sure I understand all that I heard."

"When you take me to lunch, I'll explain everything."

"Now?"

"I'll get my jacket. And we're *not* going where your little girl friend works," Mom said. "I don't want to make her jealous."

"You do know everything."

"I have my sources." She handed me her jacket and I held it while she worked her frail arms into the sleeves. Taken individually, the constituent pieces of the woman were all fragile and insubstantial, but their sum was nonetheless imposing.

"The Skyway, then," I suggested.

"That'll do." She clung to my arm as we climbed the stairs. "Whoa down there, boy. Not so fast. I'm not fifty anymore, you know."

"Sorry."

"Everything gets harder as you get older," Mom said. "You been around long enough to notice that?"

"Well, some things, sure."

"Of course, by the time I was your age, I had five half-grown kids. Tell the truth, I've spent the last thirty-seven years recuperating from the first forty."

Mom was so tiny not too much of her showed above the table at the Skyway. She settled into our green booth like a witch into a cavern. Yvonne was on duty and nodded to me, but we weren't one of her tables, and lunchtime was the Skyway's busiest hour.

"Know her too, do you?" Mom asked. "You seem to have a way with the waitresses."

"With the ladies," I amended. "I've even got a lunch date."

"Some date," Mom pouted. "You haven't even mentioned my new teeth."

"Good dentures should go unnoticed. I didn't notice. So that's a compliment."

"My kids chipped in and bought 'em for my birthday. Took me to a dentist up in Portland. Seems the grandchildren had taken to imitating me with the old ones."

"These are an improvement."

"I'll say they are. I can eat most anything I want to with these new teeth."

"Good," I said. "In that case, order anything you want. And then tell me who Orville Mason is."

"Hard to believe there's anybody doesn't know," Mom said. "Orville Mason is the senior brother of Mason Brothers Dairy. Orville Mason is Chevrolet Bonanza. Orville Mason is the president of the Kilchis County PUD. Let's see, he's also past master of the Masonic Lodge, past president of the Kilchis Chamber of Commerce, and a pillar of the church."

"Busy," I said.

"Powerful," Mom said.

"I gather he wants to reclaim Seasound from the sea."

"Orville Mason hates to lose on a business deal, even if it's nature that outdoes him. The Masons bought out J. D. Horner when Horner's wife got homesick for the Midwest. The next winter but one, the hotel ended up in the ocean."

"Orville's old then?"

"Orville's medium. You might say the Masons are a dynasty hereabouts. First one set foot in Kilchis over a hundred years ago. There's Masons and half-Masons and quarter-Masons all over the county by now. I'm a quarter-Mason myself," Mom said, "though I don't set too much store by it, except when I'm in the market for a new car. Folks of the blood get discounts."

"What do you drive?" I asked her.

"One of those little ones with the cute names. I never can remember. It's yellow," she said. "Things were easier when they called them by letters—Model A, Model T."

"I bet."

"So tell me about your romance," Mom said, the small eyes piercing.

"I never discuss one lady with another. It's not good form."

"So she's a lady, is she? Looks pretty skinny to me."

"You're not exactly Rubenesque yourself," I pointed out.

"I was the runt of the litter," Mom said complacently. "But I've got a lot of good points besides my size."

"So does Marty."

"You in love with her, boy?"

"Is that your business?"

"Partly. I've got a niece you could do worse than hook up with, provided you plan to stay in Kilchis and you're not in love."

"Thanks, Mom, but I'll pass for now."

"For which reason?"

"I don't have to tell you everything."

"No harm in asking, is there, boy? If I was fifty years younger, I might just set my cap for you myself."

"If you were fifty years younger, I'd be delighted if you did."

"There's something about you, boy. I don't know quite what."

"Thanks for saying so."

"Maybe you'll bring that young waitress of yours around to see me sometime."

"She's not really a waitress, Mom. Or she is, but she only waits table to support herself so she can paint."

"An artist, is she? Never marry an artist, boy. They're difficult and cold."

"We weren't thinking of marriage."

"In this case, it's probably a blessing," Mom said. "Tell me, when are you going to break down and get yourself a job?"

"When my money runs out," I told her. "Soon."

Chapter 21

On movies, consummation (sun sets, surf pounds) is a resolution. Nothing happens *after* lovemaking. All is assumed to be well. In life, consummation is an at best temporary solution to the single, simple problem of lust. Lust is, admittedly, a condition of immense concern if allowed to go too long unrelieved but can't, considered with a cool head, hold a candle to war or even taxes as problems go. Becoming lovers, Marty and I created as many problems as we solved.

Take loneliness. Take jealousy. Take, simply, sleep. Given painting, given waitressing, the portion of Marty's life available to a lover was necessarily small, while my days still loomed long and empty. I was still lonely. Euclid as confidant, companion, shrink left something wanting. He was a good cat, and willing enough to hear me out, but monologue is an unnatural mode, all give and no give back. Marty didn't want to live with me. She didn't even want to see me every day. She made it clear that I entered her life in addition to and not in place of everything else that was there already. There was so much else already there that our relationship was far more a scheduled than a spontaneous affair.

I'm whining. I whined then, though I tried hard not to. The time we spent together was good, very good, as long as I didn't waste any of it in complaints. We talked and made love prodigiously, with an intensity that owed much to the restrictions of time. Maybe that's the excitement of an adulterous affair, too. All I know is, Marty had another lover in her art, and much as I admired her gift and her discipline in using it, I was often jealous as hell.

One got to know the woman through the work. Marty was maddeningly reticent about her past life, volunteering nothing, and what I did learn, I had to piece together from her paintings. That her mother had left when she was very small and her father remarried, that she had little use for him and his new wife I learned from a picture of a rumpled female adolescent, a suitcase in each hand, wandering wide-eyed among the neon come-ons of the Tenderloin; Marty had left home at sixteen, headed to San Francisco, never looked back. Where the home she'd left was, she wouldn't say. That her former husband was a medical student, I learned from her painting of an ordinary hall closet, where a grinning, fully articulated skeleton hung among the winter coats. There was a portrait of her Idaho grandmother, long since dead, tossing corn to a few seedy chickens gathered at the faded front porch of an old farmhouse where Marty had spent a couple of reasonably happy childhood summers.

An early series of psychedelic canvases, more abstract and pretentious than her current work, memorialized her flirtation with the drug scene in the Haight. I liked most of her Waitress Series. Some were simply portraits of women at work, while in others, areas of the paintings melt away into the waitresses' fantasies as they serve the soup du jour. In one, called "Difficult Customer," a fire-breathing demon in a leisure suit singes a matronly waitress's apron with his exhalations. I laughed out loud when I saw it, but Marty dismissed it, saying, "The symbolism's way too obvious." That was about it, by way of biography; time sequences, transitions, how she got here from there, I was left to imagine.

If she was allowed to be mysterious about the past, I wasn't. Marty pumped me often and artfully, not for words so much as for images, and it was intoxicating to find I had them and could share them, a kind of validation of my life as art that lent coherence to my memories. She wanted to *see* Barney Crews and the neat paired army of Barbara's many shoes bivouacked on the closet floor; she wanted my mother's courthouse cubicle rack for rack, and all the interiors of our South Boston apartment. She was frustrated that I knew so little of my father's life. What was the *name* of the bar he died in, Schuyler? What color were his eyes? She studied his picture, and Verna's again and again, and loved to speculate about my mother's relationship with Jack Willets. His letter to me she read over and over, searching for more information than he'd chosen to put in.

"Let's go through his trunk, Schuyler," she begged. "There might be letters, or a journal."

It was rarely I who refused Marty, but then I did.

"Don't you want to know, Schuyler?"

"Know what? Their favorite positions? What little endearments they used? They're dead, for Christ's sake."

Marty tilted back her head a little, so that she seemed to be sighting me down her nose, a mannerism she used to increase the impact of what she had to say. "Did it ever occur to you that your father might not be your father? That all those violent genes you brood about might not be part of the mix at all?"

"That's ridiculous."

"So letters would prove it's ridiculous."

"Shut up, Marty."

She looked as though I'd slapped her. I felt as though she'd slapped me. We glared at each other, and the space between us turned cold. Then, never one to concede a point, she started in again. "I just don't see why . . ."

"Butt out, Marty."

". . . you don't want to know who you are."

"I KNOW WHO I AM. WHAT I WANT TO KNOW IS, WHO THE HELL ARE YOU?"

She had no answer, except to pick up the big canvas satchel she carried for a purse and to head out of my living quarters into the pavilion, toward the door. Seconds later I heard her car start, her tires spin a little before they gripped in the mud. I picked up the two framed pictures of my parents from the dresser and heaved them, one after the other, against my plywood wall. The glass shattered obligingly and I let it, and them, lay where they fell, pulled on a sweat shirt and slid down the dunes to the beach.

The rain had stopped, but the air was misty, almost

tangible with moisture. A mid-month misshapen moon, edges blurred by the mist, glared down. The tide was as far out as I'd ever seen it get; a quarter mile or more of dense wet sand stretched out smooth from the colony of small boulders and broken pavement at the foot of the dunes, and blowing over from the bay side, I caught the randy, rich smell of exposed tideflats. Gray by day, the dead trees, two of them still rooted in the beach itself, shone white in the moonlight. Fired with anger, I chugged up the beach, breathing steam until I got to the far end of the peninsula, where you could stand and see ocean and bay at the same time and hear them, along a longitudinal ridge of swirling white water, hiss back and forth.

It was not a scene, by the cold light of the moon, to encourage self-importance. The power of the water, the eternal confrontation was absolute and didn't need me to make it real. I KNOW WHO I AM, I insisted to the waves, to the night and to the pines, to the sand and rocks and moon and any living creature that might have been in earshot, under the rocks, burrowed deep in the sand, afloat on the tide. I said it several times, louder each, and the lack of response was gratifying somehow. The forces I invoked didn't give a flying fuck whether I knew or not. Needing to exhaust myself, I ran the three miles home, watched over by the uncaring moon, and collapsed, still panting, into my sleeping bag.

Four days later, I heard from Marty, by way of a terse card in the post office box I'd finally got around to renting. It said, simply, "Call me. M." I waited another day and a half to demonstrate my indifference, then called her at her apartment an afternoon she usually had off work. I was cautious on the phone, deliberately cool and distant, doing my own bad imitation of the Bogart antihero. Marty, on the other hand, was warm and unaffected, eager to show me a painting she'd just finished. I agreed to stop around her studio and take a look, figuring, I guess, that the painting in question was more an excuse than an end in itself.

I was wrong.

Verna, my mother, was in the foreground and behind her, almost in another plane, were two men, one to each side, one clearly a sharper if improvised rendition of my paternal blur, the other a stranger to me. Verna's head and shoulders were at least eighteen inches high, and each of the two men's at least a foot. In the right foreground, where early Renaissance painters showed their pious patrons kneeling, stood an uncannily accurate portrayal of Schuyler, greatly detailed, fully bodied, and no more than four inches tall from head to toe. The background was yellow, poor man's gold.

Marty watched me watch it carefully. "Do you like it?" she asked.

"Clever," I said.

"But do you like it?"

"Very clever, to make it a trinity. The gentleman on the left is, I assume, Jack Willets?"

"I asked if you liked it."

"Terribly clever to put the illicit lover on the left. But aren't you afraid the subtlety will be lost on folks from Kilchis?"

"Schuyler . . ."

"To answer your question, no. I don't like it at all."

Marty's cheeks flushed. She grew animated in defense of her work. "But it's a good painting, Sky. It walks that line I'm so interested in, between realism and absurdity. And it's more than an exercise. I feel good about it."

"I feel ripped off," I said.

Her eyes dropped quickly from mine, then rose again, along with her chin. "Don't you see? I've made them all contemporaries. The same age. And I really like the idea of putting a love triangle in the traditional trinitarian form. It's really highly stylized." She smiled in spite of herself. "In my own style."

"Paint trees," I told her. "Paint cows. Leave my family alone."

"Schuyler! Don't deny me my ideas just because you happened to trigger them. All art comes from life eventually."

"In this case, I wish it'd taken a more circuitous route." I stood to leave.

She exhorted me, hands eloquent. "Schuyler, don't be so literal. Or so touchy. It's one of the best paintings I've ever done."

"Congratulations. Now that you've got a good painting out of me, I suppose it's good-by."

"No one else would ever know it looks a little like your mother."

"It looks a lot like my mother, you bitch. And I bet that looks a whole lot like Jack Willets, too. The only thing you made up was my father, and that's only because the photograph's bad."

"That's not true. Besides, I don't have to defend my ways of working. You can't copyright life. Not unless you make it art."

Her passion gave her color, and color made her beautiful. For the moment, I hated her. "You had no right," I told her.

"I had every right," she came back. "Did you ever think maybe the painting was a gift to you, or trying to be?"

"Don't do me any favors. If the painting's mine, then I'm free to burn it."

Suddenly meek. "I wanted to hang it with my Portland show. It's a fine painting, Sky. Don't make me deep-six it."

"You've got time before the show to give these people new faces. Any faces you want, just as long as they don't look like me or any member of my immediate family."

"It wouldn't be any good. It wouldn't be real."

"Aha! What you're saying is, you don't have any imagination." It was the cruelest thing I could think of to say. Marty's spine turned to steel, her eyes burned with anger.

"The hell I don't. I'm a better painter than you'll ever meet again. I'm a better painter than you are an anything."

"It's easy enough to be good plundering other people's privacy. Besides, good isn't the issue here. Decent is the issue."

My back stiffened to match hers. I felt self-righteous enough, hurt enough, to strike out. She made it impossible by wilting, by saying, "Oh, shit, Sky. I wanted to *please* you. I hoped you'd like it."

"Would you like it if somebody did that to you?"

Now she cajoled, as if speaking to an intractable, slightly irrational child. "I didn't do it *to* you. I did it *for* you. There's a difference. I wanted to show you that I understood."

I laughed. "You don't understand anything, sister. You wanted your painting more than you wanted me. Even I understand that."

"That's not true," she protested. "You know it's not."

"What I know is that you've taken things I told you in confidence and put them on public display. If that's art, I'm Zorro."

"*Buenos días,* Zorro," Marty said. "Art doesn't come out of a vacuum, you know, and it isn't always nice."

"Neither are artists."

"No," she agreed. "It was never my intention to be nice. Nice people live in nice houses in nice suburbs and have nice children. By that standard, you're not very nice yourself."

"At least I don't rip off my friends."

"If you did, I wouldn't mind," she said. "I'd probably be honored, instead of throwing a temper tantrum. Go ahead, put me in an equation and see if I object."

"One times zero is zero," I said. "Go fuck yourself." It sounded so much like an exit line I decided to take the cue and left. Our positions were irreconcilable; there was no point in further wrangling. When I slammed the door, it made a final sound. I wondered how Marty, on the other side, felt, what left with me, what stayed behind with her. Wondered, but not enough to ask. I went and went.

Chapter 22

*S*aturday brought lots of riders. I spent it selling purple tickets. At four, when we shut down, Jean's mother appeared to cart her off to celebrate a great-aunt and uncle's fifty years of more or less peaceful cohabitation. Tony, not family, was not invited. He came out of the core to tell her good-by, and when she was gone, turned to me. "I told you the gears needed greasing," he said.

"Yeah."

"You didn't do it."

"I forgot."

He'd been wiping his hands on an old rag. Now he heaved it into the dirt at my feet. "Jesus Christ, Schuyler, this merry-go-round's the best thing in Kilchis County, and you treat her like a piece of shit."

"Temper, temper," I told him. "Just because you got sacked four times and managed to lose the first game of the season doesn't mean you get to take it out on me."

He had an answer, of course. "Just because you couldn't keep your woman satisfied doesn't give you any right to ruin a beautiful machine. Jack Willets'd cry if he could see how you keep this thing."

I could ignore the dig about Marty—it wasn't his first— but the charge of neglect stung me. I studied the carousel. "She looks okay to me."

"The brass needs polishing."

There was a lot of brass on the merry-go-round, all the upright poles, and they seemed good and shiny to me.

"Jack Willets polished the brass twice a year. The sea air corrodes it otherwise."

I picked up the grease rag and squished it into a ball. "Tony, I'm getting a little sick of hearing about Saint Jack.

Why don't you just back off? Get yourself a beer."

Tony squared himself to confront me more directly and didn't budge. "He sure made a mistake when he left her to you."

"Maybe you're right. Maybe I never should've come to this godforsaken backwater. For two cents, I'd sell this heap to the junkman, and you'd be out of a job." Anger flared, then passed. "I'm going to get a beer," I said. "You want one or not?" He followed me out to the cooler, his own anger still palpable. I took out two beers and passed him one. "Here. Drink up. Or are you afraid of breaking training?"

"I'm not afraid of nothin." He ripped off the ring and drank conspicuously, flushed when he came up for air and wiped his mouth dry with the back of his hand. So there.

"Okay," I said.

"You think you're big stuff, don't you?"

"No," I said. "I don't. I do think you're spoiling for a fight, but you're not going to get it out of me."

"Afraid?"

"I'm not in the mood."

Tony's scowl joined his two eyebrows into one, a dark straight line above his eyes. "That's what I mean about you, Sky. You've got a smart answer for everything. But you don't *do* a goddamn thing."

"What would you have me do, Action Man? Smash a few beer cans?" I dropped mine in the dirt and crushed it with my boot. "How's that? Or maybe you'd like me to walk on water? I'm a little old for football, or I'd show you how it's done. The quarterback's supposed to be the one with brains, you know."

"I'm going to polish that brass." Tony turned and stalked away, into the pavilion. I opened myself another beer, sat and drank it down before I followed him. He was already hard at work, spreading white paste on a round brass pole, then scrubbing so hard it seemed as if furies drove him. Maybe they did.

He held up his rag to show me the green-black streaks on it. "See? It's filthy. I told you so." The brass, where he polished, began to shine like gold. I watched him work for a few minutes, then brought the cooler out and put it on the platform, found myself a rag and started on another pole, emulating Tony's method of spread and rub. It *was* satisfying to dispel the grime, to release the shine of the brass. It was also hard work. My fingers cramped early on, applying so much force to so small a surface.

For a long time, an hour or more, we scrubbed and drank in silence. I concentrated on the process, learning that to rub in small circles yielded the best shine, that so much paste and no more worked efficiently, how often it was necessary to find a clean spot on my rag. I found I could polish ambidextrously. Sometime in the second hour, Tony rubbed his rancor away and he started to talk, thick-tongued with Bud.

"This's French brass, Sky. It came all the way from France. Jack Willets told me."

"Most French things do," I said.

He stood back and studied the poles we'd cleaned. "Looks just like solid gold, doesn't it? And all those jewels. They aren't real, but they look real, don't they, Sky?"

I nodded. "It's a splendid illusion. And not a piece of plastic on her."

"She's old," Tony said. "Seventy years or more, Willets said. They didn't have plastic back then. All the rides today, they make you sick. You ever ride the Bullet? I blow lunch every time."

"Why do you do it, then?"

"To prove I'm not afraid," Tony said. "I think I'm getting drunk." He weaved his way to the chariot and sprawled on the bench, his legs spread wide apart. He rolled his head backward. "You know, when I close my eyes, I go up and down, just like I'm riding."

"You are drunk."

He opened his eyes and grinned up at me. "Y'know, Sky, I love this machine. It's the most beautiful damn machine in the whole damn world."

I turned to look at her, half her brass polished, the horses poised. "I think you might be right," I said. "You know, sometimes I think about the guys who made the horses. Where they lived, how much they made at it, what they did for fun. It had to beat working in a cigar factory. Did Willets ever tell you anything about the horses?"

But Tony didn't answer. When I turned back, I found him hard asleep in the chariot, still spraddled, hands joined across his stomach. I eased him down on the bench and tucked his legs up, covered him with a blanket and let him sleep. While he snored softly, I finished polishing the brass myself.

Chapter 23

9 had a secret vice. At night, alone, I'd start the merry-go-round, play the organ, and I'd ride into the music, sometimes for hours at a stretch, feeling like an exiled king to have such an elaborate entertainment for my exclusive use. Weird? No doubt. But I consoled myself it would be weirder still to live day and night with a merry-go-round and never ride it, as unnatural as living with a woman and never making love to her, as having a steak in the refrigerator and eating only beans. It gave me peace, to ride, it dulled the tight ache in my stomach for a while. It freed my mind. Willets must have done it, too, ridden solo. I convinced myself he did.

Three visitors, all unexpected, caught me at it. The first was Mom. The band organ thrummed away, drowning the sound of her car engine, and she was quiet in her sneakers, so that, on completing a revolution, her wizened presence took me by surprise. For a moment she stared, then, with an amazing combination of agility and care for bones made fragile by age, she hopped on board and eased herself onto the horse next to mine. As she went up, I went down. She pitched her voice above the piccolos and asked me how I'd been.

"Fine," I reported.

Her look challenged me. "Just staying home with the horses, eh? What's happened to your waitress?"

"A disagreement."

A sage nod, as she rose and I sank. "I won't say I told you so. You probably wouldn't want to hear it."

My answering nod.

"I haven't seen you in town lately. Nobody has."

"You have spies?"

Her desiccated laugh. "Of course."

"You were concerned about my health?"

"Your sanity, maybe. Shut this big toy off and I'll tell you my news."

I obliged. She dismounted and we sat facing each other in the chariot drawn by dolphins. I asked her if she'd like a beer, if she'd be more comfortable in my living quarters, and she said no, decidedly not. She had her reputation to consider.

"Orville Mason's been asking about you," she said.

"The King of Kilchis County? What does he want?"

"He wanted to know who owned Willets's property now."

"And you told him."

"It's a matter of public record. I also told him you were a real smart fellow." She managed to convey the conviction that she'd stretched the truth in my behalf.

"Thanks a lot."

"He wanted to know if you wanted to sell. You want to sell?"

The question answered itself. "Not right now."

She grinned approbation. "See? You are smart. Know how to drive the price up."

"What does Orville Mason want with a merry-go-round?"

"Nothing. Not a damn thing. He wants your land. Don't you ever read the paper?"

I shook my head. No.

"Then you're not so smart. Things are moving right along.

The county joined the lawsuit against the Corps of Engineers. It heated things up enough that they pushed a bill through the Senate appropriating funds to build a second jetty. Which means that if Mason and his friends can sell their little scheme to the county planning commission, and I don't doubt but what they can, Seasound City is about to rise again. Which makes *you*"—a knob-knuckled finger pointed—"a rich young man."

I thought it over. "What if I don't want to sell?"

Her mouth opened so wide to let the laugh out I could see the base of her tongue. "Very good," she congratulated. "That should be good for another twenty, fifty thousand. But don't try to fool old Mom. You'll sell when the price is right."

"I'm really not sure that I do want to sell. I've gotten kind of attached to this place."

"So make them give you one of those fancy condominium apartments, boy. You can name your price."

"What about the merry-go-round?"

"You'll have enough money to move it anywhere you want," she said. "I keep telling you, you're going to be a rich man."

I had to listen to make my acclimated senses hear the sound of the sea. "It wouldn't be the same," I said.

She appeared to listen, too, and looked fondly at the horses around us, stationary now. "No," she agreed. "But the old gives way to the new. You can't fight it."

"Why not?" I asked her, not simply for the sake of argument. Why not?

The old hands held each other in her lap. "Because you can't. I've lived in this county more than three quarters of a century, and I've seen changes come that would break your heart, if you'd let 'em. But you can't do that either. Progress always wins."

"And what's progress, Mom?"

She looked up from the knotted puzzle of her fingers to face me straight. "It's money. Money looking to multiply itself."

We both thought on it awhile. Then I asked, "Why'd you come out here?"

She planted her red sneakers and stood up. "Because I don't like Orville Mason. Never have. He used to beat up my second boy, Bobby, back in the third grade. Bobby wasn't born quite right," she said. "He's gone now."

No matter how long Bobby had been gone, her voice still missed him. "I'm sorry," I said.

Her laugh was brittler than usual, high and dry. "Don't be sorry. We gave him a good time while we could. He used to love to come here for a ride." She got the words out, but a spill of tears came with them. Awkwardly, I moved toward her, to offer comfort, but she backed away, leaped lightly from the platform, dismissing the tears with the back of her hand. "I'm a foolish old woman," Mom said, "and I should be home in my bed." A quick salute, and she was gone.

A few days later, another nocturnal visitor sought me out. Orville Mason was short and stout and florid, a prosperous country boy. At least by night, he wore cowboy boots, maybe for the elevation of the heels, and one of those string ties held together by a diamond-studded disk of gold. If he had a hat to match, he'd left it in his rig, along with the rifle slung in the rear window of the cab. He called out when he came in, and his baritone reached me above the music. I stopped the machine to ask him what he wanted.

His hands were as broad as long, and his handshake was an accomplishment. "Name's Orville Mason. Schuyler Rykken, I presume?" He laughed as though he'd said something clever, and waited a beat for my answering laugh, which I omitted to provide. I told him hello.

He jerked his head toward the merry-go-round. "Looks like you're a little short on customers tonight." He had small bright blue eyes that watched me coolly around the practiced twinkle.

"It's very relaxing," I told him. "Would you like to try it?"

Again, the laugh of a man used to leading laughter. "Not

at my age. A man's supposed to put away childish things. The Bible says so."

"So it does."

"Tell me," he said, all inside and interested, "you make a living with that big toy?"

"I haven't been in business very long."

"Jack Willets pursued that hobby for twenty, thirty years and he never, to my knowledge, made a living from it."

"Unh," I said.

"You got another line of work?"

I told him something I hadn't told another soul in Kilchis, except Marty. I told him I had a Ph.D. in mathematics. It was rash, I know, but since he was flashing his wealth, I wanted to show him I respected a different kind of currency.

"That's mighty impressive. Yes, sir, it is. Not that we have much call for doctors of mathematics around these parts. You know, I had a fellow with a master's degree in— what was it?—anthropology, come looking for a job at my car lot. Can you beat that? An educated fellow like that, wanting to sell cars. I asked him what made him think he *could* sell cars, and you know what he said? 'Hunger,' he said." Mason paused to laugh at his story, then shook his head. "Nice fella, too. But I couldn't hire him. You know why? Because he was overqualified. He would've been bored selling Chevy pickups."

I was finding Mason a hard man to talk to. His conversation was a kind of performance, with little opportunity for answering dialogue. The only rejoinders I could think of were too snotty to say out loud, so I bit down on them and simply listened. The shrewd little eyes zeroed in. "I was thinking you might be having some of that trouble yourself, son. Hunger, I mean."

"Inflation takes its toll," I said.

"Inflation, hell," Mason said, temporarily candid and with a small flare of scorn. Then he reminded himself to be jovial. Jovially, he said, "I can see you're a proud man, Mr. Rykken. That's a fine quality. I like to meet a man who knows his own worth. On the other hand, the Bible tells us pride goes before a fall."

"The Bible tells us," I pointed out, "that we're all already fallen."

"True enough," he said. "That's true. But I didn't come all the way out here to discuss theology with you. What I had in mind is more of this world than the next."

Mason liked to do business at closer range than I found comfortable. He advanced and I backed away until the backs of my calves touched the merry-go-round platform. I sat down on it. "Shoot."

"I'd like to buy this hunk of ground from you. Take it off your hands, as it were." A big favor, that was his tone.

"Would you?" I said.

He stuffed his hands in the distended pockets of his slacks and gave me what he must have considered a disarming grin. "Yes, sir. I'm prepared to offer you fifty thousand dollars, cold cash, if you want it that way."

I couldn't meet his eyes and stay sober, so I looked below them, at the diamonds flashing on his fraternal tie-holder, and said, "The horses on the merry-go-round are worth more than that, if I wanted to auction them off to collectors." I didn't know if it was true or not, but I said it with enough authority that he appeared to believe.

"I'm not especially interested in your carousel. I'd let you move it out of here, if you wanted. I'm more concerned with real estate than amusement park rides."

Schuyler neutral.

"Fifty thousand and I pay for moving your ride someplace else. Maybe they'd let you lease a piece of the county fairgrounds to put it on. That'd be a good location for your kind of business."

"I kind of like it here," I said. "I've gotten attached to the view." I wanted to see if he would, as Mom predicted, offer me an apartment in his high rise. It was interesting to watch him flounder; he was prepared to offer, but to bring it up at this early point in the negotiations would be to put one card too many face up in front of me. He could still hope I thought his offer was more or less disinterested.

"Nice view," he agreed, "but not the only nice view in Kilchis. A fellow like you, I would have figured you'd want to settle up in north county, where there's more educated folks and artists and that kind of thing."

"I had my fill of that kind of thing back east," I told him. "I'm ready for some peace and quiet." I was being amiable and he was getting frustrated, trying to figure out if I was shrewder or stupider than he expected. Mason was handicapped by his belief that all men are greedy; it probably says so someplace in the Bible.

Probably because it would have shaken his world view to conclude otherwise, he decided to believe I was being shrewd. His grin gave me credit. "You drive a hard bargain." He stepped closer still and lowered his voice, even though we were alone. "Tell me, how much do you want for this piece of land? You tell me your price."

I feinted left. "No price. Jack Willets left me this place. I figure if he'd wanted it sold, he could have sold it himself easily enough."

"Jack Willets was a fool," Mason said, then tried to amend by adding, "not to speak ill of the dead. He was a nice man, but he wasn't a businessman. Even with that thing," his thumb jerked toward the merry-go-round, "he'd give a free ride to any kid who didn't have the fare. Now, I believe he thought he was doing the right thing," Mason said, "but you know what the Bible says: the Lord helps those who help themselves."

"It might help you to know, Mason, that I know why you want the land."

"You do, eh? Well, that does make a difference." He rocked back a little on his high cowboy heels. "That does put a different face on things. Maybe my partners and I, we could let you put up the land as an investment in Seasound Enterprises, Inc. Call it, say, an even hundred thousand. I think I could talk the board of directors into that." He'd become conspiratorial, and it appeared to be much closer to his natural mode. "Why, I bet we could even find a place for you in the organization, a man of your background. You're pretty good with the figures, are you?"

"Give me a calculator and I can balance my checkbook."

"Haw haw," Orville Mason said. "There's money to be made here. Big money. The good Lord only gave us so much coastline, if you know what I mean."

"Blessed be the name of the Lord," I said.

"Yes. Well, He does provide for those of us with a little hustle and a few brains. Think big, that's my motto."

"Interesting," I said. "It was Napoleon's motto, too."

He took a minute to compute, then decided it was a compliment. "Well, he didn't do too bad, either, did he? Folks remember his name."

I didn't laugh, by God, and I didn't mention Elba. Mason beamed at me. "You could do worse than be a partner in Seasound Enterprises, Inc. In fact, it's a golden opportunity for a young fellow like you. Play your cards right, make a few smart investments, and you'll never have to worry about money for the rest of your life."

Now he was quoting Satan, only he wasn't offering to make me king, just rich. For the first time, I was grateful for the space of years Verna booted me out of bed at nine and sent me packing off to Sunday School. At twelve I rebelled, and was reprieved, but I was glad now to know the language of the enemy. With a straight face, I told Mason, "The Bible says that money is the root of all evil."

He'd heard that one before. It was "Haw haw" again. "You know, I always figured that was a misprint. I figure what it meant to say was, 'Money is the root of all,' and some crazy monk or other copied it wrong."

"An interesting interpretation."

"Everything in its place," Mason said. "How about it, son? Shall I tell the board you want to buy in?"

"I wouldn't do that," I said.

"Need a little more time to think it over, do you? Well, I

can understand that." He pulled a glossy black cowhide wallet out of his hip pocket and selected one of several business cards. "You decide your terms and give a call here, to the showroom. If I'm not there, they can take a message and I'll get right back to you."

I took the card. Embossed in red script it read, "Orville Mason's Chevrolet Bonanza, Orville Mason, President." There was also a phone number, an address, and a picture of a ten-gallon hat. I put the card in my pocket. "Tell me, Mason," I said. "What are you going to do if I won't give up my land?"

"Oh, you will." Mason grinned. "I have ways of assuring you will."

"Such as?"

He raised his eyes and scanned the ceiling. "Don't imagine the fire department could get all the way out here too fast if you had a fire."

"I could go to the county sheriff and tell him about that little threat."

Mason rocked some more, his grin complacent. "So you could. Good man, the sheriff. Good husband and father. My sister's been married to him for almost twenty-five years. They'll be celebrating their silver wedding anniversary come spring. Ought to be a good party. Yes, sir, I do look forward to it."

"There's nothing like family."

"No, sir. You're right there. It's too bad you don't have any around these parts."

I had a father in my blood urging me to sock the son of a bitch in his squishy red face. I also seemed to have an Uncle Jack telling me to simmer down and think it through. Mason looked at his fancy big-faced watch. "If I leave now, I can just make it home in time for *Charlie's Angels*. I do like pretty girls. Haw haw."

"Haw haw," I said.

He headed for the door and I pursued him at a distance. Mason turned at the door to say, "You think it over, now, and let me know what you decide. I do have faith in your good sense."

By the light from the door, I saw him heave his bulk into the front seat of his pickup. It was when he put on his brights, in the crosslight, that I saw his gun.

Marty came in and watched me ride for a while with no greeting and no comment. With her hair down, her face sober, her denim coveralls a long blue vertical, she looked like a peasant madonna in El Greco's astigmatic eye. I waited for her to speak. Instead, she turned away and walked back to my living quarters. When I turned off the machine and followed, I found her sitting, waiting, on the car seat that was my bed. I think I smiled; it was good to see her, but her face stayed long.

"How was the Portland show?"

"It was okay. Three sales and one good review."

"That's great."

"It's okay. I didn't hang your picture."

"I appreciate it."

"I need to talk to you, Schuyler."

"Talk."

"I'm pregnant," Marty said.

"Oh, shit."

Two red spots appeared over the cheekbones to decorate her pallor. "I didn't expect you to be thrilled, but I didn't expect shit. And don't ask if it's yours either. It has to be."

I think I would have preferred tears to her dry-eyed desolation. I touched her arm. "I didn't mean it like that. What I meant was, I just put virtually all the rest of my money into fire insurance yesterday, after Orville Mason threatened to burn me out. Jack Willets didn't carry any."

"I wasn't asking you for money," she said.

"How did it happen? I thought you . . ."

"The usual way. And I did. Only my diaphragm was old. One morning when I went to wash it, the rubber ripped away from the rim. Two weeks later, I missed my period."

Her voice was flat, the words almost without emphasis. There were no signals in her behavior to tell me what to do.

"I don't know what to say," I said.

"Neither do I."

"Would you like a beer? Some coffee?"

"A beer, I guess."

I got two out of the ice chest, grateful for a task. We were both glad of the prop, and drank in silence for a while. Then I asked Marty how she felt.

"The same as always," she said. "Fine. The doctor says I'm an excellent physical specimen."

"I'd have to agree with him there." I meant it as a compliment, but her eyes flashed anger. She was obviously in no mood to be reminded of the pleasures of sex. I don't remember ever feeling quite so helpless, or so unmanned. Much as I wanted to help her, I didn't know how. No role came naturally. I'd always subscribed to the feminist doctrine that a woman's body is her own, never questioned her right to abort an unwanted fetus, and yet . . . The yet was, I suppose, a small pride of paternity, an interest vested in the fate of my genes. I looked at Marty, quiet on the car seat, and saw her differently, less, for a moment, as a person than as genetic potential, a conglomerate of reproducible traits.

"What are you looking at me like that for?" It was a complaint.

"I was just thinking that you have nice eyes. Nice hair. A baby could do worse than have us for parents. Genetically speaking."

Now she looked surprised. "I've thought that myself. I shouldn't let myself, I know, but . . ." She stood and turned away from me, toward the dresser. Her words came to me over her shoulder. "I'm not getting any younger, Schuyler. Something in me *wants* to have this baby."

My sudden excitement felt sexual and religious at the same time. I wouldn't have expected it, but there it was, a sharp flash of perhaps the strongest stimulation I've ever in my life felt. *My* baby. This woman wanted to have it. What a hit. Nature is canny enough to make all the steps to propagation pleasant, not just the first. The rush I felt was, I'm sure, no aberration of an individual ego, but a programmed force as basic and ancient as lust itself, designed to secure my complicity in the act of reproduction.

"Shouldn't you sit down or something?" I asked Marty. "Should you be drinking beer?"

"Oh, for god's sake, Schuyler." She turned back to me, lips pursed around a half-smile. "I *should* be making an appointment to get an abortion."

Doom followed elation. My stomach gripped. "It's your choice, Marty, but I wish you wouldn't. I *think* I wish you wouldn't," I qualified.

"How could I raise a baby, Sky? Artists aren't supposed to make good mothers. What if I resented it? What if I stopped painting? If I stopped painting, I think I'd die."

"Then you wouldn't stop painting."

"But people do. Why do you think there are so damn few women artists?"

"Men? Lack of talent? Lack of training? You tell me."

"I don't know, damn it. I'd feel better if I did. I have this vision of myself fat and harried, buried in a pile of diapers and never being able to paint, unspeakably frustrated and terminally dull." The works spilled out faster than her usual rate, impelled by an urgency I hadn't seen in her before. Then her voice quieted, almost to a whisper, and she stood very still. "I have another vision, too, of being fifty years old, maybe famous, maybe not, and all alone. Childless. Not ever knowing what it's like to hold a baby in my arms . . ." Her voice stopped, caught on tears.

"You're forgetting something," I told her.

Her chin shot up. "What?"

"Me."

"What about you?"

"Well, I imagine I could take care of a baby as well as the next person. Besides," I said, "they have to sleep sometime. Aren't babies supposed to sleep a lot?"

"I don't know," she said. "I guess they must." Sniffed. "I don't remember." Laughed.

"Neither do I."

We both laughed. Laughed hard. Approached hysteria, in fact. Laughed until it helped.

"Oh God," Marty said. "None of my friends have babies. None of my friends *want* babies. It's just not done."

"That's just an overreaction to all those years it was the only thing to do."

"Maybe. But I hate to be a pioneer. What if everything they say is true? Life is hard enough already. What if I had a baby and hated it?"

"I hear they grow up," I said. "With luck, they start school."

"That's five years of servitude. Do you know how much it would set my career back to lose five years?"

"If you lost them."

"That's easy for you to say."

"Yes. But there must be *some* rewards involved. Otherwise people wouldn't do it."

"The current theory is, there's a conspiracy of silence. Because misery loves company."

"What do you *want* to do, Marty?"

"I don't know." She sat back down beside me and pulled on her beer. "Yes, I do. I know exactly what I want. I want to have a baby and a brilliant career. I want to be rich and famous and glamorous. I want to be loved and respected."

"Is that all?"

"Not quite. I also want to live forever."

I whistled, then said, "It strikes me that out of the eight things you mentioned, one is impossible and six depend on luck. You only have a clear choice about one."

"The baby, right?"

"Right."

"Right back where I started."

I picked her hand up off her denim knee. "I'm willing to get married if that makes it any easier to decide."

Her eyes widened. Embarrassed? Pleased? Definitely surprised. Then she took back her hand and said, "I've already been married, Sky. It's a drag."

"You've never been married to me."

"No. But my first husband was also a man."

"So you're sexist."

"So I am," she conceded.

"If we didn't like being married, we could always get a divorce. But in the meantime, the little bastard would have a name."

"There's nothing wrong with my name, if it comes to that," Marty said. "Besides, pregnancy is no excuse for marriage, especially not at our age."

"At our age, it's probably the only excuse."

"We hardly know each other, Schuyler."

"Some of the world's happiest marriages have been arranged."

"Are you really so eager for an heir?"

I thought about it. "Yes, I think I am. I'm also right next door to loving you. I could go over the line at any time."

Marty squirmed. "This is absurd, Schuyler. Love, marriage. My God, that stuff went out with pedal pushers and musical comedies."

"Put it this way, then. Do you like me?"

"Sure I like you."

"Okay. Do you like making love with me?"

"Yes," she said. "As a matter of fact, I do. You've got good range."

"So what else is there?"

"You're copping out," Marty accused. "You're just looking for something to give your life meaning."

It sounded true and I admitted it. "What's wrong with that? You beat Scientology all to hell."

"Thanks."

"Let's face it. I'm tired of fucking around."

"You're tired of being alone."

"That too."

"You're practically insolvent."

"I can get a job."

"You're moody."

"So are you."

"Would you want to marry me if I wasn't pregnant?"

"That's irrelevant, immaterial and—what else did they used to say on *Perry Mason?*"

"Incompetent, I think. Did you watch *Perry Mason*, too?"

"Incompetent," I said. "Biology is destiny, I believe."

"It won't solve anything, Schuyler," Marty warned.

"Is that a yes?"

"Oh, damn." She sprawled against the seat back and closed her eyes. Excited and terrified, I studied her face, bristly dark eyelashes, blue veins like random pencil marks on the pale eyelids, brows slightly unkempt. Fine uniform pores visible in the unsubtle light. A stranger's face, and one I was proposing, with ridiculous abandon, to look at for the rest of my life. It was a gambler's high I felt, fate perfectly balanced, for an instant, between probabilities. Reason suspended. Responsibility waived. Hope irrelevant.

Marty opened her eyes. "Let's live together for a while first, Sky, and see how it goes. We've got a couple months before I start to show. There's even some leeway on an abortion."

"You're deciding not to decide."

"Not really. I'm deciding to try again. For me, that's big." This said, she put her head on my shoulder and burrowed her face into my shirt.

"I probably smell," I warned her. "If I'd known I was going to propose, I would have gone to the Y and taken a shower."

Marty smiled up at me, irises deep brown around the black dots of her pupils. "If I'd known you were going to propose, Schuyler, I probably wouldn't have come," she said.

Chapter 24

*O*verqualified."

"Overqualified."

"Just filled the job this morning."

"Sorry, Rykken, but I'm afraid you're overqualified for this kind of work."

Everywhere I went to apply for work, I was considered "overqualified," which struck me as somewhat mysterious, since on the job applications (all identical, sold on perforated pads of thirty each at the local dimestore) I never recorded any educational achievements past my high school diploma, or any jobs beyond the usual collection of undergraduate menialities and, of course, my most recent stint as a taxi driver. I signed my name without guilt on the dotted line attesting to the truth of all statements made above; everything I wrote was true and in this case, given the gravity of the situation, I considered omission no sin.

Finally I asked one prospective employer, the owner of the local feed store, who was looking for a stock clerk, just why he thought I was overqualified to fill his shelves. Oldish, baldish, not bright enough to lie facilely, he stared dumbly at me while he searched the cobwebbed stockrooms of his brain for a plausible alternative to the truth. The truth was, of course, that Orville Mason had used his considerable influence in Kilchis to blackball me from the fraternity of the gainfully employed. He'd given his cohorts the one word "overqualified," and not bothered to supply them any further explanation.

The feed store scion scratched a place on his head where a few hairs still grew. "Well, uh, by golly, Rykken, anybody could tell from how you talk that you was educated."

"You finished high school?" I asked him.

He thought maybe I was changing the subject, and his face brightened a little. "Well, sure. It took me five years, but I done it. My ma was real proud."

"I bet," I said. "Well, that makes us even."

"I don't rightly understand."

"Look on my application." I picked it up and shoved it at him. "Look under 'Education.'"

He read laboriously and for the first time. No list of colleges, no scrambled alphabet of advanced degrees. Again fingers scratched scalp. "I don't get it. It says here you only went to high school, but Mr. Mason said . . ." He realized his gaffe and stopped dead, pink and miserable.

"Look, I know that Mason told you to tell me I was overqualified if I came looking for work. But I'd be very interested in what else he said. Like why you shouldn't hire me."

He wrapped short arms around his fat plaid belly and looked unhappy.

"You realize I could sue you, under the Fair Employment Practices Act of"—I picked a year at random—"1971. I'd really like to know what Mason said."

His eyes clouded at the threat of litigation. He was caught between two feared powers—Mason's demonstrable local clout and the specter of federal intervention, even more terrible, that I invoked. "Look, Rykken, I don't mean you no harm. Mason just said not to give you a job, that's all."

"And you always do what Mason tells you?"

He nodded glumly. "He's got a second mortgage on the store."

"Okay," I said. "I understand. And I'm not going to sue you. Thanks."

"You won't tell Mason what I said, will you?"

"My lips are sealed." I turned to go, but he called me back.

"Say, what's he got against you anyway?"

"He wants something that I have," I told the little man. "I

140

guess he figures if I get hard up enough, I'll have to sell it to him."

He nodded knowingly. "He's a smart businessman, Orville is. He always gets what he wants, in the long run. If I was you, I'd just sell it to him now, whatever it is, and be done."

"That's probably good advice," I told him, "only I hate to be pushed around."

"Nobody likes it," he said, "but most of us put up with it. We got to."

"Yeah." Again I started for the door. His voice followed me. "Say, good luck."

The next Saturday morning, Tony came to work without Jean. I asked if she was sick. "She's not sick, Sky," Tony said. "But she's got to quit working here."

"She got a better job?"

Tony looked up from the hot dogs. "How'd you know?"

"Which one of Mason's businesses is she working for?"

"The car lot. She's receptionist, after school and on weekends. The pay's real good."

"I bet."

"She needs the money for college, Sky. She said to tell you she's sorry." Tony's hands moved steadily, dropping wieners into the pot.

"Well," I said, "when are you going to work for him?"

"When hell freezes over. My old man and Mason don't get along. They haven't said hello in thirty years."

"It's nice to know he holds a grudge."

"Yeah. My mom used to go out with Mason in high school. Then my dad moved to town, and she ended up marrying him instead. When my dad tried to get a loan to buy a yarder, Mason made sure the bank didn't give it to him. The old man went up to Portland and got his credit there."

I spooned coffee into the top of the old urn. "Tell me, Tony, you think he'd really try to burn me out?"

"He say so?"

"He threatened."

"He wouldn't do it himself," Tony said. "He might pay somebody else. You gonna sell?"

"If he'd let me think it over, like we agreed, instead of starting this little campaign to destroy me, I might have. Now I'm starting to think I'd rather give it away. Maybe to the Audubon Society. What do you think?"

It was a light day for riders, whether because of rain or boycott, I couldn't be sure. There were rarely more than three or four horses taken when the merry-go-round started up, and we'd cooked more hot dogs and made more coffee than we could sell in a week at that rate. Tony battled the attendant depression by hatching new promotional schemes at the rate of one every five minutes or so.

"Third ride free," he proposed.

"Discounts for senior citizens. That way they'll bring their grandchildren."

"How about a Name that Rabbit contest?"

"I've got it! We rent the whole place out for dances or big parties. A flat fee, with rides thrown in."

"Tony, it gets damn cold here at night. Who wants to dance in their long johns?"

The rain continued to drizzle and riders kept dribbling in, just enough of them to make each other self-conscious, too few to generate a spirit of gaiety. The children circled round with somber faces and their adults had to work at seeming to have a good time, smiling absentminded, obligatory smiles.

"How about a clown?" Tony said. "A clown's always good for loosening people up."

"You volunteering?"

"I was thinking more of you, Sky."

Around three-thirty, Marty came in. She was pale. I was solicitous. Saturdays she worked at the restaurant. "Are you all right? What's wrong?" I asked.

"Am I sick? No. Am I mad? Oh, yes."

"What happened?"

"I lost my job. Got fired."

"What'd you do, spill soup on a customer?"

"I got involved with you, I guess."

"Mason?"

"I think so. It had to be. I'm the best waitress Frank ever had, and the only one who could add."

"What did he say?"

"He'd had complaints about my attitude."

I put my arms around her, and she accepted a moment's solace before she pulled away. "It's not so bad. I can get unemployment, or another job. Whichever pays best."

"You can paint," I told her. "I'll get a job."

"Just paint, all day long? I'd feel like a kept woman."

"You wouldn't be. Not at all. Remember those three sales. It's time to concentrate on your career."

"You're not just saying that because I'm pregnant?"

In part I was, but I denied it so well I almost convinced myself. "You've got talent, woman. It's time to go for it. Generate product. If you make it, we're home free."

I'd seen days the weather over the ocean was like her face, that quickly changing, a dialogue of light and rain. "You know I'd love to, but . . ."

I dismissed the buts with such hoary wisdoms as "You'll never know if you don't try," and "Everything's a risk. You can't win without risking."

Sun: her cautionary weathers resolved into a smile. "How can I find you so convincing when I know you're a flake?"

"Because you want to. Because you know I'm right." I would have done anything to preserve that smile. "Try it for a year, and if it doesn't work out, then you can get a job."

"In a year, I'll have a baby to look after. Maybe."

"Definitely. All the more reason to break the chains of commerce now."

"Shit, Schuyler," she said, smiling still. "It's crazy. But okay. I'll paint. I'll paint my rear off."

I hugged her so hard that the couple of little boys riding the merry-go-round felt obliged to register their distaste with hooted boos, while their faded mother discreetly pretended not to notice us or them. When Tony stopped the machine, I

143

told him we were calling it a day. There wasn't another customer in sight. Boys and mother climbed off. I hailed the woman. "Say, you want some hot dogs? They're free."

Her painted red mouth twitched. The smaller of her sons tugged at the loose leg of her slacks. "They're probably poison, Mom."

"Surplus," I said. "We cooked too many. I'd hate to waste them."

She fingered the aqua plastic tubes her hair was rolled around. "Well, I do make a good casserole with wieners."

"Terrific. Tony, give the lady hot dogs."

"What if we all die?" the little boy asked, but his mother shushed him. When they were gone, I grabbed Marty and gave her a long kiss.

Tony looked up from the coins he was counting, a small pile. "What are you so happy about? According to my calculations, your net loss for the day is thirteen dollars and forty-seven cents."

"Marty lost her job."

"That is good news." His eyebrows supplied the irony.

"I'm going to paint," she told him. "All day, every day. I'm going to be a very famous painter."

"And rich," I said.

"Very rich," she said.

"And we're going to live together," I said. "And, can I tell him, Marty?"

"What?"

"You know."

"If we tell someone, then we'll have to go through with it."

"We're going to have a baby, Tony."

"I'm going to have the baby, Tony. Schuyler's going to help."

We had a lot of news, and Tony was our only audience. In the absence of parents, it became his job to legitimize our decisions by listening to them. He seemed a little overwhelmed by the task. After we finished our litany, he shook his head. "And they say kids are crazy."

"Kids are crazy," Marty said.

"If Jean and I made exactly the same decisions you two have, our folks would lock us in our rooms for a year."

"That's the joy of being an adult," I told him. "No one can lock you in your room."

"Well, I hope you know what you're doing." He still looked skeptical.

"Why don't you just congratulate us instead?"

With his new man's body and a childish candor not yet outgrown, Tony was a beautiful creature. I could remember being that young, but never so noble, so attractive in my youth. He put his reservations aside and smiled at us. "Congratulations, both of you." He looked questioningly but not lasciviously at Marty's torso. "All three of you. Can I tell Jean?"

"If you swear her to secrecy. We don't need her new boss finding out."

"I understand," he said, and left us to our untimely celebration.

Chapter 25

Ihe farther one got from Kilchis City, the weaker the poison of Orville Mason's sting became. Twenty miles north, it was weak enough that the school board was willing to give me an interview. It wasn't for a teaching job, there were none available midyear, but the assistant janitor at one of the district's elementary schools had just "passed on" and they needed to replace him. The board, or its postmenopausal members, would have preferred an aged eunuch to someone still physically capable of molesting children, I'm sure; the item on the agenda that preceded the interviewing of janitorial candidates produced heated debate over the proposed removal of several volumes from the school library shelves, *Stranger in a Strange Land* and *Catch-22* among them. It had come to the attention of the board via certain parents that sex, or ess-ee-ecks, as one hatchet-faced official referred to it, actually took place within their pages and they, the older females, vied with one another in expressing their distaste for ess-ee-ecks. They seemed to believe it was through books and not burgeoning hormones that adolescents discovered the baser human drives.

During their literary discussion, I had a chance to size up the board. Three professional virgins, two female, one male, formed the major opposition to the procreative impulse. Three more, one actually bearded, were moderate to liberal on the subject of the books. The chairman was in his cups. Alcoholically flushed, belching softly from time to time, his eyelids drooping like half-open (or half-drawn) shades, he reclined on his folding chair and when called upon to cast a deciding vote, which he no doubt often was, managed to do so while appearing totally oblivious to argument, on the theory, maybe, that if he didn't seem to know what he was doing, he couldn't be blamed for what he did.

Result: a compromise. The books would stay in the library, but be kept in custody behind the librarian's desk, like *Playboy* in some drugstores, and be checked out only to students presenting written permission from their parents. My competition for the janitor's post was a wiry young woman of about twenty-five, denim-clad. If our case came to compromise, I figured they'd hire the top half of me and the bottom half of her.

We were interviewed separately, she first. When my turn came, I tried to play to the liberals without alienating the Victorians. Marty became my wife, and I mentioned the expected child several times to underscore my pressing need for the job.

Had I ever been convicted of any crime?

Was I a veteran?

Why was I willing to do such menial work?

It's hard to find work on the coast, I pointed out, to no one's surprise. Necessity is the mother of janitors. That got a laugh from the beard. I claimed the Boy Scout virtues for my own, and tried to create the impression that I had a strong back and a suitably weak but thoroughly moral mind. All in all, it was quite a performance. Then I was dismissed to sit in the hall beside my competitor while they decided our fate.

The girl gnawed on a hangnail. She was a potter, not making it in pots. "Working for the school would be perfect for me. I'd be off in the summer when the tourists come, to sell my pottery."

I didn't feel compelled to withdraw just because she wanted the job, too. "They'll never hire a woman," she said. "That old bag with the purple hair hates women, I can tell. The Movement won't reach Kilchis County till"—she paused to calculate—"1990. The lag seems to be about twenty years."

"That makes it 1958 here now."

"That's about right," she said.

The chairman floated out and wavered in front of us like gas fumes rising on a hot day. "Rykken, you got the job. Sorry, miss. The ladies figure he's stronger."

"Sexists."

The chairman reeled at her vehemence. "That's ess-ee-ecks-ists," he said. He turned to me. "Rykken, report to work Monday. You start at seven." A bubble rose and popped in his esophagus. I said I'd be there, and he shook my hand.

The girl rose to confront the chairman. She towered over him. "Just tell me one thing, mister. Did I lose this job because I'm a woman?"

"I don't ask 'em why they vote, honey, just how."

I put my hand on her arm. "Feed store in Kilchis is looking for a stock clerk. I'd give them a try."

She stuffed her arms into her parka, told the chairman he was a creep and left. "Feisty little piece," he said. My new employer.

I drove through walls of water to get home. My wipers and

147

my headlights were powerless against the rain. Blasts of wind from the ocean side of the highway battered the van's superstructure and standing pools of water in the road grabbed at my tires. Headlights of the few oncoming cars I passed were hypnotically seductive, and it took a force of will to avoid collision. Mostly, I was elated, until I imagined trying to explain to Barney Crews just why it seemed like a great victory to win an assistant janitor's job in the Kilchis County Public Schools. It made me wonder myself.

Chapter 26

*S*everal things, and first first.

Rain.

Days of rain. Nights of rain. Fusing into weeks, months, eternities of rain. Fugues of rain, intensities and rhythms contrapuntal. Light rain, gauzy and gentle. Big rain, big drops, hard fast rain. Medium rains, like the rains of other places, ordinary, sedate, respectable rain. Wind-slanted rain. Punitive rain. Bouncing, leaping, dancing rain. Merely damp or wholly soaking. Hiss, whisper, knock, hammer. Gray-white skies, rain-stolen shadows. Puddles full and rivers overflowing, ocean reaching up to scratch rain tickle.

Winter in Kilchis was rain. October's Indian sun became a dim, fond memory as the days of rain mounted, back to back, with no relief. I had never known one weather to persist so long. Marty, a veteran, told me I might as well get used to it, become a student of the subtleties of rain. One hour's rain is not like any other's. Listen to its rhythms, she said. How could I not? It was incessant, thrumming the wood roof of the pavilion, pounding the metal roof of the van, striking my skull, obscuring my heartbeat. It was colder than snow, somehow, and my spirits and my skeleton were utterly susceptible to its bone-chill. Nothing ever seemed quite dry. Colors changed in the rain, for dark and bright. It makes common things beautiful, Marty said. See how it polishes the stones. The doors of the pavilion swelled with wet, until they no longer fit their frames. Marty's sleek hair grew rough with rain.

I hated the feel of it against my skin. I was only comfortable, only warm enough in bed, under a mound of covers and pressed close to Marty's rain-resistant flesh. Getting up was a recurring tragedy; I considered hibernation. Surely it would be better to hunker down and sleep all winter than to endure those awful, shivering minutes between bed and clothes when the body is pale and vulnerable as a plucked chicken, the genitals shrunk to child-size, bristling hairs apologetic, inadequate fur.

Wear several layers of clothes, Marty said. That's the way to keep warm. And don't get your feet wet or you'll catch cold. My feet were always wet. I always had a cold, sometimes two at once, the beginning of one overlapping the end of the last. Marty never caught them from me. She pumped herself full of vitamins and stayed warm. It took days, sometimes weeks for her canvases to dry when she painted in oil.

My glasses were always rain-spotted, and the warmth of my eyeballs and my trapped breath rising fogged the lenses from the inside, so I was rain-blind out of doors and fog-bound in. Driving after walking in the rain, I'd push my glasses up and down my nose and try to calculate my course from two differently blurred realities. It's only water, Marty said. It can't hurt you. Just accept it. In the end, there was nothing else to do.

Is it possible to be happy in the rain? Marty seemed to be, but painting made her happy, and she was painting hard. Rain didn't seem to mildew her good spirits. Some days it nearly obliterated mine. Euclid didn't like it either. He walked on wet ground as if it hurt his paws, and tried to shake them dry between steps. Over Marty's objections, I made him a cat box, so he wouldn't have to go outside in the rain to relieve himself. He lived a dry existence, which I envied him profoundly.

And if the rain itself wasn't bad enough, there were always people talking about the rain. Rain jokes. Rain questions. Rain pleasantries. Wet enough for you? Say, you order us this rain? It's twelve days now since I seen blue sky. Or eighteen. Or twenty-seven. As the count approached forty, I considered building an ark. Marty thought I was kidding, but it seemed abnormal to me that so much water would fall out of the sky, that people would live someplace it did. For the first time, I began to believe in sin. Kilchis was being punished. Abominable transgressions were hidden at the heart of the town, and the rain was retribution. I began to watch people closely, trying to guess if they, their wrongs, were responsible for the wet wrath of the gods. Orville Mason seemed to me to be a likely offender.

In addition to the rain, there was work. To be an assistant custodian is akin to being a slave if your boss, like mine, is lazy and sadistic. His name was Bruce, his body large and soft, the skin of his face pitted as if by gunshot, his jokes baldly crude enough to embarrass a marine. Bruce was no student of enlightened management techniques. It would be wrong to say he didn't recognize my humanity; he did, perversely, by offending it. There are few enough glory jobs in the custodial business, but he made sure I got to do none of them. Dirty toilets and clogged drains were my department. The kitchen, before lunch, was his turf; the cafeteria, after lunch, when the floor was slippery with spilled milk and smashed peas, clumped with sodden straw papers and candy wrappers, was mine. So was heavy lifting, floor scrubbing, window washing and cleaning the blackboards, which were green, three times a week.

If a secretary in the office needed a three-pronged adapter for her typewriter, Bruce installed it. If a kid threw up in a classroom, he ordered me to clean it up. Though he avoided plumbing and bathroom cleaning in general, he had a penchant for locating himself in the girls' restroom during recess, with a wrench or maybe a plunger for cover, and pretending to work while he peered up the skirts of the little girls who wore them. To be fair, I have to say that if my tastes had been as perverse as his, he wouldn't have stopped me from indulging them; several times he invited me to join him on what he called "bathroom watch."

The rules of the game I was playing required me to suppress and conceal my intelligence. Had Bruce known for sure what he suspected, namely, that I was something other and more than I pretended to be, things would have gone even harder for me than they did. He'd been in the army in Korea, remaining at a perenially low rank so that he had to continually, to use his words, "eat shit." As head custodian, he took his revenge by spreading the shit around.

I used the twenty-five mile drive to work each morning to exercise my brain so it wouldn't rot during the next eight hours of enforced stupidity. I survived by simply shutting down, pulling in, keeping my mouth closed and my expression blank. I grunted a reply to Bruce's growled "good morning" and tried to speak in monosyllables for the rest of the working day. I did my damnedest not to care, not to resent. To most of the faculty and staff, I was invisible; those who saw me patronized or seemed afraid of me. They spoke slowly and precisely to me, a little louder than was necessary. "And how are we today?"

"We" nodded or shrugged or mumbled "fine," whether we were fine or not. Some obviously congratulated themselves on the liberal impulse that led them to address me at all, the dumb, unsavory semi-human they assumed me to be as I slouched down the halls bearing my cross of mop and bucket. For four dollars an hour, a hundred and sixty dollars a week, eight thousand three hundred and twenty dollars a year before taxes and disregarding gluttonous inflation, I suffered Bruce's tyranny and their scorn.

The place and the circumstances called into being Schuyler Three, a fellow who shared biographical details with but interpreted them differently from Schuylers One and Two. Schuyler Three was a loser, orphaned son of a murderer, a dropout, both too stupid and too proud to prosper in academe. He'd knocked up a broad and needed money; he lacked respect for the better sort of people, the principals and bosses and car dealers of this world; he was trapped in a dead end of his own choosing and resided ungraciously there, a cauldron of resentment and resignation, stunted dreams and grandiose nightmares, a wild conviction of his own superiority, seasoned with the rue of failure. Schuyler Three stooped and slumped and skulked, rarely spoke and never laughed, took a certain perverse pleasure in his lowly tasks, feeling them somehow deserved. If he worked hard, it was to burn off an excess of sullen energy. He hated Bruce with a pure hate cold as blue fire and smiled only when imagining punishments to suit his boss's crimes of ignorance and arrogance.

Once Schuyler Three did a good thing. He stopped three sixth-grade boys from beating up on a small, fat, cringing boy they had chosen, perhaps justifiably, to despise. He did this not from disinterested humanism, but because he identified with the victim. When the persecutors were dispatched, he said to the fat boy, "I hope to god you're smart, kid, because you sure aren't anything else."

Schuyler Three's brain teemed with profanities and lurid sexual fantasies. He repaid the haughty female teachers their condescension by mentally screwing them until they wept and willed his expression, in their presence, to convey the drift of his thoughts. He had no loyalty to his employer, no respect for his country, with its bureaucratic corruptions, its unsubstantiated currency, its expedient and morally blind choice of friends and enemies, the vicious addiction to tax monies that made it rob the poor to feed its habit of profligacy. Schuyler Three was not, by most standards, a very nice person. Seven to four, Monday through Friday, he was I. I was he. I'm not sure which statement is most true, or if it makes a difference.

Coming home to Marty was a daily dose of culture shock. If I was not in love with the person she was, I was wholly captivated by the one she was becoming. Her belly wasn't swollen yet, but her body bloomed, ripened, grew soft and lush. A glow of good health, vitamins, protein and sleep became her better than makeup. She worked every day, sketching or painting, stretching canvases or making frames for finished pieces. Painting is an encumbered art, she had mounds of stuff, but she loved her tools and kept them orderly and immaculate. If she was going strong, my homecoming didn't stop her. Some days, though, she was waiting for me, with Euclid on her lap, and seemed to come to life at my return.

In the early months of pregnancy, she was susceptible to sleep; it was like a disease, stealing her away mid-sentence. Her eyelids would rise and fall with a slow flicker over staring pupils until consciousness lost the fight and was banished, leaving me her body, relaxed and unselfconscious as if she were a baby herself, the vista of her waxy eyelids with tiny visible veins. The sleeping sickness customarily overtook her between nine and ten o'clock, plucking her night-owl feathers, and our relationship existed in the space between five and nine.

We talked about work—hers, mine didn't bear reliving, ate dinner, sometimes rode the merry-go-round, saw our few friends or a movie, or, in the rare event of a rainless night, walked on the beach then. I learned not to make love to her before eight-thirty, because coming made her sleep at any hour, and I was jealous of what time for companionship we had. Our days were frantic and idyllic. We were dreaming hard and waking, chased the dream. Marty produced painting after painting, surprise upon surprise. It was the first time she'd had the leisure to paint full time, and she found it a little frightening.

"It lessens the compulsion, Sky. Suddenly there are so many hours in a day, and I have to decide how I'm going to spend every one of them."

"Sounds beautiful."

"*Sounds* terrific," she agreed. "In practice, it's exhausting, to have to make a moral, philosophical decision about every minute. To work or not to work. That's always the question."

"It must get easier."

But she denied it. "Days aren't connected. Every one's new, and you can't take it for granted because you worked yesterday, you'll work again today. You have to start all over again."

"You work every day."

She grinned. "I'm a very strong person. I also walk on the beach a lot when you're not here. Or climb on the rabbit and stare off into space."

We lived cheaply, primitively, with no margin for extravagance, and ten years earlier, our frugality would have earned us some small measure of security, but in that present the things we absolutely needed—gas for my daily fifty-mile commute, art supplies, milk and meat for Marty's and the baby's well-being, a monthly visit to the doctor—were precisely those things most witched by the curse of inflation. Paints with mineral ingredients, essential red, blue and yellow, soared in price, and the titanium in the painter's white of choice was scarce as gold and nearly as precious.

When a full bladder woke Marty at 4:00 A.M., I'd often find her still awake at five, staring at the ceiling, paralyzed by one of two great endemic fears: Will the baby be all right? Will we be able to make ends meet? Sometimes I woke to find her crying silently.

"What's wrong?"

"Nothing."

"You're crying."

"I'm afraid."

"Afraid of what?"

So many answers. Sometimes, if she was feeling brave and wanted to let me sleep, she'd manage a laugh and call it existential fear, "Oh, just the whim-whams," and let me hold her till she gave it up and slept. Sometimes the fear was big enough to require more thorough exorcism. "What if something's wrong with the baby, Sky? What if it's deformed or retarded or . . ."

"We'll cope." What if? The question haunted me, too; imperfect children, chilling sorrows visited my nightmares as well as hers, but it seemed to be my part to reassure, to provide faith when hers faltered. Could we cope? People did. People do. All kinds of people. Sometimes I cited odds, but we both understood that probabilities offer little comfort when it's one's own life, one's own child in the equation. "You're so healthy, you're so beautiful, it must be all right," I told her, and myself, again and again.

"It's so strange. Something big is happening in my body, but I can't see it. I can't help it happen. I feel so powerless."

She was afraid the drugs she'd taken, the ones I'd used, might have damaged our genes. Marty swore off coffee and joints, but feared it was too little, too late, clasped her hands over still firm belly and feared it was a monster growing inside. "Nature hates freaks," I told her, "as much as vacuums. If something was wrong, you would have aborted by now."

Clutched her belly, watched the ceiling, rode the terror. Could we cope?

Sometimes it was her work that worried her. At 5:00 A.M., it seemed like crap; she was hopelessly mediocre; there was no point in continuing.

"You're good."

"What do you know?"

Not much, I had to confess. I wanted her to be good, I had a stake in believing she was.

"If I'm so damn good, why am I starving? Why am I nobody?"

How many times can you say the road is hard, the world unfair, that luck is paramount, and still believe it? I didn't know any more than she did. Having faced, fixated on my own limitations made me doubly unwilling to consider

Marty's. She would be the genius I narrowly missed being. With application, she would prevail.

"It's the first time I've asked for anything back from my work, Sky. I'm not sure you're supposed to do that. It makes the muses skittery."

"Your muse is solid as a rock."

"Is not. And what do you know about my muse, anyway?"

"I know that you love her. Him? It?"

In the darkness, she summoned and examined. "Both. The strength and wisdom of a mother, the hardness and daring of a man. My muse is bisexual. Anyway, he/she/they don't like to be told they have to make money."

"They don't. Tell them it would be nice, damn nice, but that we don't demand it."

"I demand it," Marty said. "I won't be kept. I've always supported myself."

"And will again. I'm not about to give you a free ride, lady."

"I've never been afraid like this before. I hate it."

"Hormones."

Out of the darkness, her pillow landed on my face, a solid hit. "Don't patronize me, you pig."

"What else is a patron supposed to do?"

Another kapok pummeling. "You know what I mean. I can't stand your godlike pronouncements."

I pinned her wrists. "How about my godlike cock?"

We made angry, squirming, pelvis-grinding love, then slept.

Chapter 27

I was late for work. It rained. The van started grudgingly, coughed, choked and stopped with ominous finality. Intuition told me it was something major, but I made myself approach the problem logically. Not battery. Not wiring. The electrical system seemed to be okay. I managed a second start, ambivalent as the first and with the same result. I knew I hadn't flooded it. The gauge told me I had gas, half a tank, but the gauges on an old machine are suspect. The odometer, in its senescence, had lately taken to lying, to the tune of .2 on every mile. Because of shortages, real or manipulated, coastal gas stations were unpredictable, even whimsical about their business hours, so I kept a five-gallon gas can in the back of the van for emergency use and decided now to avail myself of its contents.

Reluctantly, I climbed out of the relative aridity of the van into the morning rain, retrieved the can and took the top off the gas tank. Turning, it felt and sounded gritty and I thought, idly, that sand must somehow have found its way into the ridges of the cap and stuck there. Looking closer, I saw a granular powder, just a little, clinging to the greasy mouth of the tank. Not sand. All the grains were the same color, white, while the local sand was variegated, blacks, grays, browns and pales. This was stark white, finer than sand. I moistened my fingertip and lifted a few grains to my tongue. The taste was unmistakably sweet.

Adrenaline finished the job my morning coffee only started. I roared back into the pavilion, all the way back to where Marty still reposed, knees almost to chin, in her own rendition of a fetal scrunch. "Some son of a bitch put sugar in my gas tank," I bellowed. "And I bet I could name the son of a bitch who did it."

Marty pulled the covers back and blinked at me. "Start again. You say the van won't start?"

"The van's probably ruined. Mason or one of his goons spooned sugar into my tank."

She sat up cross-legged in the middle of the bed. "How do you know?"

"Because they're slobs. They spilled some."

"Oh." She thought about it. "What are you going to do?"

An excellent question.

"You can take my car to work," she said. "I wasn't going anywhere today."

"Your car. Right. Jesus, I wonder if they got that, too?"

She shook her head. "No way. I had a lock put on the tank back in seventy-four, when I lived in the city." Climbed out of bed, barefoot on the dirt floor, and dug in a jacket pocket until she found her keys. Tossed them to me. "I'd stop in Kilchis on your way to work and tell the sheriff."

"Orville's brother-in-law. I expect he'll be real sympathetic."

"Do it anyway."

Sheriff Taylor, who had the sagging, baggy look of a formerly fat man, was in fact immensely sympathetic. What a crying shame. Likely to cost me a lot to get it fixed. No way to catch the culprit, either, unless I happened to be lucky enough to catch him at it. No? A shame, that's what it was. These damn kids. No respect for other people's property.

"You have any enemies, Rykken?"

"Only one."

"That's better than some of us, my friend. And who might that be?"

I looked him in the eye. "Orville Mason."

The sheriff laughed, so that his deflated jowls shook. "Orville's one of our foremost citizens. I can't see him going all the way out to Seasound in the middle of the night just to cause you pain. It's teen-agers, if you ask me. There's just no discipline anymore."

"Mason threatened to burn me out. He also did his damnedest to keep me from getting work in Kilchis."

158

"Those're serious charges. Lucky I understand you don't mean 'em. I know you're upset, Rykken. I would be too. But that's no reason to go round makin irresponsible statements."

"Your brother-in-law can do no wrong, right?"

Sheriff Taylor smiled. "I've never known him to. I'm just goin to write down 'party or parties unknown' on this report form. That okay by you?"

"No."

He wrote, ". . . or parties unknown." "There we go. I'm real sorry about your rig."

"I bet you are. And I'm glad to know that justice is blind in Kilchis, sheriff."

"I got nothin to do with justice, Rykken. I just enforce the law."

He waved amiably as I stomped out. I called the school from a pay phone and told them I'd be more than a little late and stopped by the Exxon station, which had the biggest garage in town, to order a tow truck to go pick up the van. That alone was going to cost me twenty bucks.

I started up the road to school. The rain was heavier now, fat drops, close spaced. Kilchis Bay, to my left, was turbulent and brown. Weeks of rain washed topsoil off the clear-cut hills, into the creeks and streams that carried it into the bay, so much dirt that even the twice daily flow of tides couldn't wash it clean. Wind and a foul weather mood ruffled the bay, and the rain striking made a smaller, more consistent roughness on the face of the brown water. At the opposite arc of the bay, through low-lying clouds, I could see the thin curve of Seasound peninsula. Since the pavilion faced on the ocean now, seaward of land's rise, it couldn't be seen from the highway, and the peninsula looked gray and desolate in the rain. Marty was its sole inhabitant, discounting Euclid, and I was suddenly afraid for her, stuck there in the rain with no car, the wooden horses useless for flight.

Suppose Mason chose today to burn me out. With no cars there, no signs of life, would he bother to make sure no one was home before he lit the torch? Once the thought surfaced, it haunted. I accused myself of paranoia, that prevalent sixties disease, tried to convince myself that having made one move, Mason would surely wait to assess its result before trying again. But maybe that was what he wanted me to think. No, he wasn't subtle enough to arrive at that, it was my own brain, turned criminal, providing embellishments beyond Mason's reach. In our one meeting, he hadn't struck me as being especially bright. But then, the appearance of stupidity could be a useful tactic. He had, after all, somehow managed to get a stranglehold on much of Kilchis. And maybe, consider this, Schuyler, maybe Orville Mason is mad, a genuine loony, operating according to crazy logic, or none at all, all bets off, all expectations of normal garden variety human behavior irrelevant.

At the next wide place in the road, I turned the car around. I needed to see Marty safe, I needed to warn her. Should she leave Seasound? Maybe so. We had no weapons. Should I buy a gun? My stomach, queasy already, tightened further at the thought. People who abhor violence should not own weapons. The possession of guns leads to the use of guns. Even to think of it was to admit the possibility of violence, to invalidate the rational code that prohibits one person from harming another. Make butter, not guns. I repeated all the standard liberal arguments to myself.

The van was gone, mud rutted from the tow truck's tires. The rain drowned any other sound. For a moment, I wondered if Marty had caught a ride into Kilchis with the truck. I pried the swollen door open and went inside. The light was on, but Marty was nowhere in sight, no longer in bed, not at her easel. I called for her.

"Schuyler? Is that you? I'm around here, in the chariot."

I circled till I found her, sketching. "Thank God you're all right."

"I'm fine. What are you doing here?"

"I was worried about you. I got afraid maybe Mason wasn't done with his dirty tricks." I climbed on and sat beside her in the chariot. On the sketch pad across her knees was drawn a van, my van, detailed and realistic as in the manufacturer's brochure, riddled with gremlins (not the cars, the evil spirits), odious, grinning elves, pressing malevolent faces against the windows, hunched maniacally behind the wheel. One reclined on top, propped on a scaly elbow. "What's that? A birthday card for Edsel Ford?"

"Like it?" She smudged a too-harsh charcoal line with Kleenex.

"I'm just glad you're all right."

She looked up. "You really were worried. Don't be. I can take care of myself."

"I'm glad you're so confident. I didn't realize you were fireproof."

"No point in brooding, Sky."

"Don't make me feel stupid for worrying about you. It's not nice."

"Okay." She laid her sketch pad aside and gave me a domesticated hug. "Thanks for worrying. But I'm not afraid, and you shouldn't be either. It's a long way from a little sugar to arson."

"I wonder. Why don't you let me drive you back into town?"

"Because I've got too much to do here."

"I'd feel better if I knew you were in town."

"Schuyler, there's no point in living afraid. If the bastard's got you down, sell and have done with it. Otherwise ignore him."

"Am I supposed to ignore what it's going to cost me to fix the van? Who knows what that creep is capable of?"

"You might," Marty said, "want to have a little talk with Orville Mason."

"Sure. I'll threaten to torch his car lot."

"Tell him to go to hell himself."

"I doubt if he'd oblige."

Marty picked up her sketch pad. "Well, failing that, pick up the mail on your way through town, would you? I'm expecting some cadmium yellow." With her charcoal, she deepened the black of one tire.

"Are you really so cold-blooded, or are you faking it?"

"Both," she said.

Chapter 28

*O*t was almost five-thirty, closing time, when I stalked into Chevrolet Bonanza with what remained of my gas lines in a brown paper bag. Jean, at the receptionist's desk, was preparing to go home.

"Schuyler. I didn't know you were in the market for a new car."

"I'm not. I want to talk to Mason." We could both see him through the glass wall of his office, chair turned away from us as he talked into his red desk phone.

"He's busy now," Jean said, "but you're welcome to wait. Tony told me your news. Congratulations."

"Thanks. We'd just as soon keep it quiet for now, though."

"I haven't said a word." We watched Mason hang up. "I'll tell him you're here." She buzzed on the intercom. Mason looked up and saw me through the glass, motioned me in. Jean got up and slung her purse over her shoulder. "I'm going home now. Big test tomorrow."

Mason ushered me into his glass cage. "Well, Rykken, I've been expecting you. You want to buy a car, or sell some real estate?"

"Actually, I wanted to return something you left at Seasound last night." I pushed past him and dumped the contents of my bag in the middle of his desk. Black Jell-O oozed from the clogged tubes, spread on his clean blotter, splashed the phone. It blackened the crisp pile of papers on his desk. "I would have brought just the sugar, but as you can see, it's all cooked up."

Mason's face got red, his fists clenched, then opened, as he decided to choke back anger. "That's one hell of a mess, Rykken."

"Four hundred and eighty-three bucks worth."

"Sheriff mentioned to me you'd been the victim of a prank. I was sorry to hear it."

"But not surprised."

"Kids will be kids. Bud was real sorry he couldn't help you, but a thing like that, it's almost impossible to catch who done it."

"I know who done it, Mason. And I want you to know I don't appreciate it."

His smile reminded me of the wolf's in my childhood copy of "Little Red Riding Hood," voracious and smug. "Of course, I don't know where you get the wrongheaded idea that I'm responsible. But just to show you how sympathetic I am, I'm not going to call the sheriff about you defacing my property here."

"You're all heart."

"I'm a reasonable man," Mason said. "Loyal to my friends and business partners."

"I bet."

"You could find that out firsthand, if you weren't so stubborn."

"I don't like to be pushed around, Mason."

"You like being a janitor, Rykken?"

"It's an honest living."

"Sure seems like a pity, a smart fellow like you pushing a broom. When you could do so much better for yourself and that little woman of yours."

"We're doing all right. Malicious as it is, a little sugar in the gas tank isn't going to drive us out."

Mason flashed the darkened silver of his fillings when he laughed. "What amuses me is that you think I'd stoop to hoodlums' tricks. If I wanted to force you out, you can believe I'd do it right."

"Wrong season for arson, Mason. Too wet."

"You get some that nitro the loggers use, it sets off real

bright and smolders for days. It's quite a sight, to watch 'em burn a cut." He chuckled. "'Course, you shouldn't under-estimate the little things. Little things pile up, they can wear a man down."

"Leave me alone, Mason. That's what I came here to say."

"Oh, you're alone all right, son. All alone. But I want you to know, my door is always open, any time you want to talk about selling that land of yours. Now," he said, "I got to head on home for dinner. The wife's invited company." He edged me toward the door, looked back at the mess on his desk. "That'll wait till tomorrow. One of the boys'll clean up then." He switched off his office light. "Nice seeing you again, Rykken. Only next time, don't bring me any pres-ents." Clapped my shoulder, good-ole-boy style. "I'll let you let yourself out while I lock up."

Walking past the shiny, shiny new cars and pickups in his showroom, I found myself wondering how much damage I could do them with a well-aimed sledge before they stopped me.

Chapter 29

*M*arty was wearing my jeans when I got home. "I hope you don't mind, Sky, but I can't zip mine anymore. It's really starting to happen."

My pants were still too big for her. There was room enough to stick my hands inside. It was true; her belly was swollen to a firm tight bump below her waist. "Can you feel it moving yet?" I asked.

"Sometimes I think so. Very faintly. But maybe it's only gas."

I stroked the warm convexity between her hipbones. "You're the skinniest fat lady in town."

"I can't hold my stomach in anymore. I can tighten the muscles, but the bump stays." She squeezed her hand into the jeans along with mine, felt her belly, then laid my hands, fingertips touching, over the curve. "I kind of like it. It doesn't make me unattractive to you, does it?"

"Hell, no." I took my hands out of her pants and put them on her shoulders. "It's a very attractive bump. Besides, I feel a certain pride of authorship."

"Mr. Macho Rides Again."

"Where would you be without my chromosomes? You can't tell me that virgin birth is a feminist myth. And at this point, I'd say it behooves you to encourage my paternal instincts." I stretched out beside her on the bed.

"Sometimes I feel sorry for you," Marty said. "You can't know what it feels like to be pregnant."

"You can tell me."

"Would you have a baby if you could?"

I put a hand on my own belly, its girdle of muscles inflexible. "I can't imagine it. My body can't. It's an academic question anyway."

"But would you," she persisted, "assuming you could?"

"Well, sure. I suppose so." I said it to placate her as much as anything. My body was resolutely, irretrievably male.

"I always thought that women who made out that childbirth was some kind of mystical rite were off their nuts," Marty said. "But it really is mystical. Not something you can imagine until it happens to you."

"I'm glad you like it."

"It's fascinating. There's this painting I want to do, only I'm afraid I'll wreck it."

"A pregnant painting?"

Marty turned, elevated her body on one hip-ridge, raised her head with one elbow-supported hand. "An unborn fetus, actually. Years ago, when I was just a kid, *Life* magazine ran a photo essay about human reproduction. Early fiber optics stuff, I guess. There was a very dramatic two-page spread of sperm swimming against a blue background. Do you remember it?"

"Uh uh. My mother hated *Life*. She said it was a loose publication. That's a pun."

"The picture that really caught me was of a full-grown unborn baby, still in the womb. It looked completely human, and its expression was the most wise and peaceful thing I've ever seen. It was still inside the sac, and the membrane was draped around it, over its face, like a veil. Like Mary wears in all those old religious paintings. Only this was mother and child all at the same time, in the same image." She sighed. "I want to paint it."

"Sounds hard."

"Is hard. Especially the veil. Did my yellow come?"

"Mail's on the table. I'll get it." I tossed several days accumulation of mail, hers and mine, down on the bed. She sorted it. "Bill, bill, bill, junk. Junk. Bill. Junk. Here's a letter for you, from Los Angeles."

"I don't know anybody in Los Angeles. More junk." When she handed me the envelope, I recognized Barbara's handwriting, the bold *S* and *R* she used in writing my name.

"What is it?"

"Huh? It appears to be from Barbara. I told you about her, remember?"

"Of course I remember. You lived with her for four years. Well, go on. Read it. Unless you'd rather be alone."

I tossed the envelope at her. "You read it. I've got no secrets."

Marty picked up the envelope and studied it, then passed it back to me. "I don't want to read your mail, Sky. I've got no right." She got up on her knees and crawled close to me. "Open it up. Read it. Now."

"What are you so anxious about?"

"I want to know the worst."

"Okay." I tore the end from the envelope and blew inside, then pulled out a single sheet of embossed hotel stationery, covered with Barbara's exotic scrawl. No more than four sentences filled the page. "Jesus," I said.

"What is it?"

"She's coming to visit. Tomorrow." I handed her the

letter, which said, in essence, that Barbara was shooting TV spots in several western locations for her airline account, and when she was done, wanted to drop in and see me for a couple days before she headed east again. She was arriving in Portland on such and such a flight at such and such a time the next day. Would see me then. Marty looked up from the page. "Does she know about me?"

"I haven't written her since I met you."

"So she still thinks . . ."

"I don't know what she thinks."

"Where are we going to put her?" She looked around our cubicle. The van seat now served as a sofa.

"In a motel. She can afford it."

"Do you want me to get lost, Sky? Disappear?"

"Of course not. I want you to meet her. You might even like each other." Marty was silent, her face stony. I put my arm around her. "You're not upset, are you? Barbara's only an old friend. She doesn't mean a thing to me."

"Then why is she coming to visit?"

"Who knows? She probably wants a free ride on the merry-go-round."

"Dammit!" Marty exploded. "Your old girl friend is coming, all thin and sleek, when I'm too fat to fit in my own pants anymore."

"Marty, honey, she won't care."

"I'll care. You'll care. You'll take one look at her and . . ."

I took Marty's hands in mine. "I'll tell you what. We'll go to a store in Portland before we go to the airport and get you some maternity clothes. Okay?"

"A thrift shop," Marty said. "We're poor, remember?" She smiled, though, as if I'd pleased her. "Do you really want me to come to the airport with you?"

"Of course I do. Besides, we have to take your car."

Again she landed a pillow blow on my head, again I wrestled her down and loved her, bump and all. It struck me as odd that our mating ritual always seemed to commence with mock violence, but I had no complaints about the result at all.

Chapter 30

Traitorous dreams. Whose body? Whose breasts and thighs? I woke exhausted from a night of making prodigious love to a kind of idealized Everywoman whose face changed every time my dreaming eyes beheld it. The body stayed the same, encompassing mine, while her features changed configuration as fast and subtly as the colored shards in a kaleidoscope. Barbara, Marty, Barbara/Mom, Janis Joplin, even, hard as it is to admit it by light of day, my own dead mother, not dead in my dream, these plus a dozen strangers—I loved them all. And woke to the reality of one Marty sleeping, a thigh slung over my backside, hair splayed carelessly across my shoulders as well as her own (so much hair!), the distortions of pregnancy invisible, buried against the mattress, Euclid the cat reposed in the warm crook of her knee. Woke to find one in place of many, the object of my new fidelity.

Would Barbara stir me? I was afraid of love, afraid of regret, of dissatisfaction. Marty whistled softly in her sleep, not a snore but a single high note that sounded on the exhalations. The imperfection bothered me. It made her too human, too particular, too perishable. I lay beside her and tried to love her, tried to summon all the tenderness and affection I sometimes, often, felt for her, the intense respect for her idiosyncratic self that often moved me. If only she wouldn't whistle in her sleep. If only she didn't need to sleep so much. If only I didn't feel so goddamn trapped.

My body stiffened and I tightened my fists, then opened my fingers stiffly, slowly. They felt cramped and crabbed. Somatically, Marty sensed my hostility and her body turned away as if I'd hurt her. She rolled herself into a tight, self-protective ball that shut me out. My body had its freedom and felt loss. It was cold where she had been. The cat, dislodged, tried to resettle on my disassembled lap, but I picked him up, the little rib cage fragile in my grip, and tossed him to the floor.

I was being a son of a bitch and I knew it. Didn't want to feel the way I felt. The tightness in my muscles and my nerves wouldn't let up. Son of a violent man, I wondered if I had any right to be a father. In penance for the violence of my thoughts, I reached out and touched Marty's shoulder as gently as I could. The touch convinced me, wordlessly, of her integrity, brought home the enormity of the miracle that made molecules cohere into a Marty, living and different from every other living thing, made me genuinely sorry for the ill will I'd felt toward her. At my touch, she stretched out flat on her back, extending arms and legs, and when she opened her eyes, her smile flickered with what seemed to be a simple and spontaneous joy at seeing me. It made me feel like a shit.

She squeezed her eyes shut, then opened them wide, drew a hand inside the covers and set it on her stomach. "Whew. Not a mother yet. I dreamed about the baby. It was a girl."

"Did she look like me?"

"I don't know. I didn't think about it in the dream. I was too amazed by her talking."

"What did she say?"

"Mostly she was consoling me for feeling guilty for having lost her."

"You lost her?"

"Yeah. I finally found her behind a furnace. It was all dark and sooty, but she was okay. I wonder what it means?"

She sat up, fixing the covers in her armpits to cover her breasts. She had a pretty clavicle, sculpted in the morning light. "You stay right there," I said. "I'll bring you a cup of coffee."

When I got out of bed, Euclid jumped back on and settled in Marty's lap. Absently, she scratched him behind the ears, and I could hear his purr. "You'll make a good mother," I told her.

"I practice on the cat."

"I know."

"I'd practice on you, too, if you'd let me."

I set the kettle on the Coleman stove and lit it. "No thanks. I'd rather be your man."

"Are you?" she asked. "My man?"

The question was so sincere it embarrassed me, and I answered with more conviction than I felt. "Sure. Count on it."

"I don't count on anything," she said. "Are you sure you want me to come to Portland with you?"

"Unless you don't want to."

"Well, I really don't want to. But I figure I'll be even more miserable if I stay here all day, wondering what's happening between you two." She gave the especially dry laugh she directed at herself.

"Do I detect a note of jealousy? I didn't think you were the type."

What I said lightly, she took seriously. It was going to be that kind of day. "I'm not," she said. "Not usually. It must be this." She patted her belly. "It makes me feel— dependent. And insecure."

I said nothing.

"I feel like a millstone around your neck, Sky. Your old lover turns up for a reconciliation, and I'm in the way. I'm afraid she'll think I got pregnant just to trap you."

"Did you?"

Another joke misfired. "Of course not. You don't think that, do you? I wouldn't want to get an abortion now, but I think I could raise the baby by myself. I wouldn't ask you for anything."

I could see that she was miserable. Also that she meant what she said. It wasn't intended to hurt me, but it did. I was a little miserable myself. "Is that what you want?" I asked her.

We looked at each other across what was suddenly a very large gap. There was no bridge across it, only the tightrope possibility of saying yes. Good-by. Finally, grudgingly, she tossed a question back across the void. "Is it what *you* want?"

I saw her dilemma. Pride made it hard to say no. And there was a certain excitement in the open question. One word could uncommit us, unravel the fabric of our joint reality. We could be free.

The kettle whistled and gave me a way out. I made her coffee. She took it from me. We were together for another day.

Chapter 31

I was grateful to Barbara now for a peculiar strength I used to see as a weakness—her chameleon quality, a playwright's ability to create a role, an actress's ability to play it. It was a kind of infinite social adaptability and it used to bug the crap out of me. I'd go to a party with a Barbara I thought I knew and find that, to fit the occasion, she'd turned into someone else, a Republican or an anarchist, an opera lover, a believer in astrology. Suddenly, she was an ardent fan of hockey, the Rolling Stones, sky-diving, or Zubin Mehta, when I knew personally that she knew next to nothing about her proclaimed passion, and cared less. More than once I accused her of hypocrisy.

She replied that she'd been raised believing it was right to tailor one's behavior to present company. Besides, she would be interested in astrology, in opera or ice hockey if she had the time and opportunity. I suppose this propensity stood her in good stead in the advertising business; I know it helped us all survive her visit.

Five minutes off the plane, she'd assessed the situation and found herself a role. If she had been aiming for reconciliation, if she'd hoped to rekindle our banked romance, you'd never have guessed it from how she acted. She was the epitome of old friend, selflessly delighted by my current happiness and impending fatherhood. She took to Marty immediately; she was simply *fascinated* by art. Especially women's art.

They were, in fact, about of an age, both veterans, in their way, of the Women's Movement, and shared a kind of determined feminism. The code of honor insisted that they be friends, even at my expense. Marty, stiff at first, soon thawed in the blaze of Barbara's goodwill. They discussed The Issues—ERA's chances of passage, the difficulty of making it in a man's world. I, driving while they talked, in many ways the least successful of the three, the least "self-realized," as the saying goes, began to feel left out.

On the way to Portland, I'd tried to quiet Marty's fears: that Barbara would try to get me back, that I'd be swept off my feet, that she, Marty, wouldn't know how to act or what to say. Now, instead of being the apex of the triangle (had I looked forward to it?), I was its lower foot. Eventually, Barbara tossed me a bone.

"Of course, you're lucky in Sky. I'd have to admit he's probably the least chauvinistic man I know. Apt to be a little jealous of one's work from time to time, but that's understandable. I used to be jealous of his."

Marty laughed.

"Speaking of work, what are you doing now, Sky? Living off your inheritance?"

I could see her eyes, the lids tinted a silvery green to match her green sweater, in the rearview mirror. For a second, I had the sensation they were meeting mine. "I'm assistant janitor at an elementary school," I told her.

And Barbara laughed. "Schuyler Rykken, man of the people. Where will it stop?"

Marty spoke in my defense. "Jobs are scarce on the coast. Professional jobs are nonexistent. Sky's lucky to be employed."

"I do tend to picture you in the halls of academe, Sky, but not mopping them. Say, maybe you'd be interested in the new line of products the agency's handling. Industrial cleansers, stuff like that. Supposed to make your toilets shine."

"Get off it, Barbara."

"I suppose your salary's lower than your IQ."

"We needed money. Don't comment on what you don't understand."

"Now I've wounded his male ego." She turned to Marty. "You've got to admit, it's a switch, from assistant professor to grade-school janitor."

"We're living in a backwater, Barb. What can I say? There's not even a junior college in Kilchis County, and the 4-H extension wasn't offering a course in topology this term."

"Is he serious?"

"Deadly," Marty said.

"Why stay then?" Barbara looked out the window at the rain. "It can't be the good weather that keeps you here."

"It's beautiful country, Barbara."

"How can you tell?"

"Wait till you see the ocean. It's right outside the door almost," Marty said.

"Mmm. You've got a nice house, at least?"

"No house," I said. "We live with the merry-go-round. No plumbing, either. And no phone. That's why we thought you might be more comfortable at a motel."

"So would you," Barbara said. "My God, isn't it miserable to be pregnant and live like that?"

"Not so far," Marty said. "It's not bad."

"Schuyler, you're out of your mind. Are there doctors in Kilchis?"

"No obstetricians," Marty told her. "A couple of family practitioners who deliver babies."

"What if something goes wrong?"

"You can see for yourself how healthy she is. Nothing's going to go wrong."

"Famous last words."

"Just because you're a hypochondriac."

"I don't take any chances with my health, that's right."

We rode in silence for a while. When I'd cooled down a bit, I asked Barbara about her airline spots.

"Oh, they're fun. I'm rather proud of them, in fact. And it was wonderful to get out of Boston for a couple of weeks. The snow's knee-deep."

"What did you do?"

"Oh, I assisted the director. Looked out for the client's interests. I really felt like Federico Fellini the whole time. Ate tons of wonderful food and put on five pounds."

"Me, too," Marty said. "With more to come."

"Well, it becomes you. That's a pretty top."

"Thanks. We stopped at a thrift shop before we met you and got me a maternity wardrobe."

"A thrift shop?"

"Junior League. Very nice stuff, and only worn maybe five months."

"Go to a city, Schuyler," Barbara said. "Get a nice apartment and a good job. A studio for Marty. A decent doctor. My God, you two could be on top of the world."

"Funny how old girl friends figure they have the right to give you advice."

"Good advice."

"How about you, Barb? Why don't you get out of advertising? Finish up your master's degree. Stop smoking. Get rid of your ulcer. Follow your heart."

"Very funny."

"I think," Marty said, "that maybe you two know each other too well."

"In all the time I knew him," Barbara said, "I never knew that Schuyler wanted to be Daniel Boone, living in the wilderness and such."

"I propose a truce," Marty said.

I dug a relatively clean white handkerchief out of my jeans and waved it between the seats. "I concur. Peace. Barb, I'm glad you're here."

"And glad I'm leaving soon."

"That too."

Chapter 32

*A*ll the way to Seasound, Barbara's skepticism persisted. She'd decided to be the city girl, appalled by the remoteness of our coastal world. The cows grazing in roadside pastures amused her, the city of Kilchis even more. "Look!" She pointed at the Treetopper chopping. "A pink Paul Bunyan." Of the vehicles, "Where are the cars, for heaven's sake? Does everybody here drive a truck?" A sharp intake of breath. "Oh my God. Look at that. There's a *gun* in the back of that truck."

"There's another one," Marty showed her. "And another. They're bigger than graduation tassels around here."

"I feel like I've just walked into the last episode of *Gunsmoke*. Do people really use those things?"

"For hunting, sure. And macho. Macho's big." Barbara's tourist was just right; it made me feel like a native. A few months before, her amazement was mine, vocalized. On the crude road to the peninsula, Barbara *oofed* with every rut that jounced the Volkswagen. Marty named the visible species of trees for her: fir, spruce, hemlock, cedar, alder. "You live here," Barbara said. "You really do." She didn't want to see the ocean in the rain ("I'm loyal to the Atlantic anyway"), so went on inside.

I couldn't have begged for anything better than Barbara's response to the merry-go-round. It was nonverbal, an index of sincerity with her, since Barbara believes that words are meant to be the tools of artifice. She looked, then touched, circled the platform, patting wooden necks, feeling the texture of the horsehair tails, the cool hardness of jeweled eyes.

"Turn it on," Marty whispered, and I did.

The music played, rich and martial, the lights, 104 bulbs,

burned off rain and reserve. We reveled in our toy. Barbara moved from horse to horse, riding sidesaddle or backward, standing in the stirrups, waving to an imagined throng cheering along the circular parade route. Marty chose a green horse and I climbed on behind, pressed close to the curve of her back, reached my arms around her and let my hands rest on her belly. We rode comfortably, close, while Barbara tackled the merry-go-round with manic glee, intense and unselfconscious.

Her excitement was a gift she gave us, restoring the wonder of the machine, which threatened to become, with quotidian exposure, a large wooden liability, or at best, an enormous piece of furniture we'd learned to live with and not see. Barbara became it. Put a can of beer or a pack of chewing gum in her hand, and she could have starred in one of her own TV spots. Her brand of polish, the perfect makeup, the artful hair and expensive clothes were absolutely foreign to Kilchis. She might as well have been a movie star.

Marty watched, too. She stiffened in front of me, half-turned to whisper, "She's beautiful, Sky."

"Yes."

"Don't you wish . . ."

I squeezed Marty tighter. "No. I don't." It was true; I didn't. Didn't want Barbara or her not-quite-real beauty back. Was pleased it had once been mine. And it was good to see her. As friends we were better matched than as lovers. No longer feeling a stake in her behavior, no longer feeling obliged to keep her true to a self that may never have existed and, if it had, was long past, I could simply enjoy her and hope she found the same rare ease with me. I lifted Marty's hair from her shoulders and found a pale spot of neck to plant a kiss on. We were aligned, were partners, and I had no complaints.

Finally, Barbara charged up to our charger. "Turn it off, Sky. I've got to pee."

When the band organ was quiet, we could hear the rain. Marty directed Barbara to the light-pull and the thunder mug we kept under the bed, and she disappeared behind the partition into our living quarters. The light came on. I started to ask Marty how she liked Barbara. Then, out of sight, Barbara called my name, an urgent half-scream I'd only heard once before, when the toilet in our apartment backed up and was spewing on the bathroom floor. That couldn't be the problem now. I went to see what was.

Barbara pointed to the bed, to a heap of blood and fur in its middle. Euclid's black fur, Euclid's red blood and spilled cat guts. Shot in the stomach and messily dead. It was too late to keep Marty from seeing; she'd followed me back. She sat on the edge of the bed and reached for the cat.

"Marty, don't."

"Maybe he's still alive." She picked up the torn body, then dropped it, her hands covered with blood and ooze. "He's stiff. Oh God, he's all stiff."

The bullet (it must have been a rifle; there was no splay of shot) had passed through him and on into the mattress. Our blankets and sheets showed a small hole at the center of a gory dimple.

Barbara gave a stranger's polite cough. "What's going on here, if you don't mind my asking?"

I looked at Marty. "Mason. The bastard." Marty held her blood-stained hands away from her and stared at them. "Wipe it on the blanket. We won't be using it again."

"Who's Mason?" Barbara asked. "Besides a shit who murders cats."

"It could have been you in there," I said to Marty.

"No, Sky. He wouldn't go that far."

"Not if I stop him first."

Barbara stuck two fingers in her mouth and blew a sharp camp whistle. "Hold on. Since I'm here, I think you ought to fill me in."

"Orville Mason wants tó buy Schuyler out."

"Wouldn't it be easier to make an offer you can't refuse?"

"I already said no."

"We've got to bury Euclid," Marty said. "Where's the shovel?"

"Have you talked to the police?" Barbara asked. "It's probably not against the law to kill cats, but there must be something. Breaking and entering, maybe."

Marty picked up the cat. "Get the shovel, Schuyler."

"It's in the van. And the van isn't here."

"Damn." She circled, looking for something else to use instead. Finally picked up a wooden spoon. "I'm going to bury him." She started out.

"Marty, wait. You'll be digging till midnight with that thing."

Barbara started after her, put an arm around her shoulders. "How about burial at sea? That's natural. Water to water, instead of dust to dust."

Marty considered. "Which way is the tide going?"

"Out, I think. I'll check." I left them, glad to get away long enough to clear my head. In another five minutes, it would be dark. A fresh blast of storm blew in off the ocean, driving diagonal sheets of rain. In the light that was left, I climbed down the dunes to the beach and made my way over the round stones, treacherously slippery from the rain, to the water's edge. The tide was high, there was almost no beach, and the cutting edge of foam hissed at the stones. I watched many waves rise and break, watched the smooth sheets of water they pushed up the sand before I satisfied myself that, overall, the pattern was one of recession, that, except for aberrations, each wave reached slightly less high. I was soaked within minutes of going out and the wind pressed my wet clothes around me. It chilled my anger into something like despair.

They sat on the edge of the merry-go-round platform when I returned and Marty held the cat. "Tide's going out. Now's a good time." I reached for the remains of Euclid. "Might as well let me take care of it. I'm soaked already."

Marty got up. "I want to."

"You don't want to risk a cold."

"I want to come."

Barbara shook her head. "Not having known the deceased, I think I'll pass."

178

We headed back into the storm. There was no point in telling Marty to wear her slicker; she was covered with gore. She carried the cat down the dunes. The wet stones were harder, required the balance of arms outstretched. I took the cat, while she picked her way across to the narrow strip of sand.

"What do we do now, just throw him in?"

"I guess so."

"It's so cold."

"He won't mind."

"No. You know, I never painted him because I thought it was trite."

"You were probably right."

"I wish I had."

"You're drenched. We better do it."

"I hate to just throw him away like so much garbage."

"I know. I wish I hadn't tossed him out of bed this morning."

"Was it only this morning?"

"It looks like he was asleep when they shot him, anyway. It was probably a real quick trip to kitty heaven." I stepped a pace or two away from Marty. "Well, here goes." Threw Euclid like a large rock into the ocean, far as I could. As usual, my throw was disappointing. "Rest easy, Euclid. You were a good cat."

Marty stared at the place where he sank out of sight. I didn't want to stand there until he washed up at our feet. "Come on. Let's get back. Let's run." I grabbed her hand. There was no running over the rocks, but we scrambled up the dunes, slipping in the wet sand, then raced back to the pavilion.

"Done?" Barbara asked. She cleared her throat. "Nothing of him doth remain but doth suffer a sea change into something rich and strange. *The Tempest* misquoted. Best I could do on short notice."

"We'd better get into some dry clothes."

"I'll wait here. I'm getting attached to your living room."

We peeled down to our gooseflesh, toweled it dry and

179

dressed again. Stepping into her pants, Marty looked like a child, calves thin, hair clumped wetly, the swelling below her waist anomalous.

"I'm not going to sleep in that bed."

"No."

"What are we going to do?"

"I'm working on it. I think you ought to check into the motel with Barbara."

"What about you?"

"I don't like the idea of leaving this place undefended. They may have figured on driving us away so they could torch it."

"Just how do you propose to stop them? With eloquence?"

She was dressed now, easing the rain snarls out of her hair with a brush. Half of it was restored to smoothness, the rest still rough and twisted. "I think we ought to get married," I said. "As soon as possible."

Marty laughed. I was torn between being glad to amuse her and hurt at the cause. "What's funny?"

"You committed a non sequitur."

"I wasn't setting up a syllogism. It makes perfect sense."

She put the brush down on the dresser. "Explain."

"What are my choices? I can sell to Mason. I can kill him. I can get married. It seems to me it's the only positive alternative."

"But . . ."

"But what? Consider it an act of affirmation. Our life goes on. Besides, the kid deserves a father."

"The kid has a father."

"Legal. Not biological."

"Not logical either."

"Do you want to get married or not?"

She looked at me sadly amd blew a sigh out through her nose. "The merry-go-round stops here? It's so bizarre."

Barbara's voice interceded. "Could you please hurry up? I'm getting hungry."

Marty smiled. "Did you ever propose to her?"

"No. Will you perform the bizarre act of marrying me?"

Marty worked the brush through the last strands of tangled hair. "Oh, shit. Why not?"

"Is that a yes?"

"Yeah. I suppose so. Only I reserve the right to change my mind."

"You have twenty-four hours."

"Barbara's hungry," Marty said. "We'd better go."

Chapter 33

*N*o twin beds at the Kilchis Motel. Barbara and Marty were easily resigned to a double, more easily resigned to it than my finer feelings were. Of all the strange things coming down, the idea of my old lover and my wife-to-be sharing a bed struck me as the strangest. Life tends to make the outrageous commonplace. I envied, and resented, their female flexibility.

We carried Barbara's luggage in, and as many of Marty's paintings as we'd been able to fit in the small car. She was afraid of losing them to Mason's vandalism, and I agreed. Practically speaking, they were part of our capital. Carrying them wrapped in plastic garbage bags against the rain into the motel objectified them for me; they seemed less good, less solid somehow, a ridiculously quixotic investment of energy and hope. Barbara, on the other hand, professed enthusiasm. There was one, an almost-abstract ocean, she wanted to buy. I couldn't tell if she was patronizing us or not, but Marty was pleased.

We ate in the room, a small junk-food feast procured at Dairy Queen. That done, I called Tony at his parents' house. He was just leaving to take Jean to the movies, but after a brief explanation, he agreed to change his plans and asked me to come over.

I left the women and went. In the dark and the rain, I had

a hell of a time finding the right address. Kilchis had the dismaying habit of unnumbered houses; if you don't know, you don't belong. I hated the streets as I circled through them. Finally I went back to Main Street, found a phone booth and called Tony for better directions. They led me to a newer part of town, where the low-lying ranch houses all seemed to have been produced from the same set of plans. Presumably, by day you could tell them apart by color; at night, the only obvious difference was that in every other one, the picture window and the front door were on the left instead of the right. I spotted Tony's car in a driveway and turned in behind it.

Before I was out of the Volkswagen, Tony appeared at the front door. He led me in through a small dining room, where a sewing machine was set up on the table, into a brightly yellow kitchen that smelled of dinner and pipe smoke. Tony's mother, at the sink, was elbow-deep in dishwater. His father sat at the table, drawing fiercely on a briar pipe. He pushed himself up on stocking feet when we came in, and I recognized him by the blood spot on the white of his eye. He was the guy from the men's room, my first night in Kilchis.

"Dad, this is Sky Rykken. Sky, Ben Silber."

Ben moved his pipe to his left hand to free his right for shaking. "Turns out we met before. You seem to attract trouble, Rykken."

"I don't mean to."

"Some folks is accident-prone. I'd stay out of the woods if I was you."

"I will."

Ben sat back down at the table and relit his pipe. "Introduce your mother, boy, and give the man a beer. Get me one too."

Tony's mother turned from the sink to me and smiled, one of those middle-aged women still pretty precisely because they don't fight time.

"I'm pleased to meet you, Mrs. Silber."

"Lynette," she corrected. "Seeing you're not one of Tony's high school friends."

My majority established, I sat down with Ben at the table, while Tony pulled the tabs on our beers. He'd taken a third for himself but was slower to open it. His father looked at it, at him, then nodded. "Better they drink at home than out behind the school where the sheriff can round 'em up."

Tony joined us. "Dad knows some about your trouble with Mason, Sky. I filled him in."

"If you judge a man by his enemies, you must be all right. You're welcome here. What's that Bible bleatin bastard up to now?"

"Killed my cat while it was sleeping on my bed."

Ben shook his head. "Damn coward. You hear that, Lynette? Your old boyfriend's taken to shootin house pets."

"I dated Mason some in high school," she said. "Ben's never let me forget it."

"Lucky for you I come along when I did. A man who'd shoot a cat'd beat a woman."

"He was a good cat," I said. Ben, despite his hard hands and scarred eyeball, seemed to understand: you don't hurt the helpless.

"Thinks he's God, Mason does. Been hidin behind that Bible too long."

"You think he's crazy?"

"You think a sane man kills a cat? Some guys drink, they do crazy things. But born-again Orville don't touch a drop. He don't have that excuse. He's just plain mean."

"How'd he get to be Kilchis's leading citizen?"

"Money talks," Ben said. "Real loud. But that don't solve your problem. Tony says Mason threatened to burn you out."

"Twice. I tended to think it was all talk. Now I don't know."

"He wouldn't strike the match himself," Ben said. "Chances are, he didn't pull the trigger, neither. But Orville can arrange to get things done. He wants that land bad. And

183

people around here've learned, most of 'em, that when Orville Mason wants somethin, they best bend over."

Ben's low voice was corroded by tobacco and booze. Every so often, he interrupted himself to cough, an upheaval deep in his lungs. I didn't like what I was hearing; it validated my own worst fears, but there was something reassuring in the confirmation. Tony's father wasn't a man to mistake shit for shinola. "You think I ought to sell, then?"

Ben slammed his beer can down. "Hell no. I think you ought to fight the bastard." He grinned. "'Course, it's easy to be a hawk in somebody else's war. I've hated the SOB for twenty-five years. That's partly why it tickles me to see a stranger standin up to him."

I was grateful for that bit of clarity, too. Six months didn't make me a settler; to Kilchis, I was still a stranger. Ben told me, in a friendly way, just where I stood. I was on alien ground. "I've got the will to fight, I think, but I'm not too sure about the way. Mason seems to be holding all the cards."

"Except the one he wants." Ben found that funny. His laugh turned into a cough that shook his upper body. "You got a gun out there?"

"No."

"I'd have me one."

"If a person has a gun, he's likely to use it."

"Person has a right to defend himself and his property. It says so in the Constitution. That's where I part company with all them bleedin hearts."

"I think I'm one of them," I said.

"Well, I suppose there's somethin in it, as far as it goes. But tell me what you plan to do when they show up out there again. Hit 'em over the head with an ax handle?"

"I haven't even got one of those."

Ben laughed again, without raising phlegm this time. "Tony told me you was a city boy. Guess he was right."

Tony looked at me. Was I offended? "He's right. Somehow I just can't see myself sitting out there in the dark night after night with a shotgun across my knees."

184

"Well, you won't be alone tonight." Ben put his palms flat on the table when he stood. "Shotgun's in the truck. Rifle's in the hall closet. You still got the BB gun I gave you some years back?"

"Sure," Tony said.

"Okay. We'll break you in on that. It smarts, but it wouldn't kill a man. Tony, you round 'em up."

I got up too. "I appreciate your willingness to help. But is there any point in it? How likely is it that they'll come back tonight?"

"I'd say there was a good chance, after the cat." Ben grinned. "Besides, it beats bendin over. I'm goin to get me a warm shirt and some shoes on. Lynette?"

"I know," she said. "You want sandwiches and coffee."

On his way out of the kitchen, Ben detoured to give her a fond pat on the rear. Tony left. His mother set to work, methodically building half a dozen bologna sandwiches.

"Can I help?"

"Oh, no. You just relax."

"I hate to drag Tony and Ben out on a night like this. Especially if there's no reason."

"Tony likes you. And Ben likes excitement. Whether anything will happen or not, I couldn't say." She smiled gently. "Think of it as a hunting trip. A chance for the boys to camp out."

They came back dressed for the duck blinds. Tony had a gun in each hand. He passed the smaller one to me, along with what appeared to be a milk carton full of small pellets. "You practice with that for a while, we'll let you use one of the real ones."

"I can wait for my merit badge," I told him. The BB gun felt awkward in my hands. Ben took it from me, put it to his shoulder, sighted down the barrel, then slung it down. "You know, I hope we spot our quarry tonight," he said. "Yes, sir, I do."

Chapter 34

$\mathcal{W}$e huddled around the little electric space
heater like cowboys around the campfire. We passed Ben's
flask from hand to hand and belted whiskey. We told dirty
jokes. Thanks to Bruce, I was able to contribute my share.
They especially liked the one about the guy who sticks his
cock into the vending machine that promises all the comforts
of home and gets it back with a button sewn neatly on the
end. That got a big laugh out of Ben.

Father and son seemed to be enjoying themselves immensely,
never mind that we were sitting inside in the late 1970s, that
the red coils of the heater never flickered, that the horses,
behind us, were made of wood. Tony and Ben kept their guns
close to their sides and handled them fondly from time to time.
They were perfectly willing to believe the situation was
dangerous, that the bad guys might turn up at any minute.
Insisted on it, in fact. Orville Mason grew in villainous stature
as the night wore on. He was the genius, in absentia, of boys'
night out, our excuse for giving up the civilizing influences of
women and television in favor of the vigilante's crouch.

Around midnight, the whiskey was gone and adrenaline
and talk was running low. Tony, who could put away a lot of
beer, wasn't used to hard stuff and his tongue started playing
tricks on him, twisting up words. His eyelids bobbed. So he
wouldn't feel bad, I yawned myself and suggested we take
turns keeping watch. Ben wasn't sleepy; he'd go first and
wake us for trouble or when he got tired, whichever came
first. Tony and I climbed into our sleeping bags and
stretched out on the floor. I could hear the change in his
breathing that meant he was asleep. It had been a long day, I
was exhausted, but my brain was still awake, not thinking
exactly, but chewing automatically on mental fodder the way
a cow recycles supper. I pretended to sleep.

I listened to the changing tempo of rain on the roof, andante, allegro, staccato. Trusted Ben and liked the noises he made, thinking we were asleep, a grunt, a fart, the low hum of old ballad. He dug in the paper sack for sandwiches, got up and walked around. I wanted to open my eyes and see if he carried his gun, but preserved my solitude and left him his. Somewhere along the line, I drifted off to sleep.

"Schuyler! Hey!" Ben, shaking my shoulder, was a grizzled demon in the red light from the heater. "I'm turning in now. I didn't want to wake up the boy. He's still growin."

"I understand. I take it nothing happened?"

"Not a goddamn thing. It's been quiet as a funeral parlor, except for the storm." He wrestled his way into his sleeping bag and I sat up in mine. "Help yourself to sandwiches, and for Christ's sake, wake me up if you hear tires on the road."

He fell asleep as fast as his son. Now I was the lone cowboy keeping watch. A wind had come up to whip the rain around and the ocean was loud. I wasn't sure I'd hear a fire engine if it came up the road with its siren going. Ben snored. The wind snarled. Every so often the space heater made a little pop as the flimsy metal expanded or contracted. I recalled having proposed, insistently, several aeons earlier in the day. Now, in the company of sleeping men, knee-deep in our cowboy charade, Schuyler the ardent suitor seemed like a stranger. The point of the game was to stay uncommitted, wasn't it? To avoid the noose. At all costs, to be free.

And I was rooted more firmly than ever before, to a woman, to a place, to the terrifying gamble of an unborn child. In the red light from the heater, I studied Tony and Ben, searching for similarities, some expression of common genes. Time tried to hide the likenesses. Ben was hardened and worn. The woods and the weather had worked him over, while Tony, sleeping, was, despite his prowess, still unharmed by living, skin smooth, face unlined, his hair perfectly black where Ben's was nearly gray. Would I guess, without knowing, that they were father and son? They slept exactly the same way, belly down, one leg raised up, forearm pillow supporting a face turned to the left.

Schuyler a father? It seemed impossible. Suddenly I was afraid for Marty, sure that even as I sat there, something was going wrong, the baby deciding not to live, genes mutating, under pressure of our chemical offenses, to make a freak. Renegade cells going crazy. I tried to remember what I'd learned about human reproduction in high school biology, the words and pictures in the book. There was something we did with pipe cleaners, joining and separating them: that was mitosis. Or meiosis. Or possibly both. A ball of cells that turns itself inside out. We were way past that already, up to the second page. Fetus as salamander, with a huge hunched-over head and a tiny body tapering to tail? I wanted to hold Marty. That was why I wanted to marry her. To hold her.

Nothing happened. It happened relentlessly. I began to believe that there was no Orville Mason, would have believed there had never been a Euclid, except for the small stigma in our covers to convince me. I ate a sandwich. I smoked a cigarette. It was absurd.

The wind died down for a time and then started up again, harder than before. A big splatting rain came, then passed over. I heard a shingle or two give way on the roof. The wind tugged at the wood battens on the window holes; there was give, the length of the hooks that held them, and the wind played it, sucked out, tossed back. Tony and Ben slept through the racket. The heater buzzed and dimmed as the wind ripped at the power lines, than revived. We still had juice. The ocean was angry now, hurling itself against the beach. It sounded closer and closer. I waited for the tide to turn, or the storm to let up, but both kept right on coming, something beyond weather. I thought I felt the ground move, less like the action of an earthquake than the reaction of an object hit hard. Was sure I felt it. Ben felt it, too. Broke the rhythm of his snoring, turned to his side. The pavilion shivered around us.

I crawled out of my sleeping bag, unkinked my legs and headed for the door. When I opened it, the wind caught it and tore it out of my hands, flattened it against the side of the building. When I stepped out, caught me and shoved. The beach grass and scrub pines bent over for the wind. I fought my way to the top of the dunes. Not six feet from where I stood, a wedge-shaped piece of what I'd thought was stable ground broke off and crumbled down. I didn't trust the wind. Dropped to a crouch, to make myself a smaller target, and edged up to where I could see over. There was no beach. The rocks were gone. Only water, furiously white, aroused, beating on the base of the dunes. The spray hissed up and stung my face. Every wave, breaking, sent a tremor up my legs.

Staying low, I crept back from the edge. A sharp crack, followed by a thunderous crash. One of the dead trees rooted in the beach gave way. The ocean grabbed it and threw it like a battering ram against the unfortified dunes. They shook. I shook. The wind was with me heading back. It pushed me toward the pavilion and we battled for possession of the door. Finally I managed to wrestle it shut. Inside, Ben had roused himself, was sitting up. "You been out?"

I nodded.

"Sounds like a goddamn hurricane. Sounds," he said, "like old King Neptune is fixin to outsmart Orville Mason. We safe here?"

"Your guess is as good as mine."

"Well, it's still here. I take that for a good sign."

The heater dying was a less good sign. The red faded from its coils and left us in darkness. Ben fished in his pocket for one of those disposable lighters, turned the flame up high and lit it. The change in ambient temperature disturbed Tony's sleep. He sputtered something unintelligible, tried shielding his head with his free arm, squirmed in the sleeping bag, finally grabbed on to language. "What? Huh? What's happening?" The ground trembled, the wind screamed, Ben and I were acclimated to the violence by now, but Tony wasn't. He scrambled to sit up. "Dad. Hey, Dad."

"Right here, son."

"Is the world ending, or what?"

"Hell of a storm," Ben said.

"We all right?"

"I figure so. One thing's sure. Mason ain't goin to be settin any fires tonight. He may be mean, but I never known him to be brave." He held his wrist up to the lighter's flame. "Quarter to four. Might as well go back to sleep, son."

"Maybe you'd rather go home. Your wife . . ."

"Storm's worse here. And I don't relish drivin home in the dark. There's apt to be lines down on the road." He sighed. "Sure wish we had us more whiskey, though."

I remembered a jug of wine out back and went to get it. "It's cheap, but it does the trick. You want glasses?"

Ben had the trick of raising a jug to his shoulder and drinking sideways, head cocked back. He took a long swallow, stopped for air and drank again. Passed me the jug and wiped his chin on his sleeve. "Rotgut," he said, "but full of warmth."

I raised the jug with both hands and filled my mouth. Not easy. The bottle's mouth was wide and the wine flowed fast. A trickle reached my shirt collar. I passed the jug back to Ben.

"Give it to the boy," he said. "Sleepin tonic."

Tony slurped. Back to Ben. To me. Between us, we killed more than half a gallon fast. Sometime, I thought, I'd like to pass a joint with them. Not now. The wine heated interior spaces. My kneecaps glowed with warmth. Tony inched back down in his bag. The wine blunted the storm some, mellowed its sounds. I could feel the blood move warmly in my arteries and veins, hear its steady buzz through my ears.

"I'm turnin in now," Ben said. We both bedded down on the wine-softened floor. Lying flat, it was hard to tell the crash of the real waves from the ones in my blood.

Laughter, not in my dreams, and the small throb of a right-temple headache. When I opened my eyes it was light and the roar of the storm was gone but the laughing didn't stop. I felt stiff and hollow from hard sleep on a hard bed, sat up to find the polyester apparition of Orville Mason duded up in the door frame. Seeing I was alive, he let himself in.

"Morning, Rykken. You boys goin hunting, or you been?"

When I tried to stand up, the sleeping bag caught at my ankles and I nearly tripped. The place was trashed. Tony and Ben were still heavily asleep in a stew of guns, ground-out butts, and half-eaten sandwiches. The empty wine jug lay on its side like a casualty. I felt like one. "What are you doing here, Mason?"

"I been out inspecting the damage. Looks like the storm blowed through here."

I didn't figure I owed him an explanation.

"There's lines down all over this end of the county. I got crews out all over trying to set things right."

"You come out here to fix my power?"

Mason shook his head. "Sorry to say, you're the last on the list. Could take weeks. Running lines out here at all is a luxury."

The sound of our voices got through to Ben. He growled and half-sat, hair wild and spiky, his morning voice thick with phlegm. "Son of a bitch."

"Actually, I come out here to see how things stood up to the storm. You lost some bank out there, boy."

Ben's slow scramble to a stand resembled a bear emerging from hibernation. The whites of his eyes were pink around the red spot. He leaned over and picked up his shotgun. "What's he want?" He indicated Mason with a thrust of the gun butt.

"Beats me," I said. "I didn't invite him for breakfast."

Mason looked at his Buck Rogers watch with all its fancy gauges and dials. "Already ate, Rykken. It's getting on for nine-thirty."

Tony woke green and suddenly. He fought himself out of his bag and bolted for the door. He didn't get far beyond it before we heard him puke.

"Shouldn't let children drink. The Bible says . . ."

"I don't care what the Bible says, Mason. You can shove your quotes. You want me to run him out of here, Sky?"

Mason had the advantage of clean clothes, a toothbrush

and a good night's sleep, but I wanted to hang on to what dignity I had. "I imagine he'll leave when he's said what he has to say," I told Ben.

"This place was mine," Mason said, "I'd start riprapping tomorrow. If not today."

Ben snorted. "Riprap ain't goin to hold this place together if the ocean wants to pull it apart."

"As a temporary measure. An engineering firm I got working for me says that Seasound can not only be saved, it can be restored."

"Some folks'll say anythin for money." Ben spat somewhere in the vicinity of Mason's gleaming cowboy boots.

"New York firm," Mason said. "Well known for shoreland reclamation in Massachusetts and Virginia."

"Easterners. What you expect?"

"Rykken here's an easterner," Mason pointed out. "Not here a year."

Tony slunk back in, looking small. Mason clucked concern at his condition. "Coach finds out what you been up to, he's gonna be playing his second-string quarterback."

Tony wasn't too sick to bear malice. He gave Mason what might best be described as a green glare.

"He's trespassin, Schuyler." Ben jerked the shotgun upward.

"Yeah. Right. You got anything more to say, Mason?"

Orville Mason fixed his greedy eyes on mine. "One hundred and twenty-five thousand dollars and one percent of Seasound Enterprises, Inc. What do you say, Rykken?"

Brilliant of him and disastrous for me, to quote figures in front of Tony and Ben. I could almost hear the numbers traveling synapses in their brains. Such a big sum, Mason figured and I feared, was sure to alienate them.

"You going to buy me a new cat, too?" Tony and Ben breathed, moved again. Mason was answered. I was stupid but incorruptible.

Mason's face was a study in false innocence. "What about a cat?"

"What about it, Mason? I can't think of nothin lower than killin a defenseless animal."

Mason gestured at Ben, looked at me. "What's he talking about?"

"Come on. Your flunky must have reported back to you by now. Tell him next time he comes around, I'll be ready for him."

Mason didn't bother to protest his innocence further. He called me a fool instead. "And it hurts me, Ben, you taking sides with a stranger. Just when I was about to open those four sections south of town up to be cut."

I didn't know exactly what he was saying, but I recognized the tune; Mason was playing the lucre organ again and now it was I who waited to see if Ben would dance.

"I never worked for you before, Orville, and I never will," he growled.

"I never gave you the chance before," Mason pointed out. Oh, he played well, pushing his dollars between us like a wedge.

"He's tryin to bribe you, Dad," Tony said.

"I know what he's doin, boy."

"We've had our differences," Mason went on, in his most congenial tone, "but I know you're a good man, Ben, and a hard worker. I could do worse than have you cut that stand."

"Could and will," Ben said. "Always have."

"What's Rykken to you?"

I wondered, too, how Ben would answer. Since I met him the night before, what I'd done was cost him a night in bed. Also, I was new, flaky, strange and eastern. Unproven. Unlikely to yield a profit. No timber and no track record.

"He's a man, Orville," Ben said. I didn't know if in philosophical discussion our definitions of the term would match, but under the circumstances, I considered it a compliment. "At least he don't shoot animals for spite."

"Too many cats in the world anyway," Mason said, turning cold. "And too many fools."

Ben elbowed me. "He means too many people who don't bend over for Orville Mason."

One of three things was going to happen: Mason was going to leave under his own steam; I was going to throw him out; or we were going to come to blows. For an instant, an instant only, I understood the fragility of life, how easily the stem is broken, the petals crushed. Mason wasn't a flower I cherished but still was, being human, a great deal more than the sum of his organic parts. We could have killed him then and there. The money, the influence, the smarmy Bible-quoting smugness would defect instantly once the vulnerable pink flesh was penetrated, once the enlarged heart stopped being an engine and became a piece of meat. So easy. And yet his antagonism was the center of my life; I needed it, as much as ever I'd needed standardized tests or an academic hierarchy to push against; as much as I needed love or nutriment, I needed this fat man's opposition to make me whole. For a moment, I was God and let the devil live. No dominion possible without boundaries. We were destined to oppose.

It takes too many words to write what was a second's thought. No more than three heartbeats passed before I said, "We've said all there is to say. You going to walk out of here, Mason, or are we going to carry you?" I took a step toward him and Ben, beside me, advanced too, still clutching his shotgun.

Mason backed away from us even as he searched for the zinger that would save his florid face. Which was, "There's more than one way to skin a cat, Rykken, as you're about to learn." Said ominously so that I wouldn't miss the threat.

With that, he waddled out to his Chevy Blazer, climbed in and drove away. Ben fired a shell into his tire tracks, and we watched the mud jump and scatter at the impact of the shot.

Chapter 35

*9*t took us four days and cost three hundred dollars (including honeymoon) to get married. There were blood tests to prevent the union of syphilitics, a state toll at the gateway to connubial bliss, a consideration for the judge, the price of flowers and half a case of New York State champagne. Our rings were made by a metal sculptor from Lake Oswego whom Marty knew, out of stainless-steel scraps from his latest equestrian Chevrolet. They would, he promised, never tarnish and last as well as the gold and silver that were beyond reach of our budget. We invited him to the wedding to ensure delivery of the rings.

Barbara was an enthusiastic accessory to our crime of passion, helping Marty negotiate the endless trivialities involved in getting married, while I mopped french fries off the cafeteria floor and dug mountains of soggy crap out of the school gutters. In the evenings, they tended to giggle a lot, which left me, not privy to the causes of hilarity, feeling a little estranged from both of them.

The business of getting married was as consuming as taxes the week before April 15, as a term paper the night before it's due. It swallowed up all our energy and left none for anxiety. As an act, it wasn't going to do a damn thing toward solving our problems, but it did prevent us from thinking about them for a while. The implications got lost in the details. It was something to do besides wait.

Once, Barbara and I were alone long enough for her to say, "I wish Verna could be here, Sky. She would have loved to see you married."

"You talked about it with her?"

"We did discuss what kind of husband you'd make."

"And what did you decide?"

"Your mother wasn't unaware of your peculiarities. But in general, we agreed that you're pretty good, for a man."

"If that isn't sexist, I don't know what it is."

"Women know what they know. And one of the things that we know is that in many ways, we're innately superior to men."

"Such as?"

"As a rule, we're wiser, kinder, more patient and more sensuous than men."

"You're beginning to sound like a female chauvinist pig."

How many times over the years had I looked at Barbara's eyes, honest under the frivolously blue or green or brown shaded lids? They had a new look now, both frank and shy. "I had an affair with a woman, Sky. After we broke up."

The admission winded me. The world seemed to change subtly in a few seconds before I spoke, and would not change back. "How was it?"

"It was nice." She sounded a little defiant. "Nice but difficult." Laughed. "I'm a little too straight and a little too lazy to put up with all the political hassle of changing my sexual orientation now. I probably won't do it again."

"Nicer than me?" I had to ask.

"Different from you. No competition. No anger. It always felt like we were on the same side."

"We weren't always angry. I wasn't. Were you?"

Barbara reached out and took my hand, pressed it warmly between hers. "No. It was very good sometimes." She leaned forward and kissed me on the cheek. "I'll always love you, Sky."

"Like a brother."

She gave me back my hand. "That's right. Big brother Sky, better than your average man."

"I'll buy that," I said, and did, memories, altered in retrospect, sealed off for good. I was a little aroused, a little hurt, a little horrified. Marty came back from using the thunder mug, my child, ours, manifest in her body. I watched as though she were a stranger. Had she ever loved another woman?

"I was just telling Sky," Barbara said, "how much his mother would have liked you, Marty."

"I'm sorry I never knew her," Marty said.

Because there was no electricity and no amenities at Seasound, Mom graciously offered to let us be married and celebrate the marriage in her home. Hers was an old frame house, distinguished by dormers, on an old Kilchis street, every room inside stuffed with the memorabilia of forty years' habitation; salt and pepper shakers with the profiles of presidents, dried flowers and souvenir spoons, novelty whiskey bottles and dolls in the costume of foreign lands abounded. There were not one but three clocks on the mantel before which we took our vows, none showing the right time.

The judge wore a gray suit and Mom the blue lace dress she'd married off her children in. Marty was pale in a flowing yellow dress that hid the contours of her body, pale as the white flowers wreathed in her hair. I knew she'd been nauseous and thrown up shortly before the wedding started. I wasn't sick, but wholly numb, like a man who's had his nerves removed. My hand was cold and heavy while Marty's trembled in it.

We omitted to vow obedience and the ceremony was short, with nothing to say on the subjects of divinity or fertility. We pledged our loyalty, Marty squeakily, and Barbara, a kind of unisex best person, produced our stainless-steel rings. Then it was over; the judge, of whom I remember only a scrimshaw tie bar with a minutely detailed whaling scene carved on it, instructed us to kiss. Marty almost collapsed against me in an iron hug, Mom dropped the hi-fi needle into the worn grooves of Mendelssohn, and the deed was done. I had a wife and child.

The upstate champagne produced a kind of false gaiety in a party too small to achieve real letting go. Only the ring maker from Lake Oswego was truly euphoric, owing jointly to the large quantity of dope he'd smoked in preparation for the solemnities and his relative ignorance of the real difficulty of our situation. Everyone else's blessings were mixed; both Ben and Mom came from generations to whom stability, financial, emotional and geographical, were preconditions for matrimony and our precipitate union seemed to them to be sheer folly. Which, of course, it was.

Right after the ceremony, I asked Marty how she felt. "Tired," she said. "But better. Halfway through, the terror passed. I think it's going to be okay."

"That's romantic."

"I'm not exactly a kid anymore."

Kid was a good word for how she looked, though, a tired kid dressed up to play wedding. Our hug had knocked the flower crown askew, so it dipped over her forehead toward her right eye, and the generosity of the dress that hid her condition also made her arms and neck look childishly small and thin. In her eyes, I saw a bewilderment to match my own. It was on the firm set of her chin, the clean determined line of her jawbone that I placed my hopes for a long and happy life.

Mom pushed back furniture to make a small dance floor in the middle of her cluttered living room, put a Bing Crosby seventy-eight on the turntable and exhorted us to dance.

"I like the three clocks," Marty whispered as we waltzed. "They belong in a painting."

"You're exploiting our life again." I meant it to be light, but the concern was deep enough to put an edge on my voice.

"*My* life," Marty said. "Do I have to spend it brokering what image is whose?"

The sculptor, tall, stooped, awash in champagne, picked just that moment to cut in, so the issue was left unresolved. All of the feelings I wasn't feeling—happiness, uncertainty, awe, tenderness and terror—coalesced into a single intense ray of righteous and profoundly irritated indignation that burned into my brain. The metaphor of union was only metaphor; the incantations of the judge on our behalf had no magic power to heal our rifts. I was still Schuyler, Marty was still Marty, and each of us was still alone and unalloyable. She was a thin-armed stranger there across the room, and when she found me watching her and smiled, her smile was wise to the impossibility of merger, and slightly sad.

I danced with Barbara, I danced with Mom, I danced with Jean and Tony's mother, Lynette, a progression of women through my arms in all ages of life, from Jean's incipience to Mom's decline, that seemed to predict the inevitable progress, or regress, of my own life. Around seven, under a rain of uncooked rice, we fled, tucking Barbara in the back and ourselves in the front seat of our shoe-tailed car. For most of the drive, no one said anything, just listened to the windshield wipers grate across the window and watched the dark. Fifty miles out of Portland I picked up a country and western station that flooded the car with heartbreak ballads too melodically mellow and corny to really hurt us. In the back seat, Barbara whistled high-pitched harmonies. Finally, somewhere along the road, Marty reached out of the darkness and put her hand on my thigh.

The business of writing betrays me again. I've gnawed the blue top of my Bic pen till it's flattened into two surfaces compressed together, rough with tooth marks, and I still can't get it right. I'm spitting out sharp little pieces of blue plastic. I've cracked the clear shaft with my teeth and only half the ink is gone. What I've written down is accurate enough. It really happened—the presidential salt and peppers, Marty's yellow dress, nobody talking in the car—all true. My hands were cold, I did dance with all those women and have a sense that time was passing through my arms. What I've written down is true, but doesn't *feel* true, doesn't begin to get at how it really was.

I was involved at the time, you see; what happened, happened to me, so my intake was more impressionistic than encyclopedic. Who knows why I remember what I do? If I start again, if I really focus on it, maybe get a little stoned and try harder, I could give you the faded floral pattern of Mom's carpet, I could give you Lynette's dress (pink, I think, and rough to the touch), or the worry around Ben's eyes when he shook my hand, or the taste of the frosting on the wedding cake (too sweet) and even the lemon filling between the layers. The sculptor had a big head, with a bald spot in the back, and almost no butt, his pants hung down from his belt unfilled in the back, and he had a funny way of talking, almost a speech impediment, though I couldn't figure out what caused it. Or how about the blood test? The guy undoes the tourniquet and still the blood comes, almost purple in the tube. The sound of plastic corks popping, or how truly strange Marty looked in Portland International Airport, in her long yellow dress with her old shapeless gray painting sweater pulled over it for warmth, like a backwoods muse, or how together Barbara was with her high-heel boots and matching luggage, how she fit right in with all the slick traveling folks and actually seemed to leave us as soon as we got there, before she physically got on the plane and left, and how that made me realize I'd married more than a woman, I'd married Kilchis County and the state of Oregon and a merry-go-round and being poor and the sound of the ocean in my ears at night and the rain and even possibly my push broom, though that, of everything, was easiest to divorce. How much I felt I was losing when she walked down the ramp and got on that plane, not because I'd miss Barbara personally so much, but because of how many doors were closing when I turned back to Marty in her Halloween getup with her slightly asymmetrical face and took her cold little hand in mine and said, "Well, it's you and me, kid," and could only guess what she figured *she* was losing or gaining by the whole thing.

I could tell you how the pavilion was locked up with the biggest padlock I could find and Marty's paintings and art supplies were safely stashed away in the basement of Ben and Lynette's ranch house, down where they had a little bar and a dartboard and a stuffed elk head up on the wall, and how I half-hoped Orville Mason *would* burn us out while we were away on our honeymoon so that we could start over fresh with a whole new set of rules. Or how the net effect of getting married was making me want to cry, and how I did, later, even though I'm not very good at it, in Marty's arms in a Portland motel room with the Magic Fingers going in the bed and how every tear I managed to squeeze out past twenty years of defenses stood for fifty more. How we finished our quarrel finally by agreeing to disagree and fell asleep, absolutely exhausted, holding each other tight.

Would any of that be truer than what I've already written down?

Would you care?

Would I want my child to read it?

Does it matter?

I could tell you that we all end up like Verna anyway, spilling out of a cardboard box at the bottom of some lonely ravine, only that's a cop-out, too—true, but not relevant.

Marty and I got married in Kilchis and went to Portland for our honeymoon. We had a nice time.

Chapter 36

*T*here was this locomotive running a cruel circle up my nose, around my right eye and back again. There was so much mucus in my head I could feel it squeezing my brain. My IQ dropped a full thirty points.

"I'm going to die," I whined to Marty, my wife of a week. "I want to die." My voice was thick with snot and misery and didn't sound like my voice. I lay in bed with the blankets bunched under my chin, a pillow jammed against the throbbing right side of my face. Marty, fattened by sweaters, sketching by lantern light, was no more than a complacent bedside blur. Without my glasses on, I saw a pale white circle where her face should have been.

"Think about something else, Sky," she advised me.

"That's easy for you to say. You can breathe."

"So can you. You'd be dead if you weren't breathing," she pointed out.

I waited for some expression of sympathy, but none came. I could hear the soft scratch of charcoal against her drawing pad. I could hear, too, the goddamn rain, not just on the roof, but against the wall behind me. That meant the wind was coming from the north. Pretty soon I could feel the north wind blowing through my sinuses. "It's freezing in here," I said.

I was simply stating the painfully obvious, and Marty didn't bother to respond. Mason was taking his own sweet time restoring our power; our married life commenced without heat and without light. Meanwhile, I had the worst cold of my life. "I can't think," I said finally, angling for solace. "My head hurts too much."

"Can you sleep?" she asked, voice gentler.

"No."

I saw a passing streak of white paper and red sweater as she put her sketchbook down. "I'm sorry you feel shitty, Sky, but I don't know what I can do about it."

"My mother used to read to me."

"Would you like me to read to you, Sky?" Marty asked.

I thought about it. "No."

"I could make you some tea."

"Uh uh. My mother used to give me tea when I had stomach flu. I equate it with nausea."

I heard her small sigh, and interpreted it as pity for my sad condition. What she was doing that began to help was giving me her full attention. I wanted to keep it. "I think I've got a fever," I said.

Marty got up and put a cold hand on my forehead, then on her own. At closer range, she acquired something like features; smudges of shadow and color appeared on the white circle. "If anything, you're subnormal," she reported.

"Thanks a lot."

"I remember someone saying all men are babies when they're sick."

"Pain hurts," I countered. "And I'm in pain. Besides, when else do we get the chance?"

"Maybe if you were more in touch with your needs all the time, a head cold wouldn't seem like such a big deal."

"I don't feel up to feminist cant," I told her.

Marty sat on the edge of the bed. I wanted her to stroke my hair back off my forehead, the way my mother used to. She didn't do it. "You know what?" she said.

"What?"

"I think you're really into being sick. I almost think you're enjoying it."

"So now you're a shrink. Sigmund Vanderhill. Thanks a lot."

She dodged the barbs and spoke thoughtfully. "I think people get sick because they need to. It's a kind of response to their lives."

"Terrific. And I respond to getting married with a hand grenade in the nasal passages."

"It's crossed my mind," she said.

"Bullshit. I feel miserable because some damn virus has set up shop in my head. You make it sound like it's my fault I got sick, for Christ's sake. I don't want to be sick." If I couldn't have the sympathy I wanted, the tender care, then I was willing to divert myself by fighting.

Marty wouldn't indulge me in that, either. She stuck with theory. "I wonder. Maybe you don't want to be married, either."

"I want to be married." I tried to sniff, but the stuff in my sinuses was like cement and wouldn't move. "I don't know what married is," I said.

"It's what we are. Whatever we are."

"Better or worse." I got pathos and drama running in tandem. "And this is worse."

Marty felt for the shape of my thigh under the covers and patted it. "Why don't you blow a joint, Sky? If you really don't want to be sick, then you'll feel better stoned."

"This crap in my head is no illusion," I said, but took her advice and lit the joint she brought me from our stash, coughing at first as the smoke scraped my raw throat, then feeling better, better. There was that brief and now familiar moment when I could feel my heart beat, fast as a bird heart, resonant as jungle drums. The self splitting, being comfortable split. Schuylers One and Two greeted each other like long-lost brothers. Been wanting to talk to you, buddy.

"You're under a lot of pressure lately," Marty said.

Schuyler One agreed. Schuyler Two snorted. You call this pressure? "What do you mean?" I asked out loud.

Marty drew her legs up on the bed, retrieved her pillow and pounded it into a backrest. I stoned, she blurred, Marty was an impressionist masterwork, uneven features bleeding into shadow. "Lots of things," she said. "You weren't exactly born to be a janitor."

Listen to the lady, quoth Schuyler Two. The lady makes sense. Schuyler One raised his shoulders in a cosmic shrug. "I wasn't meant to be a cabdriver or an academic, either. If destiny's been talking to you on the side, I wish you'd fill me in. What was I meant to be?"

The brown smudges lightened to beige as she closed her eyes to think. "I don't know, Sky. Something difficult. Something important. I can feel it."

Schuyler Two grabbed the floor. "You have to think that, since you married me. He's not really a janitor, Ma. He's a princeling in disguise. A displaced astronaut."

She didn't say anything. S2 went on, his voice a little whip. "And you're—what? A princess? No, no, I beg your pardon. A great artist. Picasso's reputation isn't safe with you around."

"You don't have to be snotty." Her voice was small and cool. "I don't make any claims for myself, you know. I just paint."

"I'm sorry," said Schuyler One. "It must be my cold talking." Paint us both into a corner, said Schuyler Two. Babies and palette knives. No favors, please.

"This thing with Mason," Marty said.

A vision of Orville, greed and piety, mixed with the sludge in my brain pan. Perplexity and thunderation. I didn't understand the man. I couldn't second-guess him. It was hard enough to second-guess myself. Schuyler One, pure-hearted, simpleminded Boy Scout, was spoiling for the fight. Schuyler the Cynic, the Cautious, the scorekeeper and odds maker, Schuyler-who-liked-to-sound-sophisticated-and-wouldn't-play-because-he-didn't-like-to-lose, counseled evasion. A neat side step, perhaps an abdication.

Marty's single set of eyes saw things more clearly. "If he doesn't turn the lights back on," she pointed out, "we're out of business. He can keep the merry-go-round shut down forever if he wants."

She touched the sore spot on my self-reliance, and I cried out. Ever since the storm had downed the power lines and left the merry-go-round deprived of function, no better adapted than a dinosaur to survive the political exigencies of Kilchis County, I'd brooded on dependence. I didn't like it much. "It hurts me every time I see it," I said. "Whoever electrified it ruined it," I said. "Do you realize that that thing used to run on steam? The technology that built that merry-go-round was the most beautiful goddamn thing that ever was," I said. "Mills, factories, ships and trains. We knew how to build them before that bastard Edison brewed up his magic juice and made us junkies. That's what we are, too—junkies," I said. "Half the people in this country can't pick their noses without electricity. They've got us by the balls. What kills me is, we call it progress," I said. I think I said. Definitely thought. It was a long speech. Was Marty really silent that long?

What I remember her saying next is, "It's like seeing Greek statues without their paint, or fountains without water. It's made me understand that motion can be part of art." It was a thoroughly Martyish thing to say. Our best communication was a kind of free translation between metaphors. At least I felt she shared my sense of loss.

I turned toward her and found her hands by grope. "I love you," I said. I did. I felt much better. Dope and love. The engorgement in my sinuses migrated south. For the first time in hours, I got out of bed, long enough to douse the lantern. Under the covers, in the darkness, I struggled out of my clothes and found my wife by feel, a long, cool nude beside me. I stroked her warm.

"I want you, Sky," she said, and I moved to give, not in the rowdy, randy, sweaty prepregnant way but gently, cautiously. I slipped in sideways. Marty squeezed.

"Not that way, Sky. Get up on top."

I put my hand on her belly. "I don't want to hurt you."

"It's okay, Sky. Now move. I want to feel you move."

Commanded, I wanted to obey, but it was hard to dismiss my scruples. What if I broke her water? I didn't want to hurt the kid. What if the baby could feel us making love? Marty grabbed my backside and urged me deeper, teased and tantalized until my brain shut up and all my parts and voices fused into one organ, playing her darkness. It was long, symphonic love we made, varying and reshaping the age-old themes, stopping each movement just short of crescendo. The finale was shattering. Afterward, we drifted in the dark, still coupled and breathing in time, hoarding the heat we'd made inside the covers. I had no syntax. My mind did not hypothesize. We'd reached a place beyond ambition where love itself became irrelevant. I wanted to stay there forever.

Then it was on us, music and lights so fast and bright they hurt, not just our eyes and ears but every nerve ending in our postecstatic bodies. Light flooded the ceiling and the blare of trumpets martialed the shadows and made them march. An army with its militant logic organized our hard-won chaos, and we held tight to the covers and to each other, trying to protect our nakedness from the invaders.

Marty caught on first. "It's the merry-go-round, Sky. It's running."

We got out of bed dressed in blankets and went to see it run. The horses chased each other in an unchanging cycle of up and down, eyes flashing as they caught the light, coats garish, tails aloft in the speed-made wind. Drumsticks

206

struck drumheads, drowning out the rain. A hidden piccolo trilled. Inside their frames of light, Marty's paintings were solemn as icons.

We watched for a long time, not party to its magic and divorced from its intention. Marty huddled close and laid her head against my shoulder. Feet bare on the dirt floor, various of my extremities exposed to the night chill, I shivered with as clear a premonition of my own mortality as ever shook me. Logically, being human, we were the greater miracle, but something about the merry-go-round, its energy or its autonomy, maybe, made me feel old and flabby, already on the downhill ride. It took me quite a while to figure out that I could simply step inside the core and throw a switch to stop the spectacle. When I did, the silence that followed was a deafening absence, and the darkness seemed to vibrate with remembered light.

We went back to bed. Lit shapes rained down the backs of my eyelids, and Marty pushed tight against me, fitting her curves and bumps to mine. Our power was restored. Whatever married is, we were.

Chapter 37

*B*ruce was picking his teeth with the corner of a matchbook flap when I came into the teachers' lounge. It was otherwise vacant; we, the dregs of the academic flagon, were allowed to use it only when the faculty (and I use the term loosely) wasn't. He was bent over the weekly county newspaper, the only thing, apart from porn mag captions, I ever saw him read.

"Got your name in the paper, Rykken," Bruce said. As a member of the Gull's Rest Tavern Bowling Team, Bruce got his name in the paper nearly every week—his last name, anyway, next to the sum total of wooden pins he'd succeeded in upending with his bowling ball. Never mind that the type was microscopically small—Bruce found his name, pondered it as if it were the Dead Sea Scrolls, and pointed it out to me proudly every time it got in. Such notoriety was never mine. Seeing his name objectified in print while I remained uncelebrated was, I figured, one way Bruce assured himself of the natural superiority that made him by rights my boss. I could tell now from his voice that my entry into the big time unsettled him. Not up for a fight, I tried to be casual. My sinuses still throbbed and every breath ran fingernails against the tender blackboard of my trachea.

"That so?" I said. I filled a Styrofoam cup with grease-topped coffee from the teachers' urn and sat across from Bruce to drink it. My reaction, clearly, was not sufficient.

"I always said he was a real smart operator," Bruce opined, with the kind of headshake that gives the devil his due.

The steam from the coffee was starting to loosen the blockade in my nose. I sniffed deeply, concentrating on the welcome rearrangement of obstructions. For about three seconds, air moved freely through a tiny corridor in my right nostril, while I contemplated a definition of perfection that included absence of mucus among its postulates.

"He sure is smart all right," Bruce reiterated, several decibels above his usual conversational bellow.

"Who's that?" I complied by asking.

Studiously, he removed a pulpy shard of last night's dinner from the matchbook corner and examined it closely before he spoke. "My wife Alma's cousin's brother-in-law," Bruce said.

Something told me he was talking about Orville Mason—who else dived so deep in the brackish waters of the Kilchis gene pool?—but I was reluctant to give Bruce the satisfaction of my curiosity. "Yeah?"

"He's got you by the balls now, Rykken," my boss told me, with at least as much satisfaction as when he dislodged the last big one from between his molars.

I reached for the paper, said, "Let me see," but Bruce snatched it away.

"He's gonna get the county planning commission to condemn your land, Rykken. He's giving them the money to buy you out. Gonna give it to the county for a park," Bruce said. He laughed.

I made a grab for the front page. Bruce held tight and the paper gave between us, performing a crude bisection of Orville's grin. Normally, a torn paper would have been justification for manslaughter in Bruce's ethic, but he was so sure my cat was skinned for good, he was willing to be big about the *Kilchis Signal*. "What's the matter, Rykken, huh? Is somethin eatin you?"

"Let me see that paper."

"Sure. Sure." He shoved the shreds at me and I pieced them together. Reading, I found the string on Orville's gift. He'd give my land to the county, so long as they let him use it to underpin his condos right next door. "Shit," I said.

Bruce consulted his Timex. "Recess is over, Rykken. It's time you was gettin back to work."

"You were here when I got here. You go first."

Bruce stayed encamped on his folding chair. "The toilets're callin you, Rykken."

I stayed put.

"Move it, creep, or I'll bash your ass."

"Jesus, you're eloquent, Bruce. You dazzle me with your semantic acrobatics."

That got him to his feet. He was getting ready to pound me fine as the saccharin some of the fatter teachers kept on hand to put in their coffee, to relieve the guilt of gulping butterhorns along with it, when the door opened and Miss Sackbutt, the kindergarten teacher, rolled in.

Miss Sackbutt represented a true distortion of the human form; pathologically short, she had, over the aeons, let her girth expand until it almost compensated for her lack of stature. As a result, she closely resembled a medicine ball in orthopedic shoes. Noah must have let her on the ark, out of pity or curiosity, since she'd been teaching in north Kilchis County since well before the flood, though she'd never reproduced herself, but devoted her days to socializing the progeny of others. I'd seen her in action around the school yard; the kids cowered before her face and mocked her from behind. Sometimes she wore a rhinestone flag pin, red, white and blue, on the lapel of her dusty, dark dresses.

"Time for you boys to go now," she said, and her command took the starch out of Bruce's hackles and laid them flat. Hard as it was to imagine Bruce five, or Sackbutt forty years younger, he'd told me himself more than once she'd been his first teacher. He still feared and hated her.

"We was just goin'," he muttered. He edged to the door, a bully shrunk, but Sackbutt called him back.

"Bruce, throw away your cup. It's a privilege for you boys to use this lounge, you know." She spoke in my direction as I, forewarned, disposed of my Styrofoam in the approved Sackbutt manner. "Good citizenship is a lifelong job," she told us. "And what happened to this newspaper?"

I decided to tattle. "Bruce wouldn't share," I said. On the strength of that, I was allowed to slip away, while my boss was detained, presumably to get her lecture on the sanctity of the printed word. Or maybe she wanted to correct his grammar. It was a petty victory, and one I'd pay for later, probably, when Bruce got me alone in the basement, but I enjoyed it while I could. He more than had it coming.

Driving home, I got a better grasp of Mason's scheme. The local radio station, which broadcast obituaries twice a week and played favorite polka tunes to celebrate the birthdays of local bigwigs, was having a field day with Orville's offer. It was the biggest story to break in Kilchis since a three-car collision on New Year's Eve made work for every tow truck in town, and they weren't exactly playing it as hard news. What the announcer had to say was so unabashedly pro-Orville, I concluded Mason must be related to the station owner or hold his mortgage or both.

Jobs, that was the key to it, all the jobs construction of

Seasound Village would bring to Kilchis. Increased custom for the local business folk. A broadened tax base, and a better sort of citizen hunkered down in condo heaven. Rejuvenation of the tourist trade. A goddamn renaissance, that's what he promised. All this and a park besides. His pose of beneficence clothed the scheme in righteousness, obscured the profit motive, dulled the sting of losing what had been, de facto, public lands to private exploitation. The local media were hailing Mason as a fiscal messiah, and woe betide the selfish commie malcontent who dared oppose him. By the time I got to Seasound, my stomach hurt as much as my head.

Marty wasn't in the pavilion, though her car was parked outside. For the first time since I left work, I noticed it was still light and not raining. In fact, something like sunshine showed silver under a stretch of moody steel-gray clouds, its source still an hour at least above the horizon. Misery went looking for company. I scrambled down to the beach to find my wife. The tide had turned for in, but only just. The beach was still wide, its day's graph of wave patterns mostly intact, though the water was at work erasing them. I looked south, then north, without seeing Marty, then chose a direction by instinct. In the far north distance coastal mountains rose, their black shapes dappled white with a dusting of high elevation snow. The ocean thundered on my left, its impersonal anger drawing off my own. A sea-bottom smell, the salty/sweet stink of marine decay seeped past the plugs in my nostrils and made itself known to my brain.

My foot slid under me. Something below the sand crust was slick as ice and soft as pudding. For a few steps, I tried skating on it, but the squishiness made me queasy and I stopped. Kicking away sand, I found a dense deposit of what appeared to be organic material, both dark and clear. The stench was stronger when I knelt, and I could see that what looked like blueberry Jell-O from a greater distance was hundreds of separate blobs of blueberry protoplasm up close. Nearer the water, they lay on top of the sand, and I went to inspect them. They covered the beach like millions of blue-black dots, they clung to stones and bits of broken shell—uncountable thousands of thumbnail-size creatures all alike, one rounded blue-black foot, supporting upright one small translucent sail, ribbed with series of concentric arcs. They were everywhere. Mathematically speaking, googolplex was inadequate to estimate their number. They stank. I wondered how the inhabitants of Seasound Village, if it got built, would like the smell.

Not wanting the death of helpless multitudes charged to my account, I walked closer to the water's edge where the beach seemed clear of them and the sand crunched audibly the way it was supposed to. Every so often, the deep inreach of an ambitious wave would drive me up the beach, into the slippery, stinking mass of bodies. In the crests and valleys of the dunes, the green of the beach grass, combed by wind, was sharply yellow pale.

Where was Marty? I was almost opposite the tallest of Seasound's dunes, a small hill, really, held firm by the salal that rooted in it, and I crossed the jelly flats to climb it. Big slabs of Seasound City's cobbled sidewalks protruded from the sandy base, and the wind had excavated a broken piece of somebody's wooden stairs, slivers of white paint still sticking, here and there, to the weathered boards. Rusted pipes bloomed from the sand like twisted flowers. Rooted deep, connected to God knows what, they were unpickable. From the top of the hill, you could see the whole peninsula and eastward, across the bay. If Marty was anywhere at Seasound, I'd be able to see her from there.

The last stretch of the climb was steep. I leaned into the hill and grabbed at bushes to pull myself up. When I emerged on top and stood erect, Marty greeted me. She was nested in salal, half-reclined against the silvery thick trunk of a dead tree. Her sketchbook was propped open against her knees. "It's spring," she said.

"I just noticed."

"The velella are back. Last night's storm must have brought them in."

"The what?"

"Velella. Those things all over the beach. They come in this time every year."

How easily she named them made me feel like the newcomer I was. "I thought God had sent a plague," I said.

She laughed. "They get bigger, now till May. Then those that haven't died sail off." She showed me her sketch, just one of them, bigger than life, perfectly rendered, floating on a shine of quiet water, with a low sun reflected in its sail. She'd made it beautiful.

"Too bad," I said. "I was sort of hoping the stench would drive the developers away."

"The developers might drive the velella away. They'll probably figure out a way to vacuum the beach." Marty looked contented, comfortable in her nest of brush. She squinted slightly into the western light. "I felt the baby kick today," she told me. "For the first time, I was absolutely sure." Her smile was more than a smile—it was a state of grace, a gift. "I think it's sleeping now, but you'll be able to feel it later on." She held out her arms to me. I knelt on the ground beside her and kissed her smile. "It's going to be a good spring, Sky," she said.

Only after all the subtle technicolor gradations of sunset had faded and the sky was graying into monochrome did I tell her the bad news. Her eyes, big and deep, were more distinctly visible than the rest of her in the fading light. "We've got to find some help, Sky," she said, as we clambered down from our hilltop, then nothing more. I felt one drop splat on my forehead, then several more, and more. We had to race the rain clouds back to the pavilion.

Later that night, I felt the baby move.

Chapter 38

*J*ean's Aunt Madeline was the last of the experts we consulted. She was tall and solid as a tree trunk and had in common with most of Kilchis's older women hips wider than her shoulders were. She'd been a beauty in her day, Jean told us, a redhead, though by now her hair was faded to the color of russian dressing and frizzed into little pinkish curls that looked like a doll's wig around her powder-pale face. Red circles of rouge on her cheeks and a red kewpie mouth heightened the resemblance to an aging plaything.

In her youth, she'd been engaged to a commercial fisherman. When his boat went belly up on a rough bar crossing, Madeline experienced her first vision. She was sitting at the family dinner table, in process of filling her plate, when suddenly she emitted a crystal-cracking scream and passed out in the mashed potatoes. Her lover drowned. Since then, no one doubted that she had "the power"; by the time we met her, Aunt Maddy was acknowledged to be Kilchis's resident mystic, its most gifted palmist and leading tea-leaf reader. So sure was she of her psychic acumen, she offered her customers a money-back guarantee.

Actually, it was Tony who suggested we consult her. We'd struck out with all the other, more conventional experts on our list. The marine geologist said yeah, if Mason was willing to spend the money and got all his rocks in place in one season, Valhalla on the dunes was "probably safe." Or put another way, he wasn't willing to get up in front of the planning commission and say it wasn't.

The lawyer said, sure, the county could condemn anything it damn well pleased. He directed me to the omnibus Fifth Amendment to the U.S. Constitution, where the forefathers collected all their afterthoughts. Condemnation was the last passenger to climb on board, considerably after the right to keep a machine gun in your bedroom and the gangsters' favorite bit about self-incrimination; what Thomas Jefferson and all the other good ole boys had to say on the subject was that as long as the government paid the poor jerk whose land it grabbed, it was stars and stripes forever AOK by them.

I'd also put in a call to the Planet Advocates, a Portland-based society of environmentalist do-gooders who weren't hurting for bucks and packed a punch in the state capital, but when I told Mom and Ben, my local strategists, that the advocates were willing to come plead my case before the county planning commission, they came unglued.

"Mistake," Mom cawed. "I wouldn't let 'em cross the county line. Around here, 'conservationist' means rich, selfish, and no-growth, not to mention stupid and communist."

Ben exhaled a cloud of pipe smoke, coughed heartily, then nodded. "Save a view and cost a job. That's how folks see it, Schuyler."

I tried to argue that considerably more was at stake than a view, even let myself wax demi-eloquent on the topics of natural habitat and holding resources in trusteeship for the future, but the Kilchis mind was fixed. Mom shook her head in mock despair. "Sad to say, Schuyler, Mason's got most of the good arguments on his side. People can support him and feel they're doing right. You let some fancy stranger get up and start spouting a lot of poetry about mud and bugs and unborn generations, you're going to look pretty foolish."

I snared her bright bird's eye. "How about you, Mom? You think it's foolish? You've got grandchildren. Don't you want there to be a beach left in this county where they can play?"

Her bony shoulders lifted in a shrug; a thousand wrinkles, more or less, radiated out from her grin. "The ocean's nice, Schuyler, but it's nothing new. You live here a long time, you get to taking it for granted. My daughters-in-law don't like to clean up sand, and the kids, they'd rather roller skate or watch TV."

I looked to Ben. Once again, he seconded Mom. "That's how it is, Sky. Any way you cut it, you're standin on pretty shaky ground." He was silent a moment, then brightened. "The good thing is, Mason ain't likely to burn you out now. No need to."

No need, indeed. I'd spent considerable time and effort the last few years embracing failure before it bear-hugged me; I'd learned to play the loser so well that the quality of the performance redeemed its content and I could still feel superior to the conventionally successful. This time was different; this time was real. I was angry at myself for caring, and even angrier at the ephemeral Jack Willets for putting me in a position where I had to care.

"Goddamn," I said. "I wish I could talk to that bastard for just five minutes."

Jean and Tony, Marty and I were dining out at Colonel Sanders's grease emporium on Main Street. Tony stopped in the middle of denuding a chicken wing. "Maybe you can, Sky. That's a great idea."

"I already tried calling. His number's been permanently disconnected."

"I'm serious. Jean's Aunt Maddy is psychic. If anyone can get in touch with Mr. Willets, Maddy can."

"Give me a break, Tony. Spiritualism is the last refuge of the gullible. Or hadn't you heard?"

I looked to Marty for support. She joined battle on the other side. "You told me yourself that being open to the improbable is the backbone of good science."

"I was talking about Einstein, not Madame Blavatsky."

"Remember your mother," Marty said. "What about that?" Before I could think of a suitably scathing reply, something classy like Mind your own business, bitch, Marty turned to Jean. "Do you think your aunt would be willing to help us?"

Aunt Maddy was. She didn't do seances often, because

they exhausted and sometimes scared her, but for her niece Jeannie's sake, she was willing to go a round or two with the spirit world. My willingness was not at issue; everybody else was so infatuated with the opportunity to make fools of themselves that over my protests the arrangements got made. The seance should be held at Seasound, Aunt Maddy said, since Jack Willets's emanations were likely to be strongest there, and should take place at night because, in general, that's when the Other Side was most accessible. We'd play our little game by lantern light, since in Aunt Maddy's experience, electricity tended to interfere with clear reception. Marty was utterly enchanted at the prospect of establishing communication with the deceased and I, if I was to be totally honest, would have to say my skepticism was leavened with a little fear. For the first time since I'd left, I almost wished I were back in Cambridge, hunched parabolic over the chessboard with resolutely incredulous Barney Crews.

After all the gypsy jargon, I was ready for a turbaned weirdo in necromancer's robes, but Aunt Maddy when she arrived resembled any other ordinary Kilchis lady wilting quietly if somewhat disconsolately into the outer reaches of middle age. She marched in near dusk in a pair of sensible saddle shoes, plucking one of those plastic accordion-fold rain bonnets off her pink Brillo pad coiffure, kissed Jean in aunty fashion, hugged Tony, nodded pleasantly at Marty, then seized both of my hands in both of hers and stared into my eyes. Her eyes were almost green. She turned to Jean. "He has the power. I can feel it." To me. "Have you ever had a psychic experience, Schuyler?"

Schuyler denied it.

"What a pity," Maddy mourned, peeling off her raincoat. "But it's never too late. Someday you will. Maybe tonight."

"I sincerely hope not," I said.

She wagged a reproving finger at me. "Now, now. The spirits don't like cynics. It makes them shy." Looked fondly at the merry-go-round. "What a wonderful machine. I did love to come here when I was little. I'd almost bet you old Frenchy Thibault comes back to visit it sometimes. Have you ever seen or heard him?"

"Never," I averred.

She laughed. Her laugh was giddy and a little shrill, a lot less sensible than her shoes. It also seemed to suggest she knew something I didn't, a ploy I've never found enticing. "Don't you believe in the afterlife, Schuyler?" she teased.

"I believe in the conservation of matter," I told her. "That's as far as I'm willing to go."

From her canvas satchel she produced something like a heavy-duty balloon and set about filling it with air. Inflated, it assumed the shape of a large rubber doughnut. Aunt Maddy plopped it down on the chariot bench and settled on it like a nesting hen. "Female trouble," she clucked. "It's best to be comfortable." Spread her flowered skirt around her. "Shall we begin?"

We took the seats she assigned us, Jean next to her and Tony next to Jean. Marty and I faced them on the opposing bench. Maddy gave us her pep talk: concentrate, maintain silence, believe. The spirits would speak through her. Once contact was established, we could ask them questions. Politely, please. Spirits like to be treated with courtesy.

The lantern was hung from a hook on the canopy rim, half an arc away from the chariot. Its soft white light snuck up on Maddy from behind and gave her the look of being pinkly haloed. Her face and Jean's were in shadow.

"Join hands and close your eyes," she instructed. Her palm closed on mine, warm, soft. Marty's hand, by contrast, felt small and cold. Tony reached across the space to Jean and closed the circle. Relax, Maddy told us. Think about Jack Willets.

It wasn't wholly dark behind my eyelids. Little rectangles of light jumped around in the darkness, moving stiffly as the blips in a video game. We breathed in five-part disharmony. The ocean was loud outside. Marty's hand started in mine, the same kind of sudden involuntary shudder that sometimes shakes her just as she's drifting off to sleep. My foot began to itch fiercely inside my shoe. Maddy's hand was a steady pressure, damply warm. At least a hundred times I considered letting go of it to scratch my foot. I endeavored to scratch my itch with imaginary fingers, I tried to ignore it out of existence, but when I succeeded in subduing it, another even sharper tingle sprang up on my right thigh. What the others suffered inside their respective silences, I had no clue.

Tony half-coughed to clear his throat. Aunt Maddy hissed for silence. I became convinced the itch was a mosquito, snacking on my thigh. Marty rustled, shifting; she was pregnant enough that no one position pleased her long. More mosquitoes landed, crawled on my legs. How long would we sit here before someone found the guts to say the emperor was naked? That task would fall to me, most likely. Outside, the raindrops got fat enough that I could hear them hit the roof.

Then, in something best described as a stage whisper, Aunt Maddy said, "I'm getting a message. It seems to be for Schuyler. It's a man, a fat man. I see something flashing. It's a diamond in his ring." A pause, then, "He says he forgives you, Schuyler."

"For what?" My voice was harsh after the whisper.

"For opposing him. God told him to build here. He wants to be your friend. Do you have anything to say to him?"

"Tell him to shove it."

Aunt Maddy squealed disapproval. "You mustn't be rude, Schuyler. Now he's gone."

"Good riddance to bad rubbish."

"I want you all to remember your manners," Maddy warned. We fell quiet again. Despite my message from the other side of town, I was less than convinced that something psychical had happened. Maddy hadn't told me anything new. Easy enough to fake it. Besides, I thought mediums (or is it media?) were supposed to faint or at very least to shriek and quiver, but Maddy was calm and seemed lucid.

"Jeannie, someone for you. I do believe it's Grandma, dear. She wanted to have a look at Tony. There. She's nodding. She approves. She'd like a favor, though. Her headstone is covered with moss, and it bothers her. You know what a good housekeeper she always was. Will you take care of it?"

"Sure, Grandma. Say hi to Grandpa and Uncle Art, okay?"

Jeannie sounded cheerful, conversational. I gathered it was nothing extraordinary for her to hobnob with the dear departed, Aunt Madeline serving as a kind of transethereal telephone operator, though I wasn't above suspecting that Maddy was too lazy to take her own toothbrush to the family monument and so enlisted the authority of the ancestors to pass the task to Jean. It was a good scam.

I expected the next message to be for Tony, and it was, a cryptic admonition to "Remember the end run," supposedly originating with a former Kilchis High School football coach who'd dropped dead on the sidelines of a heart attack while exhorting his players to "kill, dammit, kill!" The advice was out of season, but Tony seemed glad enough to get it. If my theory—that Maddy was a good businesswoman and her spiritualism a mildly diverting parlor trick in an otherwise dull town—held water, then Marty's number should be coming up next. I hadn't allowed for Roger.

Maddy burst into a fit of giggles. "Stop it, right now. I've told you not to say those things. No, I wouldn't like that at all, thanks very much. Sometimes I think you're just a dirty old ghost." After a few more giggles and protestations, she sent the poltergeist packing and explained: "That was Roger, my fiancé. He gets terribly lonely. There's no physical intimacy on the Other Side, if you know what I mean, and sometimes he lets his imagination run away with him."

It crossed my mind that on a cold night, in the privacy of her boudoir, Maddy just might let her imagination meet his halfway, an eminently practical solution to the constraints of prolonged small-town maidenhood. A phantom lover was probably a whole lot easier to deal with than a living spouse, and Roger as succubus probably didn't complain about love handles, or wake up in the morning with bad breath, either.

"There's someone here," Maddy said. "I can't quite make it out." I felt Marty stir beside me, as if she too had second-guessed the general agenda. I squeezed her hand. "It's a man, I think. He wants to speak to . . . to . . . that's it. He wants to speak to Schuyler."

Marty squeezed back. "What's he got to say?" I asked.

"He says—louder, please. All right. He says if it's a boy, you should name it after him. I think it must be your father."

Marty posed her favorite question: which father?

I said, "Describe him."

Maddy said, "I can't. He doesn't have a body. Just a kind of soft, blurry glow. He keeps fading in and out. Grandpa Nelson's like that too, Jeannie. All voice, no substance."

"Ask him his name."

There were a couple of quiet minutes while Maddy presumably tried. Then, "He's gone. He faded."

She was a pretty good scriptwriter, I'd give her that, and too ethical or too respecting of mystery to venture a false answer to an open question. For a minute there, my heart had beat a little faster. Just for a minute.

Quiet again, and rain. Rain. I drifted, content to listen, trying to hear the separate voices inside the ocean's chorus and the faint percussing of the rain. Maddy's grip tightened on my hand. She muttered something, a few incoherent syllables, then moaned. A dull thud. I opened my eyes. Aunt Maddy's head lolled over the back of the chariot bench, a big pink flower on a broken stem. Her eyes were closed, and her lips moved, but no words came out. Her hand was limp in mine.

When she spoke, her voice was low and sad. "I'm sorry, baby girl, I really am. You're a sweet thing, but you're not enough. I have to go. I found three gray hairs this morning. We never go dancing anymore. If I stay here, I'll get old. I'll die. Someday you'll understand."

Marty retracted her hand and broke the circle. Aunt Maddy groaned. I opened my eyes to find Marty's puckered around tears, a look of desolation on her face.

I stood. "That's enough. Show's over." Pulled Marty to me, head to waist, and held her. Jean tried to revive her aunt.

"She's out cold," Tony said.

Slowly, Marty calmed down. After we poured a shot of bourbon down her gullet, Aunt Maddy woke up, so readily it reinforced my doubts about the authenticity of her stupor. "Was it Jack Willets?" she wanted to know, fussing with her hairdo, all green eyes wide.

We told her it was not.

Aunt Maddy blew a gusty sigh through her crimson kewpie lips. "Well, things don't always work out the way we want them to. I'm sorry I couldn't help you, Schuyler."

"That's okay," I told her. "I didn't really expect you would."

After they were gone, I had to spend a long time convincing Marty that Aunt Madeline was nothing more than a cunning postmenopausal nut, and all her messages a hoax. Any answers we hit upon would have to come from us.

Chapter 39

*S*tep right up, ladies and gentlemen. Tonight, right here in Kilchis you will see, for your amusement and edification, the Magnificent Mason, Orville the Unsurpass-able, perform his most daring, difficult and dangerous feat to date. Before your very eyes, he will attempt to hold back the tides, turn sand to stone, snow five of nine civic leaders and snatch a condo village from the sea. That's right, ladies and gentlemen, seventy-one condominium units where now there's only sand and grass and wind. Can he do it, folks? Unstoppable Orville does not say die.

And in ring three, as a special bonus threat, you'll witness the pitiful and horrible spectacle of the young stranger from the East being thrown to the developers, savage creatures who will eat his deed, piss on his future and reduce him to a quivering, sniveling jelly of regrets.

Step right up, my friends. No tickets needed.

A carnival atmosphere prevailed in the Kilchis County Courthouse the night of the planning commission hearing on Seasound Village. So much of the local citizenry turned out to witness the proceedings that the hearing had to be moved from a modest basement conference room to the county's best approximation of an amphitheater—a courtroom on the third floor. The courthouse corridors and stairways were choked with Kilchisites in festive mood. As Marty and I made our way among them, I found myself wishing I had the hot dog and ice-cream concession, so the evening wouldn't be a total waste.

We took ourselves two empty seats in the front row and settled in. I dislike courts almost as much as I hate hospitals; one I associate with death, the other with injustice. The last time I'd been to court was 1968, to get myself arraigned, with a couple hundred other peace march detainees, on charges of disrupting the status quo. We all pled guilty and enriched the coffers of the state of Massachusetts by paying fifty bucks apiece in fines. Tonight's proceedings promised to cost me a good deal more.

I was surprised how many of the faces around me were familiar, and under other circumstances might have taken that as a symptom of assimilation, but that night, in that place, I knew I was still the alien. To me, the faces belonged to supermarket checkers or merry-go-round riders, to the lady from the laundromat, the assistant librarian or the guy who fixed my van, while to Orville, they were the faces of lodge brothers and blood relations, of co-religionists and employees, neighbors and debtors. A few folks nodded at us all the same. The feedstore owner who hadn't hired me sent a small condoling smile my way, a doleful welcome to the fraternity of Masonian screwees. Mom arrived on the arm of chunky commissioner Zeb, who entrusted her to us and wandered off to find himself a place in less politically questionable venue.

The planning commission members, six good Kilchis men, two honest Kilchis women, were deployed in the jury box and their chairman, a prominent dairy farmer weathered in his wide plaid tie, sat at the judge's polished bench and fiddled nervously with his borrowed gavel. Four of the nine, Mom told us, were related to or employed by Mason and would vote with him even if what he proposed was an H-bomb test on Main Street. The consciences of another four were less encumbered and one, Mom cheerfully reported, "hates Orville's guts." Mason himself arrived late and grandly, as befits the star attraction, escorting a plump matron in a fur-trimmed sweater, a large gold and diamond cross abounce on her bosom, whom I took to be his bride. Two hired guns in good suits settled in with Orville at counsel table; the not-quite simultaneous opening of their briefcase latches sounded like a string of caps exploding.

The chairman rapped for order. "Guess you all know why we're here. Orville Mason's got a presentation he wants to make." He deeded the floor to my antagonist, and the dog and pony show began.

Orville's leisure suit was the color of Chianti, his boots agleam, the diamonds in his bolo tie alive. His round face was sweat shiny and pinked with premonitions of success. I'd never seen him work an audience bigger than three, but he was at home in front of a crowd, his manner that of a benevolent uncle and the text smoked ham. His little pig eyes landed as he spoke, exacting loyalty, and then passed on. The first part of his spiel was long on benefits. To hear him tell it, Seasound Village was his gift to all the citizens of Kilchis, something he in his selfless wisdom and magnanimity was giving them because he knew they wanted it and needed it so bad. It would be the salvation, civic and economic, of us all.

Having scaled the peaks of prophecy, he paused for a moment, signaled his gear change with a grin, and sotto voce, started in again. "Now, there's those of you who say it

can't be done, and even a few who think it shouldn't"—
briefly, his eye was on me—"but let me tell you, I have it on
the best, not to say the most, expensive authority that once
that jetty's built, we're gonna be able to reclaim that land,
stabilize it, and build on it." (Pause, two, three. Hit it.)
"Just to make them earn their fancy fees, I had some of my
experts come along with me tonight." (The lion-tamer
displays his beasts.) "First of all, my architect, Ivan Perkins,
is going to show you Seasound Village."

As Orville spoke, Perkins rose and erected a portable easel
in front of the witness stand. His first exhibit was a set of
architectural plans, an intricate maze of blue geometries
impossible to read from any distance. Think of that as an
X ray, he told us, and moved on to the next card, a full-color
artist's rendering of the completed miracle.

Imagine you're in a helicopter, looking down. Here's the
seventy-one living units, the individual garages, the terraced
courtyard and the recreational facilities: the saunas, the
pool, the handball courts, the exercise rooms and tanning
salon, the community gymnasium complete with indoor
track. It can get pretty soggy jogging on the beach in winter,
ha ha.

Obediently, even though it comprised more loggers than
joggers, the crowd ha ha'ed.

Ha ha changed to ooh ah as Perkins showed us details of
the condos—gleaming electric kitchens, sunken living rooms
and gilded bathrooms, a couple of thin, tan families splash-
ing gaily in the indoor pool, an artist's conception of healthy,
happy WASP humanity at play. Orville interrupted to tell us
just how much money these sleek condo dwellers would blow
in downtown Kilchis. Perkins estimated for us how many
Kilchis coolies it would take to build this little piece of
paradise at Seasound.

That done, Orville got up and told his architect to sit
down. It was clear he enjoyed giving orders to the holders of
advanced degrees. For a couple minutes, Mason cannily
shuffled papers and whispered with his colleagues in order to
give the spectators a little space to ponder the wonders of

225

modern architecture. Then it was time for the next act.

Mason cracked his whip and another expert jumped through the hoop, a doctor of engineering geology this time. Actually, there wasn't much to choose between him and the architect, except the color of his suit and the fact that while the architect's aviator glasses had gold rims, the engineer's were silver. Was it fair to deduce from so small a sample that all Portland professional men-for-hire frequented the same tailor and the same optometrist?

Now the prop became a map of the Seasound peninsula. The second jetty was already drawn in, and my plot of land, I noticed, was outlined in red. Impersonating the sea with his mechanical pencil, the good doctor of engineering showed us how currents redirected by the jetty were going to deposit new sand on Seasound's beaches and, with the help of God knows how many tons of fill, reshape the peninsula, turning a thin clam into the fat oyster that Orville hoped to swallow whole. The only trick then was stabilization. All you had to do was riprap the hell out of it, put in a concrete seawall, and you could build a bleeding cathedral on those dunes. The profanity is mine. The doctor's gold pencil x'ed in more than a mile of rock along the beach. Beside me, Marty groaned.

"The trick is," said the doctor of rocks, "to anchor that seawall to existing bedrock. Core drilling tells us that bedrock is most accessible here"—the pencil landed—"and here, and here." The last "here" was my land. He tapped it again. "The basalt foundations *here* are the key to the whole project. With them in place, it's my professional opinion that Mr. Mason's development will be absolutely safe from erosion by the ocean."

He didn't mention that his opinion wore a price tag, and it didn't much matter. The young stranger had sustained a staggering blow. True or not, his words came down like gospel. Behind me, I could hear snatches of hymns in praise of riprap rising. "Looks bad, Schuyler," Mom told me, and I passed the message along, whispering "Ouch" in Marty's hair-hidden ear.

Moments later, Mason moved in for the kill. I was his prop; he stood near and regarded me with a paternal look of fond sadness he'd probably copped from an Illustrated Children's Bible rendition of the Return of the Prodigal Son.

"So what stands in our way?" he rhetoricized. "Only the bullheaded selfishness of one young man." To me. "You wouldn't deny, would you, Schuyler, that I've made you several more than generous offers for that land of yours?" Scrutinized, I blushed. Orville shook his head sadly. "Now, I suppose we really can't blame him, folks. He's not from around here, and I suppose we can't expect him to understand how important this development is to us in Kilchis. Why should he? He's got no family here. We're not his kin." Back to me, Big Daddy again. "And I respect your reluctance to part with that piece of real estate, I really do. Ordinarily, I'd say, 'Okay, young fella, if you don't want to sell, I understand. It's your right.' But not when there's a greater right involved. There's more than just a piece of ground involved here, there's the future progress and prosperity of all the people of Kilchis County. And when you weigh the property rights of one young stranger against the larger needs of a whole community on the great scales of justice" (a rueful grin), "well, Schuyler, you come up a little light, my boy."

More than four of the planning commissioners smiled at that, and I heard chuckles in the rows behind me. Through most of Orville's performance, I'd kept my eyes trained squarely on the upper regions of his belly, watching his color-coded cowboy shirt expand and contract; as he laughed at his own wit, the checks leaped wildly. Remembering what he said, I see checks, smallish wine and white ones stretched tight, slightly shiny, over his gut.

"Because this young man refuses to sell his land, and because Seasound Village can't go ahead without it, and because I know how important this project is to all of Kilchis, I have a little proposition to make you tonight." He made it. His friends and neighbors and debtors applauded, not just because he wore the flag so well; he'd pushed them

227

to their upper limit for speechifying, then released them. They were grateful to be released.

If the audience needed to chat and squirm a little, that was all right by the chairman. He took the chance to swivel in his chair and blow his nose. Orville's timing was superb. The hearing was in danger of disintegrating right then and there. So was I. I had the feeling I was watching us all, myself included, on the late late movie; I was mesmerized by bad dialogue and all those dizzying close-ups of Orville's checks; I was fascinated into passivity. The whole plot seemed inexorable. Even Marty touching my arm was foreordained. If you turn off the set, does the story still go on, beyond your seeing?

After a while, the chairman came to and banged for attention. "Thank you, Orville." Plucked at his tie knot. "Does the commission want to vote on this tonight?"

While the commission consulted its watches and weighed its wants, Marty tapped my thigh. "Aren't you going to say anything, Sky?"

I had a vague feeling that the character named Schuyler had a scene to play, but damned if I could make the connection between him and me. I couldn't remember his lines.

"What do you want to do?" the chairman asked his fellows.

"Do it now," Marty urged me. "This is it."

"Do I hear a motion?" the chairman asked.

To communicate her sense of urgency, Marty pinched me. Speak now or forever shut your mouth. In what felt like slow slow motion I stood up. Said, "Uh, Mr. Chairman, excuse me. Can I say something?"

It got quiet in the courtroom. The chairman appeared to find it interesting that I could talk. "Well, sure, I guess so, Rykken." He looked to Orville for guidance. Orville looked at his space cadet wristwatch, then at me. "I got no objection. Only try to keep it short, okay, Rykken? No point in belaboring a lost cause. Billy Graham at Madison Square Garden's coming on TV at ten, and I'd surely hate to miss it."

Laughter.

"You can always leave early if I'm not done," I said. That got a few laughs, too, not as many as Orville, but a few. I looked out at the audience. Kilchis looked back at me with the same mild curiosity the chairman had, detached, but not hostile; a kind of wonderful neutrality sat on the role-familiar faces. Waiting.

"I'm Schuyler Rykken," I told them, "and it's my land that Orville Mason wants. Have you stopped to think about why he wants it so bad? Do you really think it's because he can't bear to leave this world without a Mason Park in it? Is the tax write-off that important to him? I've thought about it a lot and I don't think so. It's simpler than that. No land, no bundle for Orville."

I made the mistake then of stopping to breathe. Mason took full advantage of my pause. "Whoa down there, boy. I never denied for a minute I stand to make some money out of Seasound Village. Of course I do. I'm not exactly one of your philanthropists." He pronounced each syllable with equal weight, so the word in his mouth sounded as foreign as it was. "After all, the Bible says charity begins at home." (Kilchis snickers.) "Maybe you know of an eleventh commandment somewhere that says 'Thou shalt not make a profit,' but it's news to me."

Even Orville had to swallow. Up to speed, I jumped. "A big pile. That's what's at stake. You want to tell us just how much it is, Mason? No? I didn't think so. Well, after all my thinking, I've decided it just doesn't cut it to kill a living beach to make a buck for Orville Mason. Somehow that's not what I call public good."

People listened anyway; I almost imagined I saw a few heads nod. Before Orville could interrupt again, I went on. "It's also occurred to me I can't just stand up here and whine. Please don't take my land. Please. That doesn't make it either. I figure there's only one way to make my point, and that's to put my money where my mouth is." Out of the aforesaid mouth it came: "I want to make you a counter offer. Seasound is a fantastic place. Give Mason his way, and it'll be all rock. You and I won't be able to go there anymore. Our kids'll never see it as it is now, and that would be a damn shame. Besides, I'm not so sure as Mason's experts are that you can make it safe to put a Hilton on that sandbar." A deep breath and I gave it away. "Zone the beach at Seasound so that no one can ever build on it again, and I'll give you my land, free and clear, for a park."

I'd done it. I'd said too much, and not enough. What I wanted them all to see, the commissioners especially, was that wide beach, a silver arc connecting mountains, those tall dunes, ancient as rock and delicate as dreams, the blue green gray white sea. I wanted that picture to shine in their minds, for just a minute I wanted them to love it as much as I was cursed with loving it. Outside the venetian blinded windows of the courtroom, a sea gull bleated peevishly, probably lost on his way to the dump.

The silence was more confused than stunned. With rough farmer fingers, the commission chairman pushed his horn-rims back up the greased slide of his nose. Perplexity behind the lenses. Too many words had said too little. If I'd got up and slugged Orville in the gut, they would have understood what was happening a whole lot better.

"Look, I don't need the tax break," I said. "That land and the merry-go-round are all I've got, besides my wife and a broken-down van. I'm not a rich man. In fact, if somebody could let me have twenty bucks till payday, I'd be grateful."

They understood that. They were so glad to understand something that they rewarded my little joke with bigger laughter than it deserved. I felt myself smile. When I looked at Orville, he wasn't smiling. His lips had disappeared, as if he'd eaten them, and a big vein throbbed visibly, up the side of his temple, over the pink dome of his forehead. It looked like a worm squirming under his skin.

The chairman cleared his throat. "Let me see if I got this right," he said. "Orville, you're saying if we condemn Rykken's land and let you build your condos, you'll give us the money to pay off Rykken and give us his land for a park. Rykken, you're saying if we take steps to preserve Seasound in its natural state, you'll give us your land for a park. Is that it?" He looked at Mason, then at me.

"That's right," Orville said.

"That's right," I said.

The chairman turned to his peers in the jury box. "It looks like we've got us some thinking to do," he said, "about a park."

The planning commission voted to postpone their thinking until another time. The meeting adjourned. Leaving, we almost collided with Mason at the courtroom door. His usual glibness seemed to have deserted him. "You're making a big mistake, Rykken," said grimly, was his best shot.

"So pray for me, fat man," was mine.

Chapter 40

*T*wo weeks later, Mom called me at work to tell me the news: the planning commission had met and failed to decide which offer to accept. Neither Orville's proposition nor mine had won the fifth vote necessary for consensus. "The fur flew," Mom chuckled, "and Orville's scared."

Her reading was borne out when Mason himself appeared at Seasound a few nights later. His usual pink corpulence showed signs of strain, I thought, a touch of puff under the piglet eyes, a grim set to the mouth that made his jawline look as if it were made of dough, rolled into biscuits but unbaked. "You've had your fun, Rykken. Now let's get down to business."

"What's wrong? Haven't we paid our electric bill?"

Orville rocked back on his boot heels. "You want to hear me say it? Okay, I underestimated you. You're smarter than I thought. A hundred and fifty thousand, plus fifty thousand worth of stock in Seasound Enterprises, Inc. The condominium of your choice at Seasound Village. Life membership in the health club. Altogether, that's worth more than three hundred thousand dollars, and it's the best you're gonna get from me."

"I wouldn't want to be holding a piece of that condo when it falls into the sea," I told him.

"Hell, Rykken, you know that's not going to happen, not in my lifetime, anyway, and probably not in yours. I've got me the best engineers. Besides, the Lord's behind this."

"You going to name the Lord codefendant in all the lawsuits people are going to file when they find their microwaves boiling seawater? Or maybe you got Jesus to agree to be your maintenance man. I understand he's pretty good at water tricks."

Orville glared at me. "That's blasphemy, boy."

"Yeah, I know. Thou shalt not take the name of the Lord thy God in jest. That's what I don't like about Yahweh. He's got no sense of humor." I grinned into Orville's scowl. "Don't worry, Mason. If God's as fond of you as you think He is, He'll shoot straight. The thunderbolt won't even graze you."

We both waited a minute for it to fall. When it didn't, Mason said, "Look, Rykken. My lawyers are already working on the condo contract. They're putting in an airtight clause that releases Seasound, Inc., from liability in case of acts of God."

"You mean watertight, Mason?" I laughed out loud. "Don't you think God's gonna be a little miffed that you're playing it both ways?"

"That's just lawyer talk, Rykken. It means——"

"I know what it means. I imagine your customers will, too. You don't really think people will sign away their right to sue, do you?"

"We're putting it in real small print. Don't you worry. We'll be hanging a 'No Vacancy' sign on Seasound Village before the shakes are weathered gray."

"Not if the planning commission accepts my offer, you won't," I said.

"Is that some kind of answer?" Orville wanted to know.

"It is. Hard as it may be for you to believe, some things are more important to me than money, Mason." I opened the pavilion door for him. "Nice talking to you. Bring your wife along next time. Maybe she'd enjoy a merry-go-round ride."

My own wife was out back painting when I brought news of Orville's offer. She was always painting. My portrait of her in those days, if I could have painted it, would have her propped against her stool, not sitting, a thin linear vertical with a ripe outward curve, not quite the classic pregnant pear, since most of her height was in her legs, so that a space of brightly colored wool sock showed between her cuffs and shoe tops. Her shapeless gray sweater with the sleeves pushed up, unequally, on her forearms. One thick braid down her back or two thinner ones, seeming to grow out of her ears. Expression fierce, eyes slightly squinted, a look that with use imprinted itself on her face. Wielding the delicate weapon of a palette knife, the whole line curving resolutely toward the work, a directional arrow drawing the eye toward the output of the brain.

"So Mom was right about Mason getting nervous," Marty said. "Do you think he'd like my painting?"

She'd been working on it all week. Against a flat brick background punctuated regularly with small dark windows, men, women and children, all slightly overweight, frolicked with golf clubs and tennis rackets and roller skates, played video games or rode exercycles, while one thin vertical strip down the right side of the canvas showed a magnificent sunset over the sea beyond.

I considered. "The irony'd be lost on Orville. He'd probably love it. Why don't you show him and find out?"

It was a dig, but Marty was as immune to its sting as to all the others'. This painting, as all its predecessors had, would come to rest in the growing stack of paintings propped, unsold and unseen, against the pavilion walls. The archive grew around us—endless painted oceans, no two the same, and other paintings, more personal and more mysterious.

There was a beached jellyfish, one of those great irregular shiny globs of translucent protoplasm that look like the nightmares of a Steuben glass-smith, tinged red-orange at the center, faintly reflecting the face of a man, not quite modern, but an intermediate man, with a largish jaw and lowish forehead, a basically amiable but unsettling face that seemed to exist somewhere just beyond clear visual reach in the depths of the jellyfish.

There was a shiny, almost photo-real red Chevy pickup chasing a naked man and woman down a long, flat expanse of beach. The couple held hands in their flight and seemed to run awkwardly; in contrast to the solid truck, their figures looked childlike and insubstantial, as if they were refugees from another painting in another style, another time.

There was one she called "The Obstetrician." In the foreground rose a huge pregnant belly, with no head and no breasts, so it was as though the body belonged to you, the viewer. Raised thighs and tented knees framed a masked and hatted doctor, front and center, with one gloved hand raised in the iconographic blessing of a Byzantine Christ. In the other hand, he held an Italian submarine, partly eaten. Marty never was able to tell me what the sandwich meant.

There were more and more, too many to describe or even, to be honest, remember clearly, dozens upon dozens of picture postcards from the outback of Marty's brain, delivered to Seasound, there to rest. The gallery grew almost daily, and still Marty painted and did nothing about marketing her work. My janitor's paycheck was our only income; we were paying property taxes and ransoming the van and trying to save for the baby in small installments and what was left of a month's pay after these expenses was barely worth mentioning, barely enough for food and gas. For a long time I waited and had faith, expected to come home from work one night to find her wrapping canvases, loading the van, getting ready, at last, to sell her wares. It didn't happen.

In reality, I came home day after day to find her at her easel, painting away, filling yet another canvas to stand with its unsold fellows against our walls. At first my hints were broad. "I've been thinking." (Over dinner one night.) "I think I better start looking for another job. Nights and weekends. Inflation's eating us alive."

Marty looked up from her macaroni with mild surprise. "A second job would kill you, Sky. Besides, I'd never get to see you if you worked at night."

"We're poor," I told her. "We're in debt."

"Everybody's in debt these days. Deficit spending is practically de rigueur."

"I don't care if it's fashionable. Wondering how we're going to feed and clothe the kid scares the crap out of me."

"I'm going to nurse it," Marty said. "We won't have to buy baby food for five or six months."

"We need more income."

She got up and rinsed her plate. "I don't want to talk about it right now, Sky."

Another time, another tactic. "Terrific. Really nice. How much do you figure you could get for it?"

"Oh, I don't know. I hate to put a price on my work, especially when it's so new."

"How about the old work?"

"Did you notice the sandpiper tracks, Sky? I really like the sandpiper tracks."

"How was your day, Sky?"

"Same old grind. Yours?"

"I painted all day."

"I wish I had time for my hobbies."

"You don't have any hobbies."

"I might if I had time."

"Painting isn't a hobby anyway. It's my work."

"And cleaning toilets is my work. Such a fine, satisfying, creative outlet."

"You sound bitter, Sky. You shouldn't do something that makes you bitter. Maybe you ought to quit."

It was no good. I couldn't get it out in the open, and I couldn't hold it in. I resented. I felt cheated. I was being had, breaking my balls as an assistant doormat while this broad, my wife, lived for art. Maybe I wasn't Einstein, but I deserved more from life than that. A tightness grew in my stomach and wouldn't relax. It burned. A glass of milk would help put out the fire, but Marty was pregnant and needed the milk. We had to save the milk for Marty. The kid needed milk. No milk for Schuyler. We were poor, right? My crack about the condo painting was only one of many. The showdown was still to come. It did.

My quarterly performance review rolled around. The school board wanted to know how I was doing. It was up to Bruce to evaluate me. The bastard checked the "average" box in every category, except for "attitude" and "self-starter," where he marked me "below average," and "reports to work on time" where, since I always got there considerably before he did, he was forced to recognize my superiority. After he signed it himself, Bruce was supposed to discuss the review with me and get my signature to show I'd seen, understood and, implicitly, concurred in his judgment of me.

"I'm not signing that," I told him.

"For Christ's sake, Rykken, just write your name, would you?"

"Hell no. What's this average, average, average garbage? You know damn well I work harder than you do."

"You're supposed to, shithead. I'm the boss."

"Tell that to the school board. Or you want me to?"

"I'm sick of your smart-aleck crap, Rykken. I'd like to kick your ass."

"I'd like to kick yours, you lazy Nazi creep."

His face was ugly and red as a wormy tomato. He grabbed me by the front of my coveralls and shoved me against the concrete basement wall. If he hadn't grinned at the sound of my neck snapping back and my head thudding against the wall, I might not have hit him, but he did, and I did, shredding the tender inside of his lip against his teeth—even Nazis are vulnerable inside the mouth—hurting my hand in the process and glad to draw blood. He was a great target; I could hate him purely because I didn't love him too. After I hit him, I was embarrassed and he was impressed, nursing his inner lip with a big stained Handi-Wipe from his back pocket.

"Didn't think you had it in you, Rykken." Clearly he bore no grudge, but seemed satisfied to have discovered a violence in me that matched his. My self-control had been a provocation. Men fight. Friends fight. To a certain kind of man, the laying on of hands is necessary ritual in making friends. He stuffed the rag back in his pocket and extended his hand. I didn't want to be his friend. To shake his hand was to acknowledge loathsome commonality. I didn't want to do it. It was impossible not to.

Bruce had his catharsis; we practiced his ritual on his terms and he was satisfied. I wasn't. Marty was painting when I got home. Painting happily away, performing *her* ritual, satisfied. She kissed me distractedly between knife-strokes, *her* ritual. "I'll be at a stopping place in about twenty minutes. Are you cooking or am I?" Painting. Satisfied. Her way.

I threw my jacket on the bed.

Over her shoulder, not looking at me, she said, "Sky? I asked who's cooking tonight."

"I heard you."

"Well?"

"Well what?"

"I'm almost through here. I just want to get these blues in before I stop."

"By all means, get the blues in."

"Is something wrong, honey?"

"Wrong? Oh, no. It's just the blues. I've got to get the blues in before I breathe."

She turned toward me, palette in one hand, knife in the other, still wearing her painting intensity on her face. "What the hell's wrong with you?"

"Oh. Pardon me. Sorry to disturb the *artist* at her *work*. I wouldn't want to cost the world a goddamn *master*piece."

She sighed, laid down her tools reluctantly. "Something's eating you. You might as well tell me what it is."

"Don't tempt me. If I get started, you might not get your blues in."

She sat down on the bed, conciliatory, downshifting,

finding compassion among her masks. Her proximity made me angry. I bounced away.

Hurt fought compassion and lost. "What is it, honey?"

"WHY DON'T YOU SELL YOUR GODDAMN PAINTINGS? WHY DON'T YOU EVEN TRY?"

Hurt won. She blew out air sharply, as if I'd hit her in the gut. "Is that what's bothering you?"

"It's bothering me, yes. You're damn right it's bothering me. I know it's crude and vulgar and beneath you to think about *money* where *art*'s concerned, but I'm getting goddamn tired of mopping floors to support your freeloading muse."

She cried. Two big tears started down her cheeks, moving at different rates of speed. With dispassion, I watched them fall. Her eyes reddened and seemed to blur. The tears stung her pallor with red marks. She folded protective hands over the shelf of her belly, and I resented the cloak of motherhood she drew around her, making me the enemy of art *and* life. When she spoke, her voice was small: "I had no idea you were concerned about that."

"Then you've been living in a fool's paradise, lady." It was the functional equivalent of hitting Bruce, only Marty had neither expected nor asked for it. Somewhere beyond anger and frustration, I felt a stab of love.

She jumped up from the bed as though I had struck her, and turned her face from me, talking fast and mostly to herself. "Yeah, I suppose I have been. I should have known it was too good to be true. No free rides, right? No smooth rides. Only the potholes. I should have known. I've always known." She turned to face me and her eyes were dry. "I'll go."

It was an almost physical pain, loving and hating and knowing at bottom the situation was utterly absurd, both positions untenable, my ritual barbaric. Of course she wouldn't go—would she?—and of course, something perfect had been breached and we would have to learn to live with the scars. "Who said anything about going? I only asked if you were ever going to try to sell some paintings."

"You said I was getting a free ride. I was insane to expect you to understand. It's better if I go."

Suddenly I was tired, profoundly tired, and couldn't think where I'd find the energy to see through what I'd started. I was satisfied, but she wasn't. "Marty, my love, I don't want you to go anywhere. I had a bad day. Fought with Bruce. Tried to take it out on you."

"I won't be anybody's whipping boy."

"I'm sorry." It was too soon for sorry.

"I've been working like crazy. All day, every day. If you don't appreciate that——"

"I appreciate it."

"You work hard, too, I know."

"That's right."

"At least I'm doing something I like. I think I'm good at it."

"You're excellent."

"Well, not excellent."

"Yes, you're excellent."

"If I believed that, it would be easier to think about showing and selling."

"Believe it. I do."

"Maybe you're the one in the fool's paradise, then."

"I don't get it. What's all this about?"

She sat down, legs apart, to give her belly space. "I'm scared. I'm afraid my paintings aren't good enough. I'm scared to death a gallery owner will look at them and me and laugh."

I laughed; it seemed ridiculous, ferocious Marty un- starched, intimidated by the marketplace. "You can only try and see. My God, you've been prolific. You've got dozens of good things. Besides, my love, we need the money." At the mention of money, her whole body winced. "You can't just stay here forever and paint."

"No."

"Well, then."

"Remember the painting I told you about? The fetus as

madonna? I promised myself as soon as I did that one, then I'd go to Portland and start hustling."

"So do it."

Her arms, opening, echoed the spread of her legs. "That's just it. I've tried. Half a dozen times, anyway. In my head, it's so beautiful, and on canvas it's awful. An abortion every time. I can't make it work."

"That doesn't mean all your paintings are abortions. Maybe some things weren't meant to be painted."

"Oh, Sky."

"I fail all the time."

"That's different."

Was it? I wondered. Why shouldn't Marty, too, salute some limitations? It hurt that she saw me as already having lost, when I felt, most days, as though I were still in the game, holding a reasonably good hand, no royal straight flush, maybe, but a nice strong full house, kings over threes, let's say, that with smart betting and steady nerves still might win a pot. I put my hand on her back, between the thin wings of her shoulderblades and she suffered my touch. I felt her body relax a little. My anger was burned out and I was ashamed of it. I loved her deeply and was ready to recant. "Hey, I've been a jerk, insisting on my own integrity. You and the kid are more important. Tomorrow morning I'm going to call the planning commission and tell them I take back my offer. We'll sell to Mason."

She stiffened again. "The hell you will."

"Listen, it's about time I grew up. With Orville's bucks in the bank, you could paint all you wanted and never have to worry about selling a damn thing." I stroked the knobby ladder of her spine. "We could buy us a very nice life somewhere."

"I want to stay at Seasound," Marty said. "We've got a nice life here."

She let me take her hands in mine. I looked into her orange-brown eyes. "You know we're going to have to move on sooner or later. Why not get paid for it?"

"No," she told me. "I won't be responsible for you going

240

back on your word. You'd hate me for it, and so would I."

"I'd never hate you, Marty. Besides, if we take Mason's money, we'll at least be able to move the merry-go-round when the time comes. We can send the kid to Harvard. It's the only way."

Her eyes darkened with indignation. "It is *not* the only way. Don't you dare discount me that way again."

"I was only being realistic."

"No kid of mine is going to Harvard or anyplace else on dirty money. I'll pack up the van tomorrow and start hitting galleries on Friday. I'll show you I can sell my paintings. I'm a very good painter, Sky, no matter what you think."

I wrapped my arms around the whole wrought-up, knocked-up bulk of her and kissed her, hard and full, on the lips. "I never doubted it for a minute, Marty love," I said.

Chapter 41

*M*arty's birth talisman was a smooth, flat rock, one she'd spent weeks finding on the beach at Seasound, and the most perfect circle that nature could describe. The talisman, an object to focus on in the extremities of labor, was one of several props prescribed by our reassuringly ordinary natural childbirth teacher when we took a six-week series of self-help classes in the basement cafeteria of the Kilchis County General Hospital. The key to the method was breath control; with proper use of breathing techniques, a woman could overcome fear and tension and ride out her labor without medication. We were forbidden to use the word "pain"; women had contractions instead, and birth was a beautiful and natural thing. It all seemed reasonable enough under the matter-of-fact fluorescence of the cafeteria lights, in the company of a dozen or so other couples willing to believe.

Now, with Marty lying beside me, clutching the rock in her fist, the skin of her belly stretched so taut I thought it might crack open and the baby simply hatch, her slow, regular breathing a lighthouse flashing aural patterns in the dark while the storm outside lashed the pavilion walls with rain, loud and irregular, none of it seemed to matter or make much sense. "It" was beginning, and "it" remained a mystery, the little rituals we'd practiced as hopelessly inadequate as a matchstick dam against the inexorable onrush of a flooding river.

"Should I rub your back?" I asked periodically. "How about your front? Is there anything I can do?"

"Just wait with me. Be with me. I just hope I recognize it when it happens."

"They say you can't miss it."

"*They* said I'd have morning sickness, too, and I didn't."

"You scared?"

"Shitless."

"Can you sleep?"

"I'll try. Don't go away, Schuyler."

"Schuyler's here."

I must have dozed off myself. Deep in the night, I felt Marty stir beside me. She jackknifed, stiff as a broken board, and gave a little whimper. Slowly the tension passed.

"That was the first one, Sky. The real thing."

"How was it?"

"I blew it. I tensed instead of relaxing and completely forgot to breathe at all."

"You'll do better next time."

"What they didn't mention was, it hurts like hell."

"Want me to watch the watch?"

She managed to laugh. "Not yet. They're supposed to start slow. In an hour or so, we'll keep score."

Rain battered the roof. We both stared at the ceiling, waiting out the uncharted interval before the next contraction. Marty's profile was sharp in the faint red glow from the space heater. It could be as much as ten minutes, as little as five. It didn't seem that long before she grabbed my hand.

"Breathe with me, Sky."

"They say you should hold off using the techniques as long as possible."

"Don't talk. Breathe."

We breathed, the rhythm of Marty's choice, four in, four out. She let go of my hand and pushed frantically at her hair, as if it was strangling her.

"If this is the beginning, I don't think I'm going to make the end."

"You'll get used to it." They taught us to say that, us husbands, in natural childbirth class.

"And don't talk to me. I've got to concentrate."

"The books say . . ."

"I don't care what the books say. I could no more play cards right now or go for a walk than I could fly."

And it was on her again. This time I breathed without being told, loudly, feeling stupid, hoping it helped.

Her breath shallowed at the end. "That was a little better. I rode it better. Schuyler, will you braid my hair?"

"I haven't braided anything since I made a lanyard for my fifth-grade girl friend."

"I don't care how it looks. Just get it out of the way."

"I'll need the light."

"Okay."

When I turned it on, I was surprised to find her face shiny with sweat. It was damn cold in the pavilion. "You'll have to sit up."

She held out her hands to me and I pulled her up; her legs dangled, thin and pale, over the edge of the bed. I found her brush and stroked her hair, too gently. She took it from me and raked it, savage and efficiently, through the sleep snarls. "There. Now braid."

"Is it two strands or three?"

"Three!" Her sharpness was an index of my inadequacy. Asked to perform a simple task, I faltered. Why had I ever imagined, why had she, that I'd be useful, helpful, good to have around in this extremity? My fingers trembled, dividing and subdividing her hair.

Then suddenly she made a noise, an almost outraged *ahh*, greeting the onset of the next contraction, and bent forward over it, pulling the hair loose from my inept hands. Her breathing was ragged again and it scared me to see her hurting, treading the edges of control. I put my hands on her shoulders, at the base of her neck, and kneaded the rock-hard muscles, breathed like a bellows in four-four time. She started when I touched her, then submitted, gasped once and caught my rhythm. Windy as the storm, we blew and blew. Slowly the shoulder muscles relaxed, yielding not to my massage but to the passing of the pain. She panted like a runner past the finish line. I tackled her hair again, separating it first in two parts, and the two into three.

"Never mind that. Just pull it back with a rubber band. And get the watch. This is happening entirely too fast."

Side by side on the edge of the bed, we watched the second hand sweep round the face of the Timex, once, twice, three times. Ten seconds into the third minute, she tapped my thigh and started breathing hard. I fixed my eyes on the watch, heard the wind scream outside, while Marty closed her eyes and contained the pain. Another rap on my leg. "How long?"

"Ninety-four, ninety-five seconds."

"Jesus. I thought the first ones were supposed to be short. I better get dressed." She pushed herself up and wobbled to the makeshift closet, grabbed a smock, yanked off her nightgown and pulled it on. "Sky, can you find me some underpants?"

Once again, I was too slow, still fumbling in the dresser when she said, "Never mind." Supporting herself with one hand on the table, she had one leg in her jeans when it hit again. She dropped to a crouch, palms flat on the dirt floor, her belly supported on a platform of thighs, and rested her forehead against the metal table leg. I grabbed the watch and counted. Not quite, no more than four minutes between.

244

When the contraction passed, she used the edge of the table to pull herself up, got the second leg into her pants, pulled on wool socks. It was time to go.

The Volkswagen suffered from wet wiring and wouldn't start. The road from Seasound, rutted and puddled, the wind blasts from the ocean, grabbed at the van and bounced it like a toy. The irregularity of the ride fought against control. Marty clutched her stone and cried with frustration.

I was prepared to be relieved by the hospital, but it felt hostile, too bright, too loud, too busy. The admitting desk was full of questions we'd already answered and the clerk, an ancient lady with a face unyielding as a wall, expected Marty to stop labor to respond to them. Finally, an orderly wheeled her off to the birthing room, helped me roll her onto the bed and left us there.

Marty lay on her hip with one knee raised, her face against the blanket, a huge cocoon, stared unblinkingly at her round rock and rallied enough to breathe when the pains came. She didn't speak and she didn't move. I was just smart enough to understand that in silence, in immobility, she found mastery; I let her be.

All that was broken when the little nurse scuttled in with her small talk and required tasks, not the wise and gentle matron I'd envisioned, but a pert girl in her early twenties, tiny-waisted and loquacious, who looked at Marty huddled on the bed with more pity than empathy. She had to be undressed, she had to shower, move, talk, submit to the myriad procedures the hospital deemed necessary to giving birth. Marty's whole body resisted the disruption and she blinked uncomprehendingly at the barrage of smiles and words the nurse flung at her, stumbled through the physical obstacles routine required. When she was back in bed, smelling of pHisoHex, her pubic hair shorn, the nurse checked her cervical dilation, told us to expect a long labor, and left.

Marty sprawled on the bed, diagonally, in one of those back-flap hospital gowns. I sat with her, breathed with her, rubbed her back, held her hand, stroked her hair. Once I got up to use the toilet, but she called me back. Otherwise, she didn't waste much energy on words, except to tell me, once, that she loved me, and once that it was hard; she didn't think she'd last six hours more. Hard, and getting harder. For a long time, she was motionless, only her lungs active when the contractions came, inert and saving strength between them. Dutifully, I watched the watch, recording information no one seemed to want.

The contractions stayed long, about a minute and a half, and slowly their frequency increased, till the space between them was equal to their length. They left us alone. We managed. Time passed slowly, measured out in breaths, in pain. After an hour, Marty was weak and haggard. Her teeth chattered and her legs began to tremble. I rubbed her arms to keep her warm, wondered at the awful elasticity of time, felt essential and felt helpless both.

After an hour and a half, the nurse came back. "How are you folks doing?"

"They're coming fast now. She's pretty tired."

"Uh huh. Has her water broken?"

Marty spoke from the bed, her voice shaky. "Please tell me how long."

The nurse consulted her watch. "You were checked less than two hours ago. Usually, we only check at two-hour intervals. First labors tend to be very slow."

"Please," Marty said.

"Well, all right. Just roll over on your back and we'll see."

Marty tried to roll and couldn't. I brought her round. The nurse pulled on a rubber glove, and by the time she was ready to insert it, Marty was contracting again, her legs shaking hard. The nurse waited out this inconvenience, then felt inside. "She's all the way. I'll call the doctor." And she left.

"What'd she mean?" Marty asked.

"I'm not sure."

"Hold me, Sky."

Hold her, God, yes; I was moved by the simplicity of her

request and ached to help her, would have held her through holocausts, only the logistics of it were less easy than the impulse to comply. She was a heap on the bed, exhausted, and the slightest movement seemed to break her concentration, a commodity I respected highly, having watched her wield it, for hours now, as her only means of mastering both fear and pain. It was an absolute, her concentration, as the ocean is, or the rain, something strong and transcendent, yet housed in her weary body, delicate, too, as a blossom in the wind. It stood between us, between her and frenzy, between her and chaos, no screams, no cries, no thrashing, no yielding to the cataclysmic process that made her body tremble as if earthquakes passed through it, as if volcanoes erupted, unseen, inside her. I did the only thing I could do, climbed on the bed beside her from behind and pressed myself close to her backside, enveloped her as best I could with my angular dressed self, pulled off my belt so that the buckle wouldn't hurt her, kicked off my shoes so that they wouldn't soil the bed. Marty pulled my arm around her and held my hand tightly in both of hers, between her breasts. So close, I could feel the contractions when they came, like an electrical current passing through her, while she willed her body to passivity, tapping an immense negative strength to not react, to not resist.

After a while, the trembling, which had been constant, stopped. She moved her head. "I think they're letting up a little, Sky. They're not so hard now."

I hugged her gingerly, not wanting to jeopardize this new equilibrium.

"I think I could sleep now. I'm very tired."

"Go for it," I said. "Sleep if you can."

She was quiet. I trimmed my breathing to hers, felt the intense moist warmth where our bodies met. I was doing nothing, and all I could. When my nose itched, I forbore to scratch it; when my lower leg went to sleep, I let it go.

The doctor bustled in to dismantle our tableau, tall, thin and frenetic, wearing his surgical greens. His name was Ordman; we'd met once for a handshake and he'd seemed amiable enough behind his horn-rims, about my age, though balding, homely in a likable way and loose-limbed, the surprising length of his forearms reminding me vaguely of some animal who's only lately learned to walk erect.

"Well, well," he said. "I understand we're speeding right along." He pulled a rubber glove over his long fingers. "I'll just see for myself." To Marty. "I'll need you on your back again." To me. "Has her water broken?"

I disengaged myself from Marty, half-sat, and told him no. Marty didn't move.

"Come on now. Over you go."

"She's awfully tired."

"The worst is over. Come on. We've got to see about getting this baby out." To me, as though Marty were not sentient, "No time to waste now. A hard fast labor puts the baby under heavy stress. The sooner we get it out, the better." And to Marty, in his soothing kindergarten-teacher tone, "Now spread your legs. That's right. Good girl. Okay, you're ready. I'm just going to break this membrane. There." A rush of fluid left Marty's buttocks in a puddle, slowly leached into the sheets. "You get behind her and support her back."

I braced myself against the headboard, sitting erect, and spread and raised my knees. Marty inched back between them and lay against my chest as if I were a chair, my legs the arms. She drew her own legs up, mirroring mine, and I put my hands under her thighs to give her something to push against. The nurse wheeled in a small surgical tray.

"Now when a contraction comes, you push like hell."

We waited.

"Come on now."

Marty's head stirred against my chest. "They're so much lighter now, I'm not sure I can feel them."

"The nurse will help you." He dispatched her to Marty's side and had her put her hand on Marty's belly. "When it gets hard, you tell us."

"Now."

"Now push."

Marty swallowed air and held it down. She grasped her knees with her hands and her whole body stiffened and strained.

"All right," the nurse said.

Marty exhaled and went limp in my arms. She flexed her fingers, stiff from gripping, and I could see the deep red circles they left on the pale skin of her legs.

"Again."

The force of her pushing jammed my spine against the headboard and hers against me, her weight multiplied a hundredfold, it seemed, by the strength of her effort.

"Harder."

Marty pushed harder. Utterly exhausted, completely focused, she was stronger than me. I marveled at her strength. It was crushing me. I breathed with her, I pushed, too, as much to ease my own pain as to encourage her. My hands were locked around her thighs, and when she pushed, her muscles tensed to metallic hardness. Between efforts, she was limp and felt boneless.

"Come on, hard. Really hard."

Marty lost it, exhaled too soon. Against my cheek, her hair was wet as when she washed it. "Can I rest awhile?" she whispered.

"Rest after," the doctor said. "Now you work. I want to see the baby's head this time."

She pushed. The doctor took her hand and put it between her legs. "Feel it? That's it. Let's get it out now."

How many pushes? How much pain? I don't remember. The intelligence that keeps score turned off. No overview possible, no part of me uninvolved to comment or observe. For the first and only time in my life, I existed wholly, exclusively in the present instant. Marty was beyond the present, in deep space, outside the reach of time.

"Push!"

"Give it everything you have. This is serious. Push, dammit!"

The doctor picked a scalpel off his metal tray. "I'm going to make a cut this time. Now push."

I heard his knife slit skin, a little escape of breath from Marty. The doctor lunged forward. "I've got the head. You see the head?"

Marty tried to raise her own head, to see the baby's. All I could see was blood, staining the sheets.

"Now push."

Marty quivered with the effort, her muscles hard as ice. The dome of her belly deflated like a popped balloon. I heard two small animal cries. The nurse pushed up Marty's nightgown to bare her torso, and the doctor laid a small slimy bloody big-headed humanoid on her stomach, trailing the shiny sausage of the cord.

"A girl," the doctor told us.

Marty held the thing, a girl, against her. It cried again, louder, high pitched and clear.

"Can you see her, Sky?"

"Sort of. Not really."

"Come around."

The nurse helped to ease Marty down while I slipped out from under. Deftly, the doctor cut the cord and clamped it. The blood was bright on the sheets around her bottom and darker, stickier on her arms and hands and belly where she touched the child.

The nurse reached out to take the baby from her. "I'll clean her up before you nurse. Maybe you could sponge off your wife." She bathed the baby and I worked on Marty, wiping her face, her hands and arms and stomach, flat again and soft between her hipbones. While we washed, the doctor drew out the placenta, that mysterious life-sustaining organ in its opalescent membrane, and dumped it unceremoniously in a steel basin, garbage, now its purpose was fulfilled. Then he began his stitchery, repairing the cut in Marty's perineum. I didn't like to watch, or to hear the faint pop as his curved needle penetrated flesh.

Marty touched my arm. "Go see your daughter, Sky."

"Are you sure?"

"Go on. I'm fine."

I stood behind the nurse as she scrubbed the baby's hair,

dark and wet, much harder than I thought she should. The body was long, androgynously barrel-chested and slim-hipped, with a protuberant round belly, unmistakably female where two plump pink petals closed around the flower of her sex. The little matchstick limbs came clean, the skin was healthy pink and not nearly so wrinkled as I'd expected. The downy eyebrows pinched together. My daughter opened round blue eyes and looked at me.

It convinced me that she was alive. Something rose up in me and passed to her, an investment of love as real as if it had been tangible. For a few seconds, I forgot to breathe. The nurse lifted the baby out of the shallow tub and toweled her dry, wrapped her in a faded flannel blanket and held her out to me. "If you'll take her to your wife, she can nurse her now."

My arms were stiff as tree limbs. The baby seemed to sense my fear of fatherhood and gave a soft cry, whether protest or reassurance, I don't know. She seemed almost weightless—I'd felt heavier baseballs and beef roasts—but motion gave her mass. She squirmed a little in my arms. Marty, sewn up now, in her own yellow nightgown, appeared wonderfully restored, all memory of pain gone from her face, her smile so eager and welcoming, both of me and of the bundle that I carried that she acceded to beauty, not metaphoric, not like the beauty of anyone or anything else in the world, but her own, hard won. Her resilience was as great as her strength. She was someone's mother now.

I put the baby in her waiting arms. She guided her nipple into the baby's mouth and stroked the dark wet fur on her head. "I think she understands. She's beautiful, isn't she, Sky?"

If all there was beautiful, that she was. Marty, blessedly, seemed unafraid of her. The nurse moved Marty to a chair while she stripped off the bloody sheets and remade the bed. The doctor put silver nitrate in the baby's eyes, as law required, and then they left us alone.

It was five o'clock in the morning of the first day of Theodora Vanderhill Rykken's life and still raining outside. We ate the sandwiches and drank the grape juice from

Marty's bag, intended for me in case of a long labor, and explored the baby at our leisure, with timid fingertips and hungry eyes made the long-awaited stranger real, exclaimed over the tiny fingernails and the dark eyelashes long enough to cast a spiny shadow on her rounded cheeks. When she moved, as she sometimes did, little reachings-out and small determined flails, Marty claimed to know the motion from having felt it inside. For her part, the baby seemed content enough to be alive, untraumatized, despite a few bruises, the battle scars of birth, and willing to accept the situation as she found it. I wondered if I'd ever lose my awe of her. She made everything in my life to date seem irrevocable, the future perilous and promising.

Dawn happened gradually and unremarkably, gray and wet, outside our window, like the slow successive lifting of a hundred gauzy curtains. We'd rented the birthing room at the Kilchis County General Hospital for twenty-four hours and so far used it only six. Marty rested her head on my chest and nestled the baby in the crook of her arm, sang a simple lullaby, not quite on key, that soothed us all. All three of us had reason to be tired, and we slept.

Chapter 42

*M*om insisted, and I agreed, that it would be both stupid and cruel to take a convalescing mother and a brand-new baby home to the primitive conditions at Seasound—no running water, no plumbing and precious little heat, at least right away, and so got her guest room ready to receive our little family. Before the birth, Marty had argued valiantly that she could cope just fine at Seasound: didn't women in Asia have their babies without help in the rice paddies, strap them on their backs and return immediately to work? Hadn't our forebears, till relatively recently, managed quite well without these luxuries?

"They coped because they had to," Mom told her. "And they didn't live to my age, either. If you'd given my grandma the choice between a covered wagon and a nice RV with gas heat and a flush toilet, she would've taken the Winnebago, hands down. Now, no more foolishness. You stay with me."

Marty didn't like the idea of being in Mom's debt.

"One of these days, you paint me my portrait, and we'll be square." She laughed her crazy broken laugh. "It tickles me to think of my daughter-in-laws fighting over the damn thing when I'm gone, over who doesn't have to live with Mom."

"I could paint several," Marty said.

By the time we left the hospital past noon on Sunday, the anesthesia of excitement had worn off and Marty was more than a little sore between the legs, more than a little tired from the marathon of birth and glad enough to be going to a heated, plumbed house and placing herself in the care of a maternal veteran. Mom put her straight to bed in a pink room with a big four-poster and tucked the baby in a worn but sturdy cradle where all her children had slept in turn. Marty gratefully accepted tea and Jell-O and within twenty minutes was fast asleep, trusting Mom's promise to wake her in two hours to nurse the babe.

Mom sat me at the kitchen table with two roast beef sandwiches and a quart of milk. The price of her ministrations was listening to her advice.

"Good woman you've got there, Schuyler, even if she is an artist."

Chewing, I nodded agreement.

"Where's her mother now, if I might ask?"

I shook my head. "No deal. Marty ran away from home at sixteen. From what I can tell, nobody tried too hard to find her."

Mom nodded. "Doesn't talk too much about it, does she?"

"Like pulling teeth."

"Just as well. Pretty baby. And a big responsibility. Being a father changes a man's life."

"I've been thinking that."

"You can't go on living like you have been, you know. Like, well, I don't like to say it, because I don't think you are one, but like hippies."

My laugh blew milk up and out my nose. I hadn't exhaled milk for more than twenty years.

"I'm serious."

"I know. But we've got plans. Marty's got her paintings in three different galleries up in Portland now. As they sell, we'll make improvements."

Hearing our plans with Mom's uncompromising ears made them seem properly chimerical. "If they sell," she said.

"They will. Marty's very good."

"Schuyler, I don't pretend to know much about art, good or bad, but I do know it's a risky business. How many of those so-called great artists died without a penny?"

"A lot, I guess. But this is different. This is us. We'll make it."

"Hmmm."

"What are you suggesting? That I sell to Orville Mason and let him ruin Seasound?"

"Maybe you understand better now why people do."

"I never didn't. I just don't want to be one of them."

"You've got that baby to think about now."

I put down my sandwich. "And I'd like to think there'd be one beach left in the world where she could play. Where she could see how the world was before man fucked it up. Pardon my language."

"I'm seventy-eight years old, Schuyler. I've heard people say that word before. Don't get me wrong, I'd love to see you outsmart Orville. I just don't see that you can afford to be that kind of hero right now. Purity has a price."

"Why the hell did Jack Willets leave me the damn thing, then?"

Mom fingered a long hair that sprouted from her chin. "Maybe so he wouldn't have to compromise himself. I'll never sell this house, you know. I plan to die here. There's fifty-eight years of junk stowed in the attic and the basement and the closets that I couldn't stand to throw out. It'll take my daughter-in-laws one weekend and a dump truck."

"The sins of the fathers are left for the sons to commit? That doesn't seem quite fair."

"Schuyler, at your age I hope you're not still expecting things will be fair. That's for children, idiots and saints. The rest of us get by as best we can." Her aged face cracked in a smile that showed the perfection of her new teeth, white, well-formed and shining, youth hostage in decay. "It's possible, too, he hoped you'd make it. Folks do get foolish as they grow older."

"You haven't." In context, it was an accusation.

"I hope you make it, too. I just don't see how you can. If I was you, I'd call up the planning commission right now and tell them you never meant to make them that offer."

"I wish they'd never invented money," I said.

"Goats messed up the banks, Schuyler, and they're awful hard to mail."

The baby cried, and we heard the creak of bedsprings, Marty rising. "Those two are your business now," Mom said. "Jack Willets would've understood that."

Marty and Theodora flourished under Mom's care, so well that by Wednesday, I was banished back to work. We needed the money, and they didn't want me underfoot; I was mostly extraneous to the process that was taking place, if not actually in the way—Marty gaining physical strength and confidence in mothering, becoming expert at diapers and baths, at distinguishing cries of hunger from cries of pain from cries for the sake of crying. It was as if someone had put a new lens on her camera; her vision narrowed to a laser beamed on minutiae. She was game, she was good, patient and tender and gravely foolish, and I loved her for her fears—that the baby would strangle in her blankets, or starve to death if Marty slept four hours at a stretch, that her milk might be full of environmental poisons or her singing, with three key changes in every bar, might permanently damage the kid's ear for music. She worried about rashes and drafts and colic, about crib death and birth defects not immediately obvious to the naked eye, about rolling over in her sleep and crushing the baby, about her own ability to perform the continuous small tasks of nurture. Don't get me wrong; I found the baby fascinating, too, but not endlessly so; my planet kept slowly, steadily, orbiting the sun, the school toilets continued to need cleaning, I still read the newspaper and ate and shat and slept, while Marty stepped through the mirror into the skewed domain of motherhood. The glassy surface stood between us, shining. It was a beautiful and lonely time.

"It's time to go home, Sky," Marty said on Friday. "We're ready, both of us."

I looked at her, reposed in the pink room, hair and sheets and nightgown clean, her sandals on a throw rug on the polished hardwood floor, the baby dozing in a sling of soft covers between her knees and saw Seasound, the bare board walls with their coating of cobwebs, the hanging light bulb, the packed dirt floor and makeshift furniture, the sparseness and not exactly ugliness but the nonbeauty of it. "I don't know. I've been thinking."

"You've been talking to Mom."

"She's probably right."

"I've been thinking, too. The key is organization. With organization, everything is possible."

"Possible is not necessarily desirable."

"The kid is loved. She doesn't need a castle."

"That's lucky. I'm fresh out of castles."

"Abraham Lincoln was born in a log cabin."

"It probably had a fireplace. I feel selfish, expecting you to live in that big drafty white elephant. I feel like a jerk."

"I've also made a list of improvements. First we enclose the space. Put in a floor. Insulate the walls. Buy a secondhand wood stove."

"If we sold it, then we could afford to fix it up."

"I've got twelve paintings hung in Portland. People have got to buy at least a couple. And the Mall Show's coming up this spring. I should be able to get juried into that." Speculation turned to certainty as she spilled it out; she willed fate to be accessory to her plans.

"I thought you didn't want to put an economic burden on your art. Besides, you know better than to count unhatched chickens. They could be sterile."

"Come on, Sky. I want to go home."

The word imploded, tossing up a hundred small fragments of hurt and pleasure that ricocheted inside me. I saw the small apartment kitchen of my childhood, the sooty windowsill and towers of dishes, dirty and clean, erected by accretion, my Barbara-nest and Marlborough Street burrow, mosquito netting hung in masculine subequatorial company barracks, Jack Willets's spartan and provisional bachelorhood and Marty smiling, wanting to go home. Such a potent word, hard to look at without pain, except obliquely. The baby stretched one pink, tubelike arm above her head and half-turned, without waking, her baby-Buddha face pinched with displeasure, as if she were a natural receiver of my thoughts and their sudden swift crackle impinged on private dreams.

"She's old enough for her first merry-go-round ride, if I hold her," Marty said.

"Okay. We'll try it for a week. You pack. I'll get the van."

It was late by the time we finally got there, dark and drizzling. Mom had to feed us first, stuff us full of protein and advice and make us swear solemnly if we couldn't hack it, we'd come back. She made us take the family cradle, on loan, wouldn't be needing it herself, she said, short of a miracle. Marty was quiet all the way to Seasound, sitting on a pillow to protect her stitches from the ruts, except to tell the baby some about the merry-go-round and how much she was going to like it.

I had them wait out front in the warm van while I went in to turn on the lights and get the heater going. The door was open a slit, the way I'd left it in the rush to the hospital. I saw the light was on, too, out back, another oversight, this one expensive; Orville didn't exactly give his kilowatt hours

257

away for free. I was halfway across the pavilion, just parallel with the merry-go-round, when the feeling of something wrong caught up with me. I looked into the shadows, among the horses, looked hard until I saw a human form, standing very still, inside the platform, beside the organ. My insides hitched up, I took a deep breath and called, "Okay. Come out where I can see you and tell me what the hell you're doing here."

The shadow responded by reaching out and ripping the drumstick off one of the big mechanical drums. I saw he had a hammer in his hand, just before he smashed the claw end through the face of the drum. My adrenaline took the cue and pumped up for mad. I remembered thinking I didn't want to fight, not again, before I started for him. He decided to run for it then, but the hind leg of the green horse tripped him up and gave me time to cut off his way to the door. When he raised his face, scowling, I recognized it—Tommy, the sheriff's kid, the one who'd tossed the chowder in my face at the Treetopper, my first night in Kilchis. I put my hands on my hips and pretended I was bigger than I was. "Your uncle Orville send you, punk?"

He shot a juicy wad of snoose somewhere in the vicinity of my boots. "None of your damn business." He took a step forward.

I shifted my screen to block him. "That's where you're wrong. This happens to be my property, and you're trespassing."

"Tell it to the sheriff." I thought I heard just a catch of fear in his cocky laugh.

"Your daddy's as much of a miserable, spineless crook as you are, kid. But the law says a man's got a right to defend his property and his life. Who'd you come planning to kill this time?"

"Ought to kill you, Rykken, and get it over with. I'd be a hero around here."

I leaned forward, arms out, trying to remember the few moves that kept me from getting pulverized on the junior high school playground. I never was very good; my main

weapon was speed, only this time I wasn't running. "Try it,"
I said.

He had to think about that one. He took a misstep
backward that told me he'd been drinking. "You getting paid
for this, or you doing it for fun?"

"I had my fun," he said. "I wrecked your music box good."

"Fine. I hope you can afford to get it fixed, asshole."

Venom and stupidity mixed in his voice. "You think you're
so smart, don't you, coming out here and gettin in everybody's way with your fancy ideas and your big words."

"Is asshole too big for you? I'd be happy to define it. It's
where the shit comes out."

I let my mouth run; he was bigger and stronger but I was
smarter. Words slowed him up, trying to catch hold of them.
I kept them coming. "Appropriate, don't you think, for
cowards who sneak around killing cats in their sleep? What
do you do on a date? Shoot rats at the dump?"

"I ain't no coward, you son of a bitch."

"Could've fooled me. I thought it fit you like your
skivvies."

He decided to make a move, stepped forward. "Get outa
my way, Rykken, or I'll bash your head in with this
hammer."

I stood my ground. "Try it," I said again, hoping he
wouldn't. "The wood part there's the handle, You use the
metal end for bashing."

He lunged at me, but slow. I simply stepped aside,
wishing I hadn't eaten so much dinner, and he stumbled
over his own boots. He was still wearing his logger's calks; I
could see the pattern of his hobnails in the dirt. He dropped
the hammer, lurching, and I managed to kick it away, like
they do with guns in the movies, before he got ahold of my
arm and ripped at it. Thank God for sockets; my shoulder
joint withstood the stress, and I gave him my best shove,
which only served to make him madder. In close, I was at a
big disadvantage. I gave myself some fast advice—dodge what
you can, stay conscious and look for openings. I thought I
had a shot at his groin and raised my knee, but he grabbed it

and threw me over on my back in the dirt. He climbed on my chest knees first and it felt like a piano landing on a postage stamp; I thought I heard a rib crack. With my one free hand I pounded back at every beefy surface I could reach. He ripped my glasses off and threw them aside before he broke my nose.

A voice cut through the buzz in my head, Marty's, yelling "Stop it. Stop it right now."

The beating stopped temporarily while he looked toward the door and I tried. There she was, a defocused vision of mercy, the blue of her nightgown and red parka the most I could make out. I thought, I was afraid she held the baby in her arms, and I swore to myself that if he touched either one of them, I'd contrive a way to kill him, despite my infirmities.

"Stop it," she shouted again.

I felt him pause, trained well as the next brute to revere mothers, and then he got up off me and I thought it was over, but he didn't, not until he kicked me in the side, at the base of the ribs, with his calk boot. I don't think it was his best shot, just a kind of reflex physical last word; at least by then I hurt so much in several places that my other aches acted as a counterirritant and cut down on the pain of that particular blow.

Then I saw his bulk recede, approach the door, push Marty aside and disappear into the dark. Seconds later, his engine stormed alive, tires squawked in the mud and the truck sound got slowly fainter. Without moving much, I tried to assess the damage to my body. I hurt all over. Even my dignity deserted me, and I threw up my fish cakes and Mom's apple pie, an especially odorous blend.

Marty knelt over me, assuring herself I was alive, holding the baby, howling now, as far as possible from the remains of Schuyler. "Yes, honey," she said, "Daddy stinks but we love him anyway. Schuyler, we better take you to the shop and get you fixed."

I was glad for her composure, and the blurred sight of her concern. "Welcome home," I told her. "I think I peed in my pants." Suddenly the whole thing struck me very funny, and I laughed like a loon, never mind the burning in my chest. There was something weirdly exhilarating about hitting bottom, and I saw that all my previous attempts to get there, my elaborate renunciations, were mere sophistries compared to the real thing. The real thing was ridiculously simple, in no way intellectual, blood and barf and urine, a dirt floor and an uncorrected astigmatism and finally, a huge, uncomplicated relief at being still alive. "By all means, get me to the body shop."

I laughed until the tears came. If only Barney Crews could see me now.

Chapter 43

Tommy had left a nail or two upstanding on the barrel, and through his oversight, the organ was still good for about six random notes. To this crippled music, the baby Theodora took her first merry-go-round ride, astride the rabbit, in her mama's arms. I wish I could say she took to it naturally, but it isn't true. She bawled.

At the emergency room, they'd X-rayed my battered rib cage and swathed me in yards of adhesive tape, so with my shirt off, I looked like a half-wrapped mummy, embalmed in Tylenol 3. Another fancy bandage in the middle of my face kept the rain off my nose, and I had to tape my glasses on over my ears so that they could ride the bandage without getting thrown. They told me I'd mend in something like six weeks, so I expected to be functional again the same time Marty's doctor lifted the prohibition on postpartum sex. Work was out of the question; I couldn't move freely enough to push a broom, but luckily, Bruce was so pleased by the sight of my misfortunes that he decided to be expansive and recommend that the school board give me a leave of absence without pay instead of canning me. His wife's cousin, who was between jobs, would fill in. Meanwhile, I dedicated myself to the business of seeking justice.

The first thing I did was go to see Orville Mason at the car lot. He beamed at my bandaged nose and necessarily stiff posture.

"Well, well, Rykken. Looks like you tangled with a grizzly bear and lost."

"Cut the crap, Mason. I've got a witness, and I've got a hammer with Tommy's fingerprints all over it. I'm here to say I won't press charges if one, you pay my doctor bills, two, you pay to fix my organ, three, you reimburse me for lost wages and four, you withdraw your proposal to the county about condemning my land. Those are my terms."

Orville Mason laughed. He laughed as hard as if I'd been all Three Stooges rolled into one, slinging pies at myself, laughed until the shiny Blazers rang. He wiped his eyes with the broad back of his stubby hand. "That's rich, Rykken, it really is. You threatening me. It's nice to see you're developing a sense of humor."

"I fail to see the humor in it. I'm damn sick and tired of being messed with, and this time I've got you dead to rights."

"Rights" set him off again, but it was a shorter spasm this time. "A couple things, Rykken. First one is, assuming Tommy did rough you up some, and I don't admit it, mind, you've got no way of connecting him to me. Second thing, you know who his daddy is. Man doesn't cotton to accusations against his own flesh and blood."

"And I don't cotton to you and yours making Kilchis County your private little kingdom."

Mason's little pig eyes opened wide as they could in a kind of practiced mock innocence. "I've been a good king, Rykken. Ask the peons. They'll tell you."

"King Shit," I said. "Is that your answer?"

"I reckon it is, Rykken. I reckon so. You can't stand in the way of progress forever. Those that try get mowed under. That's America, boy, and that's what makes her great."

I half-expected him to salute the red, white and blue

bunting that festooned his showroom. He sounded absolutely sincere, aligning himself with that glorious band of great rapists of the North American continent, and for a moment, I wondered if he wasn't right, with recorded history and the propensity of the species to back him up. Democracy, after all, allows the majority to assent to rape. Gang-banged America, convulsed in one great orgasm of development, cheering the bulldozer and the pile driver dildo, presenting her tenderest parts for pillage, on her knees and panting hard, begging for more. Do it again, Orville! It feels so bad it's good.

Let's git that bastard Nature!

(You tell 'em, Orville.)

Let's make profit!

(*aaaaaahhhhh*)

Let's make jobs!

(Just one more time, puh-leez.)

Let's make *love*, goddamn it!

(And our neon babies will multiply and subdue the earth.)

Ah-men.

I left Mason to his pornographic fantasies (or were they mine?)—still chuckling at my impotence and my injuries—and went to see his brother-in-law, the sheriff. Once again, he was sympathetic. Once again, he was helpless to help me. Once again, my antagonist was recorded as "person or persons unknown."

He looked up from the report form, his slack jaw creased deeply with a grin. "You know, it's not my place to give advice, Rykken, but it seems to me a smart man knows when he's licked. You've made yourself some enemies. There's plenty of folks wishes you'd go back to where you come from. If you stick around, I can't promise to keep you safe. I got a whole county to look after here."

I thanked him for his words of wisdom.

A phone call to Marty's friend in Lake Oswego produced the name of a lawyer who was supposed to have a scrapper's penchant for the underdog. He urged a double-barreled attack: we could bypass the sheriff and file a criminal assault charge directly with the county prosecutor. At the same time, we'd file a civil suit against Tommy for medical bills, lost wages and damages for pain and suffering. We would, he said, apply for a change of venue in the civil suit, and if the county prosecutor didn't give us satisfaction, well, we'd make a big stink with the state attorney general about malfeasance in office. Hell of an opportunity, he said. What did I think?

"It sounds expensive," I said.

"It is," he said. "It is. I'd have to charge you thirty-three and a third percent of your damages. Plus costs, of course."

"What if we lose?"

"Just costs."

"You mean to say, you work on spec?"

The operator broke in to ask me to deposit another sixty-five cents. The phone ate my coins, belching metallic thanks.

"Of course," the lawyer said. "If we didn't, no poor man could afford to sue. Contingent fees are the great leveler. At least in theory." He laughed.

"You make it sound so simple."

"It's not, believe me. It'll take a long time, things being what they are, unless we get a settlement out of court. One more thing, too, you might not like. Publicity. As much as we can rake up."

"You running for something?" I asked him.

"Not this year. But the way I see it, it's the best way to keep you safe. I wouldn't want to lose my client before the trial."

I told him I'd think it over and fed the last of my coins into the phone to settle up.

I drove through the storm back to Seasound to share the news with Marty. On the radio, between the Rolling Stones resurrected and Melissa Manchester, the announcer said a major storm was on its way to Portland; on the coast it had already arrived. Lightning ripped at the darkness. Circling the bay road, above the radio, over the familiar noises of the engine and the windshield wipers, the gusts of wind like the long sighs of a giant and the fusillade of hail pelting the van's flat roof, I could hear the ocean, its continuous, simultaneous grumble, all dissatisfactions given one voice, out there, somewhere, in the dark.

I was glad to reach the brightness. Marty was lying on the bed, awake and still, with no other purpose at that moment than to be a pillow for the babe, who was asleep inside the circle of her arm. My arrival made her start, spring into motion, and I was sorry to make her guilty, wanted to tell her it was all right simply to be, but already she was sitting, was on her feet, smoothing her hair, lifting the baby's limp body into her crib, searching the shelves for dinner makings, asking to hear my news, apologizing for time not spent in industry. On her easel, in the shadows, I could see the start of new work. I persuaded her to sit down again to hear my tale.

The prospect of justice, the promise of recourse excited us, as much as the idea of reward for being victims seemed strange. We weren't above spending it though, the 66⅔ percent that would be ours after the lawyer took his cut. Orville would pay, we reasoned, and Orville owed us. Inside, we couldn't see the lightning, but thunder rolled loud and angry through our talk. It scared the baby awake, and I watched while Marty nursed her back to peace and sleep, enchanted by their wordless intimacy but impatient, too, to have Marty's full attention for myself.

We drank wine, a California chablis so cheap it was yellow in our glasses, piss-colored, and ate indifferent chili from a can, talking about steaks and new shoes and a stroller and a raincoat for the kid. I think it was still early when we turned out the light and settled into bed under our eclectic pile of covers; time was elusive at Seasound, almost irrelevant after a few drinks, except for the gross measures of light and dark, and the turning of the tide. Marty snuggled around my backside, careful of my ribs.

"I can tell I'm healing," she said. "I'm starting to want

you again." Her movements were small but provocative. Her desire, and mine, were largely symbolic, under the circumstances, but it was satisfying somehow just to imagine both being whole and horny again.

We slept until the baby woke us, hungry again, and Marty brought her back to bed to nurse. The wind was high, out of the southwest, howling outside our walls like a stranger outraged at being excluded from our nest. I remember thinking how warm we were, the three of us, and how safe.

I was on a ship, in my dream, and the ship was on high seas. My cabin was at water level, deep below the towering wedding-cake structure of the decks, and when the sea was absolutely calm, which it wasn't, and the ship at equilibrium, which it wasn't, my one round porthole was precisely bisected by the waterline, with sky above and sea below, pale blue and translucent green, the color Coke bottles used to be, the old molded ones, thick bottomed and curvacious. It made me uneasy to know, in such rough seas, that Barney Crews was captain of the ship, by dint of his measurable superiority. Oh, he could read the charts, all right, and operate the esoteric instruments to perfection, could calculate the course in his head, if he had to, was dazzling in his white uniform, clanked as he walked from the chestful of medals that attested his merits (I saw them briefly, close up—a first-place finish in a junior high school spelling bee, a National Honor Society torch, his Phi Bete key, a round red-and-white button that said "Mensa" on top and "genius" on the bottom, plus many others, more grand, whose raised lettering I couldn't read). Barney Crews was the pinnacle of technological man, his intellect unmatched, and yet I knew that under his captaincy, we were doomed.

He had no respect, no understanding, no love of the sea. In extremity, he would fall back on reason, and his rationality would cost us our lives. There was a great secret to survival, which only I knew, and it was my job, in the minutes that remained before we crashed and sank, to reach him on the bridge and share the secret. It was up to me to save us, and the obstacles between us seemed insurmountable.

The ship reeled; I was hurtled from wall to wall of the endless narrow passageway and the ladders, as I tried to climb them, broke and fell away. Huge burly guards in navy whites and calk boots pursued and tried to stop me. My legs were heavy with fear and every step I took required lifting them against a tenfold force of gravity.

God knows, I tried, but I never reached the bridge and Barney never learned the secret of survival by hearing my dream-self speak it out loud. I was too late. There was a gigantic crash, the ship's autonomy was breached, and I could hear the sea race in, millions of gallons of green water rushing in to occupy and obliterate the fragile human ambient. The baby and Marty cried out at once, and dream melted into reality. The ship was gone but the sound of angry seas outlasted sleep. The pavilion shook as if it were being rammed by an eighteen-wheeler doing sixty. The timbers cracked. It sounded as if we were inside the ocean.

The heater was cold and the light bulb didn't go on when I pulled the string. I found our flashlights and pulled on my jeans by their light, left one with Marty and took one when I went outside to see what the hell was going on. What I saw beyond the door, I saw all at once, and have to tell in stages, one slow word at a time. The dunes were simply gone; the seaward face of the pavilion sat flush on the edge of a new-made cliff. The old gap, to the south of us, twice mended with fill, was breaching. What hours before was solid ground was now a deep pit, with the ocean ripping at its sides. The road still stood, a high ridge above the hole, but the water was eating away at its underpinnings with enormous force. Each new onslaught of waves broke higher than the last, shooting curved walls of cold white spray twenty feet or more above the road. The hiss of the water almost deafened me. Marty's Volkswagen was gone, the ground where it was parked collapsed into the pit. Shining my flashlight down, I caught a glimpse of one upended yellow fender, one lone tire;

the rest was already buried deep in rocks and sand. Where I stood, the water assaulted me from two sides, the frontal attack on the beach, the advance battalion eating out the pit. In seconds, I was drenched. As I stood there, the ocean tore out a huge hunk of the pavilion's foundation and carried it away. When lightning flashed across the horizon, I saw the enemy, the vast and troubled ocean advancing like a great army, bent on destruction. The sound of the pavilion tipping seaward was swallowed by thunder.

For precious seconds, I'd been a watcher, absorbed by the pure spectacle of power, but the pavilion shifting made me husband and father and refugee all at once. Half of the floor was gone, and crests of spray reached up inside the building. The pavilion was skewed like a crazy house, and water eddied ankle-deep around the merry-go-round. Marty had used the time to dress herself and wrap the baby in blankets; she stood on the carousel platform, holding tightly to a brass pole for support. The seaward half of our living quarters was already gone, the closet and shelves, Marty's paintings and the food supplies. By flashlight, I saw the bureau break against the rocks below and sink. Our scattered clothes and papers did a round dance on the surface of the water until a natural maelstrom sucked them out of sight.

I took Marty by the hand and pulled her off the platform, away from the edge. The baby cried, I think, but the roaring of the water drowned out her cries. Almost as soon as we moved, a volley of waves broke over the front of the merry-go-round, so that only the proud heads and raised forelegs of the horses and the ears of the rabbit showed above the white water. The carved dolphins seemed to leap through the spray. The next assault ate away the floor under it, and the merry-go-round, too, began its long descent toward the rocks below. The water climbed our legs now. We waded for the door, but there was no longer any ground beyond it to receive us. For a time—two minutes? ten?—there was no way out. We were trapped. Marty rocked the baby back and forth, back and forth in her arms, while I simply cursed myself for slowness and stupidity and swore I wouldn't blow another chance if it came. We trained our flashlights on the merry-go-round as it went down. The last of it I saw, below the ripped canopy, was the final panel of Marty's frieze, the man and woman silhouetted on the beach, and then that, too, was gone. The water climbed past our knees and a strong undertow, even there, tugged us toward the edge.

There was nothing to do but watch it, feel it happen. The edge approached us. Then, suddenly, with more of its foundation gone, the pavilion pitched forward again, began its slide into the sea. I flashed my light behind us and saw that the shift had jacked the southeast corner of the building up, raised it about three feet off the remaining ground. I crawled out first and took the baby from Marty, then helped her out. The van was parked on the road and we steadied ourselves against it. The water was so turbulent inside the gap it was impossible to tell by the flashlight if there was enough fill still under the road to support the van.

"What do you think?" I shouted to Marty. "Once the road goes, the whole thing goes. We'll be cut off. But we might be able to find something to hold on to on the bay side."

Another flash of lightning lit up the sky and we looked at each other in the brief silver glow. I could see the rain between us.

"I don't know if the baby could stand the exposure. Her blankets are soaked already. We better go for it."

I nodded and we climbed into the van. For a sickening minute, I couldn't find the keys and thought I'd put on the wrong pants in the dark, and they were gone. Then I felt their bulge in my back pocket. The van's engine sputtered and coughed. On the fourth try, she turned over. I nosed her toward the gap. A crash resounded behind us. Marty turned around to look.

"It's gone," she said.

We reached the edge of the gap. Waves broke over the road, throwing up sheer walls of water, white and sparkling, even beautiful, in the headlights. "You sure you want to try this? I can't see a damn thing."

"I'm sure," Marty said. "Try to make it in the space between."

My hands were so tight on the wheel I wasn't sure I'd ever be able to pry them loose. I let a couple of waves break, watching for patterns, trying to figure how long we'd have to get across those hundred yards. Not long enough; even if the road held, we'd have to take the impact of at least one wave.

We watched another one break. As it peaked, Marty said, "Go. Now." I hit the accelerator and we drove slowly into the blinding spray. I stayed as far left as I could, by feel, just fractions of an inch from the row of pines that lined the bay side of the road. We were enclosed by water. I drove ahead into it, slowly, inch by inch, waiting to feel the road give way, to fall. For a brief moment, the spray lightened, and I could see the darkness beyond. Then an awful roar on the right, the next wave coming, coming. Marty fell toward me when it hit, my body toppled left, the baby screamed. The water broke over us, and the outflow tried to take us with it. I steered left as hard as I could and accelerated, fully expecting to be swept away, to die. The pressure lightened, we passed through, suddenly there was ground, not much, but blessed ground to the sea side of the van again.

We said nothing all the way into Kilchis, because there was nothing much that needed saying. Inland, the storm was less violent, a heavy rain, a strong wind, but away from the ocean, it was only weather. In the neoned streets of Kilchis, it seemed quite tame. As we headed for Mom's house, I found myself wishing I'd slept long enough to learn the secret of survival. It would have been a useful thing to know.

Chapter 44

So, Theodora, my bumptious princess, Daddy's story catches up to the present and is told. Your mom's got an art class tonight, teaching a bunch of beginners how to draw the human nude in thirty strokes or less, while I sit at home with you and try to be blasé about the fact that one of her models is a man. I'm sitting in an armchair with a tablet spread open across my knees, and in front of me, you dance, chubby legs pumping, trying to seduce me away from writing or, failing that, to steal my pen. You should have been in bed an hour ago.

Two loose ends dangle. Why have I written this? What does it mean? The first one's easy. I've written all this down so that even if I get mugged or stabbed or Saturday-night-specialed tomorrow, even if I walk into a manhole and disappear from the face of the earth, you, my incontinent elf, will know your father better than I knew mine. I'm trying to save you the pain of speculation. This is your father speaking.

Number two is tougher. As I've said before, Daddy's no philosopher. Drawing morals isn't exactly my strong suit, and besides, if you can take a few liberties and apply Heisenberg's uncertainty principle to human affairs as well as to physical phenomena, which I'm willing to bet you can, then it becomes obvious that any conclusions I might come to would be not only highly suspect, but subject to change without notice. After all, *I'm* still changing, not so fast as you are, but steadily enough that what I think is true today will probably be vastly different from what I see as truth six months from now. Hell, in twenty years your mother and I could be socking away our money to buy a condo at

Seasound Village, if Orville Mason ever does manage to get it built, which I doubt, and planning to retire there. The odds are slim, but strange things happen in this world.

Okay, but what do I think today, right now? If you forced me to venture an opinion, I'd say, well, your mother and I lived in Eden for a little while, and were expelled, and that Eden probably isn't a very tenable idea, anyway. Life is a series of retrenchments. I'd even add that it's probably better to retrench with honor than without it, though in a universe as utterly and randomly mechanical as my merry-go-round was, I couldn't tell you why that should be so. Don't hold me to any of this, kid. A wise man I am not.

After the ocean breached Seasound and took the merry-go-round, we retrenched, and as retrenchments go, this one ain't bad. There's more plastic and less weather, less poverty but fewer birds. It's a good long drive to the ocean, but still, Eugene is a nice town. Your mom paints and teaches art classes a couple nights a week, and my undergraduate math majors are all right, not as smart as Barney Crews or even I was, but for the most part decent and hardworking kids. At least I don't have to take Bruce's crap anymore, or mop it up when someone in the third grade barfs. My students call me Dr. Rykken.

You seem to be a happy child. Your mother spoils you, and your father spoils you worse, and you delight in teasing your Uncle Tony, who as a freshman in the dorms is always glad to cadge a free meal when he can, and in getting all those extravagant presents from your flaky Aunt Barbara back east, whom you've never seen at all. Thanks to her, you're the only kid on the block with a four-foot-tall stuffed giraffe in her bedroom. The little house we sit in now is probably, barring further calamities and given current rates of interest and inflation, where you'll grow up.

I see you've given up on me, fallen asleep in front of the fireplace, wearing your little blue union suit, one arm clutching your favorite blanket to you, the other curved gracefully up beside your head. The fire's just coals now, sinking fast, and above the mantelpiece one of your mother's paintings hangs, of a shapely green horse with deeper green carved saddle and silver harness, a fierce blue sapphire eye, lying on its side at the foamy edge of a gentle tide, with just the slightest hint of rainbows in the bigger bubbles, to suggest the sun is shining down, washed up on a gray sand beach somewhere, among smooth dark flat stones. The horse fills the frame diagonally, its head to the lower left, its tail, twined with dark green strands of seaweed, still lazily awash and flecked with foam.

It above, you bluely asleep below, the glow from the coals pinking your baby pallor make a pretty picture, one I hate to disturb, but duty calls. I don't want your mother to come home and think I've been neglecting you. In just a minute or so, I'll scoop you up and tuck you in your bed.

Sleep well, my little one. Your daddy's here.